MASON'S REGRET

Odessa Lynne

TITLES BY ODESSA LYNNE

*Forthcoming

For an up-to-date list, visit odessalynne.com/books.

MASON'S REGRET

WOLVES' HEAT
BOOK 8

Odessa Lynne

ODELYN PUBLISHING

Published by Odelyn Publishing
odelyn.com

odessalynne.com

First Electronic Publication December 2017
First Paperback Edition December 2018

ISBN-13: 978-1-9834-4521-7

MASON'S
REGRET

Chapter 1

THE DAY HAD TURNED to night without him noticing. The light filtering through the cracks between the dusty oak boards that made up the walls of the twenty-foot square shed wasn't enough to illuminate the packed earth under Mason's feet, but he could see the outline of his hand fisting the hem of his yellowed t-shirt and the dark shadow of blood on the toe of his left boot.

"Goddammit," he breathed. His arm wasn't going to stop bleeding without more compression. He might not be able to see much, but he could see that.

Feel it, too.

He leaned forward and the thin metal of the overturned toolbox under him creaked, a faint sound that got lost under the rising whistle of wind forcing its way through the gaps in the walls. He exhaled and squinted against the swirl of dust he could feel and smell and taste in the heavy air.

A storm was coming, chasing the wind with ferocious speed. He'd been ready to take shelter anywhere he could find it, but a hundred-year-old shack wasn't going to protect him for long. Not from the storm, and not from the trouble that was coming up on him faster than the wind gusting outside.

He jabbed the short blade of his pocketknife through the fabric a few inches above the hem and tore a long strip free.

The air was cooling, but inside the shack the chill wind hadn't yet chased away the trapped heat of the day.

A sudden gust of wind rattled the walls. The knife slipped out of his hand and only a quick reflex kept him from dropping it.

He blew out a tight breath and snapped the knife closed against his thigh then clipped it into the front pocket of his jeans. Biting down on one end of the strip of fabric let him pull the makeshift bandage tight as he wrapped his forearm, closing the four-inch long gash.

His stomach roiled and he had to blink a few times to get his bearings. He didn't think the injury was going to kill him, not quickly anyway, but every time he looked at his arm, his stomach twisted, a visceral reaction he couldn't seem to tamp down.

Lightning flashed bright and stark outside and he paused. One…two…three…

Thunder rumbled, shivering up his spine.

As if to prove there was some kind of goddamn curse on him, the howl of wind died suddenly and the rev of an engine cut through the temporary lull.

Another flash of light speared through the shed's walls.

Not lightning this time, but headlights to go with the distinct rev and hum of an engine running on halfgas.

He lurched to his feet, taking precious seconds to tuck the end of his makeshift bandage tight. Pain lanced up his arm and his next breath didn't come easy. He pushed through it and grabbed his rifle off the floor beside him.

Voices rose outside the shed and something heavy slammed into the door, shaking the rickety walls. "I know you're in there, you motherfucker! Get out here or I'm going to blow that fucking shack down around you!"

Stan. That son of a bitch.

Should've guessed it'd be him leading the pack.

Adrenaline fired through Mason's veins. He raised his rifle and sighted on the rattling door. It was his fifth and final bullet. But five had always been his lucky number. *Good riddance, motherfucker.*

He pulled the trigger.

Light exploded around him. Thunder shook the ground under his feet just before his feet left the ground. He didn't have time to wonder what had happened. He slammed into the shed's far wall, every last gasp of breath leaving his lungs in one sudden blow.

The shed collapsed, the remaining walls too weak to withstand the howling wind.

One moment he was gasping for breath through the hard knot of pain in his chest and the next he was staring into the trees above him, branches whipping in the wind, the moon just a pale glow behind a bank of dark clouds.

Conscious thought coalesced into something resembling sense. Headlights shone into the trees on the other side of the shack. He blinked against a sudden patter of rain and tried to roll to the side, but a weight on his legs stopped him.

Part of the shed's roof had fallen across his lower legs.

How long had he been out? He had no idea.

He swiped rain out of his eyes and tried to move again. He needed to get out of there before—

A flashlight streaked across his face, momentarily blinding him.

"There he is, the fucker! Drag him out."

Not Stan. Lavi.

Mason shoved at the boards holding him down. His injured arm protested with a sharp stab of pain that stole his breath. He lost track of the voices.

A lean silhouette stepped close. "Get out of the way."

The weight on Mason's legs intensified, and he gasped.

Thunder rumbled loud and long overhead and the patter of rain turned into a deluge, beating at his face. He turned his head away, trying to keep the water out of his nose.

The weight on his legs eased. Ten seconds later, a hard boot caught him under the ribs and he gasped and rolled over.

Rough hands yanked him up by his arms, dragging him to his knees.

He screamed before he could stop himself. His injured arm throbbed in time to his heartbeat, a hot, deep ache, and he struggled to shake off the disorientation that had him in as tight a grip as the men holding him.

They dragged him away from the fallen shack and across the uneven ground. His knees burned under the fabric of his jeans and his head throbbed.

He glanced up, catching a glimpse of thick muscle and barrel chest.

Rock. Rock and Lavi.

Lavi shoved Mason hard toward Stan who was

propped up against the side of the utility vehicle the three had rode in on.

"You fuck—" A cough interrupted Stan's ragged words. His groan got lost in the gurgle of his next breath.

Shit, yeah. From the sound of that cough, Stan was as good as dead.

Mason laughed into the flood of rain.

Rock grabbed a handful of Mason's hair and jerked him forward. Mason's eyes prickled at the sharp pull and his knees slipped on the wet ground. He fell face first into Stan's lap.

He tried to shove himself upright, but Rock stepped on his back and forced him down. He sucked in a piss-scented breath and clenched his teeth.

The sorry bastard had pissed himself at some point. Mason exhaled another weak laugh. Couldn't say he didn't enjoy knowing that.

Rock yanked Mason upright by the hair again, hard enough to make him gasp. He struggled for balance, digging his sore knees into the soft, wet earth, and squinted through the blowing rain.

Hate glimmered back at him from Stan's dark eyes. "You're dead, Waters. Gonna blow your fucking brains out myself after we get what we want out of you." He was forcing the words out, but that was Stan, stubborn to the last goddamn gasp.

"You're just as dead," Mason said. "Nobody'll fix you tonight and you won't make it 'til tomorrow. Good enough for me."

"Your brother gave me a message for you, right before I gutted him. Don't you want to hear it?"

Rage swallowed Mason whole. "Goddamn you!"

He tore free of Rock's unyielding grip and slammed his fist into the side of Stan's face.

Lavi lunged toward Mason. "Shit!"

Rock reached Mason first. He backhanded Mason so hard Mason's vision grayed out.

Mason fell on his ass just as one of Lavi's boots plowed into his gut. He hit the ground hard, splashing into a rivulet of rain rushing down the hillside. His cheek throbbed and his head spun. He couldn't catch his breath.

"Shoot the fucker! Let's get this done. There could be wolves nearby."

Wolves.

Mason had hardly had time to think about them, even though everything that had happened had been in part because of them, because of the people who didn't want to share Earth with aliens who lived by rules no human should have to tolerate. Three years ago, Mason had been one of those people. He'd been a renegade, sure he was doing what was right and just, in a world that didn't seem right and just any longer.

When the wolves had arrived, their similarity to humans had changed the world. Their freely shared technologies had offered unlimited promise for the future of humanity.

Then the wolves' first heat season came. It had ruined everything—destroyed the peace, put an end to free will —cracked the world, he'd thought.

He still thought it, but he'd stopped trying to fight back. His own leader's capitulation had shown him how inevitable it all was. If they could turn someone as strong as Brendan, what hope did any of them have? Brendan had been persuasive and cunning and absolutely convinced that the continued resistance of the renegades was the only thing protecting humanity from becoming slaves to the aliens they'd allowed to make a home on Earth.

The government had given in years before—the American Protectorate belonged to the wolves and there would be no going back. Ever. The wolves weren't leaving. Mason's own home sat one mile from the border of the protectorate—too close to be safe during the heat season and too far away for his family to have been offered anything in trade to move after everyone realized just how dangerous living so close to the wolves could be.

It was Lavi who'd spoken—of course. He was terrified of the wolves. But only a fool wouldn't be, especially now. The wolves' heat only came around once every three years, but it had finally come again. The first notices had gone out five days ago—the very same day Marcus had disappeared.

"We're not going to...shoot him yet," Stan gasped. "I need him—I want him to—" But a deep, wet cough stole the rest of his breath and he didn't finish what he'd started.

"He'll suffer," Rock said. "Don't worry."

Rock's heavy boot landed on the back of Mason's head, grinding down with enough force to push Mason's face into the wet earth. Rock was a large man, heavy and muscled, his goddamn neck thicker than Mason's thigh. Water filled Mason's nose, and he started choking. He grabbed wildly for Rock's leg but couldn't get the leverage he needed to get out from under Rock's massive boot.

He wasn't used to fighting alone. Marcus—

But Marcus was gone and the dagger of grief that thought brought made him gasp for breath. Water burned its way into his lungs and he thrashed furiously, trying to break free.

"Stop, goddammit."

Mason could just make out Stan's voice, garbled and weak.

"Bring him here."

Rock put his foot down, splashing water into Mason's face. Mason rolled, coughing desperately to clear his lungs.

Son of a bitch obviously had a thing for pulling hair, because he grabbed Mason by his head again and shoved him onto his knees right in front of Stan. Lavi jerked Mason's arms behind his back. The move put pressure on Mason's injured forearm and Mason only managed not to scream by clenching his teeth.

Lightning flashed and thunder cracked overhead and the rain became a river of water down his face and neck and back. He shuddered, soaked through, the wind stealing every bit of heat his body could generate.

He said a quick prayer for Gillie, Brecken, and his mom. They'd be okay, even if things got harder for a while. Once Matthew found out they were alone, he'd help them out. That's what family did. Matthew might just be a cousin, but he was loyal to a fault, and Mason's mom had practically raised him.

Mason wished he'd been able to stop Marcus before it was too late. He wished—

A lot of things, goddammit.

He tried again to jerk free.

Lavi's grip slid to Mason's wrists and Rock wrenched

Mason's head sideways, leaving Mason gasping for breath at the sharp pain in his neck.

"Just get on with it," Lavi said. "I want out of this fucking rain before the wolves come."

Stan pressed his hand to his chest, wheezing. "They can't track in the rain." Wheeze. "Stop bitching."

Mason clenched his teeth. Goddamn bastard had better die.

In his agitation, Lavi jostled Mason forward. "The fuck they can't. D'you think I'm stupid or something?"

Out of the corner of Mason's eye he saw Rock knock his fist into Lavi's shoulder. Lavi muttered under his breath and then went quiet.

Stan's eyes glittered in the indirect glow of the utility vehicle's headlights and the shadows behind him made his expression appear darker, harder than ever as he stared at Mason. "You sorry yet...for what you did?"

"I'll never be sorry."

"That brother of yours...sounded sorry enough."

Mason lunged toward Stan again, but Lavi and Rock were ready for him this time and all he managed was to pull on his shoulder too hard, sending pain stabbing all the way up the side of his neck. He regained control of his temper and stopped struggling to sit back on his heels, breathing hard while the gusting wind blew the rain directly at him.

Stan made an aborted move to raise his hand but dropped it back to his chest instead. "Ready...to talk?"

"I can't wait until you're dead and buried, you goddamn monster."

Stan's eyebrows rose. "Monster? I'm a...goddamn patriot, Waters. You used to be. Don't know...what happened…to you." Stan started coughing again, bending almost double as he did. "Not—"

His coughing stopped, as suddenly as it had started.

Mason waited, one, two, three heartbeats. The wind swirled, whipping rain into Mason's face.

Stan didn't move.

"Aw fuck," Rock said. "Goddammit!"

Satisfaction surged deep into Mason's heart and he clenched his fists behind him and tried to shake off Lavi's hold. "The son of a bitch is dead. You should—"

Before he could tell them what he thought they ought to do—let him go, for starters—Rock slammed Mason to the ground. Lavi's hold on him jerked loose and his cheekbone connected with a slab of sandstone jutting out of the wet earth.

Stunned almost senseless, he couldn't react fast enough before Rock's knee plowed into the middle of his spine.

Rock felt like a two-ton truck on Mason's back.

Thunder clapped. Lightning flashed so close that the bright spark of light blinded him. A tree cracked and the long, slow fall of a broken trunk shook the forest.

Rock grabbed Mason by the hair again and yanked, bowing Mason's spine and raising his chest off the waterlogged earth. The cold edge of a blade pressed at Mason's throat.

He was about to die, at the hands of a man he'd once thought he could count on to protect his back. Talk about fucking irony.

Rock's hot breath hit his ear. "Stan was worth twenty of—"

A gunshot ricocheted through the woods. Mason jerked.

The knife slipped from Rock's fingers. His hand tightened in Mason's hair and he staggered sideways, dragging Mason with him.

Mason spent too many seconds not knowing what the hell was going on.

"What the—"

Another shot reverberated on the air, cutting Lavi off mid-exclamation. Lavi crashed to the ground.

Mason's brain finally caught up with his change in circumstance. He jerked free of Rock's weakening grip and shoved the heavy man to the side. Rock dropped to one knee, groaning. He'd been shot, no doubt about that, but Mason couldn't see well enough through the shadows created by the utility vehicle's headlights or the pouring rain to pinpoint where or how bad the man's injury was.

A quick glance in Lavi's direction said he probably wouldn't ever move again. His eyes stared sightless up at the night sky.

Mason lunged toward the utility vehicle on his hands and knees, impossible escape in his sight.

A man stepped in front of the vehicle's headlights, rifle in hand. "I thought I recognized that name of yours."

Mason stopped, pushing himself up onto his knees, his heart thundering as loud as the rain beating at his head and shoulders. "Who the hell are you?"

The man crossed the distance between them, leaning his rifle on his shoulder as he came, his stocky build stirring an unsettling sense of recognition deep inside Mason's gut.

"I'm surprised you don't remember," the man said. "We hunted wolves together."

Before Mason could react to that statement, another voice came from behind him.

"He'll remember me."

Now that voice? That voice he recognized, and it sent a chill down his spine that had nothing at all to do with the driving rain and the flash of lightning that chose that moment to light up the night sky.

Chapter 2

IT WAS A GODDAMN curse, Mason was sure of it. He looked over his shoulder. Sure enough, there stood Jay in the pouring rain, the wind dragging at the man's jacket and the headlights of the utility vehicle outlining his wiry frame and the gun strapped to his thigh.

Mason had survived his encounter with Stan, Rock, and Lavi, despite his certainty that death was just around the corner, but he'd survived only because he'd been saved by a man he knew only as Jay.

Mason clambered to his feet, raking mud off his face as he did. His forearm throbbed and pain sizzled along his nerves but he shunted it aside. No time to deal with it. No time to deal with the dizzy spin of his head or the weak feeling in his legs either.

Jay was here.

Jay. His own goddamned devil.

Three years ago, he'd almost sold his soul to Jay for a few hundred gold ten-dollars. The only thing that had stopped him had been circumstance. Even now, that thought brought with it a gut-churning splash of shame.

"What are you doing here?" Mason wasn't sure what strange fate had brought Jay back into his life, but he didn't like it. That part of Mason's life was over—or had been, until Marcus fucked up.

He exhaled a shaky breath. Marcus was still out there. Mason would have to go get him. There was no way he was leaving him behind.

Jay adjusted the hood on his jacket against the gusting rain, looking toward his companion. "Just passing through."

Mason made sure he could see both men. He didn't want either one of them at his back.

The other man moved the rifle, slinging it over his shoulder by the attached strap, and said to Mason, "Waters, right? Which one are you?"

"Mason." Mason eyed the man, trying to remember what the hell his name was. Nothing came to him.

Jay gestured toward Stan's body where it slouched against the utility vehicle. "Who were they?"

Mason glanced behind him, but Rock hadn't moved. If he was still groaning, Mason couldn't hear it, not over the gusting wind and torrent of rain.

Jay stepped closer. "You going to answer?"

Mason started forward. "I've got somewhere to go. I don't have time to answer questions."

He hadn't gone more than three feet when Jay caught him by the arm.

Mason jerked free.

"I wouldn't do that again," Jay's companion said.

Mason stopped moving. The man's rifle had come down, aimed dead center at Mason's chest.

"Not very grateful, is he?" Jay said.

"Doesn't look that way," the other man replied.

"Now," Jay said, Mason's own shadow hiding Jay's expression from the glow of headlights. "Thank me for saving your life."

Mason clenched his fists and stared straight at Jay. "Thank you for saving my life."

"Now answer my question." Jay gestured toward Stan again.

Mason breathed deep. "They're guys I knew growing up. They claimed my brother took something from them and they wanted it back. Marcus called me asking for help. I came. I found them instead."

"Renegades?"

Mason shrugged. "Don't know."

Jay's hand reached for the holster on his thigh.

"I've been out of that shit for years now." His voice turned hard. "Like I said, I don't know. Shouldn't you be the one answering that question?"

The other man moved and Mason tensed, but it was only to squat down and start going through Stan's pockets.

At that moment the utility vehicle's headlights flickered and the engine's hum stuttered before picking up speed again.

Mason gave Jay a stubborn look. "I'm getting out of here before that thing runs out of halfgas. If you want to come along and ask questions, that's fine, but I've got a body to collect."

He didn't wait for Jay to respond, just started moving toward the vehicle.

The other man raised his head, then quickly rose to his feet as Mason pushed around him. Mason jumped into the driver's seat of the utility vehicle.

"We'll tag along," Jay said, tugging his hood closer.

"I hope you've got fast transportation," Mason said, "because I'm not waiting on you."

With that, he put the machine in gear and gunned the engine. Stan's body flopped to the ground as the vehicle shot off.

He turned around by driving a circle around the collapsed shed. He stopped once, thinking he saw his rifle in the shadows of fallen boards, but it was just the end of a branch. By the time he pulled away, Jay and his companion were nowhere to be seen, but he could hear the rev of another engine off in the trees ahead of him.

Shit. He'd really hoped he'd seen the last of Jay three years ago, but seemed like nothing ever worked out for the good these days.

On the other hand, there were still men alive inside that lab somewhere and Mason wasn't letting any of them stop him from recovering Marcus's body. Jay and his companion might come in handy if Mason had to fight.

Marcus hadn't liked Jay. He wouldn't like the idea of Mason taking help from the man either. But sometimes you had to make a deal with the devil to do what needed done, and Mason wasn't too good to accept that. Marcus would forgive him. He always had.

It was Mason who'd never been able to forgive himself.

◌

"There," Mason said, pointing at the hulking shadow in the distance. Dark windows ran the length of the building, half buried in the middle of a forest of trees. Half the building was nothing but a burned out husk, while the other half…

Suffice to say, the other half should've been burned

out too, but no one had come back to do the job all those years ago, and the reasons for that were lost to a history Mason didn't know. The great quake had done some of the damage, he was sure, and the massive forest fires that followed had probably done the rest.

Or maybe not. It was just as possible someone had taken advantage of the destruction from the quake and burned the place down.

The hell if he could remember. His education had been good enough, but he hadn't been a good student. He'd spent most of his life avoiding a competition he couldn't win.

Mason raked his hand over his face, mixing the cold rain with the hot burn of tears.

Fucking Marcus. He'd always had to be the smart one.

The rain had eased during the last half-hour. The lingering drizzle ran down the back of his newly acquired jacket, but the cap he'd found along with it in one of the utility vehicle's storage boxes had kept the water out of his eyes while he led the way to the last place he'd seen Marcus alive.

Sebastian—Mason had finally gotten the man's name —climbed off the ATV he'd parked beside the utility vehicle. He stopped next to Jay, who was standing beside Mason just to the outside of a copse of oak trees.

Jay shared a look with Sebastian, before glancing again at the building. He spoke to Mason without taking his eyes off the dark windows ahead. "What is this place?"

"It's an old biolab."

"And your brother's in there? What was he doing here?"

"They brought him here."

Jay's thumb moved over the rear sight of his gun, again and again, while he seemed to be lost in thought. Finally he said, "I'm going to need more than that."

"Marcus said they've been trying to create some kind of weapon. Something to use against the wolves."

Jay finally turned his gaze to Mason. "Now that's interesting."

"Your brother knew what it was?" Sebastian asked.

Mason chose his words carefully. "He said they were part of something bigger, didn't say what. I didn't ask. He's my brother. He wants help, he gets it. I don't give a fuck what he's part of." His voice choked tight. "He's my brother."

They're going to burn down the whole goddamned world, Marcus had said. *If I can't stop them, you have to, you hear me?*

Jay shared another look with Sebastian.

Just then, Mason sneezed twice in quick succession. He barely covered his face in time and then had to wipe his hand on his wet and muddy jeans. The goddamned rain and wind was getting to him. He didn't have time for this shit with Jay.

He decided to head off any more questions. "It doesn't matter what they're doing. Marcus is dead. I want him back and I'm not leaving this goddamn place until I have him. You either help me or don't, but I'm going in after him."

He'd seen Marcus fall at Stan's feet, although it'd been from a distance. He'd rushed Stan, but their fight had taken them far away from Marcus's body, and then he'd ended up on the run.

Hours had passed. The storm had blown in and time was short.

Marcus had been clear that things were happening in the early morning hours, before dawn.

Mason had to get his shit together and take care of this, one way or another.

Sebastian leaned his rifle's barrel against his shoulder, his hand cradling the stock. He made a noise in his throat, then said, "It might be just what we've been looking for. Could go back with something, anyway."

His gaze drifted to Jay, who looked back with steady resolve.

There was a story there, but Mason barely cared what it might be. He searched the building's exterior for signs of movement but he couldn't make out anything through the swaying branches and drizzling rain.

He moved to the utility vehicle and dug with his right hand through the box where he'd found the cap. He was trying not to move his left arm more than he had to because every time he did his stomach rolled over, while his makeshift bandage had barely held together through the struggle with Rock and Lavi.

Sebastian lowered his rifle but didn't go so far as to point it at Mason.

"We'll go in with you," Jay said. "We'll find the weapon, then your brother."

"I don't give a damn about the weapon," Mason said as careless as he could manage. "I want my brother. You two can do what you want."

His fingertips brushed something hard buried under a thin blanket. He pulled out what he'd found. Binoculars.

He raised the high-tech device to his face, close enough to see details.

Whoa the fuck down. He sat back against the utility vehicle and wedged the binoculars between his thighs. He activated the thermal imaging cameras. "They're getting supplies from somewhere. Nobody I know around here can afford this shit. These are hard to come by."

"We'll stay together," Jay said.

Mason raised the binoculars to his face and directed his view toward the dark building. "I told you—"

"I know what you said."

Mason heard the distinctive whish of a gun coming out of a holster and he stilled. He knew what kind of man Jay was: he was a man who kept his promises, even the unspoken ones.

"Fine. We'll go in together."

Mason turned back to the utility vehicle. The storage box contained several extra magazines but no gun. The only weapon he found was a sheathed blade three-quarters the length of his forearm.

He took it out. The sheath still had a harness attached and when he pulled the blade free he snorted in disgust. Whoever it belonged to hadn't even bothered to clean it before putting it away.

Still, it was better than his pocketknife, even if his pocketknife did have a few special tools attached. Being able to start a fire or unscrew a panel wasn't going to help him defend himself against someone determined to put an end to him.

He realized quickly enough he wasn't going to be able to get the strap over his shoulder with only one good arm so he yanked the strap free of the sheath and tucked the sheath into his boot.

Jay's voice came from above him. "That won't do you much good."

"You got something better for me?"

Jay glanced over his shoulder. "Sebastian does."

Mason looked over at the other man. He was closing a bag tied to the back of the ATV. A moment later, he crossed the distance between them and held out his hand. The holster was so dark Mason had to squint to make out its outline.

He reached for it. "Thanks. Can't say I won't need it."

"Looks like we're on the same side here." Sebastian's teeth flashed in the dark. "But I will want it back."

Mason flipped the holster, the weight of the gun reassuring in his hand. "Hate to ask, but I'm going to need one of you to strap this on me."

"I'll do it," Sebastian said.

Sebastian stepped back and Mason stood. He held the holster in place over his thigh while Sebastian squatted in front of him and strapped it in place. Rain drizzled off the bill of his cap and pattered onto the dead leaves and pine needles at his feet.

"Thanks."

"You loaned me your sleeping bag once. You remember me yet?"

Mason straightened as Sebastian rose. "I remember."

And he did, now. He hadn't, though, not until Sebastian brought it up. Mason had shared a bag with Marcus that night, after half the guys in the group had lost their supplies because the trailer carrying those supplies to a new location got picked up by county police. Of course, back then the police had still had some jurisdiction in the protectorate. Now the wolves ruled everything.

Jay spoke up. "Let's see if we can get in there without

anyone noticing. I want to get my hands on whatever it is they're making."

Mason watched Jay gesture to Sebastian and him and then start wending his way along the edge of the woods, toward the left side of the building where the least fire damage had occurred. As Mason walked behind, he eased the gun out of the holster and checked the magazine. Half-full.

It was a small caliber weapon, but still, deadly enough against a human.

He tucked it away and picked up the pace.

Time was not just running short; time was running out.

Chapter 3

THE INSIDE OF THE secondary lab had been ransacked. The primary lab had burned to the ground fifty years ago. Whoever was supposed to be guarding the tertiary lab had moved on and left it open to anyone who walked by.

Mason wasn't sure what to make of any of it. He'd expected resistance. He'd expected to find *people*.

What he found instead was a quickly deserted facility that might as well have been a tomb.

What he didn't find was Marcus.

The closer they got to the burned out half of the building, the tighter Mason's nerves coiled. Something wasn't right and he suspected Jay and Sebastian knew it too. Neither man had said a word in the last ten minutes.

Ahead, Jay stopped. The binoculars Mason had found had fit him without adjustment and the display was as sharp as any *veo* screen Mason had ever seen, so he was able to see into the night-dark halls and rooms without the aid of the flashlight Jay was using. When Sebastian looked over his shoulder, Jay gestured with his flashlight for Sebastian to come forward. Sebastian made a motion with his chin, and Mason moved into Sebastian's position to keep an eye on the hallway behind them.

His back was to Jay and Sebastian but he could still hear the quiet whisper of their voices. He wasn't sure they realized the binoculars had targeted sound amplification—he sure as hell hadn't told them when he'd put the binoculars on and discovered that fact.

"If this was where they were making the bullets, they've managed to take the whole set up with them," Jay said. "If it was something else, I don't know what it could've been just from looking at the junk left behind."

"So you think he was telling the truth? These are the people we've been looking for?"

"Enough of a chance to make it worth coming back later to search the place in the daylight."

"What about the brother?"

Jay's voice lowered further. "Forget him. A dead man isn't going to tell us anything we need to know."

"Like Matthew? You shouldn't have—"

"You'll keep your fucking mouth shut about that when we get back, understand me?"

Mason's heart took up a rapid, thudding beat. What the hell were they talking about? *Who* the hell were they talking about? There were a lot of Matthews in the world, but Mason only knew one, but how the fuck would they have—

"She wanted him alive." Sebastian's whispering turned fierce. "We both have to answer for that."

"We didn't find him. That's all that needs to be said."

"You know that's not all that'll be said."

"We have a problem here?"

"No, we don't. But I still think you went too far with him."

"That's my fucking business. Now it's time to go. We're not going to find anything here in the fucking dark."

"We should take him—"

A sudden gust of wind rattled the roof and drowned out the rest of whatever Sebastian was saying. Then a howl rose on the wind.

"Goddammit!" Mason turned. "Wolves."

Jay had obviously picked up the sound too and he swung around, gun held firm. When the sound didn't repeat, he shifted his attention to Mason.

He didn't lower the gun.

Mason clenched his jaw.

"Shit." Sebastian fumbled something out of his pocket. "Turn your phone off. We're out of range of the signal blocker."

"It's not on," Jay said. "Why the fuck is yours?"

Sebastian flinched but didn't answer. He tucked his phone back into his pocket and looked at Mason. "You?"

"Don't have one on me."

Jay stared at Mason a moment, then gestured down the hallway. "You'll have to draw them away."

"Are you fucking serious?"

"You're injured and you've been bleeding." His flashlight's beam bounced off Mason's left arm. "Your blood's all over that jacket. If we try to get out with you along, you'll draw them right to us."

Mason bit off a curse. Not that he wanted to leave with Jay and Sebastian, but he didn't want to play bait to the wolves either.

Sebastian held his hand out. Mason blinked, then glanced at Sebastian's face.

"The pistol. Since we're parting ways and all."

Goddammit. Anger flared bright and hot in Mason's chest. He yanked at the strap holding the holster to his leg. When it was free, he tossed it at Sebastian.

Sebastian caught it one-handed. He nodded. "Good luck."

"Fuck you too."

Sebastian just shook his head. Jay maintained his alert position, waiting.

Mason took a deep breath and walked away, back down the hallway they'd just traveled. For a few moments, he could hear Jay and Sebastian's cautious footsteps heading in the opposite direction, but then the oppressive silence returned, broken only by the occasional gust of wind and the pitter-patter of rain on the building's roof.

He hadn't gone far when he heard another howl, this one seeming to come from inside the building and the hair at the back of his neck prickled. A spark of fear brought adrenaline rushing to his veins and for one brief moment his vision grayed to almost nothing.

God. He shouldn't forget how much blood he'd lost. He wouldn't be able to run if the wolves found him—not that running was ever a good idea. But he sure as hell hated that the choice wasn't going to be his to make.

A door loomed to the right and he took it, pushing past the entrance and deep into the old bathroom. Stalls lined the room, left and right, and although the room was pitch black, he was able to see the faint outline of every opening with the help of the binoculars.

He stripped off the jacket, careful of his injured arm, and dropped it to the floor. Whoever had been using the building had cleared the floor and gotten the water working. Of course, the water might not last because the pumps were probably tied in to a generator that was no longer running, but for the time being he had fresh water and he drank several handfuls before he turned to cleaning mud off his face and neck. The rain had washed most of it away, but not all, and his one-handed scrubbing helped clear his head.

When he was done, he kicked the jacket into the corner and left it there.

As good as it would feel to just sit down and not get back up for a week, hiding in a bathroom wasn't going to find his brother.

❧

Mason took his time returning to the ransacked lab, making sure every corner and corridor was clear before he risked his position. His scent would lead the wolves to him eventually, no doubt about that. Heat season had started; there was no way a wolf in heat wouldn't recognize a human nearby. But every second he bought himself was another second he could spend searching for clues Marcus might have left behind.

The lab door had broken into a million tiny pieces of tempered glass and so had the windowed wall that stretched from the doorframe to the wall on the right. They'd all searched the room earlier and found nothing useful. Mason wanted another chance at it, this time without Jay and Sebastian watching his every move.

He started in the far corner, where a series of long tables ended next to a column of glass-fronted cabinets that had been emptied of everything they'd once held. He drew his fingers down the length of one of the tables, feeling for any hint of dust.

Nothing.

Despite the abandoned look, someone had been using this lab as recently as today.

He reached up and adjusted the thermal settings on the binoculars to their highest sensitivity. A warning flashed in front of his eyes. The new setting was going to drain the power quickly and there'd be no recharging in the dark without a power station. If he drained all the power, he'd be stuck in the near pitch black building without any way of finding his way out until daylight arrived, but it was a risk he was willing to take.

A freestanding cabinet on wheels had been pushed close to the wall. He stared at those wheels for a few seconds, considering what he saw, then moved toward it. One careful shove and he'd exposed a narrow vent set low in the wall. There were matching vents near the ceiling, just as small but to reach them he'd have to stand on a table.

He squatted in front of the low vent, pulled out his knife, and pried at the edges. The vent snapped away from the wall easily, the fasteners too brittle to hold on after all this time. Unfortunately, all he found was an empty hole and a steady draft of rain-cooled air. The ventilation system probably exited somewhere in the burned out half of the building.

He slid his knife back into the sheath in his boot but didn't bother sliding the vent back into place, dropping it quietly to the floor beside him instead. He twisted around on his heels and tried to make sense of what he saw in the rest of the room.

Warm spots at the edges of the tables, several in a row. Hot spots along one straight stretch.

Maybe…someone had held the edge of the table for

support, making his way along the surface until he reached that spot there, when he'd given in and leaned...

Mason rose and crossed the room quickly, touching the table's edge.

Nothing.

Except...

He ran his fingers under the lip of the table and something slick smeared under his touch. He raised his fingers to his nose. One sniff and he knew what he'd found. Blood.

He followed the trail of residual heat on the table and stopped at one of the cabinets. They'd gone through them when they found the room, but in a hurry, and it was entirely possible they'd missed something.

He swung the nearest cabinet open and reached inside. He ran his fingers over every surface and into every corner, and finally, on the second shelf from the bottom, he found something.

The EP display was so thin the only way he could get hold of it was to pry it up with his fingernails. No wonder they'd missed it. He dragged the flexible screen out of the cabinet and dropped it to the table. The screen flared to life, one short burst of light, then went blank.

He needed a charging station.

The binoculars flickered another warning, more urgent than the last: *Automatic Shutdown in 00:03:00*.

Goddammit. Three minutes was too soon. He reached up and lowered the sensitivity as far as it would go. It'd buy him some time, but he needed to get out of this building and he needed to do it now. He quickly rolled the screen and shoved it into the waistband of his jeans at his side. The wet denim was stiff as hell, but it would create enough friction to hold the screen in place as he moved.

He started for the doorway, walking between two long tables, glass crunching under his boots. He was halfway there when a quiet shuffle behind him brought him up short.

His blood thundered through his veins. Somehow, someway, someone had gotten into the lab without him hearing it earlier.

The shuffle came again, closer than before, along with the faintest hint of glass cracking underfoot. The hair at the back of his neck prickled.

He turned slowly between two long tables and stared at the image before him.

Humans didn't burn that hot and humans didn't breathe that fast.

Humans didn't have claws that screaked against metal and clicked against the floor with every step.

Every muscle in his body tensed for flight.

"Are you going to run?" The question came through a gentle accent, and swear to God, the wolf sounded almost hopeful.

"Don't think that'd be a good idea, now would it?"

"I would try not to hurt you if you did. I promise."

An abrupt, humorless laugh escaped before Mason could stop it. "Are you serious?"

"If you submit when I catch you—"

"Which you'll do by jabbing those claws in my spine."

The wolf raised his hand and stared a moment at his fully extended claws. "You are probably right." A sigh carried softly through the air. "But mating is so much more thrilling when my mate forces me to prove myself. I'll miss the challenge."

"So I'm no challenge, huh?"

"You are human. Humans are too fragile to be a challenge. We expend so much energy holding back our mating instincts that we can't enjoy the mating."

Nothing about this confrontation made sense to Mason. But the wolves did have repression drugs that helped them control their reaction to human scent and kept them from succumbing to the frenzy of uncontrolled lust that had proven deadly to both human and wolf.

He asked, suspiciously, "Are you drugged?"

"At the moment. But I've been away from my pack too long, without my own supply. And your scent taunts me." He took a subtle sniff of air and Mason could've sworn he saw a shudder pass through the wolf's powerful body. "I tried to resist, but I couldn't. It is...hauntingly familiar."

At that moment, the binoculars' display flashed another warning: *Automatic Shutdown in 00:03:00.*

His pulse fluttered wildly at his throat. He'd gained time—then lost it. He wouldn't even have enough time to get out of the building, unless—

"If you want me to run, you're going to have to give me a head start."

The wolf dropped his arm to the table next to him and his claws raked across the surface with a metallic screak.

Mason jumped.

Shit. *Shit.* This was going to be impossible. He wouldn't get away.

"You shouldn't tempt me. I'm at the edge of my control already. I can taste your fear and it's as intoxicating as any *reigeiesteisa* I've ever swallowed."

The wolf had dropped into his own language, his words taking on an exotic sound that tickled at Mason's eardrums. Like every human he knew, he'd used the wolves' learning technology to learn the wolves' language. He understood enough to get by and could even get out a few phrases when he had to. He hadn't had to in a very long time.

Three years, to be exact.

Automatic Shutdown in 00:02:30.

An edge of panic started to push at his thoughts. He spoke fast. "So do we have a deal?"

"A deal?"

"I run, you give me a head start?"

The sudden rumbling from deep in the wolf's chest raised every hair on Mason's body.

"You want me to hunt you despite the danger to yourself?"

"Yes or no?"

"I should say no. You're human. You don't know what you're risking."

Then the wolf growled low in his chest and dropped to a crouch, his sharper-than-human eyeteeth a jagged line in the display covering Mason's eyes.

Mason staggered back a step, heart pounding as if he were already running.

"But I won't," the wolf said. "Now run, so I can catch you and claim you to mate."

Chapter 4

MASON HAD NEVER run so hard in his life. His feet pounded on the debris-strewn tiles and his lungs ached with the weight of every desperate breath he took. His headlong rush for the entrance of the building left his already weakened body absolutely depleted of energy by the time he tore through the building's abandoned lobby.

He barely missed slamming right into the algae-coated glass door.

Clouds blocked the moon but the night wasn't as dark as it had been as the early morning hours crept toward daybreak. Mason ripped off the binoculars just as the warning flashed red and the countdown hit 00:00:00. He tossed them to the ground as he crossed the threshold.

He had no idea how long that wolf was going to give him before he started after Mason, but Mason could guarantee one thing: that wolf would outlast Mason in any chase. Mason had to get back to the utility vehicle and get the hell out of there before it was too late.

The task he needed to do for his brother would have to wait.

He heard something crash through the pines to his left and he veered off the straight path he'd planned to take back to the utility vehicle.

His legs trembled and he stumbled. Everything spiraled around him as vertigo slammed into him with all the power of a wolf on his back. He couldn't catch his balance. His knee hit the ground and he threw out his arm to catch his fall.

Wrong arm.

He barely cut off a scream with his clenched teeth.

It took precious seconds to get his breathing under control—to stop the swimming of his head. Drizzle teased the back of his neck and the base of his spine where his shirt had ridden up. One...two...three... four...

He shoved himself up on his good arm and staggered to his feet. The dark closed in on him. The trees all looked the same.

He'd lost his bearings. He wasn't sure which way to go. If he chose wrong, he'd be on foot—and as good as dead unless that wolf actually could control himself enough not to rip out Mason's spine.

Shit. *Shit.* That knife he'd found would never save him.

His breath came in harsh gasps and his feet crunched through the dead and dying leaves. He thrust aside a thick limb with his right forearm, holding his injured arm tight to his chest.

Where the hell was the goddamned utility vehicle? Had he gone past it?

He could feel that fucking wolf breathing down his neck as he searched desperately for a vehicle that should be *right there* but wasn't.

"Goddammit!"

They'd taken it. That goddamned Jay and Sebastian had taken it and left him here as the distraction so they could get away—he should've realized what they'd do the moment they decided to use him as bait for the wolves, but he'd been too distracted by the search for his brother, too worried about what he was supposed to do to stop something he didn't even understand.

He didn't have time to stand around and curse so he picked a direction and ran until he couldn't take another damn step. Then he stopped and bent double, one hand on his knee, head hanging. Standing upright was better for his lungs but his muscles burned and his head spun and—

His knees gave out and he dropped to his ass on the cold, wet ground. Son of a bitch but he was almost at the end of his rope.

He struggled to listen over the harsh sound of his own breathing. Rain dripped from the leaves with every rustle of wind and the night felt as deep and dark as a cave even though daybreak couldn't be more than a couple hours away, if that.

Somewhere in the distance, the thrash and rattle of leaves grew louder. Mason concentrated on that sound, then jerked as he realized something was definitely headed in his direction. He rose to a crouch, but had to stop before he'd reached his feet because of his swimming head. He dropped back the ground with a quiet "umph."

Fuck it. He wasn't going anywhere. Not this time.

He'd had one chance and that had been the utility vehicle. Without it, running would just inflame the wolf further and leave Mason in dire straits.

He eyed the shadow of the tree across from him. He scooted around until he could rest against its broad trunk and stretched his legs out in front of him, crossing his ankles. He eased his injured arm down across his stomach, hissing through his teeth until he'd settled comfortably.

He leaned his head back against the rough bark and closed his eyes.

The wind shifted. A shiver raised gooseflesh on his arms and he tucked his good arm across his chest and held onto his shoulder, trying to conserve what warmth he could while soaked to the bone from the rain. He clenched his teeth against the chill breeze and thought it might not be so bad to end up under a lust-crazed wolf.

As hot as the wolves ran, at least he'd be warm.

Maybe it was the blood loss or the simple fact that he'd found himself in this situation after a morning so ordinary and dull he'd been ready to stick a pitchfork in his foot for a little excitement, but he laughed, hard.

What a damn mess Marcus had made for him.

His laugh turned to something else and he choked it back with every ounce of control he had left. Goddamned feelings. If he could burn them to the ground, he'd do it in a heartbeat. He didn't have time for that shit.

If I can't stop them, you have to, you hear me?

He didn't want to believe Marcus was dead, and he had no definitive proof that he was, but if Marcus wasn't dead, where was he? How the fuck was Mason supposed to find him?

And what had he meant when he said *they're going to burn down the whole goddamned world?*

Marcus hadn't explained enough of what was going

on to make things easy for Mason, that was for damn sure. *Get there before dawn. They're moving the weapon. I'm going to try to stop them, but it's going to be tricky. They've got six men on it and one of them's that tough motherfucker who used to live on Smith Road. Remember him? A goddamned sociopath if you ask me.*

He'd told Mason to get there, anyway he had to, as quick as he could, because he needed Mason in case his plan went south. He'd included a map to the old biolab.

Mason scrubbed his hand down his wet face, unable anymore to stop the shivers wracking his body. He wished he'd kept the jacket. Fucking amateur move to toss it. The blood loss had obviously affected him more seriously than he'd thought.

Leaves crunched nearby and Mason's heart started beating double-time. He sat up straighter. He was going to get this right, because he wasn't up to facing the consequences if he didn't.

He'd made too many fucking mistakes. He couldn't afford any more.

Mason pushed himself to his feet with his back to the tree's trunk and stood there, waiting. But if it was the wolf who was pushing his way through the brush and trees that made up this part of the forest, he didn't seem to be in a hurry, and Mason finally got tired of waiting.

"I submit!" he called out. "If you're looking for a mate, I'm right here." He almost said more, and more aggressively too, but caught himself at the last moment and shut his mouth.

He pressed his spine into the bark. *Just calm the hell down.*

Only an idiot would antagonize a wolf during heat season, and then only one with a death wish.

Like most of the people he knew, he'd been to one of the heat cycle survival training sessions and he'd heard the rules: *Submit if you want to live. Don't run unless you want claws in your spine and teeth in your neck and two hundred pounds of lust-crazed wolf on your back. The wolves don't want to hurt you, but during heat, they're not reasonable. They either want to fuck you or kill you. Do whatever you have to do to survive. Remember: you fight, you die.*

He didn't believe it, not the part about the wolves being reasonable people. Because they weren't. They were manipulative bastards who'd gotten the upper hand and they didn't intend to give it up.

They brainwashed their enemies. They stole a man's free will.

They turned passionately patriotic men into traitors.

He only had to look at Marcus to see it.

But Marcus was his brother and that was that. Marcus got away with his divided loyalties because Mason couldn't bring himself to call him on them. Not after what he'd demanded of Marcus.

And that insidious whisper again: *Not after what Marcus gave up for you.* Marcus hadn't been the same in the three years since, and all that was Mason's fault. Every last second of it.

The thick branches of a pine tree thrashed wildly to his left, no more than ten feet away, and then a figure pushed its way through, the shape lost to the dark.

A beam of light streaked across Mason's face, blinding him to everything before focusing at his chest.

"You know you just grossed me the hell out, right?"

"Oh fuck. Marcus. My God." Mason's thighs gave out and dragged him down the trunk at his back, bark scraping his spine the whole way. He almost sat on his ass before his legs regained enough strength to stop his downward slide.

He let his head fall back against the trunk and sucked in a ragged breath. "It's you. You're alive. Thank God."

Marcus came closer, putting his hands on Mason's shoulders, and the light strapped to his wrist blinked out. "We have to get out of here. Wolves are everywhere. I don't know what's going on but they're out in force. Maybe they've heard something about this weapon and they've come looking for it."

Mason pushed upright, reaching up with one hand to clasp Marcus's hand to his shoulder. Marcus was real. This wasn't a hallucination. Mason strained his eyes trying to see through the dark. "What happened? How are you here? I saw him stick that knife in you."

"I shouldn't be. That's the goddamned truth. I should be dead." Marcus grabbed Mason's wrist. Pain shot along the gash in his arm.

Mason jerked. "Not that one," he said, voice high and tight.

The hand Marcus still had on Mason's shoulder squeezed. "What's wrong?"

"I sliced my arm open when I wrecked the damn four-wheeler trying to get away from the guys I thought had killed you."

"The other one, then. You have to feel this." Marcus took Mason's other hand and pressed it to his midsection. "Feel that?"

Mason's fingers skimmed over a ridge of flesh nearly as long as his hand. A shudder passed through him at the knowledge of what it was. Marcus was right. He should've been dead.

"It just started healing, faster than anything I've ever

seen. I don't know what's going on but it's a fucking miracle. I thought I was dead. They left me lying in a pool of blood and my own guts and took off after you. A few hours later, I was making my way out of the woods where I'd dragged myself off to hide from the lot of them when I saw you come back. I waited for you to come out, but when you did you were running like you had a wolf at your back. But no one followed you out."

Mason started shaking his head. "I do have a wolf at my back. The bastard was nice enough to give me a head start."

His sarcasm wasn't lost to Marcus, who exhaled sharply through his nose. "A wolf has your scent?"

"Oh yeah." Mason wiped at his rain-damp face. "He talked like a determined motherfucker too. He's going to hunt me down and claim me for a mate."

Marcus darted a look over his shoulder. "Got an ATV behind the—"

Mason grabbed Marcus by the arm to get his attention. "What the fuck is going on, Marcus? What are we doing here?"

"Later. Let's just get out of here. I have an ATV hidden behind the lab. I left it because I didn't want it making noise that might attract the wolves until I knew you were safe. We'll have to go back the way you came at least part of the way."

"Not a good idea. I have no idea how much of a lead he's planning to give me. Thought you were him when I heard the—"

A wolf's howl echoed in the air, coming from somewhere deep in the woods.

An answering roar came from somewhere too goddamned close.

Marcus's whole body tensed. "Shit."

"You have to go," Mason said. "If I go with you, that wolf'll dog our trail for miles."

"I hope you're not fucking serious, because you know I'm not leaving you behind."

Marcus grabbed at Mason's shirt and turned.

Mason refused to budge. "I can't. Just go. I owe you this."

Marcus swung around and grabbed both Mason's arms. "Goddammit, Mason! You don't owe me *anything* for what happened three years ago. Stop wallowing in your fucking guilt over it. It was just the way things go sometimes. We thought we were in a war, for God's sake. But we weren't. We aren't. You need to let it go. Get over this shit. I did it because I wanted to. You didn't make me."

Mason jerked his arms free of Marcus's grip. "I know you did, but if I—"

"In fact, I liked it," Marcus continued. "I liked him. He changed my mind about a lot of shit and I don't care. I'm glad it happened."

Mason stared at the dark shadow that was Marcus, breathing hard into the chill air. The rain had finally stopped, and the trees shed water with every last gasp of wind from the storm.

"I know," Mason said, so softly that the words felt like a sigh. "I know you are, I know you did, and I can't seem to forgive you for that."

"Goddammit," Marcus breathed. "I knew you were hiding something. I just didn't think it was this."

Chapter 5

MASON OPENED HIS mouth to respond, but a violent rustle of leaves directly behind them cut him short.

Marcus turned, too slow, as something large burst from behind the trees only a few feet away. Mason threw Marcus hard to the left. Marcus hit the ground just as a deer charged by them, panicked and breathing hard, racing away from whatever it was that had put the fear of death into it.

Mason stared into the woods beyond, throat tight and heart pounding, while Marcus exhaled a groan, then rolled to his feet.

Marcus limped to Mason's side, his hand pressed to his stomach. "Shit, that hurt. But thanks."

Mason didn't take his eyes off the woods. "They're out there. We can't go back the way you came. They've probably caught your scent now too."

"What about towards that wolf of yours?"

"Fuck you. He's not my wolf."

"Not yet, he isn't. But if it's a choice between him and a whole pack, we're going with him and hoping he can get us the fuck out of here. If he wants you, he'll want to protect you and keep the others away. If we let a pack of them hunt us down, we'll end up in the middle of a mating frenzy—and one alien cock in my ass at a time is plenty, thank you very much."

Mason narrowed his eyes on his brother's shadowy expression. He hadn't missed Marcus's sudden shift in tone and he knew Marcus well enough to suspect exactly what Marcus had planned. Marcus thought he was going to find a way out of this, and if that didn't work, he would try to take control of the situation—but if he thought Mason was going to let him sacrifice himself the same way he'd done three years ago, he was fucking out of his mind.

Mason had fucked up three years ago. He wouldn't be doing it again.

"Your plan sucks," Mason said, "but it's all we've got, so alright."

He turned and started walking, then hesitated, looking the other way.

Goddammit.

He turned toward Marcus. The dark of night had faded in the coming daybreak so gradually he hadn't noticed the light creeping into the woods, but he noticed then, because he could just make out the grin on Marcus's face.

"That way," Marcus said, pointing in the direction opposite Mason's intended path.

"Shit," Mason said. He turned and shoved aside an oak sapling that stood in his way, muttering under his breath.

Behind him, Marcus said, "Not like we're trying to be quiet or anything, huh?"

Mason bit back a curse and shut his mouth. Marcus was right, as usual. The rolled-up EP display shifted at his side and he tucked it more firmly into place as he walked—much more cautiously than before.

He'd let his emotions get the best of him. He didn't need to let that happen again. Too much at stake.

They walked, and it wasn't long before the quiet of the forest became so deep and unnatural that Mason was having to force himself to keep moving. Every step he took felt too firm and too loud, and he found himself hesitating to put his foot down into the wet, slick bed of pine needles that covered the ground in this part of the woods.

Marcus slipped, landing on his knee with a soft thud and a grunt beside Mason.

Mason grabbed for him, but Marcus waved him off.

"You're okay?"

"Yeah. Goddamned boots don't have any tread left on them."

Mason understood that. His own weren't much better. There was a crack in his left boot that had let water in and his sock was still wet and uncomfortable. He'd been trying not to think about it.

Marcus regained his feet and started knocking pine needles off his damp knees.

"This isn't the way I came," Mason whispered. "We're lost."

"No," Marcus whispered back, "this is the way, we're just a little further to the east, that's all."

Mason gave him one hard look, then turned back to making his way through the trees.

Several minutes later, he said, "We should've come out near the building by now."

"We're almost there, I'm telling you."

Mason grunted but let the subject drop. A few more minutes passed—too many—and the hair at the nape of his neck started to prickle. He twisted around, looking behind them, but nothing stood apart in the shadowy forest to explain the sensation.

"You feel it too?"

Mason looked at Marcus, then scanned the distance, squinting so hard his eyes burned.

A limb thwapped somewhere ahead.

He turned, quickly.

Shit. *Shit.*

Something was there, but he just couldn't—

A wolf jumped down in front of him, straight out of the trees.

Mason yelled and fell back, his ass hitting the ground hard enough to rattle his spine.

Marcus grabbed Mason under his injured arm and yanked him backward, nearly falling over him in his effort to put himself between Mason and the wolf.

Mason hissed at the sudden pain in his arm but grappled hard with Marcus, getting his good arm around Marcus's neck and trying to sling him to the side. "Goddammit, Marcus! Get out of the way!"

"Submit!" the wolf roared.

Mason stopped moving, his elbow locked around Marcus's throat. Marcus stopped trying to pry Mason's arm loose.

The wolf lunged toward them.

Mason cringed sideways, raising his shoulder instinctively to protect his throat, half-hiding Marcus under him. "I submit!"

"I submit!" Marcus said at the same time, his heels

scraping at the ground as he tried to get out from under Mason.

The wolf tilted his head, sniffing at the air, then crouched over them both, his sharper-than-human eye-teeth gleaming in the low light, his eyes an incandescent glow. "What is this?"

His clawed hand came out toward Mason, only to end up on Marcus's chin instead. He stared with those soul-searing eyes at Marcus's face for only a few seconds before his nose scrunched and he flicked Marcus's head to the side.

Marcus didn't fight the dismissive gesture; he hardly breathed. Mason didn't blame him. There were rules. Follow them and live. Ignore them and death became more than a possibility—it became damn near inevitable.

His pulse spiked when those glowing wolf eyes turned on him. Even through the faint light of early daybreak, Mason didn't have any trouble at all recognizing this was the wolf from the biolab come to claim his mate.

"He looks like you," the wolf said, "but he isn't you."

"That's right." In different circumstances, Mason might have been happy to finally have someone take notice of that fact. Everywhere he turned, he was mistaken for his brother—but in the end it was never Mason they wanted.

"Your scent," the wolf said. He hadn't taken his gaze off Mason. "There's something about it that I cannot fathom. It haunts me as a memory that does not exist." He nodded sharply, as if he had come to some decision, his gaze fiercely intent on Mason. "We'll travel somewhere safe before we fuck, while I still have some control over my instincts. It will be safer for you and your kin that way. It will give me time to contemplate this memory I do not have. It troubles me, because we do not forget."

Mason's nod was hardly a nod at all, but the wolf returned it as if Mason understood everything he'd just said and then rose to stand over them.

Mason felt the moment Marcus started to open his mouth. He squeezed his arm tighter around Marcus's throat and then spent several tense seconds wrestling to keep Marcus in place with his leg.

"Stop," Mason hissed.

The wolf's gaze shifted to Marcus.

Marcus stilled, but even through the shadowy light, Mason could see the stubborn look on Marcus's face.

"Fighting for my favor won't change your situation. I've already chosen my mate."

The wolf returned his heated gaze to Mason and the inhuman glow in those eyes unsettled Mason to his core. Soon it would be too bright for the wolf's eyes to glow, but although daybreak had come, sunrise hadn't.

Marcus struggled harder, jerking Mason's attention back to him.

"Your kin seems angry that I chose you over him," the wolf said.

"He's used to getting his way," Mason said, "but he ain't winning this time. You're mine. He'll just have to find his own mate."

The wolf made a sound low in his throat and a rumble emanated from his chest. The vibration tingled along Mason's nerves and he shivered, his body's reaction sudden and unexpected.

Marcus made a strangled sound and tapped frantically at Mason's elbow.

"You calling uncle?" Mason asked.

Marcus wasn't able to nod but Mason felt him trying, so Mason eased the chokehold, letting Marcus suck in several deep breaths.

"Oh come on," Marcus said hoarsely. "That's pretty damn funny."

Mason was half a second away from choking him again, because he couldn't help how the wolf's rumble affected his body—he'd heard that half the human population had an involuntary physical reaction to that particular sound—but the wolf moved, bringing Mason's attention back to him abruptly.

The wolf had offered his hand, palm up, wicked claws jutting from beneath the dark material that made up the wolves' fingernails. "Come."

Mason didn't take his wary gaze off the shadows of those claws even as he released Marcus.

Marcus scrambled to his knees and started rubbing at his throat.

Mason should've taken the wolf's hand. He knew that. But instead he rose on his own, on shaky legs, and started trying to knock the leaves off his wet jeans. It was a waste of time. He was covered in mud and the leaves were stuck to him like they'd been glued in place.

A delaying tactic. He knew it. The wolf knew it. And if that shadowy, cautious look from Marcus was any indication, he knew it too.

Mason straightened, unwilling to take things too far. He wasn't ready for what was going to happen, and yet… one look into those fierce eyes, even as hard to read as they were, told him it was definitely going to happen at some point, ready or not.

"You're going to figure this out eventually," Mason

said, "but since I don't want you getting pissed at me later for misleading you or something, you should know I'm not gay. I've never had sex with a man." He shrugged one shoulder and gave the wolf a tight smile. "Unless you count my own hand. I've done that often enough."

The wolf's fingers curled and his eyes narrowed with what appeared to be surprise. He lowered his hand. "You aren't attracted to males of your species?"

"No. I'm not."

"Then it's fortunate I'm not of your species."

"That's not—"

But the wolf cut Mason off with a sharp look. "Don't concern yourself with irrelevant details of your sexual nature. Pleasure is pleasure, no matter where it originates. I'll prove it to you when we mate."

Goddamn, but he was an arrogant bastard.

Mason forced a deep breath. An argument was out of the question. Of course, there was one argument that he'd be willing to take up no matter what the consequences. "I'm not leaving my brother behind. He won't be safe out here, and he needs medical attention."

Marcus finally stumbled to his feet. "You're the one that needs medical attention. I'm fine."

But Marcus wasn't fine, because Mason had seen him wince and almost reach for his stomach. He'd stopped, probably only because Mason would've called him on it if he had.

"We won't leave him," the wolf said. Then he said to Marcus, so gently that Mason had to look at him to make sure it was still him talking, "I have more control over my need to fuck than I expected to have at this moment, but two humans in such close proximity will be dangerous. Do not forget that. My claws are sharp and your spine is weak."

The words sent a chill down Mason's spine and not even the shadows hid Marcus's wide-eyed look that said he found the wolf's warning just as disquieting.

Then the wolf snagged Mason by the hand, drawing him forward. Mason wasn't prepared and he stumbled, but the wolf steadied him so quickly Mason didn't even have time to suck in his breath. Then the wolf buried his nose against Mason's collar and sniffed in a deep breath.

Mason's back went stiff, his reaction instinctive, and his palm flattened against the wolf's hard chest. The wolf growled, hauling Mason even closer by curling one hand tightly around the back of Mason's neck. The wolf trailed his nose down Mason's chest and up again, then across Mason's shoulders, hesitating for a deep sniff at Mason's underarm, and down Mason's injured arm.

It wasn't easy for Mason to accept the wolf's inspection without complaint, especially when he felt the bulge of a hard penis he wasn't interested in getting to know better pushing at his groin, but he did it because he had to. He'd made it through a similar inspection three years ago, and by God, he could make it through again.

Keep still. Keep calm. Keep breathing.

That last bit was important, both an order to himself and a promise.

The wolf took one final sniff at Mason's arm, then raised his head. "Your injuries aren't limited to this cut. You're bleeding under the skin. Here."

The wolf pressed the palm of his hand to Mason's left side where Lavi's boot had caught him under the ribs, and Mason sucked in his breath.

He probably had a size twelve bruise, so yeah, lots of blood under the skin. Might possibly have a cracked rib, too, but he couldn't be sure. He would have expected more pain if he did, but he knew pain wasn't always the best indicator of injury.

He'd hardly noticed his broken wrist three years ago, until that wolf had made another grab for him.

But those were old, well-worn thoughts and he didn't have time for them now.

The faint pre-dawn light didn't let him see more than hints of the wolf's expression, but Mason didn't have any trouble seeing the shimmer of those sharp eyeteeth. Warmth bled through Mason's cold, damp t-shirt to the flesh beneath where the wolf's hand lingered on his bruised ribs.

Goosebumps rose on his skin and a small shudder coursed through him. It was only one patch of skin heating up at the wolf's touch, but it was the warmest he'd felt in hours.

The hand at the back of Mason's neck moved and fingers slid into his hair. Claws scratched gently along Mason's scalp. Mason's entire body tightened as a tingle raced down his spine and out along his nerve endings.

The goddamned wolf was *petting* him.

"I shouldn't have breathed in so much of your scent—but it was impossible to resist. I want to fuck you, here, now. But I hear the challenge of another alpha nearby and smell his eagerness to find a mate. My priority must be getting you and your kin to a safer location before I give in to my urges."

"That'd be good." Mason wished he hadn't sounded so weak and breathy, but he couldn't seem to relax his stomach with the wolf's hand still pressed so firmly to him.

Marcus moved a few cautious steps closer. "We have transportation, if we can get to it."

"The den isn't far. We will walk. It will give me something to focus on besides my need to fuck your kin."

"But—"

A growl rose in the wolf's chest.

"We'll walk," Mason said quickly. "No problem. Right, Marcus?"

Marcus was quiet for a moment. Then, "I guess we're getting the hell out of here on foot."

"Do not worry. We'll travel quickly. I'm eager to show my new mate how much pleasure his submission will bring him."

Before Mason could react to that statement, a gust of wind shook the trees and the howl of a wolf echoed off the nearby ridge.

The wolf's chin rose, his eyes glowing with a fierce light. He sniffed deeply of the cool, damp air, then growled softly. "We must go now. A fight will burn off what's left of the repression drugs. I won't be able to maintain my control over my instincts when your human scent triggers my urge to mate. I do not want that." The wolf's claws flexed against Mason's scalp. "And with your inexperience mating other males, neither do you."

Mason swallowed past the sudden tightening of his throat. "No. Don't think I do."

"Then we will go," the wolf said, and they did.

Chapter 6

THE HIKE THROUGH the forest was grueling. Mason was tired into his bones, and it didn't take much watching of his bother to see that Marcus wasn't doing any better.

Daybreak finally came, and with it, a heavy fog. Although the wolf ranged ahead a few times, he never disappeared from Mason's line of sight for more than a few minutes.

"Hey," Mason asked breathlessly at one point, his voice echoing off a landscape he couldn't see, "you want to tell us your name?"

The wolf spared him only one glance before returning his attention to the impenetrable fog ahead. "You can't pronounce it."

Mason shared a look with Marcus, who shrugged before puffing out another breath on the sharp incline they were struggling to get to the top of.

"Come on," Mason said. "I've got to call you something."

The wolf paused ahead of them, turning to face Mason. "Five."

Mason puffed out another breath. "Huh?"

"Call me Five."

Five? What the hell kind of name was that supposed to be?

"Gotcha. Five." He shared another look with Marcus before grabbing the trunk of a young poplar the width of his thigh and hauling himself another few feet up the steep grade. He was still favoring his injured arm, but it had stopped hurting a while ago. He wasn't sure whether to be worried or grateful about that.

He turned, putting his back to the tree for leverage, planted his heels firmly in the soft earth, then leaned down the steep grade and thrust his hand out.

Marcus pushed off his knees where he'd been bent double and straightened, taking hold of Mason's wrist.

Mason used his grip to haul Marcus up beside him.

They'd been taking turns leading. Mason would have given up halfway up the mountainside if not for his brother. The wolf, Five—what the hell, why not?—had spent most of the climb in what appeared to be a hyper-alert state, watching, listening, *sniffing* for God's sake, leaving Mason and Marcus to follow his effortless climb in any way they could.

They kept falling behind, and Five kept backtracking, but Mason assumed it was better than the alternative. Five seemed to know what he was doing, and Mason had quit worrying that a wolf pack was going to sneak up on them.

Besides, his brother had it right: one wolf wanting to fuck was better than a pack of them.

A glance over his shoulder told him Five had moved

ahead again. Mason could just see his back through the thick bramble growing between the trees.

With the changing seasons, the underbrush that crowded the woods had lost most of its foliage. But as Mason turned and started up the incline again, the briars still tore at his clothes and the thorny vines pricked at his skin and the tang of pine was so thick on the air it burned his lungs.

He didn't know how Five stood it, with his inhumanly acute senses.

"Goddamned pine trees," Marcus said.

"Could be snake season," Mason said.

"I'd take a fucking snake over this shit. My hair feels like it's glued to my skin. You know how pine trees make me itch." To prove the point, Marcus started scratching at his forearm, cursing under his breath.

Mason grunted and pushed off the tree as Marcus passed him.

It took another ten minutes to reach the top.

Mason was breathing heavily when he stopped beside Five and looked out through the trees toward a one-story house in a field on the other side of a dip in the terrain. All he could make out was a solar roof rising above the heavy fog, but he could see the first rays of the sunrise in the distance.

Marcus came up beside Mason and put his hand on the trunk of an oak tree for support.

"The den," Five said. "My pack has been waiting for my return."

"Your pack," Mason said.

Marcus looked at him sideways. "You had to know this was coming."

Marcus was right, of course. Wolves didn't live alone. They lived in packs.

Packs, just like the one they'd hoped to avoid by submitting to this wolf.

Goddammit. Why didn't he seem to have any ability at all to think ahead? He glanced down. That knife was still in his—

Five reached over and gripped the back of Mason's neck, interrupting Mason's thought before it was fully formed.

Mason tensed. It was impossible not to—Five had claws that pricked at Mason's skin, and he didn't seem to know how to keep them sheathed.

Five applied pressure, inexorably drawing Mason closer, and Mason wondered just how much he could resist before—

Five did not allow him to resist.

Mason stumbled forward, until he was chest to chest with Five. He licked his bottom lip, dry from a long night without enough water and too much exertion.

Five's eyes glittered like the deepest ocean in the darkest waters. "I'm trying to make allowances for your fear, but do not let it goad you into doing something foolish."

Mason reached behind him for Five's hand.

Five allowed Mason to drag that hand around and turn it so his claw-tipped fingers were in the air between them. "You're right. I am afraid. You'd be afraid too if you knew one wrong word was all it took to put you at the end of a set of claws like these."

Five's eyebrows rose. He stared at his claws for a moment, then let out a soft breath. His eyes darkened. "But I have faced claws like these," he said. "Many times."

Mason tried not to show his annoyance. He wasn't sure he succeeded.

But Five only let out another soft breath. "My pack won't hurt you. Not intentionally. Not if you follow the rules meant to keep you safe. We don't seek out violent confrontations with humans during the heat. Confrontations happen because humans seek us out."

Mason wasn't brave enough at that moment to say what he was thinking. But Five probably saw the truth in Mason's eyes, because he settled one of his hands at Mason's lower back and the other he slipped into Mason's hair.

He leaned close. Hot breath grazed Mason's earlobe. "You need an alpha to protect you, to lead you, to teach you the rewards of submission. You belong to me now. You'll come to understand the benefits of having a strong mate. After we fuck, and you come to understand all the pleasures we can share as mates, we'll *mate*."

With that, Five sucked Mason's earlobe between his teeth—and bit down.

A sharp tingle raced through Mason from scalp to toes. His whole body shuddered, hard enough to make his goddamned, traitorous cock twitch.

Fear. That was all it was. A rush of adrenaline, a reaction to the sensation crawling over his scalp and down his spine.

Fear? that goddamned, traitorous voice in his head echoed.

Fear, goddammit. Nothing else made sense.

"Uh, guys?"

Mason jerked. He shoved his hands up between him and Five so he could take a goddamned breath.

Five tilted his head, his lips pulling back from his teeth in a snarl. "He followed us."

"I can see that," Marcus said behind them, his voice high and tight.

Five released Mason and gave him a light shove in the direction of the field. "My pack will protect you while I fight. Go. Now."

Mason glanced at Marcus who was still standing at the top of the steep incline, looking down.

The trees shook, too close.

Marcus raised his head, his eyes wide and worried. He hurried over to Mason and shoved his hand against Mason's shoulder, hard. "Let's go."

Mason staggered a few steps backward, eyes stuck on Five's fierce expression, then he spun around and started running, his blood already pounding through his veins.

Behind him, Five roared a challenge into the trees.

The answering roar came from much too close, savage and powerful.

Mason stumbled when he heard that sound, but Marcus was there to shove him forward and keep him on his feet.

The rising sun blinded him when he burst out of the trees and into the field, Marcus at his side.

Another roar reverberated through the air, and a harsh, guttural yell that sent a chill racing down Mason's spine. Behind him, he heard a loud thud and the sound of leaves rattling with the shake of a tree. Birds cawed, taking to the air with fast and furious abandon.

Mason slowed, then stopped, gulping in air. He bent double, hands on his knees, trying to catch his breath.

Marcus pulled up short. "What the fuck are you doing?"

Mason straightened and looked over his shoulder. "We can't run into the middle of a pack of wolves without the alpha. You know what could happen."

Marcus was already talking over him. "Don't be a shitbrain. You're not doing this. You heard what he said could happen if he gets in a fight. We have no guarantees he'll win the damn thing!"

"I heard." Mason turned back.

Marcus grabbed Mason's arm and yanked. "Goddammit, Mace! He doesn't need us. He could end up fucking you right in the goddamned woods before it's all over!"

Mason jerked free. "You think it's going to matter where we fuck? It won't."

"It will, goddammit."

"Did it matter where you were when it happened to you?" He glared at Marcus. "If we face his pack without him, one of them could end up taking you for a mate and it'll be last heat season all over again for you."

Marcus's mouth became a hard, flat line. "We're not going back."

"The hell I'm no—"

He barely dodged Marcus's fist in time.

"What the fuck, Marcus!"

But it was a feint and Marcus used the distraction to kick Mason's knee out from under him.

Mason hit the ground with a pained grunt.

"You goddamned shit."

He tried to roll into Marcus's legs but Marcus pressed his advantage and jumped on top of Mason, wrestling him into a chokehold—the same goddamn chokehold Mason had used on him earlier.

"Son of a bitch!" Mason yelled.

He grappled for the back of Marcus's head, his fingers sliding out of hair that was essentially identical to his own—too soft and too short to use for leverage.

"Good for the goose," Marcus said, wrapping his legs around Mason from behind and holding tight. "Now shut the fuck up and listen. We're not going back. He will fuck you—and there's probably no way out of that. Been there, and when one of them wants a mate, he takes a goddamn mate. But you're not going to be a fucking martyr about it because of what you think happened three years ago. Got it?"

Marcus's arm had tightened, choking off Mason's airway until Mason had no choice but to agree or let the spots forming at the edges of his vision completely overtake him.

He pushed it as far as he could before he nodded.

Marcus exhaled a heavy grunt and released Mason.

Mason coughed, then sucked in a few deep breaths and stared up at the bright morning sky. After a moment, he rolled over and let his head stop swimming, then pushed to his feet.

Marcus hurried to his feet beside Mason, watching the edge of the woods behind him.

Mason took one glance toward the woods, then turned to face the houses in the distance, still too far away for him to tell whether or not anyone was watching them come—or waiting for the opportunity to strike.

"I fucking hate you right now," Mason said, but there was no heat in the words.

"Sure you do." Marcus shoved at Mason's shoulder. "Move, goddammit."

Mason moved.

Four minutes later, Mason and Marcus stumbled up

the path that led to the front door of the closest house. Mason was breathing hard, exhausted to his core from running up the slope that looked a lot gentler—and shorter—from the tree line than it really was. He scanned the front of the house, then the neighboring houses, but saw no one.

Still, his neck prickled and he couldn't stop feeling like they were being watched.

He made it to the front door first, almost collapsing against the wood frame. Shiny, clear windows let him see straight into the front room.

No one waited inside. Only masses of pillows piled high at the edges of the room, eight straight-backed chairs, and a dark, round dining table.

"This is creepy as fucking hell," Marcus said quietly beside him, his hands framing his face so he could see through the window. "I expected a welcoming party at least, claws out maybe, but not this…"

"We'll try the—"

The lock released at the first touch of his hand on the flat panel, startling him into silence.

Marcus raised his head and looked at Mason. "Didn't expect that."

Mason nodded, then curled his fingers around the latch and cautiously opened the door.

The hinges were silent, but the wood floor creaked under his weight as he stepped over the threshold.

"Anybody home?" His voice cracked and his words echoed off the bare walls. He cleared his throat. His mouth was so dry he was lucky he could talk at all.

Walking through the empty room felt like walking into a trap.

The kitchen wasn't far. He could see counter space

and a sink through the opening between rooms, and a shiny spout in the wall above it. He could almost taste the cool, fresh water that would pour out when he turned it on.

He glanced over his shoulder at Marcus, who was busy looking toward the opening at the other end of the room that seemed to lead deeper into the house—where shadows lurked in a dark hall.

Something moved in the corner of Mason's eye. He jerked around, a startled grunt escaping before he could stop it.

A golden-eyed female wolf stood at the edge of the kitchen, her claws fully extended, her full curves and long, loose hair doing nothing to make her look soft as she stared at Mason.

"If you came here to do us harm, you'll be disappointed." Her melodic voice seemed at odds with the fire in her eyes. Her gaze drifted to Marcus.

"We're not here to hurt anybody," Marcus said, stepping forward. "I promise."

"You promise?" Her head tilted. "What does a human promise mean coming from a human who smells of weapons and death?"

Marcus patted down his chest and his pockets. "I don't have any weapons—unless you count my looks and charm." He smiled. "I'm available as hell for anything you might have in mind, beautiful."

Mason directed a sharp look at Marcus and wondered what the fuck he thought he was doing.

Her arched eyebrows rose and she drew in a careful sniff of the air.

A deep, accented voice came from behind them. "Your human scent won't tempt my mate, and neither will your attempts at flattery. But if you want a challenge, I can offer that."

Mason closed his eyes for one brief moment, then re-opened them and turned. Two male wolves stood at the edge of the dark hall, nearly lost in the shadows.

"Well shit," Marcus said under his breath.

Mason didn't say anything, but he sure as hell didn't disagree.

Chapter 7

THE WOLF WHO'D spoken separated himself from the other and strode toward Mason and Marcus. He was looking directly at Mason when he said, "This one has a knife in his boot and something in his pocket."

Mason nodded, his gaze flickering toward his brother who was standing silently beside him. Marcus hadn't taken his eyes off the wolf, who was tall, broad, and dressed in a dark t-shirt and dark trousers.

No wonder he'd been hard to see in those shadows. Only his eyes stood out, bright green and alight with an unspoken command as he stopped in front of Mason and put his hand out.

Mason unclipped his pocketknife and handed it over.

Marcus did the same, wincing as the burnished metal left his hand. "Take care of 'em," he said. "We'll want those back."

The wolf was still watching Mason with those fierce eyes of his and didn't acknowledge Marcus's comment at all. He let his gaze drop to the small knives and he studied them for a moment. Then he tucked them away into his own trouser pocket and returned his gaze to Mason.

That look said everything Mason needed to hear.

Mason hunkered down and drew out the knife in his boot, then offered it handle first to the wolf. "It was for protection."

The wolf held the knife in his hand for a moment, turning it, feeling the weight. "Feeble protection at best."

Then he threw it, and the sudden motion made Mason lurch sideways and shield his head before he realized the knife wasn't coming at him.

The blade buried itself with a thunk and twang in the back of one of the straight-backed chairs.

Mason rose carefully, eyes on the vibrating knife, while Marcus dragged his hand down his face and muttered, "Holy fucking shit."

"*Aiahaleaeille*," the wolf said, the alien word coming and going quicker than Mason could grasp, "it's safe for you to question them now."

Safe? How? What did they think he and Marcus were going to—

The renegades. Goddammit.

Back when Brendan had been in charge, he'd been more than willing to send in his people to get inside the wolves' dens with the hope their trackers wouldn't be found before their capture gave him the location of another den to raid.

Without anyone to tell them differently, that was probably what these wolves suspected of Mason and Marcus.

The female wolf came forward. The male caught her by the back of the neck with his hand and he pulled her close to nuzzle at the side of her neck. Her eyelashes lowered and a soft sound came from her throat, along with a quiet rumble at a gentler, less cock-twitching pitch than the one that came from her mate.

Mason stared straight ahead, a knot in his throat and a slight flush rising into his cheeks.

Despite his experience three years ago, he had no idea what to expect from the wolves in this setting. He'd spent his entire captivity with the wolves in a locked room. After that first heat season, he'd hardly seen any wolves at all until he'd joined the renegades. What he had seen, he couldn't trust. Nobody with any sense trusted what made it into the *veo* streams.

But even before that, the wolves had shared almost nothing about their intimate lives. People had wondered and speculated, but no one had suspected anything like what the reality had turned out to be. It was one reason everyone had been so caught off guard when the wolves' first heat came after so many of them had settled on Earth.

He knew only that they could be savage when they mated, that humans—especially men in their mid-twenties—had a scent the wolves found impossible to resist—a scent that could set off a chain reaction in the wolves' brains that had terrifying consequences for any human caught in their midst.

But at the sight of the male wolf gently holding the female's stomach, rubbing his face tenderly against the long line of her neck, something in Mason's gut clenched.

He didn't want to feel empathy. He didn't want to imagine they could love, just like humans. He didn't want to imagine that what Marcus had given up because of him might have been something *real*.

But he was losing his ability to pretend otherwise, and had been for almost three years now.

The alphas fought for dominance and their chosen mates surrendered, just like he'd done to secure safe passage through the woods. They stole human choice and Mason wasn't ready to forget that. He wasn't ready to forgive them for cracking his world, even if Marcus seemed to have already done it.

Mason would let that goddamned wolf fuck him but that didn't mean he had to like it.

And that niggling voice came back, drilling a hole in his head with whispered words: *Marcus liked it. He said so.*

Mason inhaled a deep breath, forcing back that goddamned voice and waiting impatiently for the wolves to end their show of affection and get on with the questioning.

The other male wolf spoke from the edge of the dark hallway, his impassive gaze on Mason, as if he knew exactly what Mason was thinking. "It's to reinforce their bond so *Ishikeille* can more easily resist your human scent."

Mason had nothing to say to that so he just let his gaze wander back to the female, wishing they'd hurry the hell up. He hadn't had a sip of water since the bathroom in the biolab and his mouth was so dry he didn't want anything as badly as he wanted a drink from that kitchen sink.

Then with startling speed the softness in the female's gaze disappeared and she straightened away from her mate. He released her just as easily as he'd held her, except for the hand at the back of her neck—that he left in place and she seemed content to have it there.

Her gold gaze shifted between Mason and Marcus. "Two from one. Uncommon for humans." Her gaze settled on Mason. "But you...I smell *Weketekari* on you. Why?"

The context of her question told Mason he might have just heard Five's real name. But Five had been right —there was no way for Mason to reproduce the pitch of the female wolf's voice and recreate the sounds he'd heard.

"He was sniffing me?" Mason said. "I don't know. We got close."

Marcus shot him a dark frown.

Mason sent Marcus a dark glare of his own.

"Tell them," Marcus said. *Shitbrain* might have remained unspoken, but Mason heard it all the same.

"Yes," the female said. "Tell us."

Her mate was giving Mason a hard look.

Mason wiped the palm of his injured arm on his jeans and blinked her into focus again. His forearm was also itching, but he didn't dare scratch at it through the filthy bandage. What if the cut was already getting infected?

"Are you afraid to answer my question?" Then, her voice going flat. "Why are you here?"

At the sudden narrowing of her eyes, Mason's mouth went dry. "He brought us here, swear to God."

Just as quickly, she said, "And why is he not here with you?"

"There's another wolf out there. An alpha. They're fighting. He wanted us to leave him. It was too dangerous, he said. But you should probably send someone. He might be in trouble—"

Maybe that's what you want, that voice in his head

taunted him. *Get rid of the wolf and you don't have to submit...*

Shut the fuck up, he told himself. Just shut the fuck up. Because that wasn't true. Mason didn't want Five dead or injured, especially not because of a fight he'd taken on to protect Mason and his brother.

The female wolf's lip pulled back, showing a quick flash of sharp eyeteeth. "Did he ask you to send someone?"

Mason answered grudgingly, "No."

"I thought not."

"So he sent you to us for protection."

"That's right."

Marcus's frown only darkened.

"Then you did as you should have done." Her gaze skimmed Mason from head to toe. "So why did he send you to us for protection? Was his mate with him?"

"I don't smell a mate," her companion said. He stared at Mason with glittering green eyes so direct that Mason had trouble taking a deep breath.

Sometimes it felt like the goddamned wolves didn't even know how to blink.

The female looked back at her mate, sharing some unspoken communication that Mason couldn't decipher.

Marcus had obviously finally had enough. "You goddamned idiot," he hissed toward Mason. "Tell them you're his mate."

Mason was watching the male wolf when Marcus spoke. The wolf's nostrils flared, not too much, but noticeably, and it seemed as if all the air went out of the room.

"I see," the female said. "That's...unexpected."

"It's not official or anything," Mason said. "If there's

one of your people waiting on him, I can step aside, no problem. Just put us somewhere out of the way and—"

Marcus jostled him from the side and gave him a fiery glare said *shut the fuck up*.

Mason took that advice, rubbing his hand on his jeans again. His stomach churned and the room felt hazy with the sudden spill of bright morning sunlight through the windows.

The other male was still watching silently from the shadows on the hallway, but the female's mate had something to say.

"He should be honored Alpha chose him over all the others. Instead, he insults us and Alpha. He's unworthy of being Alpha's mate."

"Honored," Mason said in a flat, hard tone no one was going to mistake for friendly. "I've got another name for it."

The wolf growled, and the sound skittered along Mason's nerves, raising the hair on his arms and the back of his neck.

He felt Marcus tense beside him.

The female reached behind her and clasped the wolf's arm in her hand. "*Ishikeille…*"

The wolf's growl ended as abruptly as it had started.

Her voice soft, she said, "Alpha isn't here to teach him our ways. He will learn."

Mason had to bite back his reaction to that. But whatever had come over him earlier faded. Sweat beaded on his upper lip. He'd pushed too hard, let his temper run unchecked, and he couldn't make that mistake again.

Marcus made a small gesture that drew everyone's attention. "We're really tired and thirsty. Maybe we could have something to drink?"

"We'll be finished here soon," she said, gesturing at the third wolf, her long fingers making a short, sharp movement.

The third wolf turned without a word and disappeared into the dark hallway. Somewhere beyond Mason's line of sight a door opened and shut.

"If someone challenged Alpha, he'll come back ready to mate."

"We'll take precautions."

But Mason had lost track of the conversation somewhere, wasn't even sure what the two wolves were talking about. Sweat chilled his skin and the inside of his mouth tasted sour and dry.

Marcus's voice cut through a sudden darkness at the edges of Mason's vision. "You okay? Hey—oh—shit—he's—"

Mason wasn't sure what happened. One moment he was standing there beside Marcus and the next he was flat on his back, blinking up at the pale ceiling.

"I—" Whatever thought he'd had was gone too quickly to catch.

Someone was holding his arm.

"Hey, careful. He's got a—goddamn…"

The startled sound of Marcus's voice brought Mason's head off the floor.

He glanced to the side to see the green-eyed wolf peeling away the last of the blood-soaked and mud-caked fabric covering Mason's injury.

A long scab had formed along his forearm over the four-inch gash. It was hardly more than a long scratch and if Mason hadn't seen the original damage himself he would've never believed how it had looked just hours ago.

"That's not possible," he said. He started trying to push himself up on his elbow.

The wolf holding his arm didn't release him. "This should be cleaned. You could get an infection."

Marcus's laugh was almost a bark it was so hard. "I don't think that's the problem." He dragged his hands through his hair and met Mason's gaze with his own. "Shit. What the fuck is going on? None of this makes any sense."

Mason swallowed, dropping his head back to the floor. "What were they working on in the lab, Marcus?"

Marcus loomed over him, then hunkered down, taking Mason's free hand. "Nothing that could do this. I mean, I can't be sure someone wasn't working on something weird, but nothing I know about could account for this."

Because of Marcus's position, his knuckles brushed the upper edge of the rolled-up EP display tucked into the waistband of Mason's jeans. Marcus frowned, then made to let go of Mason's hand, already reaching with his other for the flexible screen.

The wolf's hand covered Marcus's just as Marcus grasped the screen. "What is this?"

Mason tried again to push up on his elbow, a hot dread welling in his gut. "It's just something I found."

He had no idea what was on that screen. It could be anything—something damning enough to make every one of these wolves turn against him, and since Five hadn't yet returned, there was no one to tell them it didn't belong to him.

The wolf pulled out the display, letting it unroll as it came free. The wolf stared at it momentarily, then let it drop to the floor. As before, there was just enough power to flash the screen to life for one brief moment. Then it went dark.

The female squatted beside them and re-rolled the screen, then rose with effortless grace. "I'll take it to—"

"It's mine," Marcus interrupted, jumping to his feet with a complete disregard for his safety and reaching for the screen. "He has nothing to do with what's on that—"

The wolf beside Mason lunged upright, swiping at Marcus so fast he didn't have time to jump out of the way.

"No!" Mason yelled, surging upright, only to have the wolf snarl and shove him with enough force steal his breath. He slid across the floor and banged into the legs of one of the straight-backed chairs so hard the back of his head cracked against one of the chair's wood slats, snapping his teeth together.

Marcus staggered backward, blood welling instantly along five vicious slashes across his chest. He looked down at his torn t-shirt, his hands coming up, fingers curling inward, his eyes shocked wide.

The female jumped in front of Marcus, thrusting out her arm. "*Ishikeille*, stop! It wasn't an attack."

Mason groaned, raising his hand to his head, then used the seat of the chair for leverage and lurched to his feet.

The male's fierce expression slowly eased. He shook his head, once, then again, as if trying to shake off a sense of disorientation. His chest rose and fell inhumanly fast and his claws dripped with Marcus's blood, leaving perfect little circles of red on the floor at his feet.

Mason stumbled the fifteen feet that were between him and Marcus, watching the wolf for any sign that he might be planning to attack again.

Instead, the wolf stepped back, once, twice, three times, until he'd put a good ten feet between him and the female, who was still holding out her arm, her own claws fully extended from beneath the dark material of her fingernails, the EP display clutched in her other hand between her and Marcus as a clear warning for Marcus to stay put.

"I am sorry," the male wolf said, looking at Marcus with as unreadable an expression as Mason had ever seen on one of their faces. "I reacted instinctively when you reached for *Aiahaleaeille.*"

Marcus stood behind the female, still on his feet, but looking down as if he wasn't sure what had happened to him. At those words, he looked up, and Mason's stomach lurched.

Marcus looked ready to drop, face pale, eyes wide, breath shallow.

Mason took hold of Marcus's shoulder. "Come on, just let me—"

He had just enough time to catch Marcus when he fell.

Unfortunately, his own balance wasn't exactly steady and he staggered under his brother's weight.

The female turned and made a grab for both of them, her inhuman strength giving her the power to keep them both on their feet long enough for Mason to walk Marcus to the table in the center of the room.

He kicked one of the chairs free, then let Marcus drop into the seat. He crouched down in front of Marcus, patting the side of his face. "Come on. Come on. You're okay. You're going to be okay."

Marcus nodded. "I will. They're not that deep. I'd feel it if more if they were, right?" He let his head drop back, taking a couple of deep breaths. "Just caught me off guard, that's all. Wasn't ready for it."

Mason clenched his teeth, sparing one ugly glance for the wolf still standing back, holding his own hands fisted at his sides, as if he were fighting to stay away.

"Get the fuck out of here," Mason said. "Go on! I don't know why the fuck you people can't just stay away from us when you're like—"

A tight hand gripped the back of his neck, almost pulling him off his feet and he ended up on his knees. He expected to feel claws but didn't, only the hard press of strong fingers.

"This was an accident. He apologized. He's already lost one mate and her children to the human renegades. He doesn't wish to lose me and ours. Be grateful he has as much control over his instincts as he does."

Her words hit him like a hard left hook. She was pregnant. No wonder she hadn't reacted to their human scent. Pregnancy ended the heat for female wolves.

Her fingers flexed at the back of Mason's neck just before she released him. "He's a strong mate. Don't blame him for fighting to protect what's his. Even humans fight to protect their mates and children from harm."

Mason couldn't help it. He glanced up and caught the male's gaze and what he saw in those eyes made his chest so tight he couldn't even breathe. His throat worked, but he couldn't swallow and he knew—knew with a certainty he wished didn't exist—that it was entirely possible he carried some of the blame for the events that had led to this moment.

He wasn't a good man, and no one knew that better than him.

Chapter 8

THE WOLF STANDING before Mason spoke quietly. "We'll care for your kin. We won't let his injuries become infected. You have my word."

Mason jerked his gaze down to focus on Marcus's chest, the heat of shame burning his face. He reached for Marcus's t-shirt, and said, voice low, "Let me look, okay? I just need to…"

Marcus pushed Mason's hands away. "I've got it. I'm okay. This was my own goddamned fault. I fucked up."

Mason sat back on his heels and watched Marcus take several deep breaths before carefully pulling his torn and bloody shirt away from his skin.

The slashes were deep. Much deeper than Mason expected. His eyes flickered up and met Marcus's.

"They barely hurt," Marcus said. "It doesn't make any sense."

Mason hesitated, then finally overcame his resistance and pressed his fingertips to the edges of one particularly deep gouge where the wolf's claw must have dug in. A small circle of blood welled up and then just sat there, as if the blood beneath had clotted as soon as Mason re-opened the wound.

"Goddamn," Marcus breathed. "This isn't normal. What the fuck has happened to me?" His gaze flickered toward Mason's arm, then up again to meet Mason's eyes. "Us," he said. "What the fuck has happened to *us*?"

Mason looked up just in time to see the female sharing a covert look with her mate. Mason pushed to his feet, suspicion swirling through him.

"What the fuck's going on here? Do you know something?"

Marcus grabbed his arm. "Shut up, goddammit. Don't antagonize them."

"Your kin is right." The wolf took that moment to wipe his bloody claws across the dark denim at his thigh, leaving behind a bloody smear. "You have other concerns right now. Alpha *Weketekari* is coming. You'll need to be ready for him. His heat will be on him."

The reminder of his current situation did nothing to take away from Mason's anger. But he still couldn't stop himself from glancing at the door he and Marcus had entered through. "You hear him coming?"

The wolf's eyebrows rose dramatically. "He's my alpha. I *feel* him."

The female turned to her mate. "Take him to Alpha's room while I deal with his kin's injuries. Quickly. Alpha isn't far." Her hand settled on her chest and she switched to the wolves' language. "He's angry. Agitated. Something is wrong."

Then she said something else, something Mason didn't have the ability to translate. He glanced at Marcus but all Marcus did was give him a weak headshake. He didn't know what she'd said either.

When Mason looked up, it was to catch her staring at him. Her gaze broke away and darted to the door.

"*Ishikeille*—" But before she could say anything more, Five appeared in the doorway, his fiery gaze zeroing in on Mason without a second's hesitation.

Five gripped the doorframe with one hand, the other fisted so tightly that Mason could see blood dripping to the floor. His eyes followed that trail before he jerked his attention up.

A cold fire burned in Five's blue eyes and the lines of his face were pulled tight, making him look hard and dangerous. Mason's nerves stretched taut. Something was definitely wrong. He'd only known Five for a few hours, but in all that time, he hadn't once felt like he was on the brink of having his throat torn out.

Until now.

Five growled, and his claws dug into the wood doorframe. "Take him away before I kill him."

What the hell?

Mason took a step backward.

"Alpha—" the male wolf said.

"Submit!" Five roared.

The tall wolf cringed, then turned quickly and grabbed Mason by the back of the neck, fingers bruising flesh.

He heard Marcus's voice behind him as he was dragged toward the dark hallway. "Don't hurt him!"

The female wolf said something too low for Mason to hear, but Marcus didn't speak up again.

Mason could have fought against the wolf leading him away but to what point? There was no real escape other than death, and he didn't want to die.

He stumbled along with the wolf, taking a quick, searching glance behind him.

What he saw, he didn't understand.

Five had turned his head, pressing his cheek to the back of his hand on the doorframe, eyes closed, every breath heavy, and he looked...

Lost.

Then the wolf holding Mason by the neck pushed him deeper into the hallway and Mason refused to let himself look back again.

∽

He was locked in a room he couldn't escape. The bolt on the door was on the outside and the single window had screws in the frame holding it in place. The screws were shiny and new, and the glass clear and clean. If he stretched his neck just so, he could see the moon high over the trees, half-hidden by scudding clouds, and when he was quiet, he could hear the faint creak of wood and an occasional grunt or growl.

He tried not to be quiet.

When he couldn't cover the noises coming through the walls, he buried his head under one of the many pillows on the bed, squeezed his eyes shut, and tried to remember that nothing except death lasted forever.

His wrist throbbed in time to the beat of his heart and the pillow smelled like sweat and body odor.

He didn't like the room. He especially didn't like the constant reminders that at any time one of them could decide he was fair game and come claim him for the same thing he heard going on through the goddamn walls.

Then the night turned to day in an instant and Mason rolled over and realized he'd been dreaming again, of the room he'd been trapped in three years ago while some wolf fucked Marcus right next door.

Considering how similar his current circumstances were to those of three years ago, he wasn't surprised. He was on a bed in a room with a locked door and windows he hadn't even tried to open. He didn't know what they'd done with Marcus, and he didn't know what might happen when Five finally came for him.

Would Five still want to kill him? Or would he be back to wanting to mate?

Mason knew which one he was hoping for.

Not that he was looking forward to mating, either. He wasn't conflicted about his feelings. He wasn't gay. He'd never been attracted to another man, and he sure as hell wasn't repressing sexual fantasies about men either. Why would he? If the thought of touching another man's penis had ever made him hot, he'd have done it without a second thought. Who the fuck cared what turned a man on? Sex was good when it was good and bad when it wasn't and that was all there really was to it.

But worry was still eating a hole in his gut and all of it stemmed from what had happened three years ago.

He couldn't figure it out. Why had Marcus come out of that experience changed, and not in the way Mason would have expected? How had that wolf gotten inside Marcus's head?

Even after three years, Mason didn't know. And that was what scared him. Not the idea of being fucked in the ass, although he sure wasn't comfortable with the idea, but being fucked in the head.

If he submitted, if he let Five fuck him and mate him, if he didn't fight any of it, would the same thing happen to him?

He rolled over onto his back and scrubbed his hands down his face, yawning with so much force that his jaw popped. His shirt had ridden up and his jeans were twisted tight at his groin, but he could feel the soft cotton sheets against his feet and he shifted until he could stretch his back and both arms, while he forced his eyes open against the streak of late afternoon sun spilling through the windows next to the bed.

He covered another yawn, then brushed his hair off his forehead as he squinted out the window. The sun was going down, and a breeze shook the limbs of a red- and gold-leafed maple tree that grew right up against the house. A squirrel ran down the trunk and disappeared below the window.

He was surprised to realize he'd slept away the entire day. Not that he'd fallen asleep right away. But he'd finally given in to the fact that he needed sleep more than he needed to spend another two goddamned hours worrying about why the hell Five was so angry with him.

"Do you ever think about the things you've done and wish you could undo them?"

Mason jumped, his heart going right into his throat. He rolled quickly to the edge of the bed and onto his feet. He stood just in time to see Five push away from the wall and start across the room, a predator in motion.

At that moment, Mason was grateful as fuck that he'd gone to bed fully clothed, doing no more than taking off his boots and socks and dropping them to the floor at the foot of the bed.

"What's going on?" Mason asked warily as Five stalked toward him.

"The familiarity of your scent has teased at my senses for two days. I knew from the moment I caught your scent that I had to have you. I would mate you, and I would keep you. I tracked your scent through the woods for more hours than I can recall until I finally found you inside that laboratory. I used up the last of my drugs trying to make sure I didn't lose control or succumb to someone else's scent before I found you."

Five was getting too close, but the bed's frame pressed against the back of Mason's knees and he had nowhere to go to escape. Five stopped in front of him and he swallowed back the knot trying to choke him.

Raising his hand, Five drew a line with the tip of his finger down Mason's throat.

A small shiver raced through Mason.

Five's blue eyes glimmered in the light. "I wish I could undo that decision."

"You wish you hadn't taken the drugs?" Mason was sure he sounded as confused as he felt.

"If I hadn't, I might have given up my search, and I might have continued the chase and chosen another mate. But what I did can't be undone, and only the universe knows why this is my fate."

"So you don't want me anymore? I can live with that. Just send me on my—"

Five caught the bottom of Mason's chin in his hand, bringing Mason's words to an abrupt end. He stared boldly into Mason's eyes. "That isn't what I said. I still want to mate you, knowing everything I know now, but I wish I didn't. Because I do not want this gift that the universe has given me."

Then Five pushed Mason's face away, as if he couldn't even stand to touch Mason.

The edge of the mattress jostled into the back of Mason's knees and he just managed to stay upright.

He blinked a few times, not sure what the hell he was supposed to say to the idea that Five wanted to reject him but for some reason couldn't. "So…"

"I was there, when the men you brought with you to your meeting with the human Ian Tucker killed two of my heat mate's pack. I remember how difficult it was to resist the lure of a human scent so enthralling I could barely think while I fought alongside the others to stop your companions from killing more."

That goddamned knot was back in Mason's throat and he couldn't breathe.

Five watched him with ocean-deep eyes that somehow made everything worse.

Mason had to work too damn hard to speak. "You're telling me you remember me—my scent—from an attack that happened more than three years ago."

"I also remember the smell of blood and death and bullets from your weapons, and I remember the sound *Iaehekielle* made when one of your men shot him so many times he couldn't heal. He was my heat mate."

Oh God.

Mason sat back on the bed, his legs too weak to hold him up. "I never shot anybody who wasn't trying to kill me. I wasn't even conscious when that attack happened." He rested his arm in his lap, staring down. He dragged his thumb over the thin line that was all that was left of the four inch long gash he'd had there less than twenty-four hours earlier. "It was Jay's influence that made everybody so goddamn blood-thirsty, Jay and Brendan."

He was just offering excuses and he knew it, but he couldn't stop himself.

"He said all of you were getting ready to make a big push outside the protectorate, to demand more territory from the government so you'd have more mates to choose from—that we were just good for sex and submission and that you'd turn us all into nothing but slaves if we didn't do everything we could to stop you—if we didn't make a deal that would keep you in the protectorate for good. Some of us knew he was exaggerating, but some of the guys, some of the women, it scared them."

He clenched his fist and looked up again. "It scared me, and I didn't even believe half of it."

"Fear doesn't excuse murder."

Mason dug his fingers into the disheveled bed and pushed himself to his feet again. "Might doesn't make right but I don't see that stopping you from taking what you want from us."

"We offered fair trade for a place to live on your world. We gave you technologies and knowledge you didn't have before, and we always tried to give more than we were given. But we couldn't know human scent was going to be such a problem for us during our heat. And now we fight to defend ourselves from you who forget the things we've done to make your lives better."

"Better," Mason said with flat precision. "You cracked the goddamned world. I don't know how that's better. And we have to follow your rules on land that shouldn't be yours and accept the fact that you're going to hunt us down during your heat and take us for mates whether we want it or not."

The curve of Five's jaw seemed carved from stone. "We don't seek out humans to mate."

"Except when we smell like a good fuck, right?"

The moment the words left his mouth, he knew he'd made a mistake.

Chapter 9

THE SUDDEN FLARE of fire in Five's gaze warned Mason he was pushing too hard. But it was too late, because the goading words had already left Mason's mouth and he couldn't take them back even if he wanted to—and by God, he didn't want to.

He meant every one of them.

But that didn't negate the fact that he'd forgotten just how touchy the wolves became during their heat season.

Five's harsh growl and sudden lunge toward Mason sent him reeling backward, and since he didn't have anywhere to go, he fell, his back hitting the mattress with enough unexpected force to startle a yelp out of him.

Five straddled Mason and wrestled Mason's arms over his head and to the bed.

It did Mason no good at all to try to jerk free, but he tried anyway, so hard he nearly wrenched his left shoulder. "Goddammit!"

Five's fingers tightened relentlessly around Mason's wrists. "Submit!"

Mason flinched, then pressed his lips together.

Five's lip curled away from his teeth, showing off those sharp, shiny eyeteeth that looked twice as danger- ous as they had any right to, jolting Mason's sense of self-preservation back from wherever the hell it had dis- appeared to.

"I submit! I submit! Please—" He snapped his mouth closed before he said more. He wasn't going to beg.

He was breathing too fast and his hands were shak- ing, and he could feel the tremble in every muscle in his body. Relaxing those muscles was almost impossible, but he did it.

He stared up at Five, hoping, praying, that it was enough.

Five stopped growling. His blue eyes glittered, his ex- pression unreadable.

But no, that wasn't true. There was something there in Five's gaze, something Mason thought he understood.

For the first time since he'd found himself flattened to the bed, he noticed the pressure and heat where Five sat over him. The struggle had brought Five's groin much too close to Mason's and now he could feel the thick bulge of a hard alien cock through Five's dark trousers.

And then Five shifted over him and Mason inhaled sharply. His first instinct was to shy away from the con- tact but he held his position. He'd already riled Five's temper. Being a goddamn sissy about cocks bumping wasn't going to make his current situation any better.

Five noticed though, and he let out another soft growl that sent a sharp tingle along Mason's every nerve.

"Fight," he said. "Fight for your right to deny me."

It was a trap.

Mason swallowed his pride, forced back his anger, and said, "No. I'm not gonna fight you."

He knew what Five was doing. He might've done it himself if their situations were reversed. Five couldn't have the justice he wanted, so he was trying to find a way around his own goddamn rules.

"I submit," Mason said. "I said I would and I do. I submit. Fuck me if that's what you want. Make me pay for what I've done. I'm not going to try to stop you. I submit."

Five stared down at him, eyes lit with some inner fire that slowly faded, until all that was left was a brilliant blue sadness that shook Mason to his core. The pressure at Mason's wrists eased.

"Fucking is for pleasure or breeding, not punishment. If I used your submission to punish you, I would be ashamed to call myself Alpha."

"So you're not going to fuck me?" Hope flared, too bright, too real, and it made him feel like a coward, afraid of something he'd been telling himself all along he wasn't afraid of.

Five adjusted his hold on Mason's wrists and lowered his head to put his mouth to Mason's ear. "I survived my heat without you this morning, but it wasn't pleasant and I don't wish to do it again. But I can't push aside this anger I feel in my heart and I cannot mate you while it lingers."

No sex. Thank God. Mason's entire body went lax under Five with the relief that surged through him. Until that moment he wouldn't have believed he was hanging on to so much nervous dread of something as common as sex, but the sudden release he felt made it impossible to deny.

"As much as I regret your past," Five continued, "I can't change it. But I can help you make better decisions in the future. And I can accept your submission when you're ready to ask forgiveness for the things you've done."

"I wouldn't."

Hot breath tickled Mason's ear. "You will."

"No. I mean I wouldn't forgive me. You shouldn't either."

He wasn't expecting the teeth that scraped over his earlobe, making a shiver race through him and causing him to suck in his breath.

"Forgiveness is earned," Five breathed into his ear, "and you will earn it."

"Will I?" Goddamn, but he sounded like his voice was going to crack at any minute. He couldn't decide if he was comfortable with what Five was doing at his ear or not, but he also couldn't say he wanted him to stop.

Five's lips touched Mason's neck and the hard line of his nose slid behind the shell of Mason's ear. "You smell like my future, and my past. Your scent sets fire to my senses."

The next soft huff of breath made every hair on Mason's body rise in reaction.

"I told you submission would have rewards."

Smooth skin brushed Mason's own beard-shadowed jaw and it was impossible to ignore the warmth spreading through him. He let out a breath a little too abruptly, a little too close to a gasp.

He made fists with his hands and tried to keep his focus on Five's words and not the feel of a hot mouth at his throat. He shut his eyes, but that only made every brush of Five's lips over his skin more noticeable, so he stared up at the ceiling instead.

Then the warm pressure disappeared, and Five released Mason's wrists and sat back.

Cool air swirled over the damp skin at Mason's throat and ear, teasing him with unwanted sensation. Mason brought his arms down and stared up at Five, wondering at the slight tilt to his mouth, wondering if he could trust the intuition that told him Five's anger wasn't quite what it had been, that Five might even be amused, although by what, Mason wasn't sure he wanted to know.

That goddamn voice in his head made sure he knew anyway. *You're not gay, remember? But you wouldn't know it by the way your dick is acting. He can feel it.*

Fuck you, he answered back.

It wasn't like his dick was hard, it just wasn't as soft as it had been. And he could probably blame the adrenaline flooding through his veins for that.

Five tilted his head, one thick eyebrow arching. "You're mine now, and your duty to your alpha is submission. You will submit, and through submission, you'll earn your forgiveness and we will mate. Until then, you'll be my heat mate, and I'll show you some of the pleasures we'll have as mates."

Mason went utterly still. He didn't take his next breath until his lungs burned.

He should've known his lack of understanding of the wolves' language was going to fuck him over. The wolves had a lot of words that translated to "mate" and "fuck" and "sex" but not all of them meant the same thing.

Somehow, someway, he'd gotten the idea that everything Five had been telling him meant they wouldn't be having sex—not now, maybe not ever.

That wasn't what Five had been saying at all.

They were going to fuck. And if the look on Five's face was anything to go by, they were going to fuck sooner rather than later.

Mason gripped the outside of Five's muscular thighs. "I'm not gay. I wasn't just saying that to convince you to leave me alone. I'm not attracted to you."

Five let out a soft snort.

Mason scowled. "This won't end well. Heat season doesn't last forever, and when it's over, my human scent isn't going to be that—Hey!"

Mason grabbed at Five's wrist, but it was too late.

Five jabbed one of his claws into the ragged bottom of Mason's t-shirt and ripped the fabric apart all the way up to the collar. He let the remains of the shirt fall open.

The rush of cool air over Mason's chest tightened his nipples.

Five's gaze fixated at the center of Mason's chest. "You should have taken advantage of the shower. Your clothes are filthy. So is the bedding. So are you."

"You didn't have to tear my shirt off." He fought the urge to cross his arms. He felt exposed, uncomfortable with the way Five was staring at him.

Five's eyebrows went up. "But I wanted to."

"And you always get what you want."

"I am Alpha." As if that explained everything.

"And I'm not gay. So what?"

"So now you take off your trousers."

"Or you'll rip them off me?"

Five's blue eyes flickered across Mason's chest and down his belly to his groin. "If you'd like me to." He sounded almost wistful. "I have no doubt I would enjoy it."

Mason shoved at Five's legs. "Get the fuck up. Of course I don't want you to rip off my goddamn pants. This is going to be enough of an ordeal without—"

Five's forefinger landed on Mason's lips. "This will not

be an ordeal. Without the thrill of a chase, it won't be all that it could be for me, but for you—"

"How the fuck is this even real? You're going to rape me and—and—" He'd sworn to himself he wasn't going to use the R word, he'd *sworn*, and yet there it was, a dead weight in the air between them, and hearing it disturbed him enough that he couldn't figure out what the fuck he wanted to say.

Five's eyes narrowed. "Expecting submission from a mate is not rape."

"You people don't even know what the goddamn concept of rape means, do you?"

"You're mistaken." Five flattened his hands against Mason's stomach, making him suck in his breath in a hurry as Five's claws poked at his skin. "If you don't wish to mate, you can choose to fight."

"And I'll lose, do you think I'm stupid or something?"

"I doubt very much that you're stupid. The "or something" I have no knowledge of. I look forward to discovering more about your strengths and weaknesses in the days and months to come."

Mason made a sound of denial. "This is fucking ridiculous."

Five reached out and feathered his fingers through the hair beside Mason's temple. His touch was strangely gentle and it stirred an odd feeling in Mason's gut. "You demand respect for your ways, but you don't give any in return."

"You take away our free will and tell us we're just supposed to accept it because that's *your* way."

Five's other hand flexed on Mason's belly. "You think we don't understand what it means to have our free will stolen from us?"

A bitter laugh escaped Mason's throat.

"I don't. I don't think you understand at all what we're going through now that you're here, making yourselves at home on our planet, demanding we submit or fight, even though you know damn well we'll die if we do."

Not a flicker of softness touched Five's expression. "The human scent steals our free will at a time when we're most vulnerable to the instincts that have ruled our lives for longer than your species has had language. And the only way we can escape that theft is to drug ourselves until we can barely recognize the scent of a mate—or better yet, to stay as far away from humans as possible. And yet…"

Mason pressed his lips together. He was going to lose this goddamn argument. He knew it and there was nothing he could do to stop it.

"Humans rail about how we've stolen their freedom and land and free will even as they invade the only safe haven we have during the heat, to hunt us and kill us, and to try to drive us off this world. You believe your free will's been taken, but I ask you to answer honestly, did you not have a choice when you crossed the border between safety and here? Because I had no choice in that. If I hadn't already had drugs running through my system, I would have claimed and mated you without regard for your human weaknesses. If you had refused to submit, you would have died of injuries I could not help inflicting. And I'm the one who would have to live with that knowledge for the rest of my days, not you."

"It's not the same."

Five's weight shifted over him subtly, his fingers flexing against Mason's skin. "An evenly matched fight inflames our senses. In a normal world, I would choose not to mate someone too weak to fight. But this world isn't normal, not for us. Human scent destroys our ability to choose who we'll mate. You've already said you believe I won't want you when heat season ends. If you don't believe my free will has been stolen, why do you believe that my senses can't be trusted?"

"I'm telling you, it's not the same."

Five tilted his head. "Why?"

"It just isn't."

"But why?"

"It just isn't, goddammit!"

"If you can't answer the question, say so."

"This is ridiculous." Mason blew out a hard breath. "Let's just fuck and get this over with. I'm tired of you playing with my head." He reached for Five's hand and dragged it down his body, thoroughly aware of the fact that the only reason he was able to do it was because Five let him. He pressed Five's hand to his groin. "Play with something else for a while."

Chapter 10

IT HAD TAKEN a lot of nerve for Mason to do what he did. So he was surprised when Five pulled his hand free and dragged his knuckles across Mason's belly before taking hold of the waistband of Mason's jeans. "Fucking will have to wait. First I'm going to clean you. Your hair smells of someone else's urine and blood and I don't want either of those scents in my bed when we mate."

Mason grimaced, remembering just how he'd come by those scents—landing face-first in Stan's piss-soaked lap.

He really should have taken a shower. But after he'd been locked in the room, he'd been worried someone would come for him, so he'd just washed his face and hands, taken a quick piss in the toilet, and swallowed as much water as his stomach could hold. After the long walk through the woods, his clothes had been mostly dry, so he'd sat on the edge of the bed and waited. Two hours later, he'd given up the wait, kicked off his boots, and stretched out on the bed. He'd been asleep within minutes.

Five climbed off the bed and dragged Mason up with him.

Mason lurched to his feet, then eyed the open door to the bathroom. "What do you mean exactly when you say you're going to clean me?"

"Exactly what I said." Five pushed Mason around by his shoulder, then stripped Mason of the remnants of his t-shirt by dragging it down Mason's arms.

Suddenly Mason was standing there in nothing but his jeans and socks and feeling so goddamn naked he wanted to grab his ruined t-shirt and hold it in front of him like some tenth-grade virgin.

Five tossed the t-shirt to the floor a few feet away. "Take off your trousers."

Mason muttered, "Goddammit," under his breath. But he reached for the zip and unfastened his jeans. Dried mud made the fabric stiff, but he got them off without too much trouble. When he looked up, he caught Five staring at his hairy thighs and a dull heat spread through him. He didn't know what to do with his hands so he rubbed his nose self-consciously.

"Your underwear," Five said, but this time his voice sounded different, the soft accent thicker, his voice deeper and more ragged.

Mason's blood thrummed through his veins, gaining speed as his heart took up a faster beat. Was this it? Was Five about to go into the lust-crazed frenzy Mason had been half-expecting from the moment they met?

Softly, Five said, "Submit to your alpha's will."

Mason jolted into action. He slipped his thumbs under the waistband of his underwear and carefully pushed the dark fabric off his hips and down his legs. He found himself hesitating to straighten and meet Five's gaze when he was done, and when he finally did, it was to find Five staring at his cock.

"You haven't cut yourself." There was a curious edge to his voice. "Why not? I've heard that some humans do."

Mason shrugged. "I don't know. I never asked."

"Who would you ask?"

Mason raised one foot to take off his sock, trying his damnedest to act like standing around naked in front of Five was no big deal. "They do it when you're a baby most of the time, I think. I guess I'd ask one of my parents, but I never did. Or if I did, I don't remember."

"It makes no sense."

"It matters to some people, that's all I know."

"I've never touched a human penis."

Five had barely moved his hand when Mason hopped back, out of reach.

Five nostrils flared and his eyes narrowed. He closed his hands on Mason's upper arms and dragged him forward.

"I've tried not to hurt you, but you haven't made it easy. Stop fighting submission and *submit*." Five's emphasis on that final submit came in a dark tone that brooked no argument. Then he closed his mouth over the base of Mason's throat, all hot breath and scraping teeth, and Mason damn near whimpered.

Maybe he did and he just didn't want to admit it.

Five dragged his teeth along the column of Mason's throat and then across his collarbone to his shoulder.

A shudder coursed through Mason. He was embarrassed to realize his cock was taking notice, and his breath stuttered out in a shaky exhale. "What'd I do?"

But he knew. He kept forgetting everything he'd learned in the heat survival training, number one being "submit." Submit, submit, submit. And that meant keeping his mouth shut, staying calm, and not—*definitely* not —making sudden movements that a wolf might mistake for a desire to fight instead of mate.

Wolves could fight and suffer horrific injuries and still live to fight another day, but not him. He couldn't heal the way—

Matthew.

And that was where Mason's thoughts skipped from one track to another and suddenly he knew that whatever was happening to him and Marcus had something to do with his cousin and the wolves.

Matthew was the link in the chain between Mason and Marcus and a sudden, inexplicable ability to heal wounds faster than humanly possible. Matthew thought no one knew about his activities with the wolves, but Mason knew. He'd known almost from the start.

He would never forget the night Matthew had come in after a three week absence with a strip of fabric wrapped tight around his thigh on the outside of his bloody jeans, a limp, and a bullshit explanation about a knife fight at one of the few bars still open two counties over. The next morning, Matthew hadn't been wearing a bandage of any kind and he hadn't been limping. Just a flesh wound, he'd said, waving away Mason's questions.

But Mason had found that goddamned strip of fabric in the trash and it had been soaked with blood. He'd known there was more to that story but he'd kept his mouth shut and let Matthew keep his secrets.

Just like he'd let Marcus keep his when he'd started going out alone, night after night without Mason, and Mason had thought it was all about the events of three years ago.

And then—

Overhearing Jay and Sebastian. *Like Matthew? She wanted him alive.*

It all made sense, in a terrifying rush of connections and memories.

Five had been dragging his mouth along the ridges of Mason's shoulder, but Mason's sudden stillness must have caught his attention, because he raised his head. "What's wrong?"

"You have to let me make a call. It's important."

Five's gaze flickered over Mason's face, as if he were actually considering Mason's request. "You cannot contact anyone outside the den until you've earned my trust."

Mason wasn't above begging, not for this. "Please. I'll do anything. Just let me make one call."

That fierce gaze softened, and for a moment, Mason thought maybe he'd get what he wanted. But no, he understood that look. He knew what was coming.

Five released Mason and took a single step backward. "What you ask isn't possible."

"You don't understand. I just realized that those goddamned men with me in that building might have hurt one of my family. They might have killed him. I need to—"

Five pressed his finger to Mason's lips.

Mason stopped talking.

Five lowered his finger. "Tell me the name of this family member."

"Matthew. Matthew Bryant. I think he's been working with your people, doing something. I'm not sure what."

Fighting renegades would've been his guess, since that

was about the only thing the wolves might find a human good for these days outside of heat season. The sharing of technology and knowledge between species had come to an abrupt end after the first heat season and it hadn't recovered in the eleven years since, not unless it was going on secretly inside the highest levels of government.

When Mason had joined Brendan's renegades, Brendan had said it wasn't. Mason had never doubted Brendan about that, since Brendan's father had been part of the government before the wolves came and had managed to hang on even after his district became part of the American Protectorate. If anyone would know about the sharing of technology, it would've been Brendan.

Mason knew Brendan had been stealing technology from the wolves during the raids against them. He'd known and he hadn't cared, not at first. He'd still been so angry about everything back then that he'd thought it served the wolves right to lose a little tech. They'd stolen so much from humans, after all, and unless someone stopped them, they'd continue to take what didn't belong to them.

Mason crossed his arm over his chest and rubbed his shoulder, trying to forget that he was standing naked in front of Five. It was impossible. He was naked and Five wasn't and all he wanted to do was grab his clothes off the floor and yank them back on.

He cleared his throat and looked at the wall over Five's shoulder. "If you could use some of that advanced technology I know you've got and track him down, I'd appreciate it a whole hell of a lot."

Five startled Mason by reaching for his chin. He turned Mason's gaze toward him. "Do not be embarrassed. You have a beautiful body."

Mason blinked a few times, then cleared his tight throat. He couldn't help it, his gaze flickered over Five's lean shape and he wondered for the first time just what kind of body Five had under his clothes. Hairy? Muscled? Then he blinked again and shoved those thoughts aside.

He met Five's gaze. "Come on. You can do it. I know you can."

"You have a lot of faith in my ability to find one man among many."

Mason dropped his arm to his side. "I spent a good part of the last heat season inside one of your dens. I know how carefully you guard your technology but I know you have it. You can do this for me."

Five's unreadable expression didn't change, so Mason said, "Please. Do this for me."

He stared at Five with his heart in his throat. He didn't move when Five reached for him and hauled him forward by the back of his neck.

Mason crashed into Five, letting out a soft "umph."

Five pressed a hard, quick kiss to Mason's lips, then just as quickly, released Mason and stepped back. "I won't allow you to make contact with anyone outside the den, but there might be something I can do for you."

Mason's lips tingled from the pressure of the unexpected kiss. "Thank you."

"Do not thank me yet. I might discover nothing of value to you. While you wait, fill the bathtub with water. I've taken the last dose of repression drugs I intend to take until after we mate, and I won't be gone long."

Mason wasn't going to make the same mistake twice. By "mate" Five meant "fuck." Still, he didn't let himself hesitate. He nodded.

Five turned to go but then turned back. "Use the time you have to relax. I'll clean you when I return." His gaze skimmed down Mason's naked body. "Do you know what it feels like to be penetrated?"

Mason couldn't fight the heat that rose into his face. "No. I don't."

Five let out a huff of breath. "While you wait for me in the bath, finger your anus and try to get used to the feeling."

Fucking hell. Mason's face flamed. He needed out of this room. He turned and started for the bathroom. He could feel Five watching him and it made his eye twitch to know his ass was on full display.

At the bathroom door, he turned. "You really want me to put my finger up my ass."

"Would you rather one of my betas prepare you?" That hopeful note was back in Five's voice, the one that seemed destined to unsettle Mason at every turn.

He gripped the doorframe. "Uh, no. No. And how about *fuck no*, too?"

Five crossed the distance between them and covered Mason's hand with one of his own. He gently pried Mason's fingers loose. "Go," he said, quiet but firm. "My control does have a limit."

Mason made himself step over the threshold into the bathroom, then turned once again. "And if I don't want to wait for you to wash me? I mean, you're asking me to put my finger in my asshole. I'd like to be clean first."

"Irrelevant. I do not shirk my obligations to my betas and mates."

"Irrelevant. Like the fact that I'm not gay."

"Exactly."

Chapter 11

THE BATHWATER WAS almost hot enough to scald by the time Mason had the free-standing tub half full. He used his foot to push the cold water lever up, opening the stream full blast, and dropped his head back against the contoured rim behind him and listened to the violent splash of pouring water.

He stretched his arms out on the sides of the tub while steam rose around him.

His house—the one he'd grown up in and still shared with his mother and brother and sister and cousin—didn't have a bathtub. But goddamn, he was going to wish it did after this. The hot water he was sitting in soothed his tired, overworked muscles in ways he hadn't imagined it could. He could even stretch out his legs if he didn't slouch too much.

He could thank Five for this. Hell, he might even do it. This was the best he'd felt in days.

Recycling a tub full of water every time someone needed to wash up was a serious waste of resources. The house couldn't be older than the water conservation laws, and high-capacity water recyclers weren't cheap. A tub was a luxury most people weren't willing to pay for when a shower worked just fine. Maybe the wolves were using some of their technology to make the recycler more efficient. However the hell they were doing it, Mason was more than willing to take advantage now that he knew what it felt like to sit in a tub full of steaming hot water.

Someday, someone would fix the electrical grid inside the protectorate, but he wondered more often than not if he'd live to see it. No one seemed in a hurry to fix what had been broken, not inside the protectorate, and not on the outer edges where he lived with his family.

Nine years was a damn long time to live on nothing but halfgas generators and solar.

The world had suffered in a way few had ever seen after that first heat season. The collapse of the economy had been the thing that had nearly destroyed the world, one country after another falling to anarchy. The U.S. had managed to hold on, if only because the U.S. government had quickly realized that giving the wolves what they wanted—more land and more rights over that land— meant the wolves would give them what they needed: help retaining control of the most critical areas of the country before it was too late to stop the fall of the government.

The worst of it all was that more people had died after the end of the heat season than during. Mason had lost friends and family both—including his father, who'd died somewhere out in the southwest when he'd tried to stop some half-assed militia from stealing his fully loaded cargo drone before he could send it off on a delivery.

While the rest of the country had recovered a measure of stability in the ten years since that first heat and what had felt like the end of the world, the outer edges of the protectorate hadn't. It was a dangerous place to live and work, even more so since the government had given over almost complete control to the wolves three years ago, because the wolves didn't seem to care at all what humans did to each other as long as they left the dens alone.

Fear kept away the people who could do the jobs that needed done. He didn't see how it could be any other way, not after what had happened, and how quickly. Everyone was worried, Mason too. That first heat had exposed a part of the wolves' society that was hard for most humans to accept.

What if the wolves were hiding another secret, one that could do even more damage than the heat?

The water finally reached the top of the tub, and Mason leaned forward to shut it off. He hesitated only a moment before he cupped water in his hands and splashed it over his face, rubbing briskly. Surely Five wouldn't begrudge him that. When he finished, he sat back and closed his eyes again.

He waited a few minutes, then lowered his hand into the water to take hold of his dick. He tried not to think about anything in particular, but it was hard. At first nothing happened. He tugged a little harder, biting his lower lip and grunting softly as he felt the first stirrings of an erection.

He reached up and flicked his left nipple with his thumb, back and forth. He wasn't very sensitive there, but sometimes it helped when he was trying to get off quickly. Not that he was actually trying to get off.

His breath started coming faster, and he thought

maybe it was time to see if he could get his finger through his anus, but—

"How the fuck—"

He tried putting his ankle up on the side of the tub, then couldn't grab the rim of the tub fast enough to keep himself from going under.

"Son of a—"

He surged upright, sputtering out a mouthful of water. He swiped water off his face, then stared across the room at the mirrored wall that probably hid a closet.

"Goddammit," he muttered, eyes on the sight of his hair plastered to his head and his naked chest.

He was supposed to relax and do this? No way in hell. This was the furthest thing from relaxing he could imagine doing in a bathtub.

Fuck it. He could take whatever that wolf did to him and he didn't need to stick his finger up his ass beforehand to do it. He dropped back, resting his neck on the rim of the tub, and closed his eyes.

The small measure of defiance felt pretty damn good.

Twenty minutes later, maybe longer, he startled out of a half-doze at the sound of the bedroom door opening.

He leaned forward with his arm on the side of the tub and tried to peer through the open bathroom door. He heard a few soft sounds that he couldn't identify, but no one entered the bathroom.

"Five? That you?"

No one answered.

"Hello?"

Unease sent a small surge of adrenaline through Mason. He rose, trying to be quiet, but water sluiced down his body and sloshed over the rim of the tub, splashing loudly to the tiled floor. He climbed out, nearly landing on his ass when he stepped in a puddle and his foot slipped on the tile. He grabbed the rim of the tub to catch his balance.

The quiet sounds coming from the bedroom continued.

Mason reached for one of the towels stacked in an open shelf between the tub and shower enclosure and wrapped it around his hips, tucking the end in tight so it wouldn't slip.

"Anybody there?" he called out.

The sounds stopped.

Mason took one quick look around the door but all he could see was a lanky figure crouched on the floor over his dirty clothes.

Mason clenched his jaw and stepped into the doorway.

The lanky figure was holding one of Mason's boots and sniffing at the laces.

"What the hell do you think you're doing?" Mason asked.

The figure twisted on the balls of his feet so fast that Mason took an instinctive step backward.

"I'm not supposed to talk to you. Alpha said I was supposed to give you privacy." Said as if that were a bad thing.

Mason frowned. The wolf's features had a softness to them that told Mason he was looking at a kid.

"Why are you here?" Mason gestured at his boot. "Put that down."

The young wolf studied the boot. "I was just trying to figure out what makes your scent so special."

Mason padded across the floor, leaving behind wet

hardwood in his wake. "Is that so?" He reached for his boot.

The wolf pulled his hand back and bared his teeth. "Don't try to hurt me. I know how to defend myself."

Mason eyed the kid. "I'm not going to try to hurt you."

"I overheard *Aiahaleaeille* and Alpha talking. You're one of *them*."

"Them." What the hell was this kid talking about?

"The human renegades. You want to kill us." He rose out of his crouch, letting the boot thud to the floor beside him. "You might think I'm weak, but I won't let you hurt me or anyone in my pack."

His arms were at his sides, hands at the ready, as if he thought Mason was going to surge forward at any moment and attack him.

Mason put his hands up, palms out. "I haven't been with the renegades in over three years. Even when I was —I'm not going to hurt you."

Suspicion overflowed from the ocean-blue eyes returning his gaze. The young wolf didn't relax his stance.

"I mean it, I'm not going to hurt you." Mason eased his arms down and glanced around the room. The bedding had been stripped but not replaced, and there were several small jars on the dresser, along with a coil of—

"What the hell is that?"

The wolf darted his gaze toward the dresser and back. "Ropes."

Anger stirred in Mason's gut. "They better not be here for the reason I think they are."

The young wolf's chin went up. "*Aiahaleaeille* says your submission can't be trusted because you're human."

Mason couldn't figure out who the young wolf was

talking about, but he didn't think it was Five. He distinctly remembered a "W" sound at the beginning of Five's real name. At least he thought he did.

Still, he had trouble getting his jaw to unclench enough to respond. "Take them away."

"Alpha told me to bring them."

Goddamn that wolf.

Mason forced his jaw to relax. If he kept gritting his teeth, he was going to crack one of them. He didn't waste a breath telling the kid to take the rope again. He could tell by looking at the kid that he would do what his alpha wanted and to hell with Mason's commands. So Mason would take care of the goddamn ropes himself.

The young wolf pointed at the bathroom door. "You should go back to your bath. I have work to do."

"Like sniffing my boot?"

The wolf flashed his teeth and growled low in his throat.

Mason refused to be cowed by a kid, wolf or not.

The wolf stopped his growling, his expression going soft. Regretful. "Alpha *Weketekari* says you're going to be his mate. I wish you would have chosen to fight." He flashed those teeth again, dropping into a half-crouch and slashing his arm through the air as if he were taking down an enemy with his claws.

Mason gave the wolf a flat look then moved to the hard chair. He sat, slouching enough to keep the towel in place, and twined his fingers together over his abdomen. "I'll just watch you work."

When the wolf realized Mason was serious, he straightened, then side-eyed Mason as he slowly made his way toward the bed.

Over the next few minutes, the young wolf surprised

Mason with the care he took doing his job. He put the blue and white striped sheets on the bed with careful precision, tucking each corner and smoothing every inch of fabric before laying out a clean quilt on top of it all.

Mason studied the kid, watching those familiar eyes.

After a few minutes, he asked, "What's your name?"

His voice seemed to startle the young wolf, who stilled before answering. "Aaron."

Mason pressed his thumbs together. "That's a human name."

"Yes."

The wolf smoothed the quilt across the bed. It wasn't quite large enough, but a few inches hung over each side. The wolf picked up the pillows piled into the corner and started placing them strategically, as if he knew where every one was meant to rest.

There were too many. That was all Mason could say about it.

"What's your real name?" Mason asked.

The wolf gave him a pointed look over his shoulder as he placed another pillow. "Aaron *er tio Skiatarweaieskg*."

Well that was impossible. Mason sighed. "So Aaron, huh?"

"*Traesikeille* wants us to take human names."

Mason made a quick guess. "You're talking about the First Alpha?"

"Yes." The wolf dropped the final puffy pillow onto the bed and turned. "I have to go now."

Mason sat forward. "Wait. You're not one of his are you?"

A furrow appeared between Aaron's eyebrows. "Do I belong to Alpha?"

"Yeah."

"He's Alpha. We all belong to him. You do too."

"That's not what I'm talking about." And he disagreed vehemently that he belong to anybody, but that was an argument for someone else and some other time. "Is he your father?"

"*Weketekari*?" Aaron snorted in an all too human way. "My father is Alpha's father's kin. We are not kin."

"That sounds like cousins to me." Which abruptly brought to mind exactly why Five wasn't there and what he was supposed to be doing. "Cousins are definitely kin-folk."

Aaron moved away from the bed, toward the pile of Mason's clothes. "Kin is kin, pack is pack. If Alpha were kin, I wouldn't be in his pack." He snatched Mason's clothes off the floor, gave Mason another suspicious glare, and left without another word.

Mason didn't object to the removal of his clothes, if only because the t-shirt was useless to him while torn in half and an objection would be just another wasted breath. Aaron had his orders. Mason wouldn't win that argument.

His gaze landed on the ropes Aaron had left behind.

Mason pushed to his feet and stalked across the room. He took the ropes off the dresser, went to the door that had just finished closing, and slid it open to see a wolf straightening away from the wall opposite the door. He threw the ropes into the hallway where they landed with a loud whump.

The wolf's head tilted, his eyes flickering between Mason and the ropes before settling on Mason in a way that made Mason intensely aware of the fact that the only thing between him and that wolf was a towel and three feet of hallway.

Eyes fixed on that unknown wolf, Mason stuck his fingers into the recessed grip of the door and shoved it closed.

Chapter 12

THE BATHWATER HAD cooled down considerably by the time Mason heard the door open again. He jerked upright in the hard chair—the only surface in the room for sitting unless he wanted to sit on the bed—*no*—or the floor—*hell no*—and uncrossed his arms quickly for balance.

As soon as he saw it was Five who'd entered, he exhaled a pent up breath and said, "About goddamn time. What the fuck took you so long?" And then, before Five had time to answer, "What did you find out? Is he alive?"

Five slid the door closed behind him. He tossed the bundle of ropes into the room and they landed with a dull thwap a few feet from the foot of the bed.

Anger burned in Mason's chest at the sight of those goddamn ropes again. "You won't need those."

"You were supposed to be waiting in the tub."

"Water's cold and I didn't fucking feel like—"

Five crossed the room in less time than it took Mason to get to his feet.

"Okay shit, goddammit, I submit!" Mason reared back

but Five had him by the back of the neck before he could move more than a few inches.

Five pulled Mason forward with inexorable intent, his deadly eyeteeth glimmering under the light and his eyes deep, dark pools of blue. Mason held his breath.

He wasn't sure what he was expecting, but it wasn't what he got.

Five turned Mason toward the bathroom door. "In the bath. Now."

A sharp exhale escaped, and the tightness in his chest eased. "But—"

"He's alive. Any more discussion of it can wait until after we fuck. If we don't do it soon, the moment my heat strikes me in full, I'll have you on your back and my cock buried deep inside you whether you're ready for me or not. Your human body isn't capable of taking me the way one of my own could. You won't enjoy it, and I won't enjoy knowing I caused you pain."

Mason swallowed—hard. He started moving toward the bathroom.

A sudden tug at his waist made him stop, but Five's hand landed heavy in the center of his back, pushing him forward. The towel dropped to the floor.

As soon as Mason reached the tub, he grabbed the rim and climbed into the chill water. Goosebumps raced across his skin.

Five reached around him and raised the lever that controlled the drain stopper. The water gurgled once, then started a silent, fast swirl down the drain. Five turned the hot water on and started refilling the tub.

"This is a total waste," Mason said, pulling his knees up. "All this water."

"We have a great deal of experience filtering and re-cycling water. Don't concern yourself with it."

Mason pressed his lips together and watched Five retrieve a washcloth and a bar of soap.

So this was really going to happen. Five was going to wash him. Just the thought of it made Mason's face hot and his stomach clench. He felt...

He wasn't sure how he felt. Not good, that was all.

Five turned the water off. Mason's heart started a slow, heavy beat. Not that he was scared, because he wasn't. He was uncertain. He didn't know what Five expected to get out of this, didn't know why it was necessary.

Five dipped the cloth into the water and started lathering the soap. A sharp, leafy scent wafted on the air.

Not unpleasant, just different. "What's that made of?"

Five answered in the wolves' language. "*Kueilateei.*"

It was a melodic word, and Mason liked the sound of it, even if he didn't have any idea what it meant. "A plant?"

"A beetle-like creature. It mimics scent as camouflage. The smell is of our home world. It was a popular harvest before the end. We saved enough to keep the species alive on our ships but their numbers are dwindling. They haven't thrived in captivity. They'll be extinct soon enough."

"Oh." He hadn't expected his question to lead to a reminder that the wolves' world was gone and hadn't thought much about what that really meant. Earth was their new home, whether the humans who shared it with them liked it or not.

Five set the soap aside, then took Mason's arm and

slowly dragged the cloth over his skin from his shoulder to his fingertips.

Mason watched bubbles slide down the underside of his arm. "I'm sorry you lost your world."

"What is, is."

Such a soft, quiet answer. "Do you miss it?"

"I hardly knew it."

"What do you mean?"

"I was born only a few heats before we set off on the ships. The ship I grew up on was my home. We had very little space for everyone and very little hope of finding a new world to settle on. And yet…" His quiet words trailed off and his touch slowed. "Some days I look at the trees and the sky and the open spaces, and I miss it."

An inexplicable ache tightened Mason's chest. "I miss the life I had before you all came."

He would never have that life again, and he would never know what could have been.

Five's eyes came up to meet Mason's for the first time since he'd started washing him. "I want to mate you. I wish I could do it with an open heart."

The intonation of "mate" had changed again, but Mason was beginning to sense the patterns in the words and this time he thought he understood. The wolves had a greater vocal range than humans. The adaptations probably weren't even intentional, just something that was evolving naturally as the wolves spoke a language so much less nuanced than their own.

He curled his fingers around the rim of the tub. "You want to mate me, but you're still angry."

"The past is the past, and I shouldn't cling to it. But I cannot seem to let it go, not with your scent memory tied so closely to the memory of *Iaehekielle*."

Five was talking about the attack where he'd first caught Mason's scent, Mason was sure of it.

"I can't change the past," Mason said. "You think I'd be here if I could?"

Water splashed as he straightened his legs. The strain on his muscles eased. Hiding was pointless anyway. Five had seen it all. He would see it again. Soon he would even touch it.

Mason repeated Five's words back to him. "What is, is."

"An impasse."

Mason rested his hand on the opposite rim of the tub and stared at the mirror across the room. Something in his own expression made him feel edgy.

"It's a goddamned star-crossed romance," he said.

Five palmed Mason's cheek and turned his head, then stared so solemnly at Mason that he found it hard to take a deep breath.

Something was wrong here, but he couldn't figure out what it was.

"I'm not gay," Mason said, ignoring the warmth of that palm against his skin and the way Five's thumb scraped at the shadow of his beard. "You don't even like me. It doesn't take a genius to know why you want me right now, but why in the hell are you so sure you want me for a mate?"

Five picked up the soap again. "Your sexuality isn't a stagnant lake, abandoned by the waters that created it. It's a river, and even rivers can change the direction of their flow given the right circumstances."

Mason laughed, a short, sharp sound that echoed off the bathroom walls. "You're an arrogant son of a bitch, you know that? It would take an earthquake of the size we haven't seen since the Great Quake to send a river running backward. I've never been interested in guys. I really don't think you're going to be the one that changes all that."

Five paused his effort to add more soap to the cloth in his hand. His gaze dropped to Mason's groin and suddenly there was fire in those eyes that started a tremble in Mason's belly. "I'm going to enjoy proving to you how wrong you are."

Mason let his frustration out in a noisy exhale that stirred the hair at Five's temple. "You didn't answer my question."

"You wouldn't understand my answer."

Mason gripped the rim tightly and propped his leg on the side of the tub. "Wash then. The water's getting cold again."

It wasn't, not yet, but Five didn't call Mason on it.

He started at Mason's ankle, washing with slow, soothing strokes. When the cloth dipped into the water and started up the inside of his knee, Mason clenched his teeth against the way his breath wanted to come faster. He almost lost his nerve when the cloth brushed the side of his cock and then—

He grabbed for Five's hand just as Five pushed the cloth under his scrotum.

Five's nostrils flared, his eyes tightening at the corners, but contrary to what Mason expected, Five eased his hand back, away from Mason's genitals.

Unnerved by his own actions, Mason released Five's hand, his own hand trembling with adrenaline. What he'd done was dangerous. Much too dangerous to repeat. He couldn't let himself forget that.

Five washed along the underside of Mason's thigh, then soaped the cloth again, saying, "Lean forward."

Mason rested his elbows on his thighs and lowered his head, arching his back at the same time. The slick cloth slid over his taut muscles and down his spine.

"We do this to calm the heat," Five said, his voice low and his touch gentle. His hand was only a few inches from Mason's tailbone.

"Does it?" Mason's voice cracked. He didn't repeat the question.

And then the cloth slid into the crease of his ass and Mason closed his eyes and took a deep breath and let it happen this time, because he'd told Five he would submit and he was going to keep his word if it fucking killed him.

It was the right move. After that, it got easier to raise his other leg and let Five wash away the last of the faint streaks of dirt his muddy pants had left behind, and then Five washed his chest and his other arm, and before he was ready for it, his freshly washed hair was dripping into his eyes and Five was using a clean cloth to wash Mason's face, rubbing the cloth over each eye with careful strokes.

"Stand up for me."

The command came in a deep, dark tone that brought Mason's head up. The light reflected off Five's eyes and the irises seemed brighter, hotter than before.

Mason had been quiet while Five washed him, no longer interested in distracting himself from the feel of the cloth rubbing across the sensitive areas of his skin. His nipples had peaked as the water cooled, and his cock had shown only minor interest in the proceedings—still, he wasn't completely soft and his face heated when he pushed himself to his feet and stood in front of Five.

"Submission has rewards," Five said. "And it has obligations. Taking care of those who submit is my obligation as alpha—and as a mate."

Taking care of Mason obviously meant more than just washing him, because Five leaned forward and pressed his lips to the soft, uncut skin of Mason's cock.

Mason's muscles jumped at the first touch, and he sucked in his breath in a startled rush, but he didn't step away from the warm lips—or the hot tongue that came out and licked away the droplets of water that clung to his skin.

His cock reacted by growing thicker and harder, and he reached out, gripping Five's shoulder for balance. He didn't close his eyes or try to hide from what was happening, and seeing those high, strong cheekbones and sharp nose dragging through his pubic hair was different enough from all his prior experience that he almost felt as if he were standing outside his own body, watching and waiting for what was to come.

But then Five pressed more kisses to the darkening flesh of Mason's cock, and something stirred in Mason's groin that was more than just acceptance. He swallowed and dug his fingers into the strong shoulder under his hand.

Five mouthed his way down to Mason's scrotum, and then over his balls. Each time Five sucked on Mason's skin, Mason's breath stuttered. He couldn't take his eyes off the way Five's eyelashes fluttered every time Five's warm lips came into contact with Mason's skin.

Despite never having looked at another man with

sexual interest, Mason's cock hardened under Five's kisses until he had a full erection.

He could have predicted this outcome if he'd suspected for even a moment that Five was going to go to his knees and put his mouth on Mason's cock. But Mason hadn't suspected this would happen—he'd been too worked up in the belief that Five thought Mason was just someone to fuck, and he felt like a fool for not seeing the clues in everything Five had been saying to him about mating from the moment they'd met.

And then Five took Mason's cock into his mouth, sucking him in deep, and the pleasure of the slick, wet heat of that mouth wound through every muscle in Mason's body. He took hold of Five's other shoulder, sure his legs were going to give out on him before Five was done.

Five sucked Mason's cock until Mason started having trouble keeping his hips still, until he couldn't stop the sounds that wanted to spill out of his throat, until he finally gave in and gripped a handful of hair and just held on.

He groaned, once, twice, then too many times to count as his body's reaction escaped the last of his control and he realized with startling abruptness that Five was giving him the best blowjob he'd ever had.

And then Five pulled off—well before Mason was ready to let him go.

Mason forced his fingers to unclench in Five's hair.

"Turn around," Five said, and the words came out hoarse and raw, nearly a growl.

"But I was close."

Five gripped Mason's hips, indicating with a push the direction he wanted Mason to move.

Mason turned, his heart thudding, his blood pulsing hot in his veins.

"Bend over."

Mason bit his bottom lip and breathed in quickly through his nose. But he leaned forward, gripping tight to the rim of the tub in front of him. Hands brushed up the insides of his thighs, encouraging him to spread his legs and take a sturdier stance.

Mason did, finding it impossible to think about anything except how exposed he felt, how sure he was that his balls were mere inches away from the back of Five's hand, how his asshole had to be right there in Five's face.

Then a heavy hand landed on his ass, drawing down his flank. Mason shivered, not sure if it was the chill from the rapidly cooling water that did it or something else.

Something else, that goddamn voice whispered in his head. *Definitely something else.*

Five leaned closer and his lips became a sudden warmth on the tight curve of Mason's ass while hands pulled Mason's cheeks apart. Mason's face burned with embarrassment and his knuckles went white but he kept his mouth shut and just breathed, trying not to sound like he was going to hyperventilate at any moment.

He wasn't scared. That wasn't his problem.

Hot breath grazed the pucker of his anus. His whole body shuddered in reaction.

He wanted to rear up and pull back. He wanted to climb out of the tub, to scramble away from that hot breath as quickly as he could, to turn and ask Five what the fuck he thought he was doing.

He wanted to know why every inch of skin on his body had flushed hot and tight and why he was quivering in nervous anticipation.

And then Five stopped teasing him and started teaching him what the hell he should've known years ago.

Chapter 13

MASON DIDN'T LIKE to think he was naïve when it came to sex. He was nearly twenty-six years old; he'd had sex and enough of it to feel like he knew what it was all about. But he'd never actually thought about what a gay man might get up to in bed with another gay man. Sure, he'd assumed the basics. Blowjobs and hand jobs and anal sex and all that, but it had never in his life occurred to him that there might be pleasure to be had from the feel of a hot, wet tongue on his asshole.

Or in it.

"Oh God," he said, so weak and so breathless he would've been embarrassed if it weren't already too late for that. His face was on fire. So was his body.

He felt as much as heard the rumble in Five's chest and he jumped at the tingle it created against the rim of his anus. Five's hands moved from Mason's ass to his thighs and he wrapped his arms around each, jerking Mason back into the position he wanted Mason in.

That was okay, because if Five hadn't been holding him up, Mason was convinced he would have been on his knees in the tub already. As it was, his white-knuck-led grip on the tub was the only thing keeping him from diving face first into the water sloshing at his knees. He was surprised he didn't feel the sharp points of claws biting into his skin, but Five hadn't let that happen.

"Oh fuck," he breathed. "Oh fuck."

Five had swiped his tongue over Mason's balls and up the crack of his ass, then darted heavy and quick through the tight ring of Mason's asshole. And then he did it again and again, until Mason's cock was so hard all Mason wanted to do was reach down and take his cock in hand and jerk himself off with fast, furious strokes.

The urge was so strong he had to bite the inside of his cheek to stop himself.

He wasn't ready when Five took one last swipe with his tongue and sat back, leaving Mason weak and shaking and uncertain what the hell he was supposed to do now.

Five rose behind him and wound his arms around Mason, pulling Mason's back tight to his chest. Mason's legs held him up, but he didn't know how.

When Five hauled him up into his arms, Mason grabbed at Five's neck with the crook of his arm.

"Whoa, whoa! Whoa the fuck down. I can walk."

"And so can I."

Mason couldn't believe how strong Five's arms felt under him, holding his weight as if he weren't a hundred and eighty pounds of dead weight.

Five carried Mason into the bedroom and tossed him onto the middle of the bed.

Mason's breath whooshed out of him. He scrambled up on his elbows, but Five pushed him flat and climbed over him, a predatory light in his eyes.

Mason put his hand out against Five's shoulder. "We're not going to be taking things slow, are we?"

That vibrating growl in Five's chest started again and he reared up, straddling Mason's knees. "It's too late to run. I should tie you to the bed in case you panic. It's my duty to protect you, even from yourself."

Mason dropped his hands to the bed and fisted them in the quilt so tightly his fingers ached. "I don't want those goddamn ropes anywhere near me. I won't be tied down for this."

Five growled softly at him, but then his head dipped and he rubbed his smooth cheek across Mason's abdomen. Mason sucked in his stomach so fast it stole his breath.

Five kept moving across Mason's body, sniffing deeply at Mason's groin, his belly, his chest and even his underarms—first one and then the other.

Maybe this was it, this was when Five would lose the last of his control to the lust craze triggered by human scent.

But Five raised his head, and even though his eyes glimmered glassy and bright and his every breath sounded ragged and too fast, he only stared at Mason, meeting Mason's concerned gaze head on.

"You need to prepare yourself." Five raised his hand and the sight of long, dark claws sent unease racing through Mason. "My control is slipping."

Mason exhaled out a sound of aggravation. "What the fuck am I supposed to do? I don't know anything about this—"

Five surged toward Mason.

"Shit!"

Mason tried to block Five with his arm.

Five shoved Mason's arm aside, then closed the distance between them and covered Mason's mouth with his. It was a slow, dry kiss until he nipped at Mason's bottom lip and said gruffly, "Open your mouth."

Mason parted his lips.

Five deepened the kiss, thrusting his tongue inside and toying with Mason, who was breathing heavily through his nose, as if he'd forgotten everything he'd ever known about kissing.

His hands fisted in the quilt again, until something brushed against his knuckles and he realized Five was tucking something small and warm into his hand. He took the hard little object and closed his fingers around it.

The slow, deep kiss became more forceful as the moments passed, until Mason was opening wide for it, pausing only long enough to gasp air into his lungs. Five's thumb dragged across Mason's nipple, once, twice, then again and again, and Mason wondered wildly if he was having an out of body experience, because it didn't seem possible that he was so goddamned turned on by a simple kiss.

By the time Five drew away, eyes heavy with arousal and face tight with something fierce that Mason couldn't put a name to, Mason had forgotten what it was he was supposed to be doing. Five pushed up on strong arms, muscles bulging, and slipped his knees between Mason's thighs.

"Your intoxicating scent is clouding my thoughts. I can't..." Five's words trailed off, then, instead of finishing what he'd started to say, Five sat back on his heels, resting his hands on his thighs, his claws extended and his fingers flexing in a way that seemed without thought or conscious control. "I want to fuck you, now, but you have to prepare yourself or I'm going to hurt you."

Mason looked down at the object he held. It was a small jar with a lid that had something written on it in the wolves' language, and it took him a second to realize what it was.

Lubricant. For his asshole. Because he was about to have a large alien dick shoved up his ass.

Rather have that tongue again, wouldn't you?

That voice in his head was becoming a goddamned nuisance.

Five stared down at Mason with glittering blue eyes. "Take the lubricant and finger your anus."

Do I have to? almost rolled right off his tongue. Luckily, his sense of self-preservation kept his mouth shut.

Mason was grateful for the distance between him and Five, until he looked down and realized Five was going to witness every awkward moment of Mason's attempt to slick up his asshole.

Breathe, he told himself. Breathe and get on with it.

He took a second to study the small jar in his hands before twisting off the lid and letting it fall to his stomach. He touched the lubricant inside with the tip of his finger, looked at the bulge at Five's groin, then went back in for a much larger glob. He might not know much about anal sex, but he wasn't stupid. It was going to take a lot of lube for a dick that big to go in easy.

Five chose that moment to drag his t-shirt off over his head, exposing strong, clearly defined muscle and a chest covered with dark hair that tapered down his abdomen and disappeared under the waistband of his black trousers. His hips thrust forward as his arms stretched over his head, and the thick outline of his cock was enough to make Mason swallow hard and hope like hell he didn't regret choosing to submit once that dick was sliding into him.

The distraction of watching Five toss his shirt aside made it easier to bend his knees and pull his feet up, then slip his hand down between his thighs and search out his asshole. He winced when he felt the cool lube smear across the underside of his balls, but then his finger reached the tight pucker of his anus and he rubbed around a bit before trying to push the tip inside.

His finger went in easy enough, either courtesy of the lube or the remnants of the saliva Five had left around his asshole. He glanced up from under his lashes to see Five's gaze riveted to what Mason was doing with his hand.

The scratch of claws on fabric tugged at Mason's attention and he glanced down.

Five had pierced his trousers with his dark claws and was digging their sharp points into his own flesh. Dark red blood gleamed on their shiny surface and had dampened the fabric around them.

The sight sent a twinge of empathetic pain tingling into Mason's gut, and he couldn't take his eyes off the sight of that blood.

The sight should have terrified him.

And yet...

He wasn't afraid. Not like he should've been. Those claws could tear into him in an instant and damage him in ways he didn't want to even imagine. He was lying naked under Five, for God's sake, unprotected by even a scrap of clothing. But Five had buried his claws in his own body to stave off his desperate need to fuck rather than force himself on Mason when he wasn't ready.

It was a sobering, eye-opening moment and his gaze flickered up.

Five was still watching Mason finger himself, those eyes a vibrant, shimmering blue under the warm glow of light coming from the ceiling.

Mason pushed his finger deeper into his ass. He wasn't sure why he did it; his asshole was as slick as it was going to get. But he couldn't seem to take his gaze off Five's expression and seeing those lips part when his finger went knuckle deep set off a strange tremble in his stomach.

Five's eyes narrowed on Mason, his breath coming visibly faster, and he bit into his lower lip, showing off his sharp eyeteeth. "Another finger."

Mason wasn't ready for another finger. He dragged in a deep breath and added another finger anyway. His asshole was so slick that both fingers slid right in.

Five closed his eyes and inhaled raggedly, tilting his head back, exposing the solid, masculine column of his throat. He moved his hands to the fastening of his trousers. His fingers trembled but it was his claws that created the biggest problem. They snagged at the fabric, poking several jagged holes in it. Buttons popped, one snapping loose to ricochet off Mason's inner thigh.

"Whoa there. You're not in a hurry, are you?"

Five's eyes snapped open and his gaze zeroed right in on Mason, too glassy, too bright.

Mason couldn't move with Five looking at him like that. He had two fingers stuck up his ass and he was staring at Five like a deer caught in a spotlight. He cleared his throat. "It was a joke. Bad timing?"

"Very bad timing." But Five sounded calmer than he'd sounded just seconds before and the sudden spark in his eyes made Mason wonder if that small moment of levity had actually helped Five regain a little of his slipping control.

He took a chance. "So…do you guys get extra credit when you mate a virgin? Because if we're talking gay sex, I'm about as virgin as you get."

Five blinked slowly at him. "I don't understand 'extra credit'."

Mason pulled his fingers out of his ass and held them up. "What do I…?"

Five snagged Mason's wrist and pulled. Mason sucked in his breath and came half up off the bed into a sitting position. He ended up sitting in front of Five, his legs stretched out on either side of Five's hips while Five wiped Mason's lubed fingers off on the visible fabric of Five's snug underwear.

Five's hot, hard penis pressed against Mason's fingers through the fabric and a soft sound escaped the back of Mason's throat.

"Explain extra credit," Five said.

Mason cleared his throat and tugged carefully with his hand. Five's fingers tightened. He pressed Mason's palm to his cock.

"Extra credit." Mason's voice cracked. "It's the thing you earn when you do something more than what you have to do and your teacher rewards you for it."

Five released Mason's hand. "I'm interested in this concept of extra credit."

Mason quickly drew his hand back and watched Five suspiciously.

Five's mouth curved up at one edge, and he leaned back on his arms, bowing his back and thrusting his hips forward. "You can remove my underwear for extra credit."

Chapter 14

MASON LOOKED ASKANCE at Five, his gaze slipping down to the bold thrust of Five's groin. "You want me to remove your underwear."

"Yes. Now."

Mason shifted until he could get his knees under him. Then, fingers not as steady as he would have liked, he took a firm grip of the waistband of Five's underwear and shuffled forward. He carefully pulled the elastic over Five's cock, then had to run his hands around Five's hips to slide the back down over Five's taut buttocks.

And my God, that was one tight ass under his hands.

He just resisted the urge to squeeze.

When he moved, Five's cock bumped his belly and he sucked in his breath. Moisture streaked along his hip as he pulled away, and his throat worked against the tightness trying to choke him.

What the hell had happened to him? He didn't understand why he found this so…arousing.

And he was aroused. He couldn't even deny it. His own cock bobbed in front of him, fully engorged and leaking from the tip, ready for the finish he'd been denied in the bathtub.

Five had a long, thick cock and heavy scrotum, so similar to a human male that it was easy to see why everyone believed there had to be a common origin for their species. Mason's knuckles grazed the dark hair that grew thick around Five's penis as Mason dragged the underwear down to Five's heavily muscled thighs.

"At least I don't have to worry about being the hairiest man in the room when you're around."

Five surged forward, startling the hell out of Mason, who jerked back and ended up flat on his back. Teeth grazed the skin above his belly button, making his stomach muscles pull tight.

On hands and knees, Five stalked his way up Mason's body. Mason tried to relax, but something about the predatory way Five was watching him made it hard to even swallow.

Five caged Mason to the bed, lowering himself to put his mouth to Mason's ear. "You have prominent male features. The hair here—"

He skimmed his knuckles up through the hair on Mason's chest.

"—and here—"

He drew his fingers down to Mason's groin and through the coarse hair there with just enough claw extended to send Mason's pulse skyrocketing.

"—and here—"

The flat of his palm grazed the upper part of Mason's thigh.

"—just makes me want to fuck you more."

Then he bit Mason right on the earlobe, not too hard,

but hard enough to sting. Mason's heartbeat thundered in his ears.

Five growled deep in his chest and moved between Mason's thighs.

"I need you." Dipping his head, he licked a stripe up the center of Mason's chest, then detoured to one of Mason's nipples. "Now."

At the first touch of Five's mouth on his nipple, a jolt of pleasure went straight through Mason like an electric shock. He gasped, his toes digging into the quilt under him.

Five sucked at Mason's nipple long enough to make Mason whimper, then Five reared up on his knees, fisted his cock, and came with a rough growl all over Mason's belly and groin.

The splatter of alien semen shocked Mason. His mouth parted on a gasp and he stared down at the semen pooling in his belly button and streaked across his cock and balls and belly.

He shouldn't have been surprised when it happened again, but he was. He let out a startled grunt when Five dropped forward on one thickly veined arm and came again, striping Mason's cock and scrotum with more of the glossy white semen that started an immediate slide into the crease of Mason's thigh and groin.

"Pull up your legs."

"Huh?"

Five didn't give the order again. He just pushed Mason's knees toward his chest. "Don't tense up."

Of course Mason was going to tense after that. His asshole clenched as Five pressed the head of his cock against Mason's hole, and Mason had time to grunt and that was it.

Five began a slow, unyielding thrust into Mason's body.

"Unnhh…" He wasn't ready, not in the least. He grabbed onto the quilt beneath him and tried to relax, but nothing he did seemed to help and the enormous pressure just seemed to get worse and then a cold sweat swept over him and his vision narrowed—

Five slapped the outside of Mason's thigh. Hard.

The breath Mason hadn't even realized he'd been holding whooshed out of him.

"It's done. I'll let you adjust for as long as I can." Teeth flashed and a low growl rose out of Five's chest. "It won't be long."

Mason closed his eyes and took a deep breath—which wasn't that deep with his goddamn knees halfway to his throat—but breathing helped. A lot.

When he looked up, Five was watching him with something approaching concern in those ocean-deep eyes of his.

Mason forced himself to relax his hands on the quilt. Then he looked down. He had Five's cock buried in his ass—and goddamn if the sight of it wasn't almost as arousing as the memory of Five's tongue working over his asshole.

He dropped his head back against the bed, letting out a soft groan.

He would never forget what it had felt like to have Five licking at his hole like that, not for the rest of his life. Then again, he didn't think he'd ever forget the stretch of having Five's cock breaching his asshole either, but the one memory was nothing like the other.

Then Five started to move, and Mason couldn't help it, he clutched his knees around Five's hips and clenched his fingers around those strong arms.

"Wait! Just a—"

Five growled at him, a sudden, harsh sound that raised every hair on Mason's body.

Mason snapped his mouth closed, breathing furiously through his nose.

Five took his time pulling out, sweat gleaming on his furrowed brow, eyes locked on Mason's face, the muscle and veins of his chest and arms bulging, and it felt okay. He wasn't dying. He wasn't even in pain. He was just stuffed uncomfortably full of cock, and then he wasn't, until Five thrust his hips forward and slid deep again, all at once.

A sudden rush of sensation lit up Mason's nerves and he gasped. He tried to lower one leg but Five caught Mason's knee in the crook of his elbow and thrust again.

The motion jarred through Mason.

And then Five thrust again, heavy, forceful, and too goddamn soon—but whatever he'd done, however he'd changed his angle, something inside Mason sparked off a bright, hot streak of pleasure that burned through him with all the subtlety of a shot of sour mash whiskey.

"Oh fuck," he gasped. "Fuck…"

For the next several minutes, Five fucked him like that, each stroke bringing with it a jolt of unexpected pleasure that Mason couldn't seem to anticipate no matter how many times Five thrust into him. Needy, desperate sounds kept escaping his throat no matter how hard he tried to hold them back, and his body thrummed with the first hints of an orgasm he wanted more than he wanted anything in the world at that moment.

He reached down for his cock.

Five caught his hand and pushed it away.

Mason reached up and grasped the back of Five's

head, dragging him close. "I need that fucking…orgasm. Either give it to me, or I'm…taking it."

Five reared up on his muscled arms, snarling.

Mason jammed his heel into the back of Five's knee for leverage, forcing Five's cock to slide deep again.

Five rested his sweaty forehead on Mason's shoulder, his breath coming fast and shallow.

"Mine," Five said in the wolves' language, and then again, with more of a growl to it, "*Mine.*"

Then he thrust his cock deep once more and came. Mason knew exactly when it happened, because he felt the warm spurt of alien semen filling his ass, and it was a hell of a weird sensation but not bad. Not bad at all.

When Five's rutting slowed and he made a soft sound against Mason's collarbone, Mason found himself petting at the back of Five's head in much the same way Five had done him just that morning in the woods. He wasn't even sure why he did it, but Five calmed against him and stopped trying to push his cock deeper into Mason's ass, giving him a few minutes to breathe without feeling like his lungs were being shoved up into his throat.

"Why don't you want me to jerk off?" Mason asked.

Five dragged his nose and mouth along Mason's skin, breathing deeply. "I want you to get as much pleasure from our mating as possible."

Mason clenched his fingers in Five's hair. "So you're not just trying to show me who's in charge?"

Five spoke quietly into Mason's ear. "Your prostate could become painfully sensitive after you come."

A shiver wracked his body but he still managed a choked, "Ah." What Five said might be true. He didn't have any experience one way or the other. All he knew was his goddamn cock was already aching for release, and his balls were tight and his skin sensitive—and he still had Five's cock stretching him out, making his asshole clench whenever he moved even the slightest bit.

His contemplation ended suddenly as Five pushed to his knees, took a firm hold on Mason's ass, and hauled him close, the move thrusting Five's cock in deep.

A hoarse shout escaped before Mason could stop it. He grabbed at the pillow under his head, raising his chest and arching his back off the bed, and Five began to fuck him again in earnest.

Mason couldn't have said how much time passed like that, but somewhere between Five's next two orgasms, he was able to wrap one of his legs around the back of Five's thigh and Five started hugging Mason to the bed, his hands clasped tightly to Mason's shoulders, their bodies as good as glued together as Five drove himself deep again and again. The new position caused Five's sweat-slicked abdomen to drag over Mason's cock until Mason was so close to coming he knew nothing was going to stop it.

Five had been right about one thing: pleasure was pleasure and Five was doing a hell of a job proving that to Mason.

One more thrust and the slick slide of skin over Mason's cock was all it took.

"Ahhh!" He came with a hoarse shout, his orgasm an uncontrollable shudder that wracked his whole body. Semen spread thick and sticky between them, smearing all over his belly and chest with Five's very next drive into his ass.

It took him several seconds to catch his breath, and even then, he seemed to be gasping more than breathing.

"Goddamn…"

Five pressed his mouth to Mason's shoulder, whining low in his throat, his movements taking on an edge of desperation. He would come again soon, Mason was sure of it. As for Mason, he was done.

Body trembling with fatigue and chest heaving, he dropped his head back to the bed and closed his eyes, body lax, ready to just take it and ride out the rest of Five's heat. But Five's belly dragged across his cock again, and Mason jerked and quickly pushed his hand between them to protect his sensitive flesh.

Five made a harsh sound against Mason's throat and warmth flooded his ass again.

Sweat cooled on his overheated skin and the quilt under him had rucked up uncomfortably between his shoulders. He stared up at the ceiling while he tried to calm his heartbeat and his breathing. He had no idea how long they'd been fucking. He didn't even know if Five was finally done.

He wasn't. He whimpered against Mason's throat and the rutting started again.

Mason choked out a humorless laugh and tried to stretch out his leg again, and this time Five was too far gone into his heat to stop him. Mason groaned at the pull in his back and used his hand to protect his cock from what had suddenly become a very unpleasant friction.

How the hell did the wolves do it?

Humans weren't made for this kind of intense fucking. He didn't even know if it was safe.

But goddamn.

He would never fuck again and not remember what had happened here tonight.

Later, when Five had finally reached the end of his

heat cycle and Mason was lying naked on top of the sheets only half aware of the air cooling his shower-damp skin and the sticky heat of Five's sleeping body pressed up against his back in the position Five had manhandled him into after his tired slog to the bathroom, one thought kept running through his head.

He wasn't gay.

Sex with Five hadn't suddenly opened his eyes to some hidden part of himself. He hadn't been hiding anything. What Five had done was show Mason that he liked having his asshole licked and that he could have an amazing orgasm while he had a cock up his ass, but he still couldn't think of any man he wanted to fuck.

Not one.

But what about an alien to fuck you? that ever present voice in his head whispered.

Mason tried to turn onto his back but his movement disturbed Five's sleep. Seconds later, he ended up half crushed under the weight of a thick thigh and half Five's torso.

He huffed, then tucked his arm under his head and stared through the shadowy darkness toward the bedroom door.

Did he want Five to fuck him again—and possibly again and again after that? That was the question keeping him awake. Just twenty-four hours ago, he would've said no without a second's hesitation. But now...

Now he was going to have to get some goddamned sleep, that was what.

Still, one thing was certain. He needed a new plan for convincing Five their romance was doomed. "Not gay" wasn't going to cut it.

Chapter 15

MASON SLEPT TOO long. He wasn't sure exactly how long that was, but he woke to the rattle of a door shutting somewhere out in the hallway and a chill working its way down his spine.

The top sheet was at his feet and one of several pillows were resting heavy against his thigh. He rolled to his back with a soft groan. His dick smacked his belly.

Great. He had an erection even after an entire evening of hard fucking.

He stretched out his leg to knock aside the pillows and dragged his hands down his face, only to frown up at the bright ceiling and immediately wonder just what time it was.

He sat up slowly, surprised to note he wasn't sore at all, not even in his abs, and he'd definitely expected to be sore after so much fucking. He pushed off the side of the bed and took a good look around, but from what he could see in the room nothing had changed since the night before.

He rounded the bed to peer out the windows. The sun was on its way up into the sky and leaves swirled through the air outside the window, falling from the maple growing too close to the house. He flicked the lock open and swung one of the hinged windows inward. Unpleasantly cool air hit his skin, making goose bumps rise.

Seven, maybe eight in the morning, he'd guess.

The scent of pine and hardwoods and earthy decay filled his lungs. The house was situated in a field of tall brown grass scattered with trees. He could make out a few more red maples and some sweet gum and a twisted old black walnut in the distance. He knocked a pile of dead maple leaves off the sill and leaned forward on his elbows, breathing in the crisp scent of fresh air and letting the chill breeze ruffle his hair.

The door behind him opened, causing a sudden change in the flow of air, and Mason straightened abruptly, turning.

Five stood just inside the room, the door open behind him. "You shouldn't stand in the open window."

"I needed some fresh air."

"You washed away my scent when you showered last night. Someone might catch your scent and try to claim you."

Mason took a look over his shoulder. The sun dappled field and shadowed woods beyond didn't look nearly so inviting anymore. He swung the window closed.

When he was done, he turned back to Five. "You going to close the door?"

Five stepped another few feet into the room. "Aaron is bringing food. Your clothes are clean. They're in the top drawer, along with some t-shirts that should fit you."

That got Mason moving. Aaron had already seen as much of him as he was comfortable with. He crossed to the dresser, passing in front of Five.

Just how soon would Five want to fuck again? Was Mason ready for another round of that, so soon after the first one? He wanted to say no, but the truth was he couldn't seem to stop noticing how Five's short-sleeved t-shirt clung to his chest, highlighting the ridges and dips of muscle and bone, or how Five's chest hair curled at the edges of the shirt's collar—hair that Mason had felt against the palms of his hands and that he knew was both softer and finer than it looked.

He'd never really paid attention to that kind of thing before and he didn't know why the fuck he had to start noticing now.

Life was already complicated. He didn't need this. He didn't want to be here and yet here he was. Stuck. He wondered how Marcus was handling their current situation. He hoped he'd get a chance to see Marcus soon, because they needed to talk. Mason still had a shit-ton of questions about what had gone down at the lab.

He opened the top drawer to find his jeans neatly folded right under his boxers. He pulled out the boxers and stepped into them quickly, determined to get his ass covered as fast as humanly possible. "I didn't hear anyone come in last night."

"Aaron's been training with Six in stealth and tracking."

Mason shook out his jeans and yanked them on with hurried, sharp movements. He forced the buttons through the holes. "Six?"

"*Ishikeille*. I told my betas to choose human names for

your benefit. Some of us already had them. Those of us who didn't do now."

Mason had started sorting through the stack of soft cotton t-shirts as Five spoke. The shirts were all the same, with deep v-necked collars and short sleeves that ended high on a man's biceps, and they varied only in color. The wolves seemed particularly fond of t-shirts and this particular style had become popular shortly after the wolves came to Earth. He remembered because everyone had spent that first year excited by every little piece of news that came out about the wolves and their introduction to the human world. Wolves had worn those damn t-shirts in nearly every *veo* stream that hit the nets and then so had everyone else.

He picked a black one and pulled it on over his head. When he yanked it down, he caught Five staring at his midsection. His stomach gave an odd little flip.

He covered his reaction by smoothing his shirt over his stomach. "Six isn't a name. Neither is Five."

"Six has a strange sense of humor. He chose his name only after hearing mine."

Mason paused in the middle of reaching for his cleaned socks. "That's brave of him."

Five's wicked sharp eyeteeth flashed when he smiled. "He's my beta. His bravery isn't in question."

Mason side-eyed Five while he separated his socks. "You don't mind that he's obviously poking fun at you?"

"His choice of name is his own. How can I find his desire to emulate me offensive?"

"Enlightened of you."

"A feared alpha is no alpha at all."

Mason couldn't have stopped his snort if he'd had claws at his throat.

Five's chin rose and he managed to look down his nose at Mason even though he wasn't that much taller at all. "You will learn."

What could he say to that? He hoped not to be there long enough to learn any such thing.

Mason pulled on his right sock, looking up from his half-crouched position. "What made you choose Five as a name?"

"You offered your brother your hand five times to help him up along the path we took."

Mason paused with his foot raised, sock halfway on, then had to adjust quickly to keep his balance. He finished pulling on the sock and straightened. "That's it? That's how you chose your name?"

"Would you rather I say it was because I was told once that the second of the fifth would be my fifth mate and that the fifth would be my last?"

Mason tried not to frown. Didn't work. He had a feeling Five was messing with him and he didn't like it, not one damn bit. "Are you just trying to be an asshole or is this your usual MO?"

"Em oh?"

"Modus operandi."

"An acronym."

"A fucking acronym. It means—"

"I know what it means."

Just then, Aaron stopped in the doorway behind Five, carrying a folded table and a slat-backed chair made of a dark wood.

Five gestured toward the window. "There."

"Yes, Alpha."

Mason moved to the side and watched silently while Aaron carried the table and chair into the room, unfolded the table in front of the windows, then placed the chair at one end. He only glanced once, quickly, at Mason, before leaving without another word.

Five picked up the chair Mason had sat in the night before and carried it to the table. The wood legs hit the hardwood with a quiet thunk as Five placed the chair right beside the one Aaron had brought in.

"Sit."

Mason eyed the end of the table where he'd expected that second chair to go and thought about what it could mean that the chair hadn't gone there. "How about I just wait until he's brought the food?"

Five tilted his head and looked sideways at Mason, before snorting softly. "You question me at every turn. I'm almost insulted."

But Five didn't sound insulted. He sounded amused.

Mason crossed his arms, feeling the pull of his t-shirt's tight sleeves across his shoulders. The son of a bitch was making fun of him.

"You said last night Matthew was alive. How'd you find out? Where is he?"

"He's safe. Anything else about his situation is irrelevant to you right now."

"Irrelevant. What a fucking useless word." He wanted to push Five for more on the subject, but one look at the suddenly firm slash of Five's mouth told Mason he'd be wasting his time.

Fine. He had other questions. Plenty of them, in fact.

"So where's my brother? Are you going to keep me locked up in here or am I going to be allowed to see him?"

"You're not a prisoner."

"In fact or in theory?"

Five placed his hands on the back of the chair and curled his long fingers around the top slat. There was a dusting of hair between those knuckles that Mason hadn't noticed the night before, and he couldn't say why he was noticing it then. But those were strong fingers. Hard. Masculine. Nothing like—

A low rumble came from Five's chest and startled Mason so hard he jerked.

When he looked up, Five was staring right at him, his brilliant blue eyes unreadable. Mason tightened his arms over his chest and forced himself to meet that gaze head on. He wasn't embarrassed; he didn't have anything to be embarrassed about, goddammit. He'd just been contemplating the differences between a man's and a woman's touch. That was all.

Given his circumstances, it was a natural thing to do. He'd had those hands all over him last night.

Had the novelty of the events of the night before been responsible for his reaction to those hands—or had it been the fault of something else altogether?

There was really only one way to find out.

"You're not a prisoner," Five repeated. "But I have an obligation to keep you safe. You're free to go wherever I go unless I say otherwise, but I won't leave you in the care of anyone other than my pack until the heat cycle ends."

Mason scowled, suddenly feeling a lot less amenable to the thoughts he'd been contemplating. "Shit. So I am a prisoner. And my brother?"

The wood under Five's hands creaked. "You are not a prisoner."

Mason unfolded his arms long enough to jab his forefinger toward his ear. "You keep saying that, but that's not what I keep hearing."

A loud scrape stopped him from saying more. He darted his gaze down to where Five held the wood slat tightly in his hands. Four distinct gouges marked the dark wood.

Mason stared at those gouges for a good long thirty seconds before raising his eyes. He tried for a light tone. "So I'm pissing you off, right?"

"You keep testing my patience as if what I have is without limit. It isn't. You aren't a prisoner. What you are is human. Breakable and fragile, and without an understanding of the instincts that drive us, and I cannot set aside my responsibility for your wellbeing as my heat mate, any more than I would set aside my responsibility for you as my *mate*."

Mason heard it distinctly that time, the change in intonation, the thing that distinguished one use of the word mate from another. Satisfaction swept through him. He had that fucking pattern nailed.

"My brother. You never answered my question. Is he a—" Shit. He's almost said prisoner again. "Is he going to be under guard too?"

Five arched one eyebrow, as if to call out Mason's subtle—maybe not so subtle—defiance. "He's just as human as you are. So yes, he'll be protected while he's here. But he won't be here indefinitely."

"What's that mean? You said he could come with us when we came here."

"And he did. But someone else has a claim on him. I explained that he could ask me to deny that claim as Alpha, but he didn't."

Mason made a fist at his side. "He wants to go." And God, he sounded so bitter about it. Was he never going to be able to let this go?

"His fate isn't yours."

"He should've stayed three years ago. I don't know why the fuck he had to listen to me when that was obviously what he wanted to do."

As if he could erase his guilt of the last three years by blaming Marcus. It hadn't worked yet, but he just kept on trying like a total fucking idiot.

"He said you wouldn't understand. Why do you begrudge him his fate?"

"I don't. He can do what the hell he wants. I'll be fine without him." Mason stared pointedly into the hallway. "Where the fuck is that kid with the food?"

"You shouldn't feel abandoned."

Faster than a forest fire set ablaze by a lightning strike, anger raged into an inferno in Mason's chest. He snapped his gaze back to Five. "Don't you tell me what I should feel. That wolf fucked my brother for no other reason than he needed somebody to fuck. He came in that room for me. If it had mattered to him who the fuck he put his dick in, why the fuck would he have settled for Marcus so quickly when Marcus stepped in front of me?"

Mason couldn't ever forget the way he'd looked to Marcus with a plea in his gaze as that wolf reached for him. If he could've gone back and stopped himself from opening his mouth, he would've done it a thousand times.

"*Marcus*," he'd said, a thick, panicked call for his brother to do something, just a half second before that wolf gripped Mason's wrist and started to pull him forward.

Unthinking, he reached for his wrist and rubbed. It used to ache: at night, in the cold, when it rained, until finally, one day, it had just quit.

"The drugs can make it difficult to trace the scent of a mate."

"He wasn't looking for a mate. He was looking for somebody to fuck. He found somebody. Me. And I—" He choked off his words, pressing his lips together tightly. Why the fuck had he let himself get so close to spilling his darkest moment to Five? Some things just didn't need to be shared.

"He would not have settled for just any mate, any more than I have. You were obviously not the mate he wanted, or he would have claimed you despite your brother's interference."

"You don't know that." Mason let go of his wrist. "Do you even know my fucking name? Because you sure the fuck haven't once asked me what it is. You think I haven't noticed that? You don't know one goddamned thing about me that matters."

"I know three things about you that matter, Mason Waters. I know you're no longer with the renegades and haven't been for nearly three years. I know you risked your life to come to the aid of your brother. And I know you harbor a deep regret for something that happened three years ago, although I don't yet understand why."

Before Mason could respond, Five turned his head a fraction of an inch to the left.

"Aaron is here."

Mason nodded. He wasn't about to start or continue an argument in front of that kid. He remembered Aaron slashing his claws through the air. That kid was dangerous—more dangerous than Mason, for damn sure. He let out a hard little laugh and got a raised eyebrow from Five.

"You'd've had to be here," Mason said.

At that moment, Aaron walked into view through the open door carrying a large tray and Five turned away.

Mason watched as Aaron brought the tray into the room and set it on the table. Glasses clinked against the edge of the platter and just the sight of the thinly sliced meat and warm vegetables made Mason's stomach growl.

He swallowed, throat bobbing, mouth watering. This wasn't the first time he'd gone without food, but it might have been the longest. "God, I'm hungry, I haven't eaten in a day and a half."

"Sit, then. We'll eat and I'll teach you more of our mating customs."

Great. Mason side-eyed Five for another moment before dragging the chair out from under the table. At the loud scrape and bang of wood hitting wood, he winced.

The edge of Five's mouth twitched but he didn't say anything.

Aaron was watching avidly from the side of the table but he was staying out of the way.

Mason sat and stretched his arm out on the table, fingers only inches from the platter of appetizing food. His stomach felt like it was going to growl its way right out of him if he didn't get something in it soon, but he wasn't sure enough of what was expected of him to dive in before Five joined him at the table.

He managed to tear his gaze away from the food in time to see Five ruffle his fingers through the hair at the back of Aaron's neck and murmur something to him in the wolves' language, too indistinct for Mason to catch.

Aaron left the room, closing the door behind him.

Mason was still watching the door when Five repositioned the other chair only a few feet away from Mason. Mason kept sliding the edge of his thumb against the smooth wood, but as soon as he realized what he was doing, he stilled his nervous twiddling.

Five sat and his long leg pressed warmly against Mason's own. A memory of the night before rushed to the forefront of Mason's thoughts. Five had strong thighs, thick with muscle and covered in dark hair, and Mason knew exactly how they felt between his own.

His breath stuttered and he sat there silently, eyes locked again on the tray of food.

He could have moved his leg, just an inch forward or back, and the connection would have been broken.

He didn't. He should have, but he didn't.

"You must be very hungry. You haven't taken your eyes off that tray since it came into the room."

Mason cleared his throat. "You could say that."

"Could I? What else could I say?" Asked in a curious and mild tone that immediately made Mason wary.

"You could say why there's no silverware, no plates, and three glasses. Are we waiting on someone else to bring them and share the food?"

The sliced meat was piled high beside a mountain of vegetables and bread, more than enough for two people.

"No."

When Five didn't elaborate, Mason said, "Just wondering what it all means."

"Look at me." The words were quiet and softly spoken, but Mason didn't doubt they were an order to be obeyed.

He finally glanced up.

Five set one of the glasses in front of Mason, the low

clunk of glass hitting wood a hollow echo. "This is water. Drink all you want."

Five set one of the glasses in front of himself. "As is this."

He set the third glass near the first in front of Mason. "This is not."

All Mason could do was ask the obvious question. "What is it?"

Five trailed his finger along the clear rim of the glass, while the sunlight streaming through the window sparkled on the surface of the clear liquid in a rainbow of color. "It is a gift. Something few humans will ever experience. A taste of my world."

Chapter 16

MASON STARED WARILY at that third glass. "Is it safe?" he asked. "For me, I mean."

"In small quantities. I've been warned that humans shouldn't drink too much, too quickly."

"I don't want to end up poisoned."

"The effects are intoxicating, not deadly. Even if you do drink too much, the worst is a few unpleasant side-effects."

So it was like alcohol for the wolves. Mason nodded, thoughts shifting to the food again. The smell was getting to him, and his stomach growled even louder than before. The manners his mother had taught him were the only things keeping him from digging in. Well, that and a healthy appreciation for Five's status as the alpha and Mason's uncertainty about what that might mean at the table.

When Five reached for the tray, Mason did the same.

Five caught Mason's forearm. "Be patient."

Mason scowled but dropped his hand to the table and watched as Five picked up what looked like a whole green bean glistening with a hint of some kind of sauce and turned in the seat just enough to face Mason. "Here."

Mason started to take the green bean in his hand, but Five shook his head.

"Lean forward."

For some reason, the first thought that popped into Mason's mind at those words was the memory of last night in the bathtub. His face heated and he pushed the thought away. He leaned closer to the green bean, wondering what the hell Five had in mind.

"Open your mouth."

Realization dawned, and Mason stared at that goddamned green bean, clasped delicately in Five's long fingers.

"Submit," Five said softly.

Mason felt the command into his bones. He shut up and opened his mouth.

Five allowed him to bite off half the bean, then fed him the other half.

Having someone feed him was a totally new experience for Mason. He wasn't sure how he felt about it.

"Why are you doing this?" he asked after another few bites.

"This?" Five tore a chunk of bread off the crunchy loaf and pressed the soft center to Mason's bottom lip.

Mason nodded and ate.

"Submission is a gift. You should be respected for it and treated with as much care as I would treat one of my own people if I had chosen one of them as a mate. I won't neglect my duties to you just because you're human and you expect so little from your mates."

"So you think our ways are inferior. You want respect for your ways, but you sure don't give—"

"First you complain that we ask too much from mates, now you complain because we don't treat you with as little respect as you treat each other."

"You're twisting my words."

"I'm giving them back to you from my perspective."

"Your perspective is—" *Wrong* was not the word he was looking for, even though that was the one that came immediately to mind, and he could see in Five's eyes that was exactly what he'd expected Mason to finish with.

"Alien," Mason said instead. "It's so goddamned alien. I can't figure you out."

The tension in Five's shoulders relaxed. "Then do not try. Accept me as I am."

It was a platitude, pure and simple, but for some reason it hit Mason hard in the chest, and he wondered just how many times he'd thought the same thing when he was trying a little too hard to be different enough from Marcus that people would stop treating him as if he were just a copy of his brother.

Five offered more bread, then took his time with the beans, feeding each one to Mason with graceful movements that emphasized the length of his fingers. Mason found himself watching those fingers, and a few times even came close to brushing his lips against them. Every time Five pulled away before it could happen, Mason's stomach tightened, and it felt a little too close to disappointment for his peace of mind.

Then a drip of buttery sauce plopped onto the back of Mason's hand. Without much thought, he raised his hand to his mouth and sucked the sauce off his skin.

Five followed the motion with eyes that had gone so deep and dark that not even the ocean could match them.

Mason lowered his hand and cleared his throat. "Maybe some of the meat now?"

"Of course."

Five rolled one of the thin slices and offered the end to Mason.

Mason ate, watching the subtle way Five's eyes flickered over him, how his eyelids lowered when he breathed deeply, how he avoided those deep breaths whenever possible but seemed unable to resist for more than a couple of minutes at a time.

Mason swallowed the last bite his stomach could hold and raised his hand before Five could reach for another slice.

"I'm good." He reached for the glass of water.

Five watched Mason empty the glass and return it to the table, his eyes tracking Mason with unsettling intensity.

Pretending a nonchalance he didn't feel, Mason stretched out his legs, clasping his hands together over his belly. "Is it really that hard, sitting here next to me?"

Instead of answering, Five raised his buttery fingers to his mouth and sucked them clean.

Mason's breath hitched and a small sound escaped his throat that made his face flush so fast he could feel his scalp tingling. All he could do was stare at the sight of those long fingers sliding between Five's lips and remember how those lips felt wrapped around his cock.

Five lowered his hands to the table, spreading his fingers wide and letting his palms rest flat on the wood surface. "Sitting next to you isn't hard."

"Huh? Uh—" Mason cleared his throat. "Then what is it? Something's wrong, I can tell that much."

"I've enjoyed taking care of your needs, but your scent does make it difficult to concentrate."

Mason glanced down at his clasped hands and his ragged thumbnails before looking up at Five. "What do I smell like to you? What is it that makes me so irresistible?"

"You smell rich and dark. Like the future...and the past. Of longing and sex." Five's fingers flexed against the table and a hint of dark claw peeked from under dark fingernails. "You smell like you belong to me."

"Those aren't smells."

"You cannot understand."

"I'm trying."

A raised eyebrow greeted his statement.

"I am."

"Try this." Five pushed the third glass of liquid toward Mason. The drink sloshed gently at the rim but didn't spill. "If you want to understand even a little of the fire of heat, drinking this will give you that."

Mason looked askance at the drink. "You said it was intoxicating. You didn't say anything about—"

"It will intoxicate you. It will arouse you. It will give you taste of the heat that burns in the blood of my people."

"That doesn't sound like something I want." He was already half-aroused and so goddamned uncomfortable with it that he couldn't even move for fear of giving it away. He refused—absolutely *refused*—to reach down and adjust himself, because then Five would know, and for some reason, letting that happen felt like the worst kind of submission.

He couldn't let this wolf get into his head.

Five's gaze was a little too knowing. "You said you were trying to understand."

Mason stilled his twiddling thumbs and looked pointedly at Five. "I don't like getting drunk. Never have. Drunks do stupid shit and I don't like doing stupid shit unless I don't have a choice."

"You have a choice. I do not ask for your submission on this."

Mason's gaze flickered up. "So it's not an order?"

"It isn't." Five reached for the glass.

Mason plopped forward, quickly gripping the top of the glass tight enough that the rim bit into the edges of his palm. "I haven't decided."

"Then decide now."

"Is it..." Mason stared at the clear liquid. He'd seen the disappointment in Five's eyes; he had a gut feeling Five would think less of him if he passed up this gift, and for some reason he couldn't explain to himself, that bothered him. "You said it would arouse me. It's going to make me want to have sex with you, isn't it?"

"Yes, it probably will."

"So it's just a way to make sure I have a good time?"

"A good time?"

"When we fuck." Mason rubbed his thumb along the side of the glass. "Since I'm just here because you wanted a mate."

"If you don't drink this, we won't fuck this morning."

Mason jerked his gaze up, locking it on Five. "Why not?"

"Are you disappointed?"

"What? No." Mason released the glass and sat back,

crossing his arms over his chest. "Why the fuck would I be disappointed?"

"You curse when you're upset. You are disappointed. Denying it is foolish." Five's teeth flashed. "But so human."

"Goddamn you." Mason scraped the chair back and stood with a suddenness that made Five's claws come out. Mason didn't care. He reached for the drink and knocked back half of it with too much anger and too little thought.

Five's hand came out, almost as if he wanted to stop Mason, but then he let his hand fall to the table again. "Foolish. A sip would have been more than enough."

Mason set the glass down hard and liquid sloshed onto the table. He couldn't breathe through the tight burn in his throat and the fire spreading through his veins.

"Fucking..." He choked on his wheezing gasp with a sudden cough and plopped down into the chair he'd left, hitting the seat so hard it jarred his spine.

"I did warn you."

Mason blinked and curled his fingers into a fist. "Goddamn."

The sweet fire burned through him faster than he could think. His eyes watered with the fierceness of the burn and the hair along his arms prickled like he was standing too close to an electric fence. For a moment, the world around him was an unreal wash of color before everything shifted into tight focus, the colors too bright, the sounds too sharp. He could hear the rasp of his every breath, feel the ghost of a breeze against his skin, and see into the depths of Five's soul through his eyes.

It was amazing.

He might have laughed. He wasn't sure.

Blood flowed into his cock and made him so hard he could almost feel the seams of fabric at his crotch straining against his flesh. Goddamn, he was suffocating. He adjusted himself and then couldn't resist rubbing at his hard flesh through the worn denim.

He slid down in the chair, his socks sliding along the hardwood with ease, and his head fell back against the chair's top slat with a dull thunk that echoed in his ears. "You weren't kidding. My God, I want your mouth on my cock. I can't think about anything else."

And he couldn't—except that wasn't true. Because the one thought that kept intruding was the thought of what might happen if he threw himself on the table and offered his ass to Five.

Would Five use his tongue on him again? Make him so desperate for something in his ass that he'd beg?

Maybe he wanted to beg. Maybe he'd like that. Maybe he'd beg Five to suck his cock or—or fuck him. Yes. He'd beg for that. He'd beg for anything if it meant satisfying the need welling up inside him.

Mason jolted at the sudden touch of a hand at his neck. He snapped his eyes open, not even having realized until that moment that he'd let them shut, and a harsh groan welled up out of his throat.

Five stood over him, his tall, lean body cradled right between Mason's thighs.

Mason closed his legs around Five and reached for the waistband of Five's trousers.

Five grasped Mason's wrist, but Mason had two hands and he gave up pressing his hand to his cock to grab at the hem of Five's t-shirt.

He shoved his hand underneath to feel warm flesh and the tickle of hair. "You feel so good. Touch me."

"I am touching you."

"Not there." Mason grabbed Five's hand. He tried to drag it forward but Five ended up grasping that wrist too and suddenly Mason couldn't use either hand.

So he used his mouth. He leaned forward and bit at the bottom of Five's t-shirt, dragging it up just enough for him to turn his face into the warm, soft skin of Five's belly.

Five sucked in his breath and his fingers clenched on Mason's wrists before he eased the pressure. "What do you want?"

"I want to kiss you." He turned his head, pressing his mouth hard to Five's skin. He bit down and felt the quiver of flesh against his nose. "Bite you. I bet you guys like it when we bite, huh?"

"It would be dangerous." The words were a caution, but Mason heard the deep hunger in Five's voice.

Mason let out a soft husk of a sound from deep in his throat and dragged his teeth across Five's stomach.

Five reacted with startling speed. He hauled Mason up out of the chair. Their bodies slammed together. "You tempt me too much."

Then he kissed Mason, taking a sharp little bite at the corner of Mason's bottom lip before sucking the sting away.

The kiss didn't last long enough. Breathing raggedly, Mason grappled with the hold Five had on his wrists. He wanted to touch Five, hold him. He wanted to bring their mouths together again.

Five forced Mason's arms down, then caged him in

with a tight hug, but it didn't stop Mason from dragging his hands along Five's waist.

Two seconds later, he was stuffing his hand down Five's pants.

Five grabbed at Mason's hand again.

Mason shoved, and they staggered into the table.

The table rocked, and the glasses of liquid skittered across the surface. Five somehow managed to push Mason off him and grab the alien drink before it hit the floor. His hand was hot in the center of Mason's chest, claws just the faintest prick through the fabric.

Mason had both hands free now, and he burned with the desire to touch Five, but the little bit of rationality he had left kicked in and he started working his fly open. "You're going to fuck me again, I know you are, but I—I want something else first. I want you to touch my cock. Suck me—lick me the way you did last night. I want to know if I'll like it as much today as I liked it then."

Chapter 17

FIVE SET THE half-empty drink on the table, the hard thud of the glass hitting wood echoing in Mason's head, and then he dragged Mason forward by his t-shirt.

Mason grabbed reflexively at Five's hips.

Five cupped the side of Mason's face. "You'll like it just as much every time I touch you."

"Will I?" He sounded breathless, needy, but he didn't care at all.

"You will. And if you don't, I don't deserve you or your submission."

Mason pushed his head in against Five's throat, breathing deeply against hot skin, pushing his hips forward, rubbing his cock against Five. Pleasure sparked through him, lighting up every nerve-ending, and his next deep breath brought with it a warm, sharp scent that flowed into his lungs.

"You smell nice," he said. "I'm going to—"

But the urge to act now and think later was too strong to resist. He touched the tip of his tongue to

Five's collarbone, tasting the salt of Five's sweat and the tang of his skin.

The sound of Five's soft gasp was a pleasure Mason didn't expect. So he did it again and felt as much as heard the vibration rising through Five's chest. He trailed kisses along Five's throat and across his jaw. Five sighed and turned his head toward Mason, letting their mouths come so close that Mason couldn't stop himself. He covered Five's mouth with his own and kissed him with a groan of hot, desperate need.

Hands captured his face, and suddenly he wasn't the one leading the kiss. Five thrust his tongue against Mason's, tangling their hot breaths and making Mason want nothing more than to climb inside Five and live there for the rest of his life.

But then Five pulled away, breathing heavily.

Mason started working Five's trousers open.

Five shook his head as if he were trying to regain his senses. He grabbed Mason's right hand. "Not yet."

Mason still had his left hand. He started popping buttons free.

"Stop," Five said.

Mason had never touched another man's penis before and he needed to know what it felt like. He thrust his hand inside the open fly and felt the hot, hard length of alien cock against his palm.

Five sucked in a harsh breath, his eyes flaring wide, teeth flashing. "Enough!"

The roar sent a pulse of something unidentifiable rushing through Mason. The pressure in his chest became almost too much to bear. He closed his eyes, hand unmoving, breath nearly stalled in his lungs. He dug his forehead into the hard ridge of Five's shoulder.

When the strange feeling in his chest faded, he asked, "Why'd you stop me?"

"If you want me to suck your cock and tongue your anus, you can't touch me the way you're touching me. I need control. Your scent intoxicates me, enthralls me, makes me desperate to have you, but your touch…your touch inflames me and makes me forget why I shouldn't push you to the floor with my claws at your spine and fuck you the way only a mate would dare." A harsh breath followed. "Prove to me that you've regained your senses, and I'll give you the pleasure you want."

Mason breathed hard into the cotton of Five's t-shirt. Under his hand, he could feel the heat and hardness of Five's cock. Now that his thoughts were slowing and the fire burning through him smoldered instead of raged, he could hardly believe what he'd admitted out loud to Five only minutes ago. Being forced to admit that he knew what he was doing seemed cruelly clever of Five—by doing so, he forced Mason to take responsibility for his own choices—and for what happened next. And yet—

Mason carefully pulled his hand free of Five's pants. "I know what I'm doing. I've known since I kissed you."

That seemed to be all Five needed to hear. He gripped a handful of Mason's hair and used that grip to pull Mason's head back. His eyes burned bright, the blue irises as dark as Mason had ever seen them, the color intensifying at the edges with unnatural brilliance.

"The sweet sound of your submission fires my blood and strengthens my control. I'll need every bit of it for what I'm going to do to you if I don't want to trigger my next heat cycle." Five turned Mason and pushed him toward the bed. "Undress."

"Shouldn't I—"

"Now."

Mason pushed away the thought that he should have a shower first and opened his pants the rest of the way, then pushed them down.

"Your underwear, Mason. I want to see the beautiful clench of muscle when you crawl onto that bed for me."

Mason closed his eyes but he did as Five said and pushed his underwear down to his thighs to tangle with the jeans.

"On the bed."

His heart was already thumping hard and the command sent blood rushing through him even faster. His skin flushed hot and it was the worst and best kind of uncomfortable. Anticipation thrummed through him.

He wanted this—but it made no sense why. Just yesterday, the idea of submission to one of the wolves had felt like a punishment he deserved, and now—now it felt like a reward he hadn't earned at all.

He wasn't that far from the bed, because the room wasn't that big. He shuffled the few feet to the bed and carefully crawled up into the mussed sheets and scattered pillows.

"Turn over."

Mason swallowed and rolled onto his back. His jeans were at his thighs and his shirt had rucked up above his navel and his cock was standing in the air, moisture glistening at the tip. He looked up to see Five's narrowed eyes on him and it suddenly felt ten times harder to swallow.

"You are mine," Five said in the wolves' language. "*Mine*."

Mason looked into that face and wondered what it

might feel like to believe you had a fated connection with someone.

Then Five came down on the bed and pushed Mason's legs up to his chest and proved to him that once was not a fluke and twice wasn't going to be enough and three times might just be the end of everything he knew about himself.

∽

The pillow hit the floor with a loud whoomp, but it wasn't the noise that startled Mason into opening his eyes. It was the sudden movement beside him, and he turned his head to see Five sitting up in bed, his long, jean-clad legs stretched out on the sheets, his feet bare, and his head tilted back against the wall above the simple wooden headboard, exposing the strong column of his throat and the prominent jut of his larynx.

Mason hauled his jeans up and zipped them quickly, then sat up long enough to yank his sweat-soaked shirt off and toss it to the floor. Then he rolled to his side and propped himself up on his arm. He could still taste the bitter tang of his own come in his mouth, put there by Five's last kiss, after he'd sucked Mason off and then licked the last dribbles of semen off Mason's belly and groin.

"I didn't think you could do this…you know, without wanting to fuck."

Five lowered his head, his eyes catching the light as they landed on Mason. "Don't misunderstand. I want to fuck. But my need to take care of you is helping me control my instincts for the time being."

"Why bother? If we're just going to fuck later, why not just fuck now and—"

"I have too much to do to allow myself to succumb to the heat early. The strongest urge to fuck comes at the peak of the heat cycle. Fucking now won't stop those natural cycles, just delay them for a short time. I can't sacrifice the time I'll spend mating now for that small benefit later. It won't be enough. I'll continue to take the drugs for as long as I can. But I have an obligation to take care of you. I gave you the drink knowing what it would do to you, and it was only right that I satisfied the desires it left you with."

"So you felt obligated to suck my dick?" Mason could hear the irritation in his voice and tried to shut it down, unsuccessfully.

"I told you that you would find pleasure with me as a mate. Proving that to you is an obligation I'm happy to meet. Are you hungry?"

"What? No."

"Did you enjoy it when I licked your anus and sucked your dick?"

"What's this got to do with my question?"

Five's eyes narrowed on Mason.

Mason cleared his throat. "Uh… Yeah. Sure. I enjoyed myself just fine." Which was so far from the truth that anyone with half an ear could hear the lie in his voice.

Five raised his eyebrows.

"You know I did, goddamn you."

The corner of Five's mouth curled. "I'm gratified by your honest praise."

Mason scooted up in the bed until he was sitting beside Five. "I loved it, okay? It was great. Second best blow job of my life."

"And the first?"

Mason clenched his jaw. "You're asking for a lot here."

"Last night, I assume?"

"Goddammit. You don't give up, do you?"

Five laughed—actually laughed—and it did the strangest thing to Mason's insides. Warmth spread through him with the slow slide of molasses, heating him from the top of his scalp to the bottom of his feet. The strangest part of it all was the fact that he started to get an erection, nothing too uncomfortable, not yet, but noticeable. He waited, breathing shallow and slow, his gaze lingering on the sight of his sock-covered foot pressing against Five's bare foot, not sure what to make of any of it.

Five flexed his toes with remarkable agility and his laugh quieted. "I'm gratified that last night's blowjob was the best blowjob of your life."

"Fuck you," Mason said, then raised his arms and crossed them behind his head. He sighed. "What now? You planning to keep me locked in this room for the rest of the heat season?"

"I have your submission. The door doesn't need a lock."

"There's a guard. Don't think I didn't see him."

"Lake guards my door to keep others out, not to keep you in."

Mason tilted his head and looked past the jut of his elbow to eye Five. "Your guys really aren't particular about names, are they?"

"Lake will be gratified that you find his choice of name interesting."

"That's not even close to what I said."

Five reached over and casually drew his claws along the denim over Mason's thigh. "Irrelevant."

Mason's leg jerked at the sharp tickle. He grabbed at Five's hand, but Five was too quick for him.

"Ah," Five said. "Six can help you improve the speed of your reflexes. He's very patient with the young ones."

Mason gave Five a dirty look while he rubbed the tingle out of his thigh. "Bastard."

Five let out a soft sigh. "I would train you myself but he'll think I've lost faith in his abilities if I don't allow him to do it."

"I don't need any training," Mason said. "I can handle myself."

Five turned with a speed that shocked Mason. Before he could even suck in a breath, Five had straddled his thighs and trapped Mason's arms against the wall above the headboard.

"You're too slow. You'll receive training to improve your reaction time whether you want the training or not."

The words had a hard edge to them, every smidgeon of playfulness gone from Five's voice. It was an unexpectedly abrupt reminder that Mason was dealing with an alpha wolf he hardly knew and it startled him into stillness while his heart thumped against his ribcage and his pulse fluttered wildly at his throat.

He wasn't afraid. He *wasn't*. But he was definitely unsettled. He didn't understand Five's sudden seriousness, didn't know why Five had gone from casual teasing to this, in the blink of an eye.

Five continued, "We leave within the hour on a mission to find the people who were working at the laboratory where I found you. When we find them, we'll destroy the weapon they've created and turn them over to your government for punishment."

Mason's fingers curled tight, his knuckles pressed to the wall above. "You're going on a mission. What am I supposed to do while you're gone? This training you say I'm supposed to do?"

"The training will have to wait until after the heat ends. I can't trust even Six with your safety now." Five lowered Mason's arms to his sides, his direct gaze never wavering. "But you're not staying behind. *We're* going on this mission. Together."

Chapter 18

"WHY WOULD—" Mason shook his head and clenched a handful of the sheet under him. "You don't trust me. You can't. You *shouldn't*. We've only known each other for two days. Why would you want me going on a mission with you?"

"I don't trust you. Yet. But if I expect you to earn forgiveness for your crimes against us, I have to give you the opportunity to prove yourself worthy of that forgiveness."

"That's damn considerate of you."

Five responded with a flat look. "There's also the fact that having a human along on this mission could prove useful. My choice was between you and your brother. Would you have preferred for me to choose him?"

"Why is it you don't seem to care about him earning forgiveness? You haven't mentioned anything about that, not one damn time."

"His fate isn't yours."

"That's not an answer." It was also a repeat of something Five had already said and it pissed Mason off because he didn't know what the hell it was supposed to mean.

"His fate is his," Five said. "Yours is yours. What forgiveness he earns is irrelevant to you."

"Stop using that goddamn word," Mason said through gritted teeth.

"Stop pretending you don't have the intelligence to understand why he requires no forgiveness while you do."

Every muscle in Mason's body went tight. "If I knew the answer to this goddamn question, I wouldn't be asking it."

If he sounded defensive, it couldn't be helped. He'd always known he wasn't the smart one, but he wasn't stupid.

One thing he did know: he wasn't interested in another goddamn lover who thought he ought to be everything Marcus was just because they looked alike.

"Mason," Five said with a touch of exasperation. "He swore fealty to *Traesikeille* three years ago and earned his forgiveness through submission to First Alpha's rule. You have to know this."

"I don't know what you're talking about. He—"

"He accepted responsibility for his actions and the actions of his betas. That's why *Craeigoer* released you without requiring you to answer for your crimes. As your alpha, it was his responsibility—"

"Whoa the fuck down," Mason said. "Marcus isn't my goddamn alpha and he never was. He's my *brother*. Family. Brendan was in charge, but even he wasn't my alpha. I only did what he told me to do when I wanted to."

"Who do you claim as your alpha then if not your brother or Brendan Greer?"

"I don't have a goddamn alpha. I'm human. Why would I have an alpha?"

The sharp light of an argument won glittered in Five's gaze. "And that is why you must still earn forgiveness for your crimes. You had no alpha who could accept responsibility for your actions three years ago. Your brother's fate is not yours."

Mason opened his mouth, then snapped it shut. He stared at the tight lines of Five's expression, realizing in the blink of an eye that he'd walked into a fucking trap.

"You really think you're clever, don't you?"

Five brushed his thumb across Mason's bottom lip and looked down his nose at Mason. "And you don't agree?"

"No, I fucking don't agree." But he sounded more like he was grumbling than about to start a fight he probably couldn't win.

"We didn't understand human packs as well back then as we do now. If we had, he would never have been able to leave with you until you had chosen your own path. But the universe has brought us together and I've offered you another chance to seek the forgiveness you should have sought three years ago. You will swear fealty to *Traesikeille* and you will find a place among us as my mate."

"Generous bastard." He figured Five was smart enough to know what he really meant: Not fucking likely.

Five smiled, but the showing of teeth was more unsettling than the fierce look that had been on his face moments before. "I'm starting to enjoy our arguments almost as much as I would enjoy a good fight. They make me want to fuck. Unfortunately, that means I have to put a stop to this before we have time to take this any further."

"Well, thanks for that anyway."

Five dropped his hand to Mason's groin where it was no trouble at all for him to trace the half-hard outline of Mason's traitorous dick. "So human."

"Arrogant asshole," Mason said under his breath.

∽

Six hours later, Mason was struggling to hold on to the limber branch of a young oak tree and not lose his footing on the steep incline he was puffing his way down.

"Why the fucking hell are we walking?" he demanded of Five's back. "Where's all that technology you guys have? What about a goddamn ATV or something? Anythi—ahhh, shit!"

Damp leaves under his boots sent him skidding on his ass for a good three feet before Five snagged the back of Mason's t-shirt and nearly choked him with it jerking him to a stop.

Mason sat up slowly, then yanked his shirt free of Five's tight grip and pulled it down, sitting there breathing heavily and trying not to feel embarrassed by his close call.

The ridge was steep and the footing treacherous and he had no interest in ending up in the gully twenty feet below.

A heavy hand gripped his shoulder.

Mason shrugged it off and used the bottom of his shirt to rub at the sweat on his face. "Give me a second."

"You're tired," Five said.

Mason craned his neck to look up at Five. "Don't get me wrong. I'm glad I'm not stuck back in that house, but…" He dragged his shirt back into place and dropped his gaze to the top of a scrubby pine tree a few feet below his position. "I shouldn't be on this mission. I can't keep up anymore."

"We're almost there."

"I don't care if it's just over that ridge." He made a vague gesture to the left where a tight growth of pine couldn't hide the steep, rocky slope that rose from the far side of the gully.

Five dropped into a graceful crouch beside Mason and pointed to the right, where the land on the other side of the gully smoothed out into flat forest. "Then it's a good thing the laboratory is that way."

Mason squinted into the undergrowth. "Thought we needed to head east."

"We did, but we also detoured far enough away from the laboratory to come in from the other side. We've been walking in a westward direction for a while now."

"Shit." Mason looked up through the trees at the sun. It was probably two or three o'clock, unless he'd completely lost track of the passage of time. He missed his phone, but he'd lost it in the accident that had sliced open his arm and it was buried in the mud somewhere underneath that damn ATV. "I hate trying to get around out here without a map or a compass."

"I'm sure you have other strengths."

"Shit," Mason muttered again with a half-laugh. He swatted at a mosquito trying to land on his arm. They were probably breeding in the gully somewhere below in the leftover runoff from the seasonal storms that never seemed to end this time of year. "I can't believe my goddamn life right now. This isn't where I thought I'd end up. I was going to pilot cargo drones with my dad."

"The ship I lived on was suffering catastrophic structural damage. We knew we'd found a possible home, but I wasn't sure I would survive the last *eiestialiel* to Earth to see it. And yet, here I am."

Mason wasn't sure what the strange alien word meant, but the context was clear. He cursed softly under his breath, "Shit."

"I'm satisfied with the gifts of the universe. I'm not sure I would like to be any place else."

Mason shrugged. "Could be worse I guess. Of course, I could do without the goddamn bugs." He swatted at another mosquito—or maybe the same one—trying to take a bite out of his neck, then pushed to his feet with a grunt of effort, digging in his heels to keep from losing his balance on the steep incline. "I'm ready. Let's go."

Five rose alongside him, looking much more at ease within the crowded scrub growing up the ridge. "Your human body doesn't have the stamina we have. If you need more time to rest—"

"I said I was ready. I'm not letting those bastards get too far ahead of me. I'll never catch up."

"Our goal isn't to catch up. Lake and the others are staying upwind of your scent because I told them to. The repression drugs aren't infallible."

Mason gave Five a look and shook his head. "I know that, but I wish to hell you hadn't reminded me of it."

He threw his arm around the trunk of a scrawny tree and started a controlled slide on his booted feet down to the next. He kept his eyes on what he was doing and ignored the rough scrape of bark on the inside of his arm.

He had his feet under him again on a much gentler grade within minutes. The next several feet of travel down the ridge only took half the effort of the last.

Near the bottom, Five said, "There is something we need to discuss before we reach the laboratory."

Mason waited for Five to continue, but it wasn't until Mason was picking his way carefully into the mud-slick gully that Five did.

"Your brother told us you don't know why he was at the laboratory. You should understand, mate or not, that if your reason for being there was anything other than to help your brother stop these people, you will have to face *Traesikeille* and he will not judge you innocent in the events to come."

The alien name had a familiar ring to it, and Mason thought he recognized it as belonging to the wolves' First Alpha—their leader—and the wolf who'd taken Brendan and turned him from a leader of the renegades and into a mouthpiece for the wolves. The thought of what Five might mean sent Mason's stomach churning.

His distraction nearly caused him to slip his foot into one of the many deep grooves that runoff from the ridge had cut into the clay soil. Only a few more feet and the gully widened out into something that looked like an old roadbed. He'd be able to think for a change instead of worrying about breaking a damn leg…

He only took a few more steps before Five's hand came down on the back of his neck and stopped him.

"You haven't asked for any details of our mission. Aren't you curious? Or do you already know what we'll find?"

Mason twisted around, careful to keep his feet placed on firm ground.

"You don't trust me. I know that. But I don't know what they were up to in that lab. I don't know what this weapon is that you want to destroy. Marcus never told me what he was doing, only that he needed me. He called, I went. If the only thing you want to hear is that I was there to play hero like my brother, you're going to be disappointed. I wasn't there to do anything except save Marcus from whatever mess he'd gotten himself into. And I didn't even manage that. I'm lucky—so goddamned lucky—he's even alive."

Five's hand flexed at the back of Mason's neck. "I want to trust you."

It wasn't what Mason was expecting to hear.

He exhaled roughly and brought his hand up, his intention to point hard at Five, but he changed his mind and scrubbed his hand down his face instead. The smooth skin at his chin and jaw was a nice change from the scruff he'd been carrying around for days. Right before they'd set out on this mission, he'd had a chance for a quick shower and shave. He only wished he had access to the wolves' shaving tech at home. There was nothing else like the close, smooth shave it could give.

He dropped his arm to his side. "Listen, I don't know what you think you know about me after two days, but you don't. You don't know me. And you *shouldn't* trust me. I've done some really selfish shit, some of it so ugly that even I'm ashamed of it. Sometimes I'm so goddamned ashamed of myself I can't even look in the mirror. But that doesn't matter, because you don't know me and you don't know if I'm even telling you the goddamned truth. You just don't trust somebody you don't know after two days and half a lifetime of being on opposite sides of a conflict."

"We've only been on Earth for eleven of Earth's years. Hardly half a lifetime."

"Don't be a shitbrain. You know what I mean." The

words were out of his mouth before he thought to stop them. It was something he might've said to his brother—definitely not something he needed to be saying to the alpha wolf in charge.

But Five's mouth turned up and the growl Mason half-expected didn't come. Five was surprising him at every turn and he didn't know what to make of it.

"I listened to you and your kin argue while we walked to the den. It's interesting how often you called him names."

Mason scowled. "Don't get any ideas."

"It's much too late for that. I already have a great many ideas about you, Mason Waters. Now—" Five turned Mason and gave him a light push between the shoulders. "Walk. The rest of the pack is waiting impatiently for us to catch up."

"I thought we weren't trying to catch up." Mason started looking for a clear path across the gully that wouldn't end with his boots stuck in the mud.

"That was before they had reached the laboratory. I told you we were close."

"I'll shut up then."

"I don't require your silence—yet. You'll know when I do."

Mason glanced back. It wasn't a smart move. His left boot slipped off the edge of a rock and only a quick catch by Five stopped him from sprawling on his ass.

"But maybe we should concentrate on the task at hand and save our talking for later," Five said, "because traversing uneven terrain does not appear to be one of your strengths."

Mason glowered up at Five.

Five helped Mason regain his footing, his wry look

doing nothing for Mason's sorely abused self-respect. He started to snap at Five, but one good look at him stopped Mason cold.

He took a breath, a small laugh choking its way out of him.

Five's eyebrows rose, and Mason's gaze drifted over him, his smile widening, his laugh mirroring the growing warmth in his belly.

Five glanced down. He hadn't escaped Mason's mishap unscathed. Not even the dark t-shirt he wore could hide the streak of clay-orange mud Mason had somehow managed to smear across his chest.

Mason wiped his muddy arm off with the bottom of his t-shirt. For some inexplicable reason, the sight of Five covered in mud filled him with good humor.

He gestured, his smile wider than ever. "That's a damn good look for you."

Five flicked carelessly at a small chunk of mud over his midsection. "It was inevitable you would eventually realize how attractive I am."

Mason guffawed—so hard it made his ribs ache.

But it was a sweet ache, and when they restarted their walk, Mason couldn't stop wondering what it was about that moment that had made him feel more alive than he'd felt in half a lifetime.

Chapter 19

"IS IT TOO LATE to ask what the hell we're doing here?" Mason whispered to his right where Five crouched next to him in the midst of the forest surrounding the old biolab.

Five's forbidding stare was answer enough.

"Shit." Mason twisted on the balls of his feet and hunkered a little closer to the ground, using his hand to keep from losing his balance.

The cloying scent of pine hung heavy over him, filling his nose with every breath he took. They'd traveled less than a mile from the gully before catching up to the other wolves, but even in that mile, the terrain had changed dramatically. The oaks had given way to more pine and thick underbrush that the changing season hadn't killed off yet. Kudzu grew in thick patches, choking out a significant swath the forest leading to the back side of the building. Another few years and the invasive vines would cover it, unless someone came and cut it back.

A movement to his left caught his attention.

Lake was crouched beside him, untying the laces of his boots. Lake was a tall wolf, taller than Five—taller than any of the five other wolves who'd come along on this mission. He had clear green eyes and the darkest hair Mason had ever seen on a wolf—not black, but the deepest, darkest red Mason had ever seen, highlighted by the late afternoon sun dappling through the trees.

Mason had barely gotten a glimpse of the other wolves. As soon as he and Five had arrived, the others had gone off in different directions, either to act as lookouts or to get away from Mason's human scent.

Mason hadn't asked which.

He should have, he saw that now. He should have asked a lot of questions.

Maybe it was because he was so used to letting Marcus lead, but he was seeing now that he was going to have to change his ways, and damn quick too.

He jerked his head toward Lake. "Why's he taking his boots off?"

"Getting into the laboratory unseen will be easiest through the second floor."

"Are we really worried someone's watching?" He hadn't seen any signs of occupation in the five minutes they'd been watching the back of the building.

"There's enough fresh scent nearby to make it prudent to be cautious. I don't want you hurt if we're discovered by enemies and have to fight."

"That's nice of you."

Mason focused on the corner of the old biolab that he could see through the underbrush. A mix of oak and pine crowded against the back of the building on a hilly slope, but several of the trees grew tall enough to get someone into one of the broken windows of the upper floors at the divide between the burned out half of the building and the half that still stood.

With a deft, quick motion, Lake tied the laces of his boots together, stood, and swung them over a chest-high limb. Two seconds after that, he hauled himself up the same limb with a careless strength that made Mason let out a silent whistle.

He glanced at Five, only to realize Five was staring at him instead of the building or Lake.

"What?"

"Nothing of concern."

Mason didn't believe that for a minute, not with that glittering gaze locked on him, but he turned his attention back to the building and ignored the quiet rustle of leaves and shaking of limbs overhead. He wasn't going to gawk, no matter how much he wanted to see exactly what Lake was doing and how he was doing it.

Five leaned in close enough for Mason to feel his body heat at his back and pointed through the underbrush.

"He'll enter there." The quiet words tickled at Mason's ear and Mason fought the shiver that wanted to slide through him. "When he's certain no one has returned to the lab, he'll signal that it's safe for you and then we'll enter with Jordan, Rain, and Cord. Francis and Gray will watch the forest."

Mason hadn't taken his eyes off the windows. If he had turned his head, he would have been almost mouth to mouth with Five.

"I can count the panes in those windows," Mason said. "It's funny how much better I'm seeing these days. You wouldn't know anything about that, would you?"

"A discussion for another time."

"Of course." Mason continued to stare at the windows he shouldn't have been able to tell weren't solar glass from this distance.

He'd been nearsighted since he was sixteen. He'd been scheduled to have the problem corrected the week the heat came and cracked the world.

Needless to say, he'd continued to be nearsighted in the decade since.

Except now, apparently, he wasn't, and he hadn't even noticed the change happening.

He hadn't noticed a lot of stuff he was noticing now. One particularly scary thought had started teasing at the back of his brain, but he kept shoving it away; he had enough to worry about without adding that goddamn horror to the list.

The silence stretched out. Mason managed to catch sight of Lake in the trees before one jaw-dropping jump and he sucked in his breath, hand clenching into a fist as he watched, sure Lake was about to break his neck, but that wasn't what happened. A short minute later, he was swinging out of the tree and sliding into the building and out of sight.

"Showoff," Mason muttered, but his pulse was still fluttering wildly at his throat and the adrenaline in his body made him want to jump to his feet and stomp around just to burn it off. The muscles in his legs started to cramp and he shifted a little to the right, putting him a few inches closer to Five.

"He's attractive when he's showing off his strengths, isn't he?"

"Sure," Mason said, then, "I mean, I guess, I wasn't really paying attention."

"Of course you weren't."

Mason looked askance at Five. "Are you jealous?"

"You belong to *me*. I have no reason to be jealous."

"Last I heard, your instincts weren't that reasona— okay, okay, sorry." Mason let out a quiet huff and turned away from Five's dark expression. "Won't mention it again."

"Jealousy is an emotion of doubt. It's unnatural to doubt a mate."

Mason flicked a leaf off the toe of his boot. "Pretty normal for humans. Last girlfriend I had was fucking around and I got jealous as hell over it. But it was my own damn fault. We weren't together that way, and she had every right to do whatever she wanted. Figured I'd better cut my losses though. She liked Marcus better anyway."

Five slid a look in Mason's direction. "She was fucking your kin."

"Yeah. He didn't know." But Mason didn't sound as sure about that as he should have. Time to change the goddamned subject. "How long do you think this is going to take?"

Five rose from his crouch with fluid grace. "It is safe."

"Oh." Mason grunted as he rose out of his own crouch, his muscles burning with the sudden flow of blood.

"This way." Five started pushing through the underbrush, moving with a quiet efficiency that impressed Mason.

He tried to do the same, but every step he took seemed to put him on top of brittle deadfall that cracked and crunched underfoot.

Halfway to the front entrance, just past the edge of the thickest part of the forest, one of Five's wolves met up with them. Mason had recognized him earlier, even from a distance, as the wolf who'd stayed in the hallway yesterday when Mason and Marcus had first entered the wolves' house.

"Cord," Five said.

Cord inclined his head toward Mason in a way that seemed more significant than a simple nod, then said, "*Zaeta*—sorry, Alpha—Francis tells me the trail you wanted him to pick up doubles back into the laboratory. He followed the second trail into the woods as far as he dared but the—"

Cord turned his head.

Five tensed, so suddenly and completely that it sent a surge of adrenaline through Mason.

He'd never felt anything like it before, as if Five's sense of danger had become his own.

He quickly scanned the woods, but didn't see anything that warranted the feeling of disquiet that had rushed over him. Without much thought, he put more of his back to Five and watched the trees to the left, away from the building.

"What's—"

Five put his hand on Mason's arm and shook his head.

Mason shut his mouth and squinted into the distance, but as far as he could see, nothing had changed.

Another moment passed, the only sounds the chirp of a bird and the hum and song of insects in the forest around them.

Cord turned. "Francis needs help."

Five's claws came out. "Protect my mate."

"Gray is already on his way."

"Gray isn't close enough. Have him return here."

Without any further discussion, Five raced away from Mason and Cord, disappearing into the forest with only a quiet rustle of undergrowth to tell Mason where he was headed.

"Come," Cord said. He started a careful walk in the direction Mason and Five had been headed in earlier.

Mason followed, but only after a long look over his shoulder at the last place he'd seen Five. "How do you know Francis is in trouble?"

"He told me."

"You have communications tech on you?" Mason hadn't seen anything, but that didn't mean much when it came to the wolves' advanced technologies. Even humans could implant tech. They didn't, not often, not anymore, but it was possible. He wouldn't do it, not knowing the little bit of history he remembered and what had happened in some place called Ontario all those years ago, but some people still braved it.

Ontario was the kind of story people told around a campfire to scare the shit out of everybody. Mason could still remember the way Tiffany Carter had curled up against his chest the first time he'd heard it. He'd gotten his first real kiss that night, three months after the wolves came—notable because it hadn't been from Tiffany, but her older sister Megan. The experience was forever tainted with the knowledge that she'd thought he was Marcus, something he hadn't discovered until she'd put her hand on his dick and whispered "Marcus" into his ear.

The worst part was that he'd let her keep touching him until guilt had finally eaten a hole in his gut and he'd hauled her hand out of his pants, zipped up, and left his and Marcus's tent without explaining anything.

He had let Marcus do the explaining later.

Cord ignored Mason's question. He held back a thick tangle of thorny vines that had lost most of their leaves and gestured for Mason to pass through. "This way."

Mason went. Cord followed.

The building loomed ahead, shadowing the forest.

They were less than twenty feet from the tree line when Mason saw the wolf leaning back against an old birch tree with peeling bark. The wolf pushed away from the trunk and walked toward them, his eyes on Mason.

"Stop here," Cord said from behind him.

Mason stopped. He didn't take his eyes off the approaching wolf; he knew trouble when he saw it coming. There was something there in that wolf's bold gaze, something that told Mason he was being challenged.

"Where's Alpha?" the wolf said, his gaze turning lazily toward Cord.

Mason had been dismissed; he knew it, and that wolf knew it.

"Francis ran into a pack of rogues," Cord said.

The wolf's eyes flickered toward the woods behind Mason and Cord. "It was dangerous of him to leave this one with you."

"This one has a name," Mason said.

"I know your name," the wolf said, his gaze flickering in Mason's direction, "but my comment wasn't meant for you."

"He's worried your scent will overcome the drugs and trigger my heat," Cord said. "It's a valid concern. I'm... between mates at the moment."

His pause and the look that passed between him and the other wolf told Mason there was more to that story.

Mason continued to watch the unknown wolf. "Which one are you? Rain?"

"Jordan."

Mason gave him a sharp nod.

Jordan had already returned his attention to Cord. "Alpha could have chosen anyone he wanted for a mate. He even had the opportunity to mate someone of First Alpha's line. And he chose this one. This human doesn't understand the honor of that, and his lack of affection for our alpha is an insult to all of us."

"What the hell," Mason said. "I'm right here."

But even as Mason spoke, Cord reached out with remarkable speed and yanked Jordan forward by his throat.

Mason jerked, staggering several steps backward.

Blood trickled from puncture wounds at Jordan's neck where Cord's claws bit into his skin.

"Apologize, *Jetarikeille*." Cord's voice was a tightly controlled weapon.

"I won't apologize for speaking the truth all of us feel. He's—"

Cord's hand visibly tightened around Jordan's throat.

Jordan struggled to breathe. He wrapped his fingers around Cord's wrist but didn't actually seem to be trying to pull away.

Mason glanced over his shoulder. Bolting was probably not a good idea, no matter how tempting the thought was at that moment.

"He's human," Cord said, "and we'll make allowances for his lack of knowledge of our ways."

"He isn't worthy of—"

"You will submit, or I'll tear out your throat in Alpha's stead." Cord sounded like he meant it, too. "Now, *submit*."

The word had power—literal power, because Mason felt it into his bones.

The worry that had been building in the back of his brain blossomed into panic and he turned, not knowing where to go or what to do. He leaned over, resting his hands on his knees, his stomach clenching. A cold sweat swept across his skin and the edges of his vision grayed to almost black.

He was going to be sick.

He dropped to one knee.

The sudden feel of hands on him, under his arms, pulling him up, shocked him almost as much as the bare hand pushing under the bottom edge of his t-shirt did.

"Something's wrong with him."

"Are you okay?"

Cord's voice, and Jordan's. Both sounding confused and concerned.

Mason locked his knees and took a deep breath, then in the next second, jerked away from the arms offering him support. "Get away from me. Both of you. Don't touch me."

A tense silence followed, and then another voice from behind them, "He's confused."

Startled, Mason turned to see another member of Five's pack standing under the knotty branch of an old pine tree. The wolf had his arm stretched above his head, his hand resting on the branch, and he was watching Mason with narrow, shadowed eyes.

Cord straightened away from Mason, pulling Jordan back with him. "Do you know what's wrong with him?"

"I hear him. His communications are scattered. Weak. But he wants me to know he's afraid."

The other wolves shared a glance that chilled Mason. The cramp in his stomach returned in full force.

He rubbed his hand across his mouth, wiping sweat off his upper lip. "Tell me what's happening to me. You fuckers are doing something to my head. I know it. I can feel it."

The newly arrived wolf said, "Alpha will tell you what he wants you to know."

"But you know?"

"I have a suspicion. We'll know soon enough."

"Then tell me!"

"Alpha will decide."

"You goddamn—" But he couldn't continue as anger rose with such a fiery heat inside him that he lost the ability to speak.

He turned around and slammed his fist into the side of the tree behind him. It was a goddamned idiot thing to do, and in the instant his knuckles made contact and he felt the crack of bone, he recognized that fact.

Too late for his hand—or his self-respect.

Chapter 20

MASON HAD NEVER been one to lash out physically when he lost his temper, so it was almost with surprise that he looked down at his bleeding knuckles and the dark bruise forming on the back of his right hand near his pinky and realized exactly what he'd done.

"Shit," he said, just as feeling rushed back into his hand.

A sharp, nerve-stabbing pain stole his breath, severe enough that he felt it all the way into his knees.

"Oh fucking—*fuck*—" he gasped out, doubling over and cradling his hand to his chest.

Hands gripped Mason's shoulders, pulling him up and turning him.

"Let me see," Cord said.

Mason tried to knock Cord away using his uninjured arm. "Leave me the fuck alone."

Jordan gripped Mason's forearm and pulled, using his superior strength to overcome Mason's resistance. Cord took hold of Mason's wrist.

"He broke his hand," Cord said.

The other wolf, the one Mason still didn't have a name for, approached. "*Weketekari* isn't going to be pleased."

"With any of us," Cord said, staring pointedly at Mason.

Mason winced. "You think I don't regret this?"

"What's done is done. Your regret isn't going to save any of us from Alpha's wrath."

"Well thanks for that goddamn platitude," Mason snapped. He tried to pull his arm back.

Jordan held firm and Cord gave Mason a sharp, disapproving look.

"Gray," Cord said. "Your shirt."

As names went, Gray wasn't so bad. The until-then unnamed wolf sighed but stripped off his shirt without any further complaint.

Mason breathed hard through his nose. "Won't it just heal, like that cut did?"

"Even we have to set our bones before we can expect them to heal properly."

"Oh, no no—don't you—*fuck*!"

Something in his hand snapped with an unpleasant pressure, and pain sparked bright and sharp, only to fade to a dull ache almost as quickly as it had come.

It reminded him of the moment he'd sliced his arm open on the barbed wire fence when he'd wrecked the ATV. At the time, he'd thought the intense pain had faded so quickly because of shock, but now…he wasn't sure. The cut had continued to hurt—he remembered that clearly enough. And when Rock and Lavi had gotten hold of him, they'd managed to make it hurt a whole lot worse, but…

He tried moving his fingers. Pain sparked again, intense enough to make him suck in his breath, but the feeling eased into a slow, deep throb too quickly to be normal.

Mason glanced up at Cord. "Is this what it's like for you guys?"

"I don't understand your question."

"The pain. It should be worse than this. This isn't the first time I've had my hand broken—well, my wrist, but close enough. It should hurt—shit! What are you—" He tried to pull away again.

Cord used Gray's t-shirt to take another swipe across Mason's bloody knuckles. "I'm going to bind your hand for the moment. But if your broken bone doesn't heal properly, we'll have to break it again."

Mason gritted his teeth and held his hand steady.

Cord did exactly what he'd said: he tore off a strip of Gray's black t-shirt and wrapped it around Mason's hand, too tight for comfort. Mason winced as Cord tied the ends into a secure knot, but the throbbing pain eased quicker than Mason expected.

As soon as Cord finished and released Mason's hand, Jordan released Mason's arm and stepped back.

"He's already slowing us down," Jordan said. "Now this. And his scent—" Jordan sniffed carefully of the air and his lip curled. He turned his head away.

"I didn't ask to come on this goddamned mission," Mason said.

"But you are here," Cord said. Then to Jordan, "If the drugs are weakening—"

"They aren't." Jordan took another step back. "Alpha's mark is enough—for now."

Still, Cord looked as uneasy as Mason felt after that, and if Mason had been asked his preference, he would not have been walking ahead of any of them as they continued through the forest toward the front of the biolab building.

He wasn't allowed that choice, though, and had to feel Cord's gaze boring into the back of his head the entire way.

Gray had taken the lead, headed toward the building's front entrance where Mason assumed they would meet up with Lake. It didn't make a lot of sense to Mason, their path through the woods parallel to the tree line, but he assumed the wolves had a reason for choosing to stay under the cover of the trees for as long as possible.

Earlier, Five had said he and Mason would enter the lab with Jordan, Rain, and Cord, so Mason knew there was another wolf somewhere nearby who hadn't made himself known yet. Mason had glimpsed him earlier, but all he'd noticed was that Rain was a perfectly average wolf. Tall, but not too tall—definitely not as tall as Lake. Dark, short hair, fit and lean.

Nothing at all to distinguish him from any other wolf as far as Mason had seen. The same as Jordan, and the same as Cord.

Only Cord had a certain something about him that made Mason think he could be counted on to keep his temper in check even when he was angry, and Jordan had already proven he didn't know how to keep his mouth shut. Lake had shown himself capable of knowing what needed done and doing it without being told, and Gray seemed ready to lead at a moment's notice.

The idea that the wolves were indistinguishable from one another was as far from the truth as possible.

Mason followed along through the prickly underbrush, looking back often enough to get a curious look from Cord.

The next time Mason had the urge to look behind him, he didn't let himself do it. Five would return when he returned and not a moment sooner. Looking back wasn't going to make a goddamned bit of difference.

It pissed him off that he couldn't shake the niggle of worry that seemed to have burrowed its way into his brain, just like whatever it was that was making him heal was burrowing its way into him in other, more insidious ways. Something was happening to him and he couldn't explain it, and goddamn him if he was going to just let it happen.

Five was a wolf, and an alpha at that. He could handle himself.

Mason, on the other hand—

Jordan released a spindly pine branch full of prickly needles too close to Mason's face.

Mason shoved it aside with great prejudice and said, "I should have a weapon."

"And yet you do not," Cord said.

Mason heard a low thwap as Cord caught the limb Mason had just released.

"And yet you do not," Mason muttered. "You fucking smartass."

"You are Alpha's mate. We'll protect you from humans—and if there are other rogue wolves, a weapon would only encourage you to make a foolish mistake. Submission is your only safe course of action."

"So what you're saying is that I'm both too stupid to do the smart thing and incapable of taking care of myself. No wonder your pal is pissed that your alpha wants me for his mate. Talk about being a goddamned lucky bastard, right?"

"Your perception's flawed. But if that's how you want to perceive my words, you're free to do so. It won't change the truth as I experience it."

"What is the truth?"

"Perception alters truth just as the choices we make alter fate."

"Forget I asked," Mason said and used his left arm to block another pine branch about to smack him in the face.

He raised his voice at Jordan's back, "Would you stop being such a fucking asshole and try a little harder not to break my nose?"

Jordan hesitated, glancing over his shoulder. His gaze skimmed Mason from head to toe. "I assumed you were capable of moving quickly through the forest. I apologize. It seems my assumption was mistaken."

"Oh you fucking—"

The firm hand on Mason's shoulder tensed the few muscles in his body that weren't already tense but effectively stopped him from saying more.

Cord spoke, his voice quiet and low. "He means what he said. If your injury is making it hard for you to make your way without assistance, I can help you."

"I can handle it."

Cord didn't look like he believed Mason.

Mason shrugged off Cord's hand. "I said I can handle it."

Cord gestured for Mason to resume walking.

Jordan also took that as his cue to turn away and resume his walk.

Mason followed, and this time, Jordan made his way through the thick growth of pines with more care.

When they reached the outer edges of the partial clearing around the biolab building, Mason started looking around more carefully. He'd been watching his step for a while, because of the number of fallen limbs—the storms the night before last had been big enough to leave behind some wind damage—and because the ground was soft and dead trees left behind big holes a man could break an ankle stepping into.

"There should be a pair of binoculars around here," he said over his shoulder. "I tossed them coming out of the building. If they're still here, I'm taking them. Damn things are worth a fortune."

He could trade the binoculars for a reasonable supply of halfgas. Gillie and his mom could use the halfgas to supplement the solar power running the generators and maybe winter wouldn't be so miserable this year.

Then again, with two fewer people using up the power reserves, this winter might not be so miserable even without the halfgas.

The wood stove kept the house warm, but it didn't run the water recycler nor the locks or the alarms. Fucking thieves were everywhere when they thought you had something they didn't because your house was bigger than theirs.

That unwelcome thought was enough to darken his mood.

Where would he and Marcus be come winter?

He didn't know. Marcus had obviously come to some kind of decision about that wolf of his, while Mason suspected Five was going to be just as stubborn about Mason sticking around after heat season as Mason planned to be about leaving.

Gray's stride halted abruptly and he turned toward the woods nearest the burned out walls. "Alpha's returning. He has a human with him."

Mason stared at Gray, suspicion blazing into a white hot certainty.

There was no logical way Gray could know what he seemed to know, just like there'd been no way for Cord to know what he'd known earlier, either. Gray had done nothing, touched nothing, made no gestures, said no words that Mason had heard. It could've been implants, sure, but now, after what had happened to him earlier...

"My God," he breathed. "You guys are using some kind of telepathy."

Cord frowned at Mason.

"Is that what's going on here?" Mason's words came out strident, too sharp and demanding, but Mason didn't care—couldn't care. He had to know. Maybe what was happening in his head had nothing at all to do with what was happening to his body. "Are you telepathic? Is that how you get into people's heads?"

Gray turned, catching Mason's gaze. Those shadowed eyes were a brilliant silver-blue that would never have looked natural on a human. "Alpha tells me what he wants me to know." His gaze flickered over Mason. "So do you. It's our purpose as watchers to watch."

Mason did get the chance to ask what the hell that meant, because Cord stepped around him to get closer to Gray.

"Francis?" Cord asked.

"He's returning with Alpha. The rogues continued on."

The tension in Cord's shoulders eased and he nodded to Gray.

Sharply, Mason said, "Now you're asking what's going on with Francis? I thought you could hear him."

"Gray is one of our most sensitive watchers," Cord said. "It's why he trains the young ones."

Gray turned and started walking again.

Cord started to follow, but Mason reached out and caught his arm.

Cord went as stiff and still as a statue. He stared at Mason's grip on his arm with glittering eyes.

Ahead of them, both Jordan and Gray stopped and turned.

Mason had been lulled into a false sense of security with the sniping and bickering, but the look in Cord's eyes reminded him with heart-pounding certainty that he was far from safe.

No one said a word as Mason let go of Cord's arm.

"I had a question," Mason said. "I wasn't thinking."

"Then ask your question," Cord said. "I can hear Lake's impatience growing."

"Are these rogues you keep talking about the same wolves that tried to make a deal with Brendan during the last heat season? Are they your enemies?"

Jordan spoke up before Cord could. "Why should we tell you these things? So you can betray us to your rene-gades as soon as the heat season ends?"

Cord's mouth tightened. "Your lack of respect for Alpha's heat mate shames us all, Jordan."

Jordan's upper lip pulled back enough for Mason to catch a glimpse of his sharp eyeteeth. "He was *there*. Alpha will understand."

"I think you're mistaken," Cord said, a gentleness to his tone that didn't touch his eyes. "You're risking your place in the pack for the momentary satisfaction of a justice you don't have a right to seek."

Jordan's gaze landed on Mason again, his pale brown eyes shadowed. "He doesn't deserve to be Alpha's mate. He hasn't earned his place. He submits, but not the way he should. You feel it too, I know you do." Jordan's voice quieted. "I don't doubt Alpha's reading of the signs, but this fate—he's worthy of better. Why him?"

Mason winced. The comments stung, but in a strange way, he understood exactly what Jordan meant. He'd asked Five the same question: why him?

"The universe—" Cord said.

"No," Jordan said, bowing his head. "Do not explain. I apologize. I'm ashamed of my thoughts and I shouldn't have expressed them here, this way."

Jordan raised his head again and looked directly at Mason. Something sorrowful glittered in those eyes, something Mason couldn't understand. "Forgive me. Only Alpha has the right to judge the truth in your submission."

Mason didn't know what to say. So he nodded, even though he didn't know if he should trust Jordan's sudden change of attitude.

"He's undecided," Gray murmured.

Mason exhaled roughly and glared at Gray.

The corner of Gray's mouth twitched upward, but he said nothing as he turned and started walking again.

With a quick look at Mason and then Cord, Jordan followed.

Mason scrubbed his left hand down his face, looked over his shoulder once out of some kind of instinctual need to know what was behind him, and then started out after Jordan.

Cord's footsteps hardly made a sound behind him, but Mason felt him at his back nonetheless, like a phantom shadow that had worked its way into his bones.

Chapter 21

LAKE AND THE OTHER wolf, Rain, met them just inside the sunlit hallway beyond the biolab's entrance. Just being inside again made Mason's stomach heavy and his heart pound. He remembered so much of that night, so clearly, not the least of which was the memory he had of thinking Marcus was dead, and it was surprising how viscerally his body reacted just crossing the threshold into the building.

The floor-to-ceiling windows allowed plenty of daylight into the facility and Mason was struck by how different the place looked in the light of day. The glass on the floor crunched underfoot, and he noticed right away how scattered it had become.

People had been inside, walking around since the night of the storm, he was sure of it.

"I found something you should see," Lake said to Cord, speaking in the wolves' language, just before taking the lead down that long hallway.

Rain stayed behind, leaving Mason to assume he was waiting for Five and Francis and whoever it was they were dragging back with them.

At the end of the hallway, Lake led them down a set of open stairs to the lower level. From the front of the building, it would've been considered the basement, but from the back, it appeared to be the ground floor. Mason hadn't explored that area with Jay and Sebastian. If there'd been more time, they would have gotten to it eventually, but there hadn't been more time, and they'd never made it past the first floor.

He was halfway down the wide stairway when a fly buzzed past his ear, startling him into jerking his hand up to swat it away. It was a bad move, reminding him with a sharp stab of pain that he had a broken bone in his hand.

"Are you okay?" Cord asked from behind him.

"Yeah, it was nothing. Just startled me."

At the foot of the stairs, a whiff of something un-pleasant stuck to the back of his tongue. Nothing overt, but it made him look around, searching for the source, but all he saw was the empty hallway and windows that looked out at nothing but trees and brush and, in the distance, what looked like an old retaining wall made of dark red brick.

Several doors lined the inside of the hallway, and Lake stopped in front of one in particular with a cracked panel set into it at eye level. In the past, the panel would have given a hint of what was behind the door, but with-out power, and broken, all it promised was a nasty sur-prise.

Dread curled tight in Mason's belly. He didn't want to see what was behind that door, but he couldn't explain why. He glanced to the side at Jordan and took notice of the suddenly stoic expression on his face.

Mason swallowed hard.

He knew exactly where these feelings were coming from—the wolves around him. This was how they'd done it—how they'd turned Brendan and Marcus and so many others—they were burrowing so deep into him that he wouldn't ever be the same. He could feel them—Jordan's dread, Cord's unease, Lake's determination, Gray's curious sadness.

It didn't make sense and he didn't know how it was possible, but by God, it was there and he wasn't crazy.

Lake opened the heavy door, the low shush of a seal releasing making Mason's scalp crawl. The smell hit him hard.

Mason turned quickly, bending at the knees and covering his face with the bottom of his t-shirt. He couldn't breathe. It was difficult to even think as his stomach rebelled at the stench of death.

A light flared behind him.

Cord gripped the back of Mason's neck, his hand warm and firm, his claws nowhere to be felt. "Will you be able to tell us anything about these people?"

Mason shook his head, unable to speak for fear of losing the breakfast he'd had that morning. He pressed his thumb and fingers tight against his eyes, forcing himself to calm down, take a breath, ignore everything except the fact that he had to get his shit together.

This was a mission. He had a purpose for the first time in years that didn't involve chopping wood and hiding from his past. He coughed a few times, fighting back the burn of acid at the back of throat, and then made himself straighten.

Cord rubbed Mason's neck lightly before removing his hand.

Mason felt the lack of contact immediately, as if he'd been relying on Cord's touch for support and hadn't even realized it.

He turned, holding his shirt to his face, and took a step forward. The sunlight streaming into the hallway illuminated the area near the door and he could see—

Too much.

Lake had entered the room, and he held a small white object in the palm of his hand at chest height. Light glowed from the center in a downward arc, lighting only the space directly in front of him.

"I found the room earlier. The door has an airtight seal so I didn't know to expect this."

A body lay stretched out on a table, only one of many. Death had come and gone, days, and in some cases even weeks, before.

Mason crossed to stand beside Lake, carefully avoiding the horrors that had dripped and puddled onto the floor near the tables while keeping the fabric of his shirt as tight over his nose and mouth as he could with only one hand. Flies buzzed around him, drowning out the sound of his rushing blood. Only sheer force of will and tightly clenched teeth kept him from throwing up.

He knew without a single doubt that nightmares about this room would haunt him for the rest of his life.

"She's been dead for several days," Lake said.

Coughing against the stench, Mason waved his bound hand in front of his face, trying without success to drive away the flies.

"She looks like a scientist," Mason said, voice muffled.

He had to draw in more air than he wanted just to speak. "That's a lab coat. Don't see a name tag."

He coughed again, and looked over at Lake, who stared with unflinching regard at the dead woman.

It wasn't until Lake had to take in a breath to speak that Mason noticed just how little breathing Lake was actually doing. "These people...the weapon killed them all."

"I thought—" Mason shook his head. "The weapon— it's not meant to kill wolves. I don't understand."

"The weapon is meant to kill humans, like your kin, humans like First Alpha's mate, and many others. Like you, as Alpha's mate."

Can't kill the wolves...that dark little voice in Mason's head whispered. *Can't kill the wolves, but the wolves have already proven that humans are the easy prey.*

Mason shoved that goddamned voice as far back into his head as he could and took a harder look at the woman's body. He didn't have the kind of knowledge he would need to know how she'd died, but whatever had done this...

"They're going to burn down the goddamned world," Mason said. "That's what Marcus told me. This weapon, it's bad, isn't it?"

"Very bad," Lake said. "They've made the kind of mistake that could bring about the end of your species."

Mason couldn't stop staring at the woman's stained lab coat. His eyes burned at the caustic odor as much as his lungs ached with his resistance to taking a deep breath. "What have they done?"

"According to the information stored on the display you found, they discovered a living sample of a virus that should never have existed in the first place. They set out to create a version of it that would infect easily but kill quickly enough to burn itself out before it could infect the population at large. They succeeded with the one and failed the other."

Mason coughed again and swatted at more flies. There were so goddamned many. They were everywhere. "What virus?"

He shifted his foot and grimaced when he heard a low squelch. So many horrible things lurked underfoot that he couldn't look down, not if he wanted to keep his shit together.

"The research documents referred to it as the 2060 influenza."

Mason would have sworn to anyone who asked that in that moment his heart lurched.

Several deadly flu viruses had swept across the world at various times in the past, but he knew almost nothing about them—expect for the 2060 flu. Everybody had heard of that one, simply because it had been one of the most significant events in recorded human history, wiping out half the population of Earth.

Human progress had sputtered and stalled as the world picked up the pieces.

If not for the 2060 flu, the world would have been a completely different place when the wolves finally found Earth. The population would have been larger, leading to more aggressive trading for land and resources. The desire for medical advancements might not have been so great and the wolves' offer of technology and knowledge so tempting.

Mason remembered one popular *veo* drama from his younger days that had imagined an alternate history of the world—one without the 2060 flu.

It had been strange and fascinating to imagine North America thriving as independent countries and the east collapsing under the threat of a fourth world war if only one woman hadn't died. He'd stopped watching before he found out if the hero could stop the spread of another, even more deadly plague that would have brought the world back to rights.

"I shouldn't be here," he said, finally bringing himself to look to the side. Some of the bodies had clearly been decaying much longer than the one in front of him.

A cold sweat rose on his skin and his throat tightened. He swallowed hard, repeatedly, and returned his eyes front and center.

Cord's hand landed on the back of Mason's neck again. The notion that the wolves knew he was struggling stiffened his spine.

"Isn't this a risk? What if I catch this thing?"

"You're not at risk," Cord said. "You've already been exposed and were likely infected. Your kin tested positive for antibodies to the—"

"What? Is he—"

"He isn't at risk." Cord's voice was calm. "Both of you are safe. Alpha would never have brought you with us if he believed you could become sick."

Sweat tickled Mason's upper lip. With a calm he didn't feel, he rubbed it away with the fabric binding his broken hand. A twinge of pain raced up his arm but disappeared almost as fast as it occurred.

"Because of what's happened to us," Mason said. "Because of whatever you've done."

For once, Cord didn't put him off. He nodded. "Because of the gift inside you. You are safe."

Mason lowered his arm. "If we hadn't had this…this *gift*…we'd both be dead, wouldn't we? Or dying."

Cord gestured to the room at large. "What do you think?"

"I think…" Mason looked down again, taking in the short blond hair and blood spattered lab coat soaked in fluids he couldn't name. "I think it doesn't matter what could have happened. What is, is."

For reasons he couldn't fathom, he had the sudden desire to turn to Five—to say something smart, to say something funny. To say anything that would take his mind away from the tragedy staring him in the face.

But Five wasn't there, so Mason looked over at Lake instead. "What are you hoping I can tell you? I'm ready to be done with this. I want out of here."

"Can you tell us if you recognize any of the people here as members of the renegade groups you were in contact with?"

Mason studied the woman, then braced himself and turned. He reached for the light but hesitated. "Can I—"

Lake turned his hand over and the light brightened, flowing into the outer edges of the room, reflecting off the ceiling and cratering shadows into the walls and along the floor. "You'll find it too difficult to control. Tell me what you want me to do."

"Just…lead me around the room. I'll look at everyone I can." He closed his eyes for a second before reopening them. "Don't skip anyone. Sometimes you can recognize a person if you've known them pretty well just by their clothes."

Lake nodded and redirected the light to the body nearest the woman.

Mason walked slowly around the room, following Lake from body to body. At one, tucked into the corner, half upright, Mason stopped and stared, not sure what it was about the man's bloated body and distorted face that seemed familiar.

"This is difficult, I know," Lake said, "but necessary."

Mason started to tap his thumb and finger together at his side out of habit, but a needle-like pain in his hand stopped him. He forced himself to stand still despite the nervy energy rushing through him.

"What's going to happen to them when we leave?"

"We'll send a pack to collect and preserve them, and study them, for the benefit of your people."

"They've got families." And then it hit Mason, what it was about the guy that had caught his attention.

He squatted and reached out with his bound hand, taking the edge of fabric at the man's collar carefully between his fore and middle finger. He tugged, ignoring the twinge in his hand, and the fabric slipped down.

Bile rose up Mason's throat quickly—almost too quickly to swallow back—but the man's flesh hadn't decayed to the point where Mason couldn't see the rest of the colorful tattoo covering the man's neck and shoulder.

A deep breath nearly undid him. The fabric of his shirt wasn't a mask and the protection it offered was minimal. The only thing it was stopping were the flies. He stood. Despite knowing his shirt wasn't really helping, he couldn't bring himself to release it and breathe the tainted air directly into his lungs.

"I knew him," Mason said. "He was the kind of guy you could count on to have your back. He was one of—uh, Brendan's guys."

Not *us*, never again.

"He was one of the good ones," he continued. *Just like Rock used to be.* "If you were on the same side."

"So he was a renegade?"

"He joined four or five years ago, maybe a few months before me and Marcus. I don't know what he's been doing since I left. Half the guys deserted after Brendan. Some of them stayed in. I didn't keep up with any of them."

"So it's possible he was unconvinced to abandon the renegades after your leader's defection?"

"Defection? Now that's a word for it."

Lake continued to watch Mason curiously, the light a steady glow that didn't hide the pale glow of Lake's own eyes. "So you don't know if he was still with the renegades?"

"Why does it matter if he was a renegade or just working with some other faction trying to get rid of you? Same shit, different day."

"Alpha will—"

"Don't give me that shit." Mason glared over his hand at Lake. "I'm looking at dead bodies and I need a goddamned reason that makes it—makes—"

He stumbled over the rest of his words as his heart jolted with one of the oddest sensations he'd ever felt. He almost lost his grip on his t-shirt but recovered at the last second and pressed it tighter to his mouth and nose.

Warmth spread from his chest outward and he looked toward the door before he even knew why he was doing it.

Five stood in the doorway, the bright sunlight from the hallway spilling around him and casting his shadow across the floor.

"You have family living at the edges of the protectorate," Five said. "If these people aren't stopped and their weapon destroyed, half the people you know may end up dead. Is that not reason enough for you to do everything you can to help us even if you don't understand why we need you to do it?"

"I just want to know it's worth the nightmares this is going to give me." He glanced around, once, his stomach roiling as he did it. "I'm not saying—"

"Our mission is time sensitive. We have to find the weapon and destroy it quickly. I expect you to do whatever you can to assist us. We all have our nightmares to face when sleep comes. I think you can tolerate a few more in service of the greater good of your entire species."

Mason swallowed, and this time it wasn't because he was trying to stop himself from being sick. No, this time it was because he could read the look on Five's face, and there was nothing good there for him. He hadn't meant what Five seemed to think he'd been saying, but defending himself, now, after Five's reminder that time was short would be selfish and unhelpful.

He nodded, turning his head back to his task. "His name was Brody, I think...Brody Rogers. Or maybe Roberts." He stared in silence at the bit of Brody's green t-shirt that was still visible. "Yeah, Roberts. He was Brody Roberts."

A fly buzzed across Mason's cheek and he brushed it away with a shaking hand. He moved on to the next body.

Lake followed.

Five didn't. In fact, Mason felt the moment Five moved away from the door and disappeared back into the hallway. Maybe it was because Five had things to do, important things even, but to Mason it felt like a deliberate rejection.

Why do you even care? that goddamn voice in his head kept asking.

He shouldn't have. But he did.

Chapter 22

"I WASN'T SAYING I didn't want to help," Mason said later. He brushed his sweaty hair back from his forehead and eased down on the ground beside Five, who was sitting cross-legged with his back against a tree a considerable distance from the building.

Five's only response was a slight raising of his eyebrows.

Mason breathed deeply of the fresh air, grateful to finally be outside, where the early evening sun shone through the canopy of trees and the crisp breeze helped him erase the feeling of claustrophobia that had been growing inside him over the last hour.

They'd finally left the building, and of course the first thing he'd done was hide behind a tree and lose everything in his stomach except the lining. He could have done that inside the building, if he'd been willing to step foot into one of the pitch-black bathrooms, but he hadn't been—not knowing what he knew now about what had gone on in that place. Instead, he'd used one of the small sinks in the lab closest to the entrance that still had water and scrubbed every inch of exposed skin, even going so far as to tear off the binding around his hand to toss it.

If he'd had a second set of clothes with him, he would have stripped everything.

The little he knew about viruses told him he hadn't done enough. He was worried, but he wasn't sure what else he could do considering his current situation.

"I just meant—" Mason exhaled heavily and stretched out his legs, crossing his ankles. Trying to explain himself felt pointless. "Forget it. What happened to you?"

Five touched the swollen side of his face where several long gashes cut across his cheek. "A disagreement about the human I brought back, nothing to concern yourself with."

Mason glanced toward the crumbling retaining wall halfway between them and the building. The other wolves had to be around somewhere but he hadn't seen them since staggering outside to find Five waiting on him. "Where'd you put him?"

A faint furrow appeared between Five's eyebrows. "The human is female. I left her with Francis. He's making sure she eats."

"A woman? Who is she?"

"I'm not certain. She was scared and getting her to talk was difficult."

"I can talk to her. If you want."

"That's exactly what I want. You'll talk to her as we travel, discover whatever you can about her reason for being here, in this area, at this time, and you'll share everything you discover with me once we stop to rest again. But right now, we eat."

Mason shifted a little closer to Five so the edge of the

rock under him would quit poking at his ass. When he'd resettled himself, he pulled up his knee and rested his arm on it. "I won't be able to keep up. I doubt she'll do any better. And there's no way I can put food on my stomach right now."

"You will keep up. I know where your brother hid his transportation. The vehicle is still there. You'll use it to follow us. And you will eat, because it's necessary. We won't stop again until deep into the night."

Mason tilted his head to the side and studied Five's stern expression, then said, "You're not afraid I'm going to take off."

"I have your submission, Mason. You won't take off."

Mason clenched his jaw and looked away. Then, forcing himself to let it go, he glanced down at his broken hand. "I don't understand what's happening to me. I don't like it."

"What's happening to you is a gift—one of the greatest the universe has ever given us. It will strengthen you, keep you healthy, and give you peace."

"How can you say that? I didn't want—it's not that I was lying when I said I—" Mason sighed. "Goddammit. You know I'll try to leave once heat season ends."

"You won't leave."

"Because you won't let me?"

"Because you'll choose to stay."

Mason exhaled noisily. "Even if—how can any choice I make be mine while this—this thing is happening to me? It's—goddammit, Five. It's changing me. I can *feel* it." His voice deepened, and his next words came out harsh. "How will I know if I'm even still me when it's done?"

"The gift just makes the bond possible. Your thoughts

are still your own. But you can't submit and expect not to open yourself to the bond."

Mason stared steady and hard at Five. "There was no fucking way for me to know this was even a possibility when I decided to submit."

"And I was supposed to warn you of this possibility even though I had no reason to suspect you were carrying the gift inside you?" Five snorted softly. "Such a human complaint."

Mason grunted.

"You would argue?"

"Of course I would argue. I didn't choose this bond. If I'd known…well, I don't know what I would've done but I would've thought a lot harder about what I was doing, that's for sure. I got fucked is what it comes down to and nothing you say now is going to change that."

The quiet felt suspiciously like—

"Oh for God's sake. Of course you have the goddamn sense of humor of a fifteen year old." He jostled his shoulder into Five's. "Shut the fuck up."

"I've said nothing."

"You're thinking it."

"I'm thinking a lot of things, Mason Waters, and you would probably be surprised by half of them." A quiet moment followed. "I certainly am."

Mason could have asked what Five meant. He wanted to. But he was afraid of the answer, so he chose instead to let those words sit undisturbed and changed the topic back to his most pressing concern. "What is this thing inside me anyway that's doing all this to me? I'm pretty sure I know where it came from, but I don't have the first fucking idea what it is."

"It's a discussion for another time."

Mason took a breath and turned, eyes on Five, hand landing on Five's knee. "Please. Just give me this one. I need a win, before I—" A harsh laugh escaped, and Mason dragged the back of his hand across his mouth to stop the sound before it became something else altogether. He'd had a trying two days, that was all. The world around him might have cracked, but by God, he never would.

Five reached around and took hold of the back of Mason's neck, drawing Mason toward him. Five's intense stare made it hard to breathe, but Mason didn't look away.

"I want to trust you with this, but there are things you cannot know until we mate."

"I deserve to know what's happening to me."

"What's happening to you is that you've opened yourself to a bond with my pack and the bond is taking hold. Nothing more. You're not in danger of losing your power over your own thoughts as much as it might comfort you to think you are." The corner of Five's mouth turned up. "Did you not remark just this morning on the possibility that Six was poking fun at me with his choice of name? Is that the action of someone who's lost the ability to think for himself?"

Mason lowered his gaze, then flicked at a spider the size of his thumbnail trying to climb onto his thigh. "Not really."

"Then accept that this isn't something we've done to you to steal your will. The fact that you acquired the gift was the work of the universe. But the choices you make are your own. For good or ill."

Mason licked his dry lips. "I wish I didn't understand why you won't explain, but I do."

"Do you?"

"I told you not to trust me. It makes sense that you don't." He left unspoken his unreasonable desire for the exact opposite to be true. It was an irrational desire and he could see that as clearly as he could see that spider scurrying away into the dead leaves beside him.

"You make it difficult for me to hold on to my anger."

"Then don't. The world isn't going to end if you let it go."

It was only after he said the words that Mason realized just what it would mean for him if Five did let go of that anger. Five would mate him, not in the way of a heat mate, but as something more, and that would leave Mason—

Where? Where would that leave him?

Five made a soft, quiet sound that brought Mason abruptly back to the reality around him.

Five leaned forward, his forehead resting against Mason's. "Reach into the bag beside me."

Mason's first instinct was to ask why, but something held him back.

Five took a shallow breath and squeezed his eyes shut. "Find the long, cylindrical object and bring it out."

The bag was tucked close to Five's thigh and the opening was a simple drawstring that had already been pulled half open. Mason stuck his hand inside, frowning with growing concern. Sweat glimmered across Five's cheeks.

"Are you okay?"

Five spoke gruffly, "Did you find it?"

"I've got it. Here." Mason tried to offer the cylinder to Five.

Five shook his head and squeezed his eyes shut even tighter. "Jab it against my thigh. Now."

The growled emphasis on now was enough to tense every muscle in Mason's body. His gaze flickered toward the object he was holding between them.

It took two seconds to make the connection.

"Oh. Shit." He jabbed the drug against Five's thigh and felt the faintest pulse go through the object.

Five went tense, pulling Mason half the way into his lap. Mason fumbled for balance, catching his weight on his arm between them, his hand slapping hard to the ground only a fraction of an inch from Five's groin. Claws pricked sharply at the back of his neck for one startling instant as Five tightened his grip and their foreheads pressed together so firmly Mason could feel a tingle in his nose.

And then Five made another soft sound, almost like a whimper, and rolled his forehead against Mason's. "I don't know how much longer—" As abruptly as he'd started speaking, he stopped.

For the next several minutes, Five sat with Mason balanced precariously over him and breathed, fast, shallow breaths that made Mason worry he was hyperventilating or something.

Mason jostled his way into a more stable position on his knees and took hold of Five's neck in the same way Five still held his.

Five's reaction was instantaneous. He pushed back into the touch and a long, harsh exhale escaped him.

Mason squeezed the back of Five's neck. "Hey, seriously, are you going to be okay?"

"I—the drug is—I shouldn't have waited so long."

"Ah." Mason released his pent-up breath in a quiet, slow exhale. "Anything I can do—well, besides the obvious. Don't think this is the place for that kind of thing. Although maybe I'd get some more of that extra credit, so there's that."

Five's eyes opened, glassy and bright. "This extra credit is an interesting concept."

Mason let himself smile. "I wasn't much of a student in school, but I was pretty good at getting Marcus to do my extra credit work to make up for the bad grades. I didn't flunk, even though I probably should have."

A second passed, then another.

"Five?"

Five blinked a few times, slowly. "I cannot decide if I should praise you for being clever as a young human or chastise you for being lazy and taking advantage of a pack mate."

Mason laughed, just a small huff of sound. "How about we play it safe and just say I was a little of both."

Five breathed in, shaky but deep, and eased the grip of his hand at Mason's neck. "You seem to know exactly how to give me back my control when it's all but lost."

"You had it in hand. I just nudged you in the direction that's better for both of us."

Five eased upright, gently releasing Mason. His cheeks were flushed but his breathing had slowed to almost normal levels. "We need to eat. The others will be waiting impatiently for us soon."

Mason rolled his shoulders to ease the tension between them and straightened his back. His spine creaked and he groaned out a low sigh as he twisted around and sat back against the tree. He rested his head on the trunk and stared at the blue sky through the interwoven branches overhead, thinking about everything Five had told him and listening while Five opened some kind of packaged food.

Despite Five's insistence, Mason didn't think he'd be able to eat anything.

That last body...

Young, male, and so close to his younger brother Brecken's fifteen years that it had made Mason absolutely sick with dread. More than anything that had happened, seeing that body ravaged by a human-made virus and left to rot in a room with eighteen other bodies had set off a firestorm of anger in his chest that he couldn't contain.

"They're fucking monsters, whoever they are," he'd told Lake. "We're going to find them, and we're going to put a stop to this shit if it's the last thing I ever do. I don't care what it takes."

Lake had simply said, "We will find them. And we will stop them."

And Mason had believed him. He'd felt the determination in those words as if it had been his own, like an iron bar stiffening his spine.

He just didn't understand how, and since Five wouldn't tell him, all he could do was go over and over the facts he had, trying to imagine how he might have opened some door to a bond he'd never even heard of before that day.

"So—" he finally said, if only to break the silence and stop the spiraling thoughts, "basically, what you're telling me is that I'm not being fucked in the head at all. That it's just me fucking myself."

The sound of rustling stopped and Mason angled his head and glanced over at Five through his eyelashes.

Five was staring at him with glimmering blue eyes lit by a streak of evening sun that had made its way through the canopy of half-naked limbs and pine branches. Leaves fluttered through the air every time the breeze kicked up and pushed the sharp scent of pine into his lungs, and somewhere in the distance, Mason could swear he heard the quiet sound of the others talking.

"Yes," Five said, sounding suspiciously neutral.

Mason sat up, away from the tree. "You have no idea what I'm talking about, do you?"

Five turned and knelt in the pine needles in front of Mason, right between Mason's spread legs. He offered two fingers worth of a stiff paste-like food to Mason. "You didn't want me to agree?"

Mason glanced at that paste and felt his stomach give an unpleasant little jolt. "Should've let Marcus have you. Don't know what I was thinking."

But of course he wouldn't have. There was no real question of that. He was done letting Marcus save him; he could damn well save himself.

Five ignored his comment, in favor of moving his fingers closer.

Mason grabbed Five's wrist.

Five stopped, giving Mason a hard stare that said patience wasn't something he had in abundance at that moment.

"I can't eat that." But instead of pushing Five away, Mason eased Five's hand closer so he could sniff the food on offer. He hadn't even gotten his nose close enough before his stomach clenched alarmingly. He dug his head back against the tree, shaking his head. "No way."

"It is necessary," Five said. He gestured to Mason's right hand where it rested on Mason's thigh. "The healing will take a lot of energy. You have to have sleep or food. Sleep isn't possible, not for a while. Food is the alternative."

"I just lost my breakfast, Five. I can't eat this right now."

"Mason..."

"I'm telling you, I can't do it."

"Submit," Five said, with a quiet power that tugged at Mason's insides.

He didn't want to give in, even though it made a lot of sense, what Five had said. He needed energy; he couldn't go all day without anything else to eat. But part of him resisted for the sheer, stubborn reason that he wanted to know he could.

Five brought his hand closer to Mason's mouth. A sweet, tangy scent wafted under his nose.

Before he thought about it too hard, he let his tongue flick out and take a small taste.

Whatever Five was offering him reminded him vaguely of a gooey desert his mother used to make, back when luxuries were affordable. He leaned forward and let Five's fingers slide into his mouth.

He didn't just eat a little of it. He let Five feed him the whole pouch. He wasn't sure what it was—he'd never tasted anything quite like it before, but it triggered his sweet tooth and by the time his stomach was full, he was licking the last of it off Five's fingers.

Warmth flared to life inside him, and his blood rushed. He slid his tongue along the tight ridge of skin covering Five's knuckles, seeking out the last of the sweet tang.

Five's soft growl brought his eyes up, those fingers still trapped between his teeth.

He quickly backed off, not sure what the hell he'd been doing. His face heated, but he doubted it was going to be noticed considering how flushed he already felt.

"We can't fuck here," Five said, "but if we were any-where else, I would already have you on your knees."

The vision those words created unsettled Mason. He would've put some distance between them if he'd been able, but he was already backed up against the tree. So he just sat there, wondering if he could trust anything Five had told him about his thoughts being his own despite the gift inside him, because it didn't make sense that his insides quivered and his jeans felt too tight and his dick too interested.

He wasn't attracted to Five. He didn't want to have sex with him. Everything he'd done, he'd done because he needed to—to survive, to protect his brother, to get through heat season. Because that's what you had to do. Submit...or die.

Maybe the wolves hadn't just managed to crack the world—maybe they'd cracked him too.

He sucked in a shaky breath, but the image in his head remained: of him, bending over for Five and letting him do whatever he wanted, not because he had to, but because he wanted to.

And once that thought took root, it was goddamned impossible to get rid of.

Chapter 23

HER NAME WAS Cecily. She wasn't what Mason expected. Thirty, she said, but she looked younger. If he'd met her in different circumstances, he'd have been attracted enough by her looks to want to get to know her better. She was dark, with dark eyes and long dark hair, and he'd always had a thing for girls who could look at you like they owned you.

She had that look down pat.

Funny how he hadn't realized until then just how often Five looked at him in that exact same way.

Five's warning came back to him and he refocused his attention on the night-shrouded landscape in front of him and made a point of thinking about what he'd seen back in that biolab to get his mind off her looks—and the way her breasts mashed up against his back.

Not that he was interested, but there was no point tempting fate.

"The human scent is the strongest trigger of our mating instincts we've ever faced, and it takes hold quickly and mercilessly. The drugs are working well for the moment but it's

inevitable that we'll develop a resistance to them. How long that takes varies from season to season with the change in drugs, but it will happen. Don't allow yourself to get too comfortable with the human. If my heat cycles resume or my instincts begin to cloud my judgment and I begin to see her as a threat, the fact that we haven't mated could put both of you into a very dangerous situation."

The ATV he drove tilted to the left as the terrain shifted and he began a cautious climb up a steep ridge. The wolves were somewhere ahead, with Francis guiding them, and Five off doing whatever alphas did.

Warm arms slid up his chest as Cecily clung to him. Her quiet gasp left a tingle at his ear as her breath tickled his ear canal.

He was unpleasantly aware of how close she was at his back and the feelings her presence brought to the surface could be laid directly at the feet of his last girlfriend. Jeri had spent a lot of time with him on his ATV, since it was the easiest way to get from job to job, and they'd both been interested in conserving their power supplies by sharing a ride whenever possible. She'd always enjoyed teasing him by rubbing her hand over his cock while they were riding on the ATV, so every time Cecily's hands moved over his chest, he felt a little jolt of memory that got him a little too close to "comfortable" for his peace of mind.

He took the next turn as carefully as he could but it still ended with them going downhill and her squishing up to his back even tighter than before.

"I'm so glad I'm not alone with the wolves," she said into this ear. "I've never been so scared in my life as I was when they showed up."

"Five's a pretty good guy," Mason said, not taking his

eyes off the ground ahead of them. One wrong turn and a wheel could end up in a hole that sent them both flying. He'd been there just a few days ago and he wasn't ready to do that again.

"That's the one that saved me. I'm talking about the others. Do you know who they were?"

"Other wolves?" Mason squeezed the handles a little tighter, his shoulders tensing as he tried to catch a glimpse of Cord through the trees.

"They came with the humans who were going through the labs."

She'd already confessed that she'd come looking for her brother, but hadn't found him. Mason had made no mention of the dead, because if one of the men inside that room had been her brother, he sure didn't want to be the one to tell her.

"Did you catch any names?"

"Not real—" Her response got cut off when the ATV jolted over a fallen log. Her gasp this time was a lot louder than the last and she clutched frantically at him.

"Sorry."

Glowing eyes appeared in the distance. Mason leaned forward, aiming the vehicle in that direction.

"You were saying," he prodded.

"The guys were weird. That's really all I can tell you."

Mason remembered Jay saying something about coming back later to search the place. "Was one of them skinny but kind of wiry?"

"I can't really—Oh." She rubbed up against him again, her hand sliding under the edge of his shirt.

Goddammit. Jeri had done a good job training him to react like a horny bastard. Five was *not* going to be happy about this shit.

Honestly, Mason wasn't that happy about it either. He wasn't exactly turned on, but he couldn't seem to stop the awareness he had of her at his back.

He was half-convinced she was doing it on purpose.

But that really didn't make any sense, because she seemed like a perfectly normal, nice girl who didn't know what she'd gotten herself mixed up in.

Who also just happened to know how to look at a man like he was hers for the taking.

Something about that just wasn't sitting right with him, and he couldn't even say why. Jeri had been able to look at him like that and the only thing it had done was make him hot as hell for her.

But Jeri had gone and fallen in love with her sister's ex and dumped Mason so fast his head had spun. That had been it for him for a while. He'd needed a break from getting his heart broken by girls that just wanted to fuck a hot guy until someone better came along. He didn't like thinking about himself as the hot guy in that scenario, because he sure as hell didn't see it when he looked in a mirror—or at Marcus who just happened to be his mirror image, but Gillie had told him that denying it made him look like a shitbrain and that self-deprecation didn't suit him.

Gillie was a fucking nuisance, but like Marcus, she was usually right.

He had to slow down so he could reach up and push aside a thick vine that there was no way around. His shirt rode up and a warm palm landed right at the center of his abdomen. He sucked in his breath and just kept from jerking.

"Hey," he said, hoping she'd take the hint.

"What's your story?" she asked. "Those wolves—are you helping them or just stuck, like me?"

Before he answered, he goosed the vehicle's engine and got them past the vines, letting them fall behind them. The headlights worked to illuminate the moonlit forest, and luckily the controls were modern enough that he'd been able to adjust the brightness with a single slide of his finger on the ATV's control panel to conserve the battery.

A straight stretch of well-worn trail appeared in front of him and he relaxed for the first time in half an hour or more.

He caught sight of Cord ahead and sped up.

"One of them wants me for a mate," he finally said.

"And you went along with it," she said. "Why?"

"Why do you think?"

"Because it's heat season and you don't have a choice."

"Something like that."

"Don't they scare you?"

He thought about where she might be leading him, then said, "Enough to know it would be a bad idea to run."

"Yes," she said.

He wondered what she meant by that. "So you're not going to try anything that stupid, right?"

She didn't answer for a moment, and whether that was because he started slowing or because she'd finally realized they were coming up quickly on Cord, he couldn't say.

"I know how dangerous they are," she finally said. "I know you're not supposed to run."

A tight knot of dread settled in his stomach. She was going to run. He knew it.

"Don't even think about it," he said. "I swear to God, I'll lay you out if you do, and I don't care what my momma taught me. I'm not watching you get us all in trouble."

She rested her face on his back and spoke so quietly he almost didn't hear her over the hum and rev of the engine. "I'm not staying here. You do what you want, but I'm not staying here."

"You'll get yourself killed." And for some reason the only thing he could think about was the pressure in his chest that he could feel coming back at him, like an echo in a link he didn't know how to tap.

"They're on the drugs," he said, "but if you take off running who knows what the fuck could happen. You know the kind of stories you hear. It could get ugly, quick."

Her chin dug into his spine and her whisper echoed into his bones. "Coward."

With that, she locked her arms around his throat started trying to choke him.

"God—*dammit!*" He slammed the brake and released the steering, nearly sending them into a tree.

It was a dirty little fight. Cecily clawed his neck with her human fingernails and dug her knee into his back, but he yanked her forward and threw her at the ground with enough force that he could hear her "umph" despite the deafening sound of blood rushing in his head.

He caught her foot before her heel could catch him in the groin, then yanked her hard, dragging her backside across the well-packed earth. Leaves crackled under them and she just about managed to pull him off-balance, but he recovered before his knee fully buckled.

"Stop it!" he said. "I'm saving you a world of hurt here, you fucking idiot."

She didn't waste her breath responding, just kicked out wildly with her other leg.

"Goddammit," he snarled, before practically falling on top of her and jabbing his forearm against her throat and his knee into her belly. He tried not to hurt her but her furious fight continued until he was ready to do exactly what he'd told her he'd do.

Only he really didn't want to knock her unconscious just to put a stop to her clawing and fighting, because part of him completely understood her fear. If one of the wolves decided she was mate material, her choices were going to be as limited as his had been.

"Get off me!" Tears had started to streak across her cheeks, and that was really what got to him.

He didn't know what the fuck to do with her. "I can't let you go. But calm down, for God's sake. I'm not going to hurt you."

"They will. I know they will." She hiccupped, so hard it sounded downright painful. "Let me go. Please." Then she looked up at him and past his shoulder and started crying again, hard, giant sobs that tensed every muscle in Mason's body.

"I'm pregnant," she said. "Get off me. You're going to hurt my baby."

Mason stared down at her, then jerked almost as if he'd been slapped. He took his knee off her stomach and pushed to his feet as quickly as possible.

"Goddammit," he breathed out. He raked his hands through his hair, turned, and saw that Five had come up on them, his eyes glowing in the bright moonlight.

"She's pregnant," Mason said, because that was the only thing he could think about.

"I heard." The calm in Five's voice was a salve to Mason's taut nerves.

Cecily rolled over, still crying, and rose on her knees. "I'm not staying. You have to let me go. I've seen the video, I've had the training. If any of these wolves try to have sex with me, they're going to kill my baby."

Mason tried to offer her his hand but she shoved his arm away. He looked around at Five, expecting to see compassion there. Maybe it was the play of shadows across his face, stark and gray, everything washed out by the moonlight and the backwash from the ATV's headlights, but the only thing Mason saw on Five's face as he stared down at Cecily was a hard jaw and a mouth carved of stone and glowing eyes that sent a shiver down Mason's spine.

Cecily clambered to her feet, limping upright.

Mason winced. He might have hurt her, twisted her knee. He remembered that hard yank he'd given her leg when he'd been trying to keep her from running off.

To Five, he asked, "What's going on?"

"She has antibodies for the virus."

"What?"

"She's infected."

Cecily looked between them, settling on Five. "What virus? What are you taking about?"

"And she is not pregnant." Five took an obvious sniff of the air. "Human females have a very distinct scent when they are pregnant."

"You can't know that for sure," Mason said, giving Cecily another searching look, "not from a goddamn sniff of the air."

A soft growl cut through the air, raising the hair on Mason's arms with a tingle. His gaze quickly returned to Five and he realized immediately he'd fucked up. The tight lines of discontent in Five's expression were enough to tell him just how badly. He shouldn't have questioned Five, not here, not now.

"If that isn't definitive enough for you," Five said, his gaze never leaving Cecily and her gaze never leaving him, "the sample of blood we tested for the antibodies did not indicate pregnancy."

Her cheeks were wet and she reached up and swiped the tear tracks away. "Where'd you get the sample?"

"It was convenient that you left one in the woods before we left the vicinity of the laboratory."

"Fucking period." She sniffed deeply and rubbed her nose. "You'd think we'd have figured out how to end them by now, wouldn't you?"

"Well if she's on her damn period, she definitely ain't pregnant. Even I know it doesn't work like that." Mason shook his head, glaring at Cecily. "You wanted me to think I could've hurt you."

Her glare wasn't pretty. "It was worth a try."

A cold fury rose through Mason but he kept a tight control over it.

Cecily covered her face with her hands. She started crying again. Behind her, across the trail and a short way into the woods, Mason caught a glimpse of movement.

"Hey," he said, clenching his hands, not sure what to do with them. He wanted to offer some kind of comfort but didn't know what kind would be welcome.

She didn't respond.

Five pulled something out of his back pocket. "Has she shown any symptoms of the infection?"

"Not that I've—hey, I'm not going to—"

"Submit!"

The forcefulness of the command shut Mason up. Tension coursed through him, and adrenaline spiked his blood, but something in his chest pulled at him, and he stared with rigid attention at Five for several seconds before he realized...

He had a choice.

He exhaled, letting the fight drain out of him, and opened his hand to take the deceptively thin pair of cuffs from Five. He hadn't seen anything like them before, but their purpose was obvious.

"I'm sorry this is necessary," Five said, "but she's infected, and if she escapes, your entire species could pay the price."

Cecily raised her head at that. "What virus? What are you talking about?"

Mason reached for her.

She backed up.

Right into Lake. She screamed, and he snagged her by the arms, lifting her so that only her toes touched the ground, stealing all her leverage when she started thrashing in his hold.

"Let me go! Let go! Stop!"

She tried to kick Mason but he blocked her and crowded close enough that it was impossible for her to get her legs up between them.

He pressed his mouth together and hauled her arm up. He wasn't trying to hurt her, but she sure wasn't making it easy to be gentle. She tried to jerk her arm back but he held on and placed the cuff around her wrist, knowing as he did it, he was probably putting a large bruise around her forearm. He'd done that to Gillie once, when he was younger, and it had made him aware of how much stronger he was than his sister. He'd never done it again.

As soon as he brought the open edges of the cuff together, it sealed around her wrist with a faint click. He barely heard it over her yelling obscenities in his face.

She tried to headbutt him.

Lake hauled her backward, even as she screamed louder at Mason. "You fucking traitor! You traitor, you fucking—" A sob broke through. "Why are you doing this? Why are you helping them? You're—you're a fucking..."

Mason gritted his teeth and placed the second cuff on her other wrist. Almost instantly, the two cuffs snapped together, locking her hands in front of her.

She struggled with that, before finally sagging in Lake's hold.

Lake turned her with so little effort that it was almost comical and hauled her up over his shoulder. Her kicking continued, but his arm wrapped firmly around the back of her thighs and she could do little but yell and jerk.

Eventually she would wear herself out. Mason could already hear the hoarseness in her voice and the slowing of her movements.

He rubbed his hands over his face, suddenly bone tired. He let his arms drop to his sides, feeling so much like the traitor she kept calling him that he couldn't even look at her. "You don't want her riding with me?"

"I don't trust her reasons for being in the vicinity of the laboratory and I don't yet understand why the rogues wanted her with them. Until I have answers to those questions, leaving her with you would be too distracting. We have a lot of distance to cover. I feel the heat teasing at my senses despite the overwhelming doses of drugs we've taken to make this mission possible. Once I fall to the heat, the others will follow. Any distraction at all is too much."

Mason nodded.

Five said to Lake, "See Gray about the drugs. If she's sleeping, she'll be more comfortable. Also, have him give you an extra dose of the repression drugs."

"Of course, Alpha." Lake jostled Cecily into a secure position, gave Five a sharp little nod, then turned and pushed his way back into the trees.

Mason watched them go, too many questions roiling in his head for comfort.

Chapter 24

CRICKETS SANG IN the night and the air smelled of damp earth and wood. Mason hadn't done much sleeping outdoors in the last three years and he had a difficult time getting comfortable with Five at his back and nothing but a thin blanket spread out under him and another pulled up to his chin.

Still, he was warm enough, and he'd started to be able to see in the dark a little. The ATV sat parked behind them, blocking his view of the sleeping form of Cecily. She'd been left alone, drugged into unconsciousness hours before, and he couldn't say it bothered him. He didn't need her to tell him he'd done something he couldn't reconcile with his own conscience.

If one of the wolves decided to mate her, he would be complicit in the act and that…that knowledge disturbed him deeply.

"She lies."

The quiet words came from Five, spoken into Mason's ear.

He shifted his arm until he could get it under his head. "About what?"

"About everything. I smell her deceptions but I can't identify their cause. She has secrets and I'm worried about having brought you along now that she's here with us."

Speaking low so as not to disturb anyone else, Mason said, "She seemed okay to me. I feel sorry for her. If she's infected…what are you going to do about that?"

"There's nothing we can do, here. I've sent for help. She'll be removed from our care early tomorrow. There are drugs that will get the truth out of her, whatever it is, before it's too late."

That sounded ominous. And like one more thing Mason was going to have on his conscience when this was all said and done.

He turned his head away and stared out at the deep, dark forest, where leaves swayed with the occasional gust of wind and an owl hooted somewhere in the distance.

"I didn't like scaring people, you know. I never wanted to hurt anybody. It wasn't fun—not for me. It just—it all seemed—it wasn't fair, and it all seemed so goddamned important that we stand up for ourselves and take back what was supposed to be ours. Can't change the past, though, don't even know if it makes sense to wish you could."

"What is, is. A result of everything that came before."

"Yeah."

A grunt whispered through the air. Mason's thoughts stopped in their tracks.

He blinked, straining to see clearly through the dark.

To the other side of Cord, Gray was sitting nearly

twenty feet away with his back to a tree, watching and listening. It was obvious what his job was—lookout.

But the others, they'd taken to the ground the same as Mason and Five, and Mason had been under the impression they were supposed to be sleeping.

Five had told him to go to sleep more than ten, maybe fifteen minutes ago.

The flash of skin he saw under the moon told him sleep was the furthest thing from Cord's mind. He and Rain had shared one of the few blankets and Mason hadn't really thought a lot about it, but he could see now that he'd been terribly naïve to think it was because they were going to share body heat.

Five's warm hand spread heavy across Mason's stomach. "You need rest, more than any of us. I had hoped you would sleep at least a few hours tonight, but if you continue to smell of arousal, I do not think sleep is what we'll spend those few hours doing."

Mason closed his eyes, and tried to breathe deeply of the chill night air. The fall had been colder than usual this year, and now that late fall had set in, it was getting even colder. If not for Five at his back, he didn't doubt he'd be freezing his ass off on the cool ground, even with the blankets.

The grunting got louder and someone let out a harsh groan. The sound of the wolves' language whispered on the air. He swore he wasn't going to open his eyes, but when another groan sounded, this one from a slightly different direction, Mason couldn't help it.

His eyelids drifted up, and his eyes zeroed in on Jordan and Francis with unerring accuracy.

Naked flesh met his gaze and his mouth parted, his breath coming in a shallow pant.

He had trouble telling Jordan and Francis apart under the moonlight at that distance, their bodies so similar in shape. But one of them shoved the other's arms up, then spent a minute grappling with him while kneeing his thighs apart. Jordan—yes, it was Jordan—tried to snap his teeth at Francis, but missed, and Francis rolled with him, taking him to his back, and shoving his hips forward, and then—

They were fucking, right there in the open, without a stitch of clothes or a square of blanket to block Mason's view, and the sound of grunting intensified and the hoarse growls deepened.

He'd never watched two men fuck before—hadn't had any particular interest in it and hadn't ever sought it out in curiosity.

But watching it now did something to him. His cock was getting hard and his body tightening.

And then hands were on his stomach, running warmly over the hair leading down. He held his breath, not moving as one of those hands slid beneath the edge of his waistband and then the other reached for the fly of his jeans.

Five flicked the button through the hole and slowly peeled Mason's pants open. "I'm going to fuck you now. It will set off my heat cycle, but I don't think waiting would gain us much time. Your scent has become too much of a distraction." He spoke the wolves' language, and the cadence of his voice was hypnotic.

Mason swallowed and could hardly complain when Five's mouth and nose brushed against the line of his throat.

He turned his head, not to get away, but to give access.

Five took advantage. He sniffed, deep and hard, at Mason's skin, drawing his teeth carefully along the side of Mason's neck.

Heat and want engulfed Mason. He hadn't closed his eyes—couldn't bring himself to give up the view he had —and he saw the way Francis's ass tightened with his thrusts into Jordan's limber body and the way Jordan tried to rock into the motion, and he could *feel* the desperate need clawing at them, barely contained. His chest ached, and he wanted to share in their excitement with a fierceness that baffled him, until he realized he must have done it again—opened himself to the mysterious bond forming between them.

A sharp, gasped cry brought Mason's attention back to Cord and Rain, who were fucking even more vigorously, Rain's back shadowed by the moonlight as he rode Cord with his head back and his chest thrust forward and his dick in hand between them.

Mason's breath came faster. Five yanked Mason's jeans down his hips and over his ass, and Mason's whole body jostled. He couldn't keep his head on his arm, so he rolled onto his stomach.

His heart started pounding with a brutal rhythm that left him breathless and dizzy.

He wasn't just letting Five fuck him—he was offering himself to him.

"Submission is your duty," Five said against the top of Mason's spine, "but your submission is also a gift."

Five pulled aside the collar of Mason's t-shirt and his mouth found the prominent bones at the base of Mason's neck.

Mason shuddered and let out a quiet breath, trying not to draw the attention of the others.

Five took Mason's t-shirt by the hem and shoved the fabric up Mason's back, then kissed his way down Mason's spine from neck to tailbone.

Mason shook with the surge of blood to his dick. He turned his head, tried to stop watching the others and concentrate on the feeling of Five parting his ass cheeks.

The unrestrained slap of flesh and the low cries coming from less than thirty feet away made it impossible.

Mason turned his head again, but a low laugh from Five tickled the hair at the crack of his ass, and he felt his face go hot with a self-conscious flush.

"Watching my betas fuck is only one of the many pleasures you'll have as my mate."

Breathlessly, he said, "You're just a bunch of voyeurs, aren't you?"

"Watching someone else's pleasure is a pleasure in itself. You're enjoying it." He squeezed Mason's ass, and Mason felt claws against his skin. "Aren't you?"

"I—yeah. I am." It felt useless to make excuses. His dick was hard and his body was thrumming with arousal and he didn't know when he'd been so turned on just from the anticipation of what was coming.

"Then watch," Five said, "while I prepare you for mating."

It was the peculiar change in pitch when Five said "mating" that clued Mason in to the fact that more might be going on here than he'd realized.

But by then it was too late, because Five put his mouth to Mason's asshole and the underside of his balls, and Mason lost sight of everything except the feel of hot, wet tongue and pressure and his own hard cock trapped between his belly and the blanket that was protecting him from the cold ground.

He was gasping into the back of his hand when Five stopped fucking his asshole with his tongue, dragged Mason up onto his knees, and started rubbing something cold and slick into the rim of his quivering hole.

Mason whimpered and bit down on his knuckle to keep from making any loud noises. He thought Five was using his knuckles, but he wasn't sure, and of course the others could see them, if they were to look, but Mason was doing everything he could to keep quiet so he didn't draw extra attention to himself and Five.

Fabric rustled behind him and then dark fabric hit the ground. He felt the blanket under him shift a few inches backward as Five moved. Mason rose on his elbows and continued to watch Rain and Cord fuck while Five stood and stripped out of his pants.

Small jolts of pleasure fired through him every time he caught a glimpse of Cord's dick sliding into Rain, and he wasn't paying attention to Five as he knelt behind him. But then Five's hand curled around the back of Mason's neck with startling speed and Mason sucked in his breath.

Five leaned over him, letting his long alien dick slide along the crack of Mason's ass. Hot and hard, Five's flesh caught at the pucker of Mason's asshole.

Mason's breath hitched. He couldn't stop himself from clenching up.

Five licked up Mason's spine, and then bit gently at the side of Mason's neck and positioned his dick, pushing the broad head firmly enough against Mason's hole to make Mason feel weak all over. "Watch all you like, but do not forget who you belong to, Mason Waters. You are *mine*."

The emphasis at the end of his declaration was accompanied by a sudden hard thrust.

The sudden pressure forced a harsh gasp out of Mason's throat, but he'd been well-fucked by Five's tongue and well-lubed, and that one thrust was enough to let Five bury half his dick in Mason's ass.

Five felt even thicker and longer than Mason remembered and his asshole clenched around the cock impaling him. He squeezed his eyes shut and gasped for breath, his head down between his shoulders, his back tight with the tension riding him. His knees dug into the soft bed of leaves and earth beneath the blanket, and the earthy smell of the forest filled his lungs.

"God," he said on a groan, not sure if he was praying for Five to pull out or push his way further in.

"Mine," Five growled. "*Mine*."

Then it was no question what Mason wanted, because Five pulled part of the way out and all Mason could do was think about how it was going to feel when—

A shock of sensation jolted its way through him.

"Yes," he hissed through his teeth. Then, groaning, "God, yes."

Five was already coming with a rough growl, but Mason knew after last night that this was just the beginning for Five; Five's dick wouldn't soften and he would keep fucking Mason for however long it took for his heat cycle to burn out.

Mason brought his head up and looked across the way.

Francis was still fucking Jordan in the ass with random, hard strokes that were being met with fierce growls while he held Jordan's arms to the ground over his head.

Jordan's body bowed every time Francis's muscular ass clenched.

Mason let his eyes drift shut again while he reached under him and touched his swaying cock, hard with the flush of blood and sensitive to the touch. He closed his fist around his flesh and let Five's fucking do most of the work for him. His shoulder took his weight on that side and his body twisted to accommodate the motion of his hand.

He jerked off to the feel of his asshole stretching around Five's thick cock, and the steady, hard rhythm into his body.

He almost expected Five to stop him the same way he'd done the night before, but he didn't. The air was cool in Mason's lungs, and he was ready to come much too fast. Five caged him to the ground, his hands landing on each side of Mason and clawing through the thin but soft blanket as his movements turned ragged with another approaching orgasm. At least, that was Mason's assumption as he felt the hard jut of bone at his spine and the warm, ragged heat of moist breath, coming fast and shallow.

Warm semen spurted deep inside Mason for the second time. His ass clenched at the still unusual sensation and he began a harder, faster pull on his cock.

Then Five pushed himself up on one muscular arm, and used to the other to grip Mason's hand. "Let me."

"I'm close," Mason gasped, not even thinking about stopping as his balls pulled in tight.

Teeth snapped too damn close to Mason's ear.

"Submit," Five growled.

Pressure squeezed Mason's chest, sending a fierce tingle shooting through him, and he jerked his hand away from his dick with embarrassing haste.

"What did you—" he choked out, before gasping as the pressure disappeared and the only thing that remained was warmth and pleasure and Five's hand curling around his stiff cock.

"Yeah," he said. "Oh fuck. Jerk me off. That's good."

Five somehow managed to not only jerk Mason off but keep shoving his dick into Mason's ass. Mason glanced up, not even intentionally looking, to see Cord's head turned his way. He met Cord's glowing gaze.

"Oh *fuck*," he said, not able to turn his gaze away from that hot stare. The tension in his whole body released at once.

He came with a strangled groan and a furious clench of his fist on the blanket beside his head. Five milked his cock with practiced strokes, not too much, not too little, and a shudder wracked Mason's entire body from the top of his head to the soles of his feet.

Things got hazy after that. He breathed hard into the blanket and Five fucked him a little too long, and at some point, Mason noticed the others had calmed but Five had barely slowed.

A while later, maybe an hour, maybe less, Five ran his hand down Mason's side and slowly pulled away from him with a quiet, tired sigh. "You should clean up, so you can rest easy."

Mason stretched out on his back with a groan before rolling to the side. "It'll be dawn soon. Not sure there's any point trying to go to sleep now."

Five's glowing eyes lingered on him. "Would you like me to help you?"

He made a choked sound. "No. In fact, *hell* no." He

pushed upright on his arm, then slowly climbed to his feet.

Five rolled to his back, resting his head on his arm. "Then go before I change my mind about letting you go alone."

Mason stumbled off into the woods, careful to choose a path that wouldn't trip him up when he had to make his way back to the camp.

He was only gone for ten, maybe fifteen, minutes tops.

But when he came back, the blanket had been removed and the moonlight spilled on the trodden leaves and the bed of pine needles where Mason had spent the last few hours, and there was no indication at all that wolves had ever been there.

Chapter 25

CECILY WAS AT his back on the ATV and Mason couldn't relax because of that—not after what had happened before. She'd tried to choke him once, and he kept expecting her to try again, even though she no longer believed they were on opposite sides.

He focused on the narrow track ahead of them and drove the vehicle slowly over a jarring hill of closely fallen logs.

One wrong rev of the engine and one of them was likely to go flying into the brush. Considering he'd known a guy who'd ended up half-blind because of a knock on the head, Mason wasn't willing to risk going any faster.

"It's a good idea," she said. She leaned closer, her mouth almost touching his ear. He tensed, turning his head away. His gut instinct was to ignore her, because he didn't believe for a minute he could trust a word out of her mouth.

He wasn't sure where the distrust was coming from,

but it was there like a spike in his chest every time she spoke.

"No, listen," she said, her grip tightening on his arms and her body swaying with the rhythm of the ATV's slow crawl over the logs.

"If you've got something else to say about it, just say it. You don't have to keep breathing in my goddamn ear."

"I will," she said, a tightness in her tone that raised all kinds of alarms in him.

He turned his head back and felt her lips brush his earlobe before she spoke again.

"I know what I said to you back there was wrong. You got us away from the wolves and I owe you for that."

Mason hadn't made any effort at all to correct her when she'd woken up to find them alone with the ATV and assumed Mason had found a way to take off and leave the wolves behind.

Mason had still been reeling from the unexpected situation he'd found himself in.

Nothing made sense. Why the fuck would Five mate him and then just leave him in the woods? Alone. With no one for company but the woman Five had straight up said he didn't trust.

"You don't owe me anything," he said. "But I told you I'm not leaving you anywhere that you could infect somebody if you've got that virus."

"I'm not sick! How many times do I—"

"You keep saying that, but—" He cut himself off as the ATV jolted. "Goddammit!"

The front wheel slid off the edge of a hole left by a decayed stump and he couldn't turn fast enough to stop the vehicle from slamming forward and then stopping hard.

Cecily smushed into him from behind, and her chin snapped hard into his spine.

"Ow, goddammit!"

The engine sputtered and revved and then died.

She hit him in the back with a balled up fist. "Would you stop being such a dick? It wasn't on purpose, you asshole, and you're not the only one that hurt."

He broke loose from her clutching hold and climbed off the ATV.

"Something's wrong."

"I bet it is. You drive like a—" But she bit off whatever insult she'd intended to level at him and threw her leg over the vehicle's seat, then hopped off the ATV. She turned and leaned over the engine. "Let's get it out of this hole."

He gave her a flat look, before he leaned forward and started pushing the ATV backward. It took a few attempts—he had to rock it hard and put his shoulder into it—but the vehicle finally rolled back.

She had hold of the bar at the back and had dug her feet in, and she had to jump fast when the vehicle moved.

"Shit," she muttered, breathless, hands going to her knees. "At least you're good muscle."

"Thanks."

"No offense."

"If you have to say that, it's already too late."

She laughed through a couple of deep breaths then waved him off as she stood. "Get it started and let's get going again. I want out of these woods before the wolves end up finding us just because you can't read a map."

"I can read a goddamn map," Mason said. He started flicking his way through the startup screen. Then, before he could remind her that the damn maps weren't there because there was no goddamn signal, a red box flashed around the edges of the screen and the ATV went into lockdown.

"Are you—fucking shit!" He smacked the screen.

Cecily came up behind him and looked around his shoulder. "Ah shit. Is this for real?"

Mason smashed his fist into the seat then propped himself on his arms and leaned his head down. He was tired, sweating, chilled by the cold breeze the lowering sun had brought with it, and hungry. He hadn't eaten since Five had fed him that mush yesterday. The only reason he wasn't thirsty was because they'd found a stream coming off a ridge a few miles back.

"The jolt under the carriage probably hit something important," he said. "It thinks we've been in an accident. It won't start unless we can hack the damn thing."

"Nobody leaves that shit active. Why did you?"

"You think this is my doing? I'm not that stupid. This isn't even my vehicle."

Her frown made her look closer to the thirty years she claimed. She wiped sweat off her forehead and managed to smear dirt across her skin.

The system that had shut down the engine was meant to stop vehicles leaving the scene of an accident or people fleeing the authorities. Mason had been confident that every vehicle he had access to had that auto shutdown system deactivated. One of his distant neighbors had made a good side job out of it. It was illegal as hell, but he had never let that stop him.

"Shit." Mason straightened away from the vehicle, balancing one foot on a root that was in his way, and rubbed his hands down his face. "I bet Marcus reactivated it so he could shut it down remotely if someone stole the damn thing." Reactivation of the auto shutdown system was much easier than deactivation, which required special codes and knowledge of the systems involved.

"So you got us lost and now our fucking transportation is gone. Great."

She put her hands on her hips and stared off into the distance.

Mason put his head back and stared up at the darkening sky. Night was coming again, and she was right. He had no fucking idea where they were. He didn't know a thing about foraging for food. And he didn't know what to do with her.

Five had said she was infected. That meant he had to keep her away from other people. No way he was dropping her into the middle of a populated area, even though that was exactly what she'd been trying to get him to do.

Of course, he had to find his way out of the woods first, and that was turning out to be harder than he'd expected.

But no wolves—which was both suspicious and a huge relief.

He lowered his head and turned, eyeing her a little more closely. "So you're not sick, right?"

She returned his look curiously. "I told you I'm not."

"Were you?"

"What do you mean?"

He could tell by the way her shoulders stiffened that she knew exactly what he meant.

"Were you sick? Before?"

Her expression closed down. "Of course I wasn't sick.

I told you I don't even know what this virus is you keep talking about."

"You're lying," he said. "You know exactly what I'm talking about."

She made to shove past him in an effort to climb back onto the ATV.

He grabbed her upper arm and hauled her around. "Were you involved in that fuck up?" he asked in a cold, hard tone he couldn't remember ever hearing come out of his mouth before when talking to a woman. "Did you have something to do with those people dying?"

Her eyes widened. "What are you talking about?"

His grip tightened.

She winced and reached up to pry his fingers off her. "Let go, you asshole."

"You're lying to me. If you want my help getting out of here, you're going to tell me the goddamn truth."

"I don't have to tell you shit. Now let go." Her gaze skimmed over him. "Or are you going to start hitting me next? Think maybe that'll make me talk?"

Mason let out a frustrated growl and released her arm. He watched her climb onto the seat and start flicking through the systems screens. "Do you know how to override the auto shutdown?"

"No."

The small kernel of hope that had been building as she flicked from one screen to the next evaporated. "Goddammit."

"No shit, cowboy."

He eyed the rapid flash of words on the screen. "What are you doing then?"

"Most of these things have a—ah." She slowed.

Mason watched, suspicion warring with curiosity. He

didn't trust Cecily, and he could blame Five for that. But he didn't want to be stuck in the woods another night if he could avoid it. Especially without Five to keep him warm on the cold ground.

He flexed his hand against his thigh, unsettled by his own thoughts. Five had left. Mason didn't know why, but last night, for the first ten minutes after he'd realized that fact, he'd just stood there in the middle of the woods under the moon and felt...

He used you, that cold, hard voice in his head sneered at him. *He hated you for being involved with the renegades. Getting you to roll over for him and offer your ass when you don't even fuck guys... Talk about a sweet revenge. Bet you feel like a fool now.*

But he didn't. That wasn't how he felt at all. He felt...

Hurt. Confused.

Worried.

Why would Five just up and leave, sneaking off when Mason was least expecting it? It just didn't make sense.

A yellow screen flashed up, the words blinking faster than he could read them from his position. He moved to her side and felt her knee pressing into his belly as he leaned forward. "What's that?"

"Emergency beacon."

He turned his head toward her. "There's no signal here."

"Doesn't need one. Goes out on HF radio."

"HF." He was pretty sure he knew what that was. "Like old phone signals?"

She gave him a look that made him wince. "No. Something else. Older. It's a backup in case the sats transmitter gets broken in an accident. Range is short but they're made to piggy back on the nearest connection it can find until it gets to where it needs to go. Now I'm going to record a message for it, so shut up, okay?"

He gritted his teeth but didn't say a word as she recorded a message that would apparently repeat until someone shut it down or the power supply failed. Their biggest problem was that neither one of them knew exactly where they were and neither had a compass or phone to pinpoint their location for the sats, while the ATV's location wasn't coming up because of a lack of signal.

"We'll just stay here tonight and hope for the best," she said. "I sure don't want to be walking off alone with the moon behind those clouds."

"Yeah," he said, looking up again with a rough sigh.

It was going to be a long night.

Fuck.

Chapter 26

MASON HADN'T BEEN able to help drifting off to sleep. The very fact that it had been well over twenty-four hours since he'd slept meant his defenses were down and his thinking wasn't clear. His hand hadn't given him trouble since the day before but his chest had been tight with unease all day.

As soon as he stretched his legs out beside the ATV and propped his back against it, he started getting groggy. He'd intended to stay awake at least until Cecily fell asleep beside him under the blanket he'd found in the ATV's storage compartment, but he'd let himself forget the fact that she'd been unconscious for hours the night before and was considerably more rested than him.

So he fell asleep and he slept hard, and it wasn't until someone was kicking him in the thigh that he jolted awake, his heart thudding painfully hard inside his chest and adrenaline spiking his blood in a fiery rush.

"Wake up, you fucker."

Mason might have played it safe—if he hadn't been dreaming so hard only moments before. He shoved hard into the man's legs with his shoulder, knocking him back with a muffled "oomph" and a strangled shout.

Mason rolled to the side before he even knew if he'd knocked the guy down. He went to his knees, wrestling the blanket away from him while leaves rustled furiously behind him.

He surged to his feet—and found himself only inches from the barrel end of a rifle pointed at his face.

He raised his hands, slowly.

"That's right," Sebastian said. "Keep them up or I'll blow your head off."

The rifle was a problem.

The four wolves behind Sebastian were an even bigger problem.

None of them were Five or Five's wolves, and Mason was breathing hard, his blood rushing. Something about those wolves scared him in a way he hadn't ever been scared around Five and his pack. Three of them looked like ordinary wolves, two with ugly claw marks on their faces and necks, but the fourth was larger and had hair longer than any Mason had ever seen on a wolf, and his eyes—lit from within like fire around a sun—were enough to set Mason's heart thundering.

These wolves looked at him like he was actual prey, something he was realizing now that Five and the others had never really done.

Jay stepped up, dusting leaves off his green and gray pants. "That's no way to treat an old friend."

Mason lowered his hands. "We were never friends. We shared a cause. That's all."

"You're right about that. But I'm going to give you a pass, this time, because you were almost one of us." Jay unholstered his gun, his eyes as cold as ever despite the casual sound of his voice. "I wasn't expecting to meet you out here. Figured one of those wolves we kept hearing would get you."

"Thanks for that, by the way."

A grunt came from behind him and a soft thud of sound. He glanced over his shoulder.

A man had Cecily in a tight grip, and he had his hand over her mouth keeping her quiet while she struggled to get free.

The man wasn't a stranger, although Mason hadn't known him well. Lamar something or other. He'd been another of Brendan's guys, obviously someone who'd decided there was as much to be gained working with the wolves as against them.

Mason had almost been that guy, bought and paid for with a few hundred gold ten-dollars. Only circumstance —what Five would probably call fate—had saved him from himself.

"Found her," the guy said, not to Jay but to one of the wolves with the slashed face. "She claims she was trying to take a piss."

That wolf stepped away from his little pack, his mouth pinching and his nostrils flaring. "She smells of…" He took a blatant sniff of the air and then crossed the distance between them, his bare feet crunching leaves underfoot. He drew in a breath along her throat, forcing her head back.

He pulled away with a snarl. "She's dying. What use will she be to us?"

Mason sucked in his breath, too loud, and the wolf turned his attention suddenly to Mason, his eyes flickering dark amber in the early morning light.

"But your scent…" the wolf said.

He left Cecily to her captor and approached Mason.

Cecily stared at the wolf's back, her mouth pressed into a flat, hard line, her eyes so full of hatred it was impossible not to see.

Mason held his ground but knew he was taking a risk doing it. The wolf had no softness about him at all. His eyes blazed with the fire of a barely satisfied heat and if Mason had to bet, he'd put everything he had on the fact that this wolf wasn't one to use repression drugs.

He'd probably burned out his heat in the ass of one of his human or wolf companions and was running on pure self-control at the moment.

Mason had always believed that the wolves were primed to combust at the slightest provocation—that was what the heat season survival training was about—and that was the danger of the human scent trigger. Five had proved that it wasn't always as straightforward as that, but this wolf?

This was a wolf ready to let his instincts loose on any human in his path and maim and murder, all in the name of preserving his alien ways.

Mason forced his pent up breath out in a slow and careful exhale.

The wolf sniffed at Mason's collar, then drew his nose up by Mason's ear. He sniffed deeply at Mason's hair and a soft growl rose in his throat. "You've been marked. I recognize the scent."

The wolf's comment brought so many questions flooding into Mason's thoughts that he had to be ruthless in shoving them aside. Right now, right here, Five and the others, they didn't matter.

His survival was at stake and he wasn't going to let himself fuck this up.

"We were with some wolves yesterday. Could have been one of them. The alpha took me for a mate, for a while, but we got away."

The wolf pulled back and stared at Mason. One look into those eyes was all it took for Mason to know the wolf knew he was lying.

Mason cracked. "They let us go. I don't know why. Just abandoned us last night."

He glimpsed Cecily glaring toward him.

The wolf looked to Jay.

Jay seemed to know exactly what the wolf wanted. "Mason Waters," he said. "He was one of the renegades I tried to bring in before Greer was captured. He didn't commit fast enough. Shit happened and by the time I got back to the group, him and his brother had gotten involved in that mess with that nuisance friend of Greer's. The deal fell through."

The wolf turned away.

Jay said, "Just take him and let's—"

"Hush. Save your orders for your humans."

Jay hushed.

The wolf returned his disturbing gaze to Mason. "You can join us—if you know your place." His hand came up and he drew his first two fingers along Mason's jaw. "I would much rather fuck you than kill you. Of course, as intoxicating as your scent is, I'll probably fuck you either way so don't base your answer on an aversion to submission. You will submit."

Whoa. Whoa the fuck way down was all Mason could think. His body shook beneath his skin. His chest ached in a way he couldn't explain. His back was ramrod stiff and his mouth as dry as a creek that hadn't seen water in a year.

"You understand submission, don't you?"

The wolf's words might have sounded like a question, but there was no damn question there.

Mason nodded, once, and the ache in his chest bloomed into a pressure unlike anything he'd ever felt.

Was he having a goddamn heart attack? He actually thought he might be.

The wolf's head tilted and a strange look came over his face, one Mason had no hope of understanding. "But your alpha has a tight hold on you, I see. Fascinating. What has the false alpha *Traesikeille* done?" He turned to the other three wolves and addressed his next words to the long-haired wolf that freaked Mason the hell out. "*Jetikima* will want this one. He is proof that the false alpha has started integrating humans into the packs."

"*Jetikima* won't be pleased," the long-haired wolf said. "*Traesikeille* is trying to turn the prophecy."

"He will not succeed." The wolf turned back to Mason. "And that dilemma is solved. Join us or not, I won't kill you. But you will come with us and you will submit."

Mason stared back, saying nothing.

"Ah. I see I'll have to treat you as a beta to be pulled to my will." The wolf's hand landed in the middle of Mason's chest, claws coming out swiftly to prick at Mason's skin through his t-shirt. Mason's backward stagger was stopped by the hard clench of the wolf's other hand at the back of Mason's neck, claws breaking the skin with a sudden sharp pain.

"Submit," the wolf said in his own language, his voice a powerful, physical thing clawing at Mason's insides.

Mason pulled at the wolf's arm, trying to pry the wolf's hold loose, but the wolf was too strong.

Those claws dug deeper, the grip tightening until Mason could swear he felt bones creaking. Pressure stabbed at his forehead, stealing his ability to think.

He couldn't breathe.

He couldn't fucking breathe at all.

"Release him," someone said, sounding very far away.

"*Paetinishikid*," the wolf holding Mason said. "Do not interfere."

"You'll break his neck. *Jetikima* will need him if she's to—"

"He *will* submit."

"Betas have to choose," the long-haired wolf snarled. "You forget the warning of the Diviners."

"My fate is my own. I'll deal with it as I please."

Dark spots swam across Mason's vision and the voices of the wolves faded in and out like a cheap *veo* recording.

"You are not my alpha," the long-haired wolf said, "and I'll deal with you as I please."

Mason thought he might have blacked out for a moment, because in the next instant someone had him under the arms and he was halfway to the ground staring up at the sky through the trees.

The long-haired wolf loomed over him, blood dripping onto Mason's chest from long, shiny claws. "Drop him."

The wolf wasn't talking to Mason and in the next instant Mason's breath jolted out of his lungs as his back hit the damp ground.

He breathed in, the pressure in his chest nowhere near as severe as it had been only moments ago. Someone squatted beside him and patted the side of his face.

"Hey, you okay?"

It was Lamar and he was looking down at Mason with a tight furrow between his eyebrows. Mason darted his gaze around, looking for Cecily. He found her, her back to Sebastian's chest, wrapped tightly in his arms, her mouth stuffed with a piece of fabric Mason couldn't identify. Sebastian said something into her ear and her expression went flat.

She was afraid, but she was doing a damn good job hiding it.

Mason was afraid too, but he wasn't so sure he was hiding it at all.

"You're bleeding," Lamar said. "Lucky you aren't dead. Those claws caught you under the chin."

Mason blinked up at Lamar. "What?"

Of course, as soon as he moved his mouth, he felt the flesh beneath his chin pull apart. He reached up, cupping his jaw, then hissed at the sting of pain.

Lamar winced. "That's going to be a bitch to stitch up. Those too." He pointed vaguely toward the back of Mason's neck. He looked over his shoulder, then back to Mason. "I have a small emergency kit in my bag. They might let me—"

"Go," the long-haired wolf said. "He doesn't need your assistance."

Lamar's eyebrows rose. He looked down at Mason one last time, then rose and moved to cluster with the other humans.

The long-haired wolf sniffed the air. His eyes narrowed on Mason. "You'll come with us."

Mason sat up. Blood coated his hand, and he could feel it running off his chin and down his neck. He needed pressure on the wounds to stop the bleeding. "You got something I can—"

"Use your shirt."

Okay, then.

Mason wadded up the bottom of his shirt and pressed it to his chin. He jerked his head awkwardly in Cecily's direction. "It's not safe to have her with you. She's infected with a virus."

"Is that why she's dying?"

Mason glanced again at Cecily. "I have no idea."

"Your alpha, who is he?"

"I mean it, she could infect every—"

The wolf reached down and dug his fingers into Mason's hair. He used that grip to tilt Mason's head back. "Just because I stopped *Haeiakim* from making a stupid mistake does not mean your situation has changed. Do not talk except to answer my questions. Understood?"

Mason swallowed hard and nodded.

The wolf released Mason's head, then took him by the arm and hauled him upright. Mason swayed on his feet but then stabilized. He didn't know if he should thank the wolf or pray for mercy from him.

His gaze strayed to the wolf lying face down on the ground only a few feet away. The back of his shirt was a long streak of bloody slashes.

"His neck is broken. He might heal."

The cold nature of the wolf's words chilled Mason to the bone.

"Now," the wolf said again, "your alpha, who is he?"

Chapter 27

MASON DRAGGED HIS gaze away from the wolf on the ground and looked up. "He, uh—" He released his bloody shirt and let his hand fall to his side. He cleared his throat. He could feel the faintest trickle of blood sliding down his neck but he wasn't in pain unless he stretched his face.

Which he wasn't going to do again, because goddammit, that hurt like a son of a bitch.

The wolf was waiting, his strange eyes glittering with reflected sunlight and the lines of his face a patient mask.

Mason wasn't going to fall for that again, though. "He calls himself Five. I have no idea what you would call him."

"Five," the wolf said, testing the word. He turned his head and looked off into the woods, before he returned his gaze to Mason. "*Weketekari ah se Taliskaeiriat*, I would think."

"I couldn't say."

The corner of the wolf's mouth turned up. "I think you could say without any trouble at all. The rush of your blood and the scent of your worry is giving you away. But it's an argument for another day." He turned to Jay. "We'll take them both. Leave their things. We have a distance to go and very little time. *Weketekari* and his pack are near."

It seemed the wolf knew Five, or at least knew of him, and was familiar enough to recognize a name Five had made up only a few days before. It didn't make sense and it was just one more question to add to the many Mason already had.

Not only that, but Five was apparently nearby and that didn't make sense either.

Mason took a closer look at his surroundings as the others herded him into a line between Jay and Lamar, Cecily and Sebastian ahead of them.

The worry he'd been carrying around all day began to morph into the burn of anger. Five had abandoned him for who knew what reason and the whole idea of it was starting to piss him off. Because if Five was here, then he had to have followed—

Mason clenched his fist as his confusion coalesced into something more.

That son of a bitch.

It was very possible Five had set Mason loose with Cecily in the hopes that Cecily would lead them right to the people they were looking for—and the weapon.

Meaning he'd used Mason as the equivalent of a god-damn beacon.

It made a twisted kind of sense. Five claimed not to trust Mason, so why tell him what he had planned? Five had been clear that he didn't trust Cecily, so why not assume she had a closer connection to the weapon and the people responsible for it than she claimed?

Except it still didn't come close to explaining Five's reason for leaving the way he had, and all Mason was left with was more confusion as his anger quickly fizzled out.

The long-haired wolf gestured to one of the remaining two wolves—the one without any injury to his face—and that wolf stepped forward and took the lead. The long-haired wolf fell back to the end as everyone followed the new leader.

They walked for almost an hour before the wolf in the lead stopped, his head coming around, his expression one that Mason had seen just yesterday on Cord's face, and Gray's. His pause lasted for several long moments and during that time, no one spoke.

Then again, no one had been speaking before that either, so it wasn't a change. Even Cecily had finally had the cloth removed from her mouth after a harsh warning from Sebastian that she had obviously decided was in her best interest to take seriously.

After a careful sniff of the air and a slow canvassing of the unusually thick pine canopy overhead, the wolf resumed walking without a word, pushing his way into a dense stand of pine trees.

And then, with no warning at all, gunshots rang out, a repeating echo that fired Mason's blood with a sharp, sudden flood of adrenaline.

There was nowhere to hide, and nowhere to go except forward into the pines.

The wolf in front of Cecily took several shots in the chest, and Mason yelled, "Get down!" and lunged for her.

She turned, the look on her face telling him in no uncertain terms that he'd been both right and wrong about her: she couldn't be trusted and fear had no place in the fiercely determined expression she wore.

She raised her arm over her head and circled her wrist, finger high in the air.

Shit. He wheeled away from her and ducked low, not sure if that was going to help or not, his hand on the ground for balance and his gaze scanning every direction but picking out nothing and no one to account for the gunshots.

Cecily wasn't watching her back, probably on the assumption that whoever was firing those weapons was doing it for her, and her overconfidence backfired as Jay yanked out a knife from a sheath at his thigh and grabbed her from behind and hauled her backward, putting her body between him and the direction of the gunshots.

"Into the trees!" the long-haired wolf roared, and in a move that would have put Lake's powerful moves the day before to shame, he grabbed a branch and hauled himself up, then raced across a branch that cracked under his every step before he jumped and went flying through the air toward a tree twice as tall.

Mason jerked his attention back to the ground just as Sebastian and Lamar took off toward the protection of the thick pines ahead.

Mason pushed forward, sprinting toward those same pines. Less than halfway there, a bullet tore through his right shoulder and he let out a startled shout. Pain sparked hot and bright and spread with breath-stealing speed.

He looked down at the welling blood, a lightheadedness stealing his ability to think. He staggered, realized he had to get down, and dropped to his knees and crawled one-armed toward the nearest tree.

More shots fired, but he got the tree at his back and

tried to breathe, but something was wrong. His arm was on fire, and his body wasn't responding like it should and the pressure was back in his chest—so sudden and complete that this time—this time he really did think he might be having a heart attack.

A crippling burn spread through him, and his gritted teeth lost their ability to hold back his whimper as he tried to pull his shirt away from the bleeding injury. His chin burned with sudden pain, and blood gathered at the crease of his neck. On top of everything else, he'd managed to pull the scabbed-over slashes apart and reopen the wounds. But it was his shoulder that—

Oh God. He shouldn't have looked.

His breath was dying in his lungs and his stomach roiled and he couldn't touch what wasn't there. He thought about the size of the bullets they'd used against the wolves and knew this was no more than he deserved, but fucking shit, he actually liked having an arm that moved.

His head hit the back of the tree. He heard voices—someone screaming—and jerked hard when he realized it was him.

Why wasn't the fucking gift inside him taking the pain away? What the goddamn hell was *wrong*? Because something was very, very wrong.

Steady. Steady. He had to get pressure on the wound. He would bleed out if he didn't.

With a shaking hand, he pulled at his t-shirt, thinking he could rip it off the way Five had ripped it off him two days ago. It didn't happen.

He clenched his teeth and changed tactics, stretching the shirt up over his left arm and his head, and trying to wedge his—

"God—" He couldn't even finish his curse.

He dragged the shirt back down, breathing heavily, feeling like he was going to pass out. The goddamned shirt wasn't coming off.

He rolled his head to the side and felt blood well through the scabs under his chin again. A crackle sounded somewhere in the underbrush to his left and he rolled his head that way. Blood made his throat sticky and every time he moved his head he heard a little squelch.

He listened—and noticed for the first time how quiet it had gotten. No gunshots, no voices, no major movement at all.

A wolf roared in the distance, making him jerk.

He couldn't help it—he groaned out in pain, reflexively moving his hand toward his shoulder, but stopping before he went so far as to touch anything.

A breeze flitted past, scattering leaves in every direction across the forest floor. One landed on the laces of his boot and got stuck there.

Mason tried holding his breath to hear better, but he was in too much pain to keep it up.

The crackle came again, much too close.

He couldn't move. If he did, the sounds of leaves crunching beneath him would give away his position—and that was assuming his position hadn't already been found by whoever was sneaking through the woods.

Shit. He was going to have to move. He couldn't just sit there and wait for some asshole to step out of the woods and take off his head.

Decided, he tried drawing his leg in slowly, but even that made a quiet crackle in the leaves, so he stopped and waited. Nothing happened.

Was Five nearby? Would yelling for him help his situation or make it worse? With those wolf senses of his, if he didn't realize Mason was in trouble... Well, he had to know. And if he knew but hadn't come to help, then Mason had to assume—

You're on your own, that ever-present voice in his head said.

And fuck you too, Mason thought back.

He'd be okay. He didn't need anybody to save him; he could do it himself.

That goddamned voice came back again: *But what if you didn't have to? Wouldn't that be worth something?*

You know what, you fucking bastard? You need to pick a side and stick to it.

A twig cracked somewhere to the other side of the tree he was leaning against and his attention snapped back into focus. Dread coiled tight in his stomach.

Goddammit, but he was in real trouble here.

He dug his fingers into the earth, then leaned on his left arm and used it to push himself to his feet. The crackle and crunch of leaves sounded too loud in his ears. Twigs snapped under his boots and the rough pine bark scraped at the side of Mason's arm. He rested his left shoulder against the tree, waiting impatiently for some sign that whoever was coming for him had heard his movements.

"Found you," came from behind him and Mason turned quickly, but an arm wound around his throat, and another wrapped around his torso.

He didn't even try to fight; the pain in his shoulder was unimaginable. He screamed.

The sound echoed loud in his ears, reverberating against his own eardrums, but it was nothing compared

to the roar of the wolf who jumped from the trees behind them both.

Mason could hardly believe it, but he would've recognized that roar anywhere. Warmth drove away the pressure in his chest, followed by a strange sense of rightness
where only wrongness had lived before.

The man with his arm around Mason's throat jerked
him around, throwing him into the trunk of the tree, his
own body smacking into Mason from behind and forcing out another unintended scream through Mason's
gritted teeth. Then the weight was gone, and the roar of
wolf accompanied a terrified yell that ended on a gurgle
as Mason slid down the tree, bark digging at his left arm
the entire way.

His right shoulder was nothing but a fiery ball of pain
shooting sparks through his whole body.

"I am sorry," Five said, in a tone of voice that told
Mason something bad was coming.

He was right.

Five pulled Mason away from the tree, shoved his
shoulder into Mason's belly, and straightened with Mason slung across his back.

Mason couldn't even speak. The blood rushed to his
head, his vision went tight, and he passed out.

Chapter 28

"WAKE UP, shitbrain, come on."

A stinging slap to the side of Mason's face finally cut through the grogginess in his brain. He lay still for several seconds. Too long, because in the next instant, another stinging slap landed on his cheek and he jolted the rest of the way to consciousness.

"Oh, thank God." Marcus got down in his face, the thin, flickering light just enough to illuminate Marcus's eyes. Mason reached out to push Marcus away so he could have a little breathing room, but his arm wasn't working.

"I'm okay," he tried to say, but even he could hear the slur in his words. Something buzzed against his face.

He blinked a few times into the dark room and turned his head.

A scuffing sound came from beside him and he realized Marcus was backing off.

Then the smell hit him.

"Oh God," he groaned.

His heart lurched and his head swam and his stomach heaved and he rolled to his side just in time to throw up beside him. Nothing much came out, but he hadn't had anything in a while; he remembered that.

He pushed up on his left arm, felt his whole body shaking as he did it, then just sat there and breathed in the rancid air.

He remembered that smell too. He spat on the floor a few times, trying to think, but it was so damn hard.

He tried to sit up straight, but couldn't balance, then realized his right arm was completely immobile—he couldn't even feel it, although he knew it was there. That weight—it was the weight of his hand pressing against his thigh, he was sure of it.

What was wrong with him?

"Five?" he asked. "I was—where's Five?"

"I'm really sorry," Marcus said. "You able to get up?"

"What?" Mason swayed a little.

"Come on, Mace, you've got to get up. I'm sorry. But you've got to."

He couldn't breathe.

Something hard hit him in the back, forcing a gasp out of him. Marcus was looming over him again.

Okay, okay, okay. He could breathe. He wasn't suffocating. He just...he wasn't sure what was going on. He smelled smoke. Why did he smell smoke? His chest hurt —so bad. Like a vice clamped to his heart that just kept squeezing and squeezing and squeezing...

Another hard smack landed on his cheek.

"Goddammit, Mason!"

Mason swayed again. "I was shot? I remember—" He looked around, but all he could see was the dark shadows of Marcus's face and the flicker of fire in one corner of the room, just a tiny fire, smoking like it was trying to burn its way through a pile of wet leaves.

And the bodies. He could see them too.

"Okay, here's the thing. If you don't get up, we're going to die in here. You don't want us to die, do you? Come on. I can't leave you here, but I can't carry you, so you've got to get up."

"What are you doing here?" He actually thought he got that out pretty clear, but the look on Marcus's face was wrong. So, so wrong.

"They shot everybody. Do you understand? None of them are healing. They're going to kill them all."

That caught Mason's attention, even though it took a moment for his thoughts to fall in order. "Is that what happened?" The smoke was irritating his throat and he started coughing. Then he couldn't seem to stop.

Marcus scooted close again, rubbing his back. Mason tried to wave him away but he'd forgotten already that his arm wouldn't move.

He finally quit coughing, but every breath he sucked in felt like it was going to make him start all over again.

"I was shot," he said, his voice coming out weak and scratchy but clearer than before. "Something's wrong."

"Don't you think I know that? You're not healing either. I thought you were dead. You quit breathing for more than ten minutes. I counted the goddamned seconds."

So much tension there in Marcus's words. Mason tried to think.

Just *think*. Why couldn't he think? Maybe...maybe his brain had been damaged. You needed oxygen to live. Oxygen to think. He wasn't thinking.

The gift. He wasn't healing. Why wasn't he healing?

Five had told him—told him—told him—what had Five told him?

Five hadn't told him anything. Five didn't trust him.

Where was Five?

"Where's Five?"

"Mason—goddammit. Mace—" Marcus sounded like he was going to cry. "Don't do this to me. I got the door open. I can't leave you here, but if we don't go soon, it's gonna be too late."

"It's okay." Mason took a breath. "It's okay. You can go. I'm okay. You don't have to take care of me anymore. I'll take care of myself."

"Please don't say that. Please..." Marcus grabbed him around the neck and pulled his head in tight to his chest. "Goddamn you."

He was trying to remember what he'd been thinking before Marcus distracted him. "Where's Five? I was with him. Why isn't he here?"

That was what he tried to say.

He wasn't sure it all came out.

His ear was pressed tight to Marcus's chest so he heard when Marcus choked back a sigh.

"Where is he?" Mason asked. "Why haven't you told me where he is?"

A hard breath shook Marcus. "He's dead, Mason. I think he's dead."

Mason couldn't breathe. "No, that's not right."

"He put himself between you and those goddamned motherfuckers. He wasn't moving. They shot everybody. They're going to kill them all."

"No." Mason drew in a rancid gulp of air. "He's not dead. He's going to—he's—I can't breathe."

Marcus was usually right. But Marcus couldn't be right.

Marcus released him, his fingers dragging through Mason's hair. "I'm sorry. Come on. It's time to get up. You can do it."

Mason's thoughts kept circling between a vision of Five dead on the ground and the memory of his broken hand. He needed to *think*. If he could just think, he'd know what was going on. He'd figure out how to fix it. Five was dead on the ground. Dead. Dead. Dead. Dead.

The wolves healed terrible and terrifying injuries. It was why they were so hard to kill. It was why he'd found it so easy to—

Why was Five dead on the ground?

"Where's Five?"

Marcus shook him. Mason's head snapped back. "God, Mason, I know it's hard, but pay attention. We have to leave. You have to get up."

When he'd broken his hand, he'd healed. So quickly. The wolves' near-magical gift had healed him. So why was he dying now? And he was dying. He could feel it in his chest—the tight, slow *thump thump* of a heartbeat that wasn't quite firing on all cylinders.

Five didn't trust him. He hadn't told him what the gift was.

The gift was the key.

Or maybe—maybe not. Something tickled at the back of his brain. Something he couldn't grasp because his thoughts weren't coming together.

He needed to think, goddammit. Why couldn't he *think*?

Marcus would know. He would've been able to figure

it out. He was the smart one. But Marcus wasn't right. Not this time. He couldn't be.

"I was shot," he said again. "They shot me. My shoulder—"

"Your shoulder's not in good shape," Marcus said, "so we're not going to talk about your shoulder, okay? Let's just get through this and deal with that later."

"They locked us up with the dead people."

"Yeah, they did. Come on, Mace, there you go." Marcus had his hands on Mason's shaking arm—the only thing holding him up. He was trying to wedge himself under Mason's armpit.

The sudden jostling movement actually caused a jolt of feeling in the shoulder he hadn't been able to feel until that moment.

Pain, so much pain. He thought he might have screamed.

Marcus was babbling, his voice high and tight and laced with panic. "Don't you pass out—Don't—No no no no no no..."

Mason needed to lie down. He tried to writhe away from the pain ballooning through his chest. His heel scuffed the floor, and the sole of his boot hit something soft and heavy. Flies buzzed around them in an uncontained frenzy.

A sharp slap knocked his head to the side.

"Don't you fucking pass out, don't you do it."

"I'm not—it *hurts*. Goddamn it hurts." He curled forward.

Marcus grabbed him and held him tight to his body, hands clutching at Mason's head and ears. "It's okay. I've got you. It's okay."

Mason forced himself to breathe—just breathe.

And suddenly he knew. "The bullet—did you get it out?"

Marcus squeezed him tighter, almost as if he were afraid to let go. "I didn't touch it. Didn't want to risk making it bleed. I'm so sorry. I shouldn't have—" He interrupted himself with a choked off laugh that made no sense. "It's bad, Mason. I fucked up. I got you into this and I fucked up."

"Get it out."

"They're going to kill you trying to get me to talk, but I've got nothing to tell. You've got to get up now, okay? The door—"

Mason tried to pull free of Marcus's hold on him but Marcus wasn't giving an inch. "It's killing me. I know it is. Get it out."

Marcus leaned his forehead against the crown of Mason's head. "If I leave you, they'll kill you. But I have to go, I have to stop them from—don't make me choose. Don't do that to me, okay?"

Mason clutched at Marcus's shirt with all the strength he had. It wasn't much.

"Listen to me. Get it out. It's killing me. It's got something to do with—with—with—" He jerked at Marcus's shirt and dug his forehead in against Marcus's breastbone. "Why can't I *think*?"

"You were dead, for God's sake! I told you!" In the silence that followed, Mason could hear the harsh rasp of Marcus's breathing. When Marcus continued, he'd lowered his voice, "You weren't breathing. I told you that."

"I'm sorry."

"You're sorry? Don't be a fucking idiot. Look—"

Marcus shuffled on his knees backward a few inches. "We have to do this quick, okay? But I'll do it." With no further warning, Marcus started easing Mason down to the floor. "This isn't a good idea. I know better than this. You're going to die and I'm going to know it was all my fault for dragging you into this shit."

Mason gritted his teeth, the movement sending sparks of pain from the back of his neck and head all the way into the backs of his legs. "Just—shut up. Shut up."

"Okay, okay—"

"Can you—"

"I can barely see a goddamned thing."

"Ahhh!"

"I'm sorry, I'm sorry. Shirt has to come off." Marcus made a harsh sound under his breath. A sob, maybe. Mason couldn't tell. His body was starting to feel like the whole thing had been put to sleep and was prickling with the sensation of pins and needles.

He was dying—he knew it.

Why he'd decided the bullet was the reason, he couldn't explain, but he knew that too. He knew it the way he knew Five wasn't dead. He wasn't—he couldn't be. They had too much to settle between them.

Marcus yanked and the shirt came off, unintentionally knocking Mason's head back to the floor.

"I'm sorry. I'm sorry."

"Just find the—" Mason broke off on a scream. And then another.

Marcus had found something, because he was digging around in the mess of fractured and splintered bone like he was trying to scoop out the insides of a cantaloupe with his fingers.

"I'm sorry, I'm so sorry," he kept saying, over and over until Mason thought he would rather lose consciousness than hear another—

A hard slap caught him in the side of the face.

He jerked, his thoughts coalescing with a sudden, painful clarity.

"You passed out." Marcus leaned close, something in his hand. Metal shone in the flicker of firelight. "I think I got it." Awe echoed in the words. Then he hissed and dropped the bullet to the floor and started rubbing his fingers. "Shit, that thing's hot."

Mason lay on the floor and tried not to notice the stench of rot and decay while he sucked in air. His heartbeat slowed, settling into a steady, even rhythm. His hands stopped shaking, and the terrible pressure in his chest eased.

It was still there, though, and that was enough to give him hope.

Chapter 29

MASON REACHED UP with his left hand and brushed sweat off his forehead. His right arm tingled, but he didn't dare try to move it.

"Did it help? Do you feel better? Can you get up? We have to—"

"Yeah yeah yeah. It's okay. I'm okay." He was breathing a little heavy still, but he wasn't lying. He was okay. He was feeling stronger by the second.

"Thank God," Marcus said, staggering to his feet, "because that's it, we're out of time. We have to get out of this fuckhole, now."

"I'm—yeah. Believe it or not, I'm already feeling—"

"That's great." Marcus grabbed Mason's wrist and hauled. "Less talking and more moving."

Mason rose all the way to his feet with that one aggressive pull, and although his legs were as weak as watered down whiskey, he maintained his balance.

Marcus hauled him in for a tight hug, stealing Mason's breath, then stepped back with a jerky movement.

"My God, you just don't know. I thought you were dead. I won't ever forget that feeling."

Mason gripped Marcus's shoulder. "I know exactly what you mean."

Marcus took Mason's hand and squeezed, then bent over and grabbed Mason's shirt off the floor. "Here, I'll help you get this back on."

The shirt was bloody and the shoulder torn, but Mason let Marcus help him pull it up his right arm before stretching it over Mason's head.

Mason sucked in his breath a time or two and hissed through gritted teeth another, but the difference between then and earlier was remarkable. The pain was bearable, and within a short minute, he had his filthy shirt back on, clinging unpleasantly cold and wet to his shoulder and chest.

Marcus started for the door. "They shoved me in here and threw you in after and I couldn't see a fucking thing when they shut the door. Took me a few minutes to calm down, but when I did, I was able to remember everything I saw."

Mason could hear the heavy rasp of Marcus's breathing. He followed carefully. It was less than twenty feet to the door but he remembered the state of the floor, and he didn't want to end up on his ass because he'd stepped in something he was better off not thinking about.

"I don't know about you," Marcus continued, "but my memory is so goddamn sharp these days I could recite the lyrics to that song Gillie was singing the day Brecken spilled milk all over the kitchen floor."

The memory of that moment came to Mason, a crisp, clear thought full of detail he shouldn't have been able to recall: Brecken had been wearing a white shirt, stained at the collar, and when the milk had puddled under the leg of the table, Brecken had looked up with that wide-eyed "what did I do?" look on his face that he'd been perfecting for the last two years. Gillie had stopped singing for two seconds and then picked it right back up as if nothing had happened.

There'd been nothing special about that day, nothing that made it inevitable he'd remember it so perfectly weeks later. But just as his vision had sharpened, his memory had too. Only he hadn't noticed any of it happening, because he hadn't known there was anything to notice.

"I used my memory to find what I needed to start a fire so I could see," Marcus said, stopping in front of the door. He took a breath as if bracing himself. Maybe he was. He would have had to feel his way through the pitch black room until he had a fire to give him some light. "That's all that matters."

"How'd you do it?"

"Pocketknife. Clothes. They burn as easily as anything else."

"They gave you your knife back?"

"Don't you have yours?"

"No. They didn't give mine back."

The identical pocketknives had been two of the last gifts their father had given them. Mason intended to get his back, but it seemed pretty goddamned unfair that the wolves just handed Marcus his and left Mason without anything.

Instead of dwelling on the unfairness of it all, Mason changed the subject. "You said they wanted answers from you? What do you know that they want to know?"

"I destroyed the lab. You probably saw it."

"Yeah." Mason watched Marcus fiddle with the panel by the door. "Go on."

"In a sec. Let me—"

Marcus quickly pulled the panel away from the wall. It had already been detached but left in place, probably to fool anyone who looked at it.

"When they caught me, I figured playing dumb was the only way to keep from ending up tortured for the information they wanted. I told them I was you, just doing what you'd asked me to do. I'd already ditched my phone so that couldn't give away the truth. Then you showed up, Stan stabbed me and took off after you, and I knew I'd fucked up. They thought you were me. I thought I'd probably gotten you killed until I saw you show up here again."

The confession stunned Mason. He thought back over his confrontation with Stan, Rock, and Lavi, and with a clarity that amazed him he was able to recall every word Stan had said to him before he'd died.

You're dead, Waters. Gonna blow your fucking brains out myself after we get what we want out of you.

You sorry yet for what you did?

That brother of yours sounded sorry enough.

Nothing that had happened proved Marcus wrong. Stan had thought Mason was Marcus, and he'd thought he was proving something to Marcus by killing his brother.

"You shitbrain," Mason said.

"I know." Marcus let out a tight little laugh that had absolutely no humor in it and lowered the panel to the floor. "God, do I know. I didn't think they'd kill you that quickly. Thought they might try to use me as leverage, thinking you were me, and that it would buy me some time. Stan might have been a goddamned sociopath, but he wasn't stupid. Or I didn't think he was. I have no idea about these people we're dealing with now. I've never seen most of them before."

He stopped talking as he took out his pocketknife and flipped the blade open with his teeth.

"You said this was bigger than just the—"

"I know. I know what I said. And it is. Somebody supplied the research for this shit. These goddamned motherfuckers were smart, but not one of them was smart enough to figure out what this place was hiding and come up with a way to get the equipment they needed to turn it into a weapon. Someone shipped it in and you know how goddamned expensive that is. Stan doesn't have that kind of money and resources. But he was the one in charge for as long as I was around."

"How the fuck did you get mixed up with these people?"

"I was having a drink with Lavi one night, got him to talking about how he was making all that money he'd been throwing around. Rock got pissed, but I said the right shit and before I knew it, I was walking the perimeter every day. A few weeks after that, I was allowed inside—that was when these—" His voice cracked before going hard. "These poor bastards started dying. Knew something was up then. Stopped going home because I didn't know what was going on and was scared as hell I would take it back with me. I think Lavi had it too, maybe Stan. Lavi was sniffling and complaining that day it all went to hell. Swore there was no damn way he had it though. Delusional bastard. He had it, he just didn't want to face the fact that he was about to die."

Without waiting for Mason to react, Marcus raised

his knife and jabbed it into the wall where the panel connected. A spark shot out and a loud pop followed. The door hissed slightly, coming open a fraction of an inch to let in a painfully bright line of sunshine.

Mason barely kept himself from jumping. "Goddamn, Marcus, you should've warned me."

"No time." Marcus jammed his fingers in the opening and pulled. The door started to open.

Mason reached for the door with his left hand to help.

Marcus pushed his arm away. "Don't be a stupid fuck. You can barely stand."

Mason grimaced and raised his hand. "Okay, okay. I'll stay out of the way."

"Just use the time to get stronger. We won't be pussyfooting around when we get out of here. It'll be a dead run at least part of the way." Marcus pulled harder and the heavy door moved another few inches.

Smoke wafted on the air, tickling at the back of Mason's throat. "Good thing the alarms don't work."

"If the generator wasn't off line, we'd be completely fucked. This door would've never opened. They locked it. That backup battery was the failsafe. I don't think they had half the systems in this fuckhole working."

"So good thing then."

"Yeah. Good thing."

"The plan is to stop these motherfuckers, right? Because I'm not leaving without Five and his pack. They're not dead until I see proof they are."

Marcus's glance was a little too full of pity for Mason's peace of mind.

Mason clenched his fist. "He's not dead."

Marcus's response was just a cold, hard, "We're going

to stop these motherfuckers, and we'll find the wolves, whatever they've done with them."

"Good, because I'd hate to think we weren't thinking the same thing here."

"Don't worry, we're not leaving until this is done, one way or another."

"Is that why you came back? To stop these people?"

Marcus peeked down the bright corridor, speaking much more quietly, "I was fine letting the wolf and his pack handle this. I had plans. You know why I'm here."

Mason was silent for a moment, staring at the back of Marcus's head. "You knew I was in trouble."

It wasn't something they talked about much, that feeling they sometimes got when trouble came around for one or the other of them. It just was, the same way they sometimes managed to finish each other's sentences or knew what the other was thinking before he'd opened his mouth.

Marcus pulled himself back in but kept his voice low. "They believed me. Didn't even make me explain why I was so sure."

Mason thought about that feeling in his chest, the one that wouldn't go away. He didn't believe Five was dead. He hoped the others weren't either, but there was a strange little hiccup that kept jolting through him every time he thought about Jordan, Gray, Lake, Cord, and Francis. Something was wrong. He knew that. He just didn't know what. But it answered one question pretty clearly as far as he was concerned.

"I could tell you why they didn't ask questions, but we should probably get our asses moving, so—" Mason ruffled the hair at the back of Marcus's head. "Love you, you fucker."

Marcus glared suspiciously at him. "We're going to be fine."

"Just in case, shitbrain."

"Alright, asshole." Marcus caught Mason by the neck with the crook of his elbow, almost pulling Mason off his feet. "I love you too. Now let's go."

Marcus released him, then braved a step into the hallway, confident as always that Mason would follow.

Mason said a silent prayer for the people he was leaving behind, already dead but not buried, and stepped out after Marcus.

The brightly lit hall stung his eyes, making them water, but the fresh air was more welcome than he could express with his careful exhale.

They hurried past the wide windows but saw no one outside watching, and instead of heading for the open stairs, Marcus led him to the opposite end of the corridor where a door stood closed.

"Maintenance," Marcus said. "I dug up the old plans for the building after Rock showed me the place. Had a feeling I might wish I had someday."

Mason nodded and followed Marcus into the stairwell. The dark engulfed them.

The door closed with a creak behind them.

"Shit," Mason said under his breath, but even that small sound echoed off the walls he couldn't see.

"Keep your hand on the rail."

"Already there."

They climbed slowly, carefully, Mason fully aware of the fact that his right arm was useless and that if he tripped, he would be in serious trouble.

"Landing," Marcus said. Then, "Shit. Spider webs, I hate those goddamned things."

Mason eased onto the landing. "Stop being a chickenshit. Most spiders are—"

Something raced across his fingers, and Mason jerked hard and let out a startled breath. "Goddammit!"

When his heart settled enough that the blood wasn't rushing in his ears, he could hear Marcus's quiet laugh.

"Shitbrain," Mason said. "Get moving."

"Trying to find the—" A low clank interrupted him. "There we go."

"You know this is dumb, right? Anybody could be on the other side of that—"

"No one bothered with this stairwell. Trust me."

Mason clenched harder at the rail. "I hate it when you say that."

"I've got my knife."

In a furious whisper, Mason said, "It's a goddamned pocketknife, Marcus."

"It's got a blade, shitbrain."

"Call me shitbrain again—"

"Okay okay okay. We're just nervous. With all the wolves—they're going to be too busy to pay attention to a maintenance stairwell. Let's just do this."

"Where are we supposed to go when we—"

"There's an old supply room just to the left. Door was open last time I was here, room has some crates in it, don't know what, but—"

"Weapons?"

"I said I don't know."

"You say that a lot, but usually you're lying."

"Not this—well, it might be weapons. I saw Rock go inside once and come back out with—"

"If there are weapons there, it won't be a good hiding spot."

"Or it's the best we can hope for, because like you said, all I got is a goddamned pocketknife."

Mason released the rail and rubbed the back of his head. "Shit."

Because Marcus was right about that. They couldn't just walk up to the gun-wielding bad guys with a pocketknife and ask them to surrender.

He lowered his arm and fumbled for a good grip on the rail again. He hadn't wanted to face the question earlier, because there'd been no answer for him, only a cold, hard will. But it was time. "How are we going to do this? You have a plan, right? I only have one working arm at the moment, and I'm not thinking running out of here and getting shot to death is how I want this to end. It ends like that and Five won't be any better off than if we'd stayed in that damn room."

"We'll still be better off. I wasn't looking forward to them torturing you to get me to talk."

Mason was quiet for a second. "Good point. Now you going to answer the question?"

The quiet was broken only by the sounds of their breathing.

"You don't have a plan. Goddammit, Marcus."

Marcus exhaled harshly. "I do have a plan. Remember when I said I ditched my phone? It has all the information I was able to get hold of about the changes they made to the virus. We send it to the right people and nobody'll be unprepared if one of these motherfuckers gets away. But we have to get our hands on it first."

"And it's in that room, isn't it?" Mason pinched the bridge of his nose. "Why the *fuck*—"

"I didn't have time to find another place for it."

"You hid that EP display so how can—"

"What? No, I didn't. Someone must have left it behind."

Mason remembered the blood that he'd been sure belonged to Marcus. "You didn't hide it?"

"No. Let's move on. We go out and—"

"No, we don't."

A deeply indrawn breath sounded in the dark. "We have to do this, Mason."

"Come on. Think. You're the goddamned smart one, you know there's a better way. I don't want anyone spreading this thing, not if it's truly the 2060 flu, but right now, we need to find Five, if he's here, and the others—*before* we get ourselves killed. Where would they be keeping the wolves? If the bullets are doing the same thing to them as that one was doing to me... We have to get those bullets out of them if they're going to have any chance of healing. And if they can heal, they can help us."

"Mason..."

"Don't you fucking tell me not to get my hopes up, because I'll punch you in the goddamned face, Marcus."

The silence lingered before Marcus's hand landed heavily on Mason's shoulder. "You like him."

"Fuck you. This is about stopping those goddamned monsters, not about—"

"He made you think, didn't he? That was how it started for me."

Mason pushed Marcus's hand off him. "When we get out of here, I'm going to kick your ass." There wasn't much heat there, though, and they both knew his words weren't a promise so much as an admission of guilt.

He breathed tightly through his nose. An idea came to him, and he looked up. Of course, the darkness didn't abate, and there was nothing to see, but—

"Hear that echo?"

Marcus shuffled closer. "Yeah, I do."

"It keeps going up."

"There's another couple floors. No one messed around in them as far as I know."

"Then we go up and see what we find."

Chapter 30

THE SPIDER WEBS got thicker as they went, and by the time Mason had reached the landing of the next floor, his hair was standing on end. But he couldn't blame it entirely on the spider webs that were stuck to him. Something in his chest had started squeezing tighter, a burn that didn't want to abate, a sense of wrongness that he couldn't shake.

"This was a bad idea," Mason whispered, so low he wasn't even sure Marcus would hear him from his position ahead.

Marcus's response wasn't anything Mason expected to hear. "I see light."

Mason strained through the darkness, and sure enough, the faintest pinprick of light shone in the distance above them.

"Let's keep going," Marcus said. "The light's coming from the top floor."

"You sure it's the top?"

"Three stories above ground, one partly below."

He recalled how Lake had climbed in a broken window on an upper floor. "Okay."

As soon as he heard the quiet sounds of Marcus moving again, he followed.

They were halfway there when the low sound of a wolf growling sent prickles of fear racing across Mason's entire body. His spine stiffened, and his chest squeezed the breath right out of his lungs. He heard Marcus's stumble and the slap of his hand against a step and a tight gasp.

The growl stopped as quickly as it had started. But before Mason had time to wonder if he'd been hearing things that weren't there, he heard a soft whine and a scrabbling sound, like claws on concrete.

He reached down blindly for Marcus, patting from his back to his arm. Neither spoke as Marcus rose to his feet just one step up from Mason.

Finally, his nerves stretched so taut he should've been vibrating, Mason said, "Who's there?"

Marcus made a strangled sound in his throat, barely audible.

"You...go..."

That voice.

Without much thought, Mason climbed the next step. "Jordan? Is that you?"

A gasping breath answered him. "Go...away."

Mason dug his fingers into the rail and climbed another step. He felt Marcus grab at his arm. He pulled free.

"You're injured. I can help. Marcus says they shot everyone. Is that what's—"

A heart-stopping growl cut him off. Goose bumps raced across his skin. His chest tightened to painful levels. He felt something. He just couldn't name it. Not pain, not anger, not fear.

Despair. The thought came to him in a sudden rush, and he could almost taste the sweet sorrow of it on the back of his tongue.

"Jordan. I can help."

"Mason, don't," Marcus said.

Mason climbed another step, pulling free of Marcus's tug at his shirt, his eyes straining so hard to see what couldn't be seen that they burned.

"Jordan?" he tried again.

Another scrabbling sound came from somewhere on the stairs above, followed by the distinct sound of shuffling.

"I'm going to help you." Mason started a careful push forward, feeling his way up the stairs.

"No!" Then, just as fiercely, "You belong to—ahhhh!" His groan was pained, his word an agony of fire.

Mason knew because he felt it. Not as an agony of his own but as a curious wash of cold through his body radiating from his chest outward. But he understood the agony, even if he couldn't explain it.

His foot bumped into something solid and he stumbled. His white-knuckled grip on the rail was the only reason he didn't fall.

"Jordan?"

But Jordan's voice came from further up. "Stop. Do not...*please...*"

A crazy worry tightened Mason's body as he tried to go around the large object—the *person*—blocking his way up the stairs to Jordan. "Where's Five?"

Only the harsh rattle of breathing answered him.

"Where is he, goddammit? Is he alive?" His voice echoed violently in the stairwell.

The scratch of claws came again. "I…your scent is…*I can't…*" The growl that followed raised the hair at the nape of Mason's neck.

And then it all made sense. Mason stopped with his foot already on the next step up and the fading growl of Jordan's voice in his ears.

"Shit," Marcus said behind him.

Mason clamped down on the adrenaline racing through his veins, took a deep breath, and resumed his climb. "I'm not leaving you here injured when I can help."

Marcus's quiet footsteps followed him up the stairs.

"No," Jordan said again, and the sound of movement became louder.

A quiet thud followed and a short cry. Jordan's movements stopped.

Mason was there, finally, and he eased down to his knees, forcing himself to release his tight grip on the rail so he could reach out his hand.

His fingers slid in wet warmth.

Jordan cried out again.

"I don't know how I'm going to do this, but that bullet…it did something to me. When it came out, I started healing again. I'm going to get those bullets out of you. Then you're going to get better."

"Your…scent," Jordan said. "*Please…* Alpha will—"

"Hush," Mason said. "Just hush. This is hard enough with only one arm. Marcus—"

He didn't have to finish because Marcus was right there, waiting. Mason heard Marcus lower himself beside Jordan on the stairs.

"Can't see a damn thing in here," Marcus said with a huff.

"I need your knife."

Silence greeted him.

"Marcus—"

"If he attacks—"

"I've only got one arm that'll work right now. I know. And he might. But I have an idea."

Jordan tried to push Mason away, but he was so weak his claws couldn't even break through the denim of Mason's jeans. "Don't *touch* me…"

A faint rustle came from beside Mason. "The idea any good?"

"It's probably the dumbest thing I've ever come up with."

"Shit."

"We'll just see if it works and if it doesn't—"

"Won't much matter anyway. Unless you're thinking you'll—"

"No. I won't. I want to find Five."

"Don't really want to fuck on the stairs here, either."

"Nobody's going to—"

Jordan let out a choked growl and made a grab for Mason's arm.

Mason quickly straddled Jordan and used his knees to hold down Jordan's arms. The very fact that what he was doing was even possible told him how dangerously close to death Jordan must be. Jordan was so weak he couldn't even fight off an injured human who had only one good arm.

"You sure you can do this?" Marcus asked beside him, his breath stirring the sweaty strands of hair by Mason's ear.

Mason shook his head even though there was no way Marcus could see it. But it was Marcus. He would know.

Mason reached out, and Marcus fumbled the pocketknife into Mason's hand.

Mason used his teeth to pry open the blade.

❧

Ten minutes later, Mason sat back on his knees holding both the bloody pocketknife and his blown-out shoulder and feeling the slick slide of blood drizzling down his arm from multiple gouges in his bicep. He turned his head to swipe his chin over his other shoulder and wipe away the blood there too.

Under him, Jordan was breathing raggedly, unconscious for the moment, his body already twitching with the first sign that he might be healing from the terrible injury Mason had inflicted upon him after digging numerous bullets out of Jordan's body by feel alone.

Mason hadn't wanted Marcus to bang Jordan's head into the floor so many times, but Jordan had not reacted well when Mason had started fumbling with the ties to Jordan's boot so he had access to the tendons between foot and calf.

It was a crippling injury, but if Jordan didn't heal on his own, it was an easy fix with the wolves' medical technology.

That's what Mason kept telling himself, anyway. At the end, it had been obvious Jordan wasn't thinking straight. He'd been under the influence of Mason's and Marcus's human scent, and even as weak and injured as he was, he'd been willing to fight to get what he wanted.

Mason had had no choice.

"I can feel the bone in my elbow where his claws got

me," Marcus said. "Doesn't hurt unless I touch it but it's still freaking me the hell out."

Mason lowered his arm so he could wipe the pocketknife's blade clean against his thigh before forcing it to close.

He handed it back to Marcus awkwardly, then spent several seconds trying to wipe as much blood off his hand as he could. There was just so much goddamn blood everywhere; he could even taste the metallic tang of it on the back of his tongue.

He clamped his hand around the railing and pulled himself upright. "Let's get out of here before he heals enough to come after us."

"Maybe you should be back here. That way he won't have to go through me to get to you."

"Fuck you."

Marcus laughed quietly. "Let's get moving before someone realizes where all that goddamn roaring was coming from."

"Assuming anyone heard it from up here."

"Somebody heard it," Marcus said. "My ears are still ringing. I tried to muffle him, but those fucking wolf teeth aren't just for looks."

"You okay?"

"Been better." But Marcus bumped his fist into Mason's back, his way of telling Mason he was okay despite what he was saying.

"Couldn't let him die," Mason said.

"I get it. Go on. Lead us out of here."

Mason started climbing the steps. He wasn't sure how far up the stairwell they'd gone before running into Jordan but the landing had to be near. He could still see the faintest pinprick of light ahead.

So Mason climbed, step by step, sliding his hand along the rail and fighting against the desire to let go when his fingertips brushed thick, clingy spider webs he couldn't see.

The landing surprised him, his foot coming down on the flat surface where he expected another stair to be that wasn't there. He let out a startled puff of breath and re-balanced quickly.

"Found it," he whispered over his shoulder. "Watch out."

"About time. Get us out of here."

Mason leaned forward, eyes tracking the faint light. He almost bumped his nose into the door as he realized he was looking at a narrow crack between the door and the frame.

He fumbled for the knob and found a panel instead.

"Oh, fuck," he said on a breath of panic.

"What's the—"

"There's no way out. Just a lock."

"Are you serious? Shit. We'll have to go back."

A low groan came from below them and sent Mason's heart thudding into his ribcage.

"Oh fuck," Marcus said.

Mason rested his forehead on the cool surface of the door and closed his eyes. "We can't go back."

Marcus shoved at Mason's shoulder. "Move out of the way. I'll find that goddamned failsafe by feel if I have to. If I can short it out…"

"You can't see in the—" Mason raised his head, a sudden surge of adrenaline making his mind race. "The other panel. This one is probably just like it."

"Exactly."

"You really think you can remember it in enough detail?"

"Only one way to know," Marcus said, pushing carefully around Mason.

Mason moved aside and let Marcus go to work.

The creaks and clacks and pops that came with him tearing into the sealed panel echoed too loudly in the dark stairwell, but it drowned out the occasional groan from below. Mason eased himself a few steps down and sat with his back to Marcus, staring into the pitch black and listening for any sign that Jordan might be recovering enough to come for them.

He tried to imagine doing what would need to be done if that happened, but something about submitting to Jordan felt wrong. So goddamn wrong. He didn't know why it hadn't felt that way with Five, but it hadn't.

He didn't want to submit to Jordan, and he couldn't see himself doing it, not even to save all their lives.

But why?

Why?

God. He exhaled roughly and started to rake his hand through his hair. His breath caught as pain shot through his right arm, and he realized what he'd tried to do. But his arm had responded, even if only a little and even if he'd paid for the move with a jolt of pain that shot all the way from the base of his neck and into his fingertips.

He twisted on the step toward Marcus, who was mumbling under his breath and making small noises that told Mason just how hard he was concentrating. He turned back to the stairwell. He wouldn't interrupt Marcus just to tell him his shoulder might be healing already.

He frowned and strained his hearing. Why couldn't he hear Jordan breathing anymore?

Other than the sounds of Marcus behind him, all he heard was a strange clicking sound.

Click, click, click…

Screeeech.

Every muscle in Mason's body tightened. He sat up straighter, then eased to his feet, staring into the utter darkness below.

His chest tightened, then tightened some more, and his hair stood on end.

He didn't know what—or who—was down there, but it wasn't Jordan.

He remembered the heavy body blocking their access to Jordan. He'd assumed…human. He wasn't sure why, but he had.

"Marcus," he said, his voice taut with concern, "you about done?"

"This goddamned—umph—fuck—" He sounded like he was talking through gritted teeth.

Click, click, click…

Mason carefully stepped up onto the stair behind him. "Somebody else is in here with us, and it ain't Jordan."

Chapter 31

FROM THE SOUND OF things, Marcus was working furiously to remove the panel, but Mason could already tell he wasn't going to be fast enough. The tight pull of dread in his chest intensified. He thought about how he'd left Jordan, helpless, defenseless.

He hesitated, then said, "You get the door open. I'm going down."

Something clattered to the landing, ringing with the sound of metal. "Don't do it, you fucker. Don't you do it."

"It'll give you time—"

"I've almost got—" He cut off with a hard yelp and a stagger, bumping into Mason's back.

Mason grabbed the rail with his right hand out of habit and his shoulder screamed in pain at the sudden pull. His hand didn't have enough strength to hold him, so he stumbled sideways into the wall, but he didn't fall and Marcus's weight shifted off him quickly.

"Sorry, sorry," Marcus was saying behind him, hands patting at Mason's back before taking a grip on Mason's waistband.

"I'm okay. I got it."

His balance, he meant, although his voice came out breathless because of the stabbing pains in his shoulder that were taking too goddamn long to ease up.

Marcus stopped apologizing and released him. Mason stayed put for a moment while he listened to Marcus's feet shuffle across the landing again.

Somewhere in the dark below, the *click, click, click* became a *click, click, clank, click, click, clank* and Mason found himself holding his breath in anticipation of whatever might come next.

His position was unsustainable though, so he pushed away from the wall, grimacing as he did. His arm throbbed and his shoulder screamed and his hand shook with fine tremors. His shoulder was undoubtedly healing and his pain was under more control than he had any right to expect, but that didn't mean he could use his arm. Every time he forgot that, he felt like he was tearing the muscles and tendons in his shoulder apart all over again.

The air was stale and dry and unmoving and there was no way whoever was below didn't know Mason and Marcus were there.

Wolves couldn't see in absolute darkness—he didn't think—but they could still hear remarkably well and their sense of smell—well, there was a reason running wasn't the answer when a wolf caught your scent. Wolves were supreme trackers and they did most of that tracking with their goddamned noses.

Something shuffled behind him, fabric rubbing against the floor—Marcus, on his knees, resuming his work on the panel, his breath coming fast enough to tell Mason he was pushing himself, working as fast as he could.

"I'm almost there," Marcus said. "Just hold off for a minute, okay?"

"It's not Jordan," Mason said again, even as that sense of dread tightened inside him. He couldn't know who was making those sounds below—*click, click, clank, click, click, clank*—if it was human or wolf, and he couldn't know if that human or wolf was friend or enemy.

But it didn't matter what he couldn't know, because he knew.

There was a wolf in here with them, someone who wasn't Jordan, and that wolf was not a friend.

"I can't," Mason said, and he started down the stairs before Marcus could stop him.

"Dammit, Mason!"

But the crack of sound that followed told Mason that Marcus wasn't going to try to follow him. He was working as fast as he could to dig his way deep into the panel's insides and save both of them.

Mason eased his boot onto the next lower tread and gripped the rail until his knuckles ached. As he closed the distance between them, Jordan's dread thundered like a heartbeat in his ears.

He couldn't understand it, why it was such a physical thing.

He hesitated before taking his next step.

Jordan was awake. His silence had tricked Mason into believing he was still unconscious, but he wasn't. A sense of Jordan's feelings pushed hard at him, like the wind in a storm.

Shame. Determination. A surge of need and want. A desire for—

Something. What? He couldn't—

Betrayal.

Earlier, Jordan had feared giving in to Mason's human scent, because he had believed it was a betrayal of his duty to his alpha. How strong would that sense of betrayal be if Jordan couldn't stop one of his pack's enemies from claiming his alpha's mate?

As soon as the thought solidified, Mason knew he'd hit on the reason for Jordan's dread. His loyalty to his alpha was everything to him. His alpha's mate was his to protect. His weakness was a shame he couldn't escape and his need to fulfill his duty to his alpha a burning rage he couldn't satisfy, just as he couldn't satisfy the heat running through him.

A growl cut through the suffocating silence, much too close. Mason stopped in place, afraid to move a muscle, wishing he'd been counting the steps. He didn't know how far from Jordan they'd climbed and he didn't know how close he was now.

Too close, that was for sure.

The other body had been a few steps down from Jordan. He remembered the feel of denim under his palm and the cool skin. Wolves didn't have cool skin. Maybe that had been what tricked him into believing the body was a dead human. He remembered the brush of hair against the side of his arm and the weight of the body, unmoving and heavy on the stairs when he'd scrambled to regain his stability while digging those bullets out of Jordan.

Not soft.

The wolf would be big. Male. More likely to be attracted to human scent.

You can distract him, the ever-present voice in his head told him with unsettling calm. *Get right up on him and all he'll want is to fuck. You don't fight and you don't cringe. You just do it, and maybe Marcus will make it out and find a way to stop those monsters from infecting the whole god-damned world and Jordan will have time to heal.*

And when Jordan healed, Mason would have two wolves fighting over him on a stairwell where one wrong step could send him plunging down the stairs.

He'd break his goddamned neck.

Not good.

Possibly better than the alternative.

It shouldn't have been funny, but he bit back a desperate laugh anyway and took another cautious step forward.

But what choice did he have? He couldn't leave Jordan to die, and he couldn't fight—not without leaving Marcus at risk once Mason was dead. He didn't doubt for a minute that the fight would be over before it had started. Definitely not long enough to benefit Marcus.

As if to prove his point, Marcus let out a string of curses and banged hard enough at the door that the reverberation seemed to travel down the rail and into the palm of Mason's hand.

Time for that distraction.

"Hey," he said. "You want to tell me who you are? Are you hurt?"

The only response he got was a quiet grunt.

Maybe he'd been wrong, maybe—

"You should have submitted," a wolf's grave and deep voice echoed in the dark, scattering Mason's thoughts like leaves in the wind. "Because now, human, all I want from you is to satisfy my heat before I tear out your throat."

A rush of *wrong wrong wrong* smacked into Mason with all the weight of a fifty pound block of ice. He took a hurried step backward before he could stop himself. Oh shit. Oh, *shit*.

It was a goddamn curse. There was no other explanation for the trouble he kept finding himself in.

Mason clenched tight to the rail, the darkness suffocating him. His voice shook. "How'd you get here? I thought you had a broken neck."

Screeeeeech.

An unpleasant tingle raced down Mason's spine.

"I followed your scent," the wolf said. "*Paetinishikid* should not have interfered, but I'm not foolish enough to stand against him when he chooses a path. So I chose retreat instead of death. And now I'm here to follow my fate."

Something shifted heavily not that far from Mason. He strained his eyes trying to see into the unrelenting darkness but it was impossible. He couldn't see a goddamned thing.

Mason's dread started to spill over. "What are you doing?"

Click, click, clack...

"Stay away." Jordan's voice echoed weakly off the walls as he finally made his awareness known.

Was he talking to Mason—or the wolf?

"Jordan?"

"No." Jordan's voice was barely more than a rasp. "He isn't yours. He belongs to...*Weketekari*."

Fear ate at Mason's stomach. Something was going on just a few feet away from him and he had no idea what.

The noises shifted so close Mason thought he could reach out and touch them. His fingers flexed on the railing, but his common sense was telling him not to make that mistake.

"This one will try to interfere. I can't allow that. It's unfortunate his loyalty to his alpha is so strong. He would have made me an excellent beta."

Click, click, clack, clack, clack, clack...

Mason took a step down. "What are you doing? Tell me, goddammit."

A loud thud echoed in the stairwell.

Jordan screamed.

Mason jerked, the sudden wash of—of—

Rage. Not his own, not Jordan's, but so overpowering it consumed him.

He threw himself into the darkness toward the sound of the wolf. His shoulder slammed into something big and solid that fell back under his sudden weight.

Mason's stomach lurched with what promised to be a long, painful fall.

But the wolf grabbed him and slammed him sideways into the wall, roaring so loud that it vibrated Mason's eardrums. He flinched just as the wolf dropped him to the stairs.

"Mason!" Marcus yelled. "What the fuck's going on down there?"

Mason couldn't answer. He tumbled down three... four...maybe five steps with his hand scrambling for purchase and his shoulder stabbing him with a fiery burn so bright and hot he thought he might vomit right there. His knees thudded against the next step down and his descent stopped as suddenly as it had started.

"Jordan?" His voice came out high and tight, his concern a fierce pressure in his chest. "Jordan! Are you—"
Dead.

Something heavy bumped into his shoulder and he

realized Jordan wasn't laid out on the stairs any longer. His body moved, twisting—

"What the fuck have you done?" Mason yelled into the darkness. He grabbed for Jordan, pulling, while something cold brushed the outer part of his arm.

What the fuck was it?

Clack, clack…hard against the wall.

"Jordan—Jordan—Answer me." Mason yanked and heard the whish of something slide along the railing. His fingers brushed a rough fabric, thick and—

A fire hose. A goddamned fire hose had been wrapped around Jordan like one of those spider webs, binding him tight.

"Leave him," the wolf growled as he hauled Mason upright by the back of his shirt.

Mason scrambled to keep his feet under him at the sudden shift in position. He struck out with his fist and his knuckles connected with a dull thud against unyielding muscle.

An arm? The wolf's chest?

Still, the wolf didn't seem to have the same trouble figuring out where Mason was and how to subdue him. He caught Mason by the throat and forced him onto his toes.

Choking, Mason grabbed at the wolf's wrist with his left hand. His right arm refused to move more than a few inches, and even that caused a burning pain to tear through his shoulder. His vision narrowed and everything around him spun in a dizzy rush.

Or maybe that was caused by the fact that he couldn't breathe. Claws bit into his skin, sending warm blood trickling down his neck.

"God…damn…you," he gasped out.

The wolf pulled him forward and sniffed deeply, his breath hot, the hard line of his nose raking across Mason's cheek.

"You chose your fate when you refused to submit the first time," the wolf said in a husky voice right at Mason's ear. "We will fuck, and if you don't die fighting your fate, I might allow you to live through the rest of the heat."

Mason tried to get one foot on the step in front of him but his balance shifted and he jerked, his body reacting instinctively to the feeling that he was about to fall backward.

The wolf took another long sniff along the side of Mason's face. "In fact, your alpha might sacrifice himself to have you returned to him. I smell his mark all over you —the mark of a *mate*." A harsh growl followed. "*Traesikeille* allows you humans an honor you do not deserve. But it won't be for much longer. *Jetikima* will see the end of the false alpha's rule."

"I don't...even know...what...you're...talking about," Mason wheezed out. He tried to drag in another breath, but it was difficult getting anything into his lungs with the wolf squeezing his windpipe closed.

"Got it!" Marcus yelled, just seconds before a bright, blinding light hit Mason in the face. His eyes burned and watered and it was impossible to see through the deluge of sunlight that spilled down the stairwell from above.

Marcus yelled again, this time nothing Mason understood, and a loud bang echoed off the walls.

Then a wolf roared, so goddamned fierce it made Mason's whole body tense in alarm.

His captor growled and squeezed at Mason's throat before half turning, dragging Mason right up onto the next step, where one of Mason's boots finally found some footing and he shoved forward with all the power he had in his leg, throwing all hundred and eighty pounds of his weight toward the wolf.

The wolf staggered and fell back into the stairs, pulling Mason down with him.

Frantic to make the most of his moment, Mason jammed his knee into the wolf's groin as hard as he could, even as he tried to catch himself with his hand on the stairs. His right arm gave out, his shoulder burning so white-hot that he let out a short, sharp scream of pain.

The wolf roared and slashed at Mason's face, catching Mason over the cheek, mere inches from his eye. He threw Mason off him, and Mason's back slammed into the wall, his head cracking against the rail hard enough to make him bite his tongue. The iron tang of blood filled his mouth.

He shook his head and the whole world moved under him. He groaned and tried to push himself up, but his body was too heavy and his muscles too weak.

The shadowy form of a lean and powerful wolf leapt into the center of his rapidly narrowing field of vision with another deafening roar.

Mason tried to blink back the darkness but it was im-possible.

Didn't matter. For the first time in two days, the pressure in his chest wasn't suffocating him.

Five was back, and he was alive, and he was going to kick that goddamn wolf's ass.

Chapter 32

MASON RETURNED TO consciousness just in time to feel himself being yanked down the stairs.

He didn't have time to think or wonder what had happened before the back of his head took a glancing blow on the edge of a stair tread, knocking him nearly senseless again.

Groaning, he tried to roll onto his stomach to protect his head, grabbing at the wall to stop the painful jarring as his body banged into the hard edge of one stair after another.

He could almost feel claws biting through the tough skin of his boots and scratching at his ankle, but he couldn't kick free.

Then a flash of something at the corner of his eye caught his attention and bodies collided, and the wolf trying to drag him into the middle of the fight was wrenched away from him with a force strong enough to tear Mason's boot right off his foot.

Five's roar of rage was so dark and full that it sent a sharp stabbing pain through Mason's eardrums. Then

Five raised his arm and brought it down in an arc, and dark red blood splattered across the wall beside them.

A surge of adrenaline finally pushed away the foggy disorientation in Mason's head and he scrambled around and started crawling up the stairs on hand and knees. He put his hand down and barely caught the edge of the next step. He squeezed his eyes shut, trying to will away the double vision, but it didn't work.

He grabbed for the rail, missed, and tried again. His fingers caught the next time and he hauled himself to his feet, a chill going through him as the sole of his bare foot touched the cold tread under him.

A few feet above him, he could see the hazy shape of Jordan struggling against the bonds of the fire hose, his upper body suspended from the rail and his bound legs pushing at the stairs without much effect.

Relief weakened Mason's knees. Jordan was alive.

"Mason!"

Mason jerked his gaze up to see a hazy vision of Marcus standing in the halo of light that spilled through the open door at the top of the stairs.

"Let's go!"

Another roar rattled the stairwell and the thud of heavy bodies followed. Mason turned his head toward the sound just as Five and the wolf slammed into the landing. Their fight had the kind of desperate struggle to it that said they were well-matched for speed and strength, and all it would take was one lucky break to determine the victor.

"Mason, goddammit! Come on!"

Mason's head throbbed in time to the frantic pounding of his heart.

What could he do? How could he help?

He turned toward Marcus. "Give me your knife!"

Marcus hesitated for the briefest moment. He might have cursed, Mason wasn't sure. But finally, after one quick look over his shoulder, Marcus rushed down the stairs.

When Marcus reached Jordan, he slammed his back to the wall and squeezed his way past.

Jordan's head came up, tracking Marcus's position. He didn't speak but a low grumble came from his chest and his movements became more agitated, his attempt to free himself more focused.

Concern tickled at the base of Mason's skull but he didn't have time to deal with it.

Marcus stopped on the step above Mason, huffing slightly. "You're being a shitbrain, you know that? That wolf can handle himself better than—"

A loud thud came from below, and Mason jerked. He looked around to see Five and the wolf fighting several steps down from the lower landing. The wolf had Five tight to the wall, and the only thing keeping his teeth from Five's throat was Five's grip on the wolf's shoulders.

The fact that neither wolf was saying a word was what unsettled Mason the most. Both were focused on only one thing from the look of things: kill his opponent.

Mason turned back to Marcus, his knees almost giving out on him before he steadied himself. He released the rail and thrust out his hand. "Just give me the goddamned knife."

Marcus was already digging into his pocket. The clip that held the knife in place snapped as Marcus pulled it free. He smacked it into Mason's palm.

Mason didn't close his fist. "Open it, goddammit."

Marcus snatched the knife out of Mason's hand, flicked the longest blade open and handed it back. "You're making a mistake. You can't do anything to help him. You've only got one working arm!"

Mason clenched the handle in his fist and met Marcus's gaze. "I never was the smart one. You know that."

"You expect me to argue any different now? This is fucking insane. You're going to get us both killed."

"You're not coming with me."

He turned away, his attention already refocusing on the fight, but Marcus's hand landed on his shoulder, stopping him before he could start down the stairs.

"Something's going on out there, I could hear it when the door opened. Wolves and guns and engines. We can't let these guys get away. If they found my phone—"

Mason looked over his shoulder. "Marcus, get the fuck out of here."

Marcus's expression turned into a tight scowl. "You're out of your fucking mind if you think I'm leaving—"

"Who's going to save the world if I fuck this up?"

"Mace, goddammit—"

"There were wolves coming to collect the bodies. Maybe they're already here. Go. This might be your best chance, maybe they're all distracted. Find your phone. I'll be there if I can."

Marcus looked over his shoulder toward the open door at the top of the stairwell. "I don't want to leave you down here alone."

"I'm not alone, Five's here."

Marcus stared at Mason too long. Mason was on the verge of turning away again when Marcus said, "Don't get yourself killed, you asshole," then shook his head, turned, and started climbing the stairs as fast as he had raced down them.

Mason was proud of his brother. Marcus could set aside his feelings to do what needed to be done. Mason couldn't. He'd proven it time and again. He hadn't cared about the world when this had all started; he'd wanted only to save his brother. Now here he was, risking the world again, for reasons that only made sense if he'd lost his fucking mind.

Mason released a harsh exhale and turned to look down the stairs again, but Five and the other wolf had slipped below his line of sight. He leaned over the interior rail, trying to see what he was about to walk into but they were under him and all he caught was a glimpse of someone's back.

Five. He was wearing the dark shirt, Mason was sure of it. Then again, the stairwell was shadowed and dark that far down and Mason couldn't be sure of anything with his impaired vision.

Behind him, he heard Jordan growl even as his frantic attempt to get free of the fire hose intensified.

He turned quickly, only to see that Marcus was sliding by Jordan without any hesitation at all.

Jordan lunged, a growl rising harsh and fast in his chest.

"Sorry for leaving you like this," Marcus said, pulling away from the wall a few steps above Jordan, "but somebody's got to stop those motherfuckers before they destroy the world."

That was all Mason needed to hear.

He began a halting limp down the steps, knife held tightly in his hand, hand dragging along the rail for balance, right arm numb at his side.

He'd lost his fucking mind, no doubt about it.

Something jarred through rail and he paused, listen-ing.

A harsh groan came from below. Mason sped up. He couldn't know what had happened, but he was done wasting time.

He rounded the stairwell at the next landing, and then jerked back as the wolf Five was fighting slammed into the wall. The roar that followed make the hair on Mason's arms stand on end.

He hunkered down, knife at the ready, and tried to make sense of the noises.

A harsh growl was followed by a clank and a screak—something like claws raking across the metal of the stair rail. Whatever it was, the sound made him cringe as his spine tingled and gooseflesh rose on his skin.

He yelled around the corner, "You guys might want to take it easy on the building!"

His answer was a roar and the sound of something big rushing for his position. He started to rise, but changed his mind and just leaned into the wall for sup-port in case the wolf—or Five—came crashing into him.

His hope was that the wolf who wanted him dead would try to use him against Five, giving Five an open-ing to bring him down.

Unfortunately, Mason recognized Five the moment he raced around the corner, blood dripping from several nasty gashes down his cheek.

"Mine!" Five roared, his eyes glassy but his move-ments fluid as he swung around just in time to stop the other wolf from barreling into him and Mason both.

The landing wasn't big enough for them all, and the wolf and Five staggered into the wall, both of them wrestling furiously for control. Mason had two seconds to question his sanity again, then he threw himself right into the fray and sliced as deeply as he could through the wolf's dark trousers and across his thigh.

The wolf reacted with a howl but the moment of distraction was all Five needed to lunge forward and dig his teeth into the wolf's exposed throat.

Before Mason could pull back, the two wolves crashed into him, knocking him backward into the stairs. His ass hit hard and then his back, and the weight of both wolves came down on top of him.

His head slammed against the edge of the stair behind him.

Light burst behind his eyes. He tried to lift his head and that was the last thing he knew until a hard tug on his injured shoulder sent pain zinging through nerve endings that should have been dead already.

He groaned and blinked his eyes open but the world around him was just a haze of color and light. He tried to focus his vision and heard himself groan again. For a moment, he had the weirdest sensation he was outside his own body.

"Shh. Shh. You're okay. Just a few more minutes. We'll have some drugs here for you soon."

Mason didn't recognize the voice, but he blinked a few more times and a shadowy figure leaned over him, and he recognized that face, even though it had been three years since the last time he'd seen Ian Tucker.

"What're you doing here?" he asked. He was surprised at how slurred his words sounded.

"Same reason you're here, I figure. Trying to stop the end of the world."

"How's that working?"

The skin around Ian's eyes crinkled. "Not so bad, actually."

A surge of relief flowed through Mason. He sighed and let his eyes close. "That's good."

A hand landed on Mason's chest. "He's in trouble here. How long?"

Noises came from somewhere that Mason couldn't pinpoint. A voice echoed, saying something Mason couldn't be bothered to hear. Ian wasn't talking to him any longer, anyway, and he didn't feel like asking questions. Then a memory of the fight between Five and that wolf floated to the top of his thoughts and he changed his mind.

He tried to raise his head.

Ian pressed his hand firmly against Mason's forehead. "You shouldn't move. You cracked your skull on the stairs and you need some serious medical attention before we try to take you out of here."

"Is that why it feels like somebody kicked me in the head?"

"For all we know, somebody did kick you in the head."

Mason tried to remember what might have happened, but everything was a jumble. The last thing he could remember easily was Five trying to hold off that wolf... "Where's Five?"

"Five?" Ian looked behind him and down, making Mason aware suddenly that he was flat on his back on the stairs, still, and he hadn't even recognized that fact until then.

An accented voice answered Ian from below. "His mate. *Weketekari*. You called him 'Second' when we brought him out."

Mason thought about trying to move so he could get a look at the wolf who'd spoken, but the gray at the edges of his vision was already closing in on him again.

"He was the second one you brought out," Ian said. "It made sense."

"Of course." But something about the wolf's voice sounded funny, as if there were a whole lot more to his answer than a simple agreement.

Ian scoffed quietly and returned his attention to Mason. "He's never understood why I called him Craig but everyone else got a number."

Mason heard quiet footsteps, and then the wolf spoke again, his deep voice closer than before. "Your mate isn't well, but he will heal now that he's receiving the medical attention he needs."

"The renegades are using some dangerous new bullets," Ian said. "The wolves don't heal the way they should until they're removed. He was injured pretty badly. Not sure how he survived the way he did."

"Stubborn bastard...one of his strengths." It was a weird thing to say and Mason wasn't even sure why he said it, but it was too late to take it back so he just closed his eyes and didn't bother listening for a reply.

Ian was one of the good guys. Nothing like Mason at all.

Three years ago, Ian Tucker had punched Mason in the side of the head and ended Mason's plans to take Jay up on the offer he'd made. Mason had been a renegade, not for money, but for principle, and he hadn't liked where Brendan was taking things. Mason hadn't been the only one who'd noticed how often the promise of alien technology played into their raids and how little it mattered to Brendan when the wolves ran instead of stood their ground, but Mason had been the only one who'd tried to do anything about it.

Jay's offer had been a good one, a few hundred gold ten-dollars in exchange for betraying Brendan. But Jay wouldn't have been any better, and Mason had only realized that after the wolves had taken him and held him against his will and he'd heard what happened with Brendan and the wolves Brendan had been trying to make a deal with.

Ian had stopped Mason from making a terrible mistake. Mason would never forget that, but he would never tell Ian.

But Five…he could see himself telling Five, someday. Five would understand what it meant for him to have one less regret to live with.

The noise around Mason faded until all he could hear was the slow beat of his own heart.

Somewhere out there, Five was healing, and that thought followed Mason into the deep, dark sleep that had been waiting impatiently for him to let go.

Chapter 33

AWARENESS CAME IN bits and pieces after that. A quiet hum, a low grumble, a sudden shout that roused him just enough to open his eyes for one brief moment. Hands touched him and people moved him, and the ache in his head turned into an explosion of light behind his eyes.

He heard Five's voice, once, and Mason mumbled his name, not sure why it was important for Five to know he was okay.

But he wasn't okay. He knew that, although he didn't know why.

A loud voice cut through the darkness once, followed by a roar and a clatter, and then more voices, too many to listen to, so Mason just drifted back down into the depths of wherever he was and waited for peace.

Peace didn't come—only a restless need to wake up and ask Five why he'd left—to ask how Jordan was healing—to ask why the bond he'd just started getting used to felt as thin and brittle as a piece of shale.

Once, Mason woke up to a bright room and a loud

crash and an unrecognized voice roaring, "Bring him down!"

It was the strangest thing, how he recognized the roar that followed without even looking. He tried to roll over, but something pulled at his head and he was tangled in a sheet and just the sound that came out of his own throat scared him into stopping.

Mason blinked the haze out of his vision and tried to make sense of what was going on around him but the noise and light were too much, and all he saw was a bunch of wolves and a man he didn't recognize.

The man loomed over him and blocked his view. The man had soft lines around his eyes, and a half smile that disappeared as he turned and threw out his arm to stop a wolf from staggering backward into him.

Mason felt the world under him jostle and he realized he was in a bed, in a room.

Then he heard Five's voice roar out, "He's mine!" just before another crash sounded across the room.

He tried again to push himself up, but the man moved quickly to shove Mason flat.

Another roar from Five, and then—

The man turned his head away. "That's the third time today! Find out what Trey wants done with him, but keep him out!"

A few seconds later the man's attention came back to Mason. He smiled. "That mate of yours is a pain in my ass. Sorry about this."

And then Mason's eyelids drooped and the commotion around him became nothing but white noise that faded under the sound of his own breath.

Chapter 34

HE WOKE AGAIN later and found that same man standing near him.

"Just Alan," the man said. "Don't try to call me doc, because doc's already taken. He gets a little testy about it when there's a mix up."

No last name. All Mason got in reply to that question was a laugh and a smile that creased lines into Alan's face.

At one point, Ian came by to see how he was doing, and then he went off alone with Marcus. When Marcus returned, he told Mason that Cecily and those of her followers who hadn't died or escaped were in custody and would be transferred to the States as soon as a safe transfer could be arranged.

Mason listened, but he couldn't really focus on what Marcus was saying. His head ached and his body didn't want to respond to his thoughts and he realized at one point that he was drifting toward sleep again, even as Marcus tried to explain that Jordan was already walking and Gray and Francis had been locked up.

Which made no sense at all.

"You cracked your head open on the stairs," Alan said at one point. "It was a bloody mess. You're alive because the biotech inside you kept you alive but none of us really knows how. Hey, you with me?"

Mason fell asleep before he could reply.

"You could have brain damage," Alan said sometime later. "It's important you understand that it's still a possibility, even with the gift."

The gift was alien biotechnology. At least he understood that. But of course it made sense, he realized later, when he opened his eyes to pale sunlight and a ceiling of wood beams.

He frowned.

"You're getting better," Alan said. "Even if you don't think you are."

"I definitely think I am. I feel…" He stared up at the ceiling, trying to catalogue how he felt. He flexed his toes. "I feel good."

"Now that's a change."

Mason fixed his gaze on Alan. "What do you mean?"

"Give me a minute. I'm going to get your brother."

Mason grabbed at Alan's arm as he turned away. His reflexes seemed perfectly normal. That was good, right? He was sure he'd been on the verge of dying. Or at the least he'd been very, very sick.

Alan pulled his arm free but stopped trying to leave. "I'm going to need to do some tests, but I'm starting to feel like we might be talking best case scenario here. Your brother is going to be thrilled."

Mason nodded. "Where's Five?"

Alan rubbed his chin while taking a quick look over

his shoulder toward the door. "I'm going to get Marcus for you, okay?"

Mason fumbled his way into a sitting position, and the quilt covering him tangled around his lap. He was naked beneath it. He hauled the quilt to mid-chest and frowned again. "I thought…"

"Yeah?"

"This isn't a hospital."

Alan let out a gentle huff of breath. "As good as. Just not one of ours."

Mason glanced around. He was in a room, not all that different from the one the wolves had held him in three years ago. Bed, dresser, low table, but there were other things too, like another table of medical tools and tech, a metal tray that reflected the light glowing warmly from the ceiling, a bench pushed up against a wall with a colorful pillow at one end that looked like it had been used recently.

"Marcus?"

"He's been here a time or two." But the way Alan said it, a quiet laugh underlying the words, told Mason the truth.

Marcus had been sleeping on the bench.

"If he worried Momma over this, I'm going to kick his ass."

"Don't know if he did or not, you'll have to hash that out with him. But he's been worried sick over you."

Mason rubbed his hand through his hair, only to wince when his fingers hit stubble nearer the back of his head. "Damn."

Alan gave him a wide smile. "It won't be hard to even it up."

"I liked my hair, goddammit."

"What about that brain?"

Mason slumped back on the bed.

Sometime between Alan leaving to go get Marcus and the two of them returning, Mason fell asleep again.

But that was okay, because it felt like a normal sleep, and his dreams were of Five and a smile and a flash of teeth, and when he woke up, the warmth in his chest had come back as a quiet pulse of something he couldn't explain and yet understood as if it were supposed to be a part of him.

Of course, the fact that he also had an erection he had to hide when he heard someone at the door wasn't so great, but at least it proved he was alive.

Chapter 35

THE FIRST THING Marcus did was accuse Mason of falling asleep on purpose. Turned out Mason had slept nearly three hours before Alan finally allowed Marcus back into the room.

Alan had brought clothes. Both men left to stand outside the room so Mason could have a few minutes of privacy.

While he was dressing, he took another look around. The room he'd been convalescing in was more rectangular than square, and the door was on a short wall, while the long wall was taken up by several wide windows. The morning sun shone through the windows and fell across the bed in a pattern that matched the thick metalwork covering the glass.

There was a bathroom attached, small but complete, and Mason made quick use of it. Then he propped himself up against the headboard and wiggled his toes and wondered if anyone thought he was actually well enough to try to escape.

He actually felt like he might be. But he wasn't a prisoner as far as he knew and escape wasn't on his mind. It was also unlikely the bars were meant to keep anyone in, considering their location on the inside of the glass and the hinges to one side.

He was wearing loose pants that were a little long, but not a bad fit otherwise, and a t-shirt that matched the dark gray of the pants and was made of the most comfortable fabric he'd ever worn.

He closed his eyes to relax for a minute, but it was only a few seconds later before Alan and Marcus came back in, with Alan clutching a few tools in one hand and a rolled up EP display in the other.

Over the next ten minutes, Alan explained the exact nature of Mason's head injury. He was thorough, showing Mason pictures of his fractured skull and using terms Mason had never heard before while Mason sat on the bed and took it all in.

It all came down to one thing: the wolves and their advanced medical technology had saved Mason's life.

He felt damn good for somebody who'd had a piece of bone stuck in his gray matter only a week ago.

When Alan finished that explanation, there was only one thing Mason wanted to know.

"Where's Five?" He glanced over Marcus's shoulder toward the door for the umpteenth time. "I keep expecting him to show up, but nobody's said a thing about him. Why isn't he here?"

Alan stepped back and crossed his arms, looking toward Marcus. "You can tell him."

Marcus muttered under his breath. Mason didn't quite catch what was said but he saw it in the way Marcus's mouth moved. A curse.

Mason frowned, looking toward the door again then back to Alan and Marcus. "He's not coming."

That feeling in his chest seemed to agree with him.

"Son of a bitch. He's not coming." Mason scooted to the edge of the bed and started to put his legs over the side.

Alan stepped up quickly and dropped a heavy hand onto Mason's shoulder. "You need to stay put until I do some tests this morning."

"That bastard knows he shouldn't have abandoned me in the woods with that sociopath. He didn't give me the first goddamned hint of any kind of plan. Just up and left, like I was nothing."

Alan said, "He tried—"

"The hell he did."

"You don't—"

"He knows I'm pissed off and he doesn't want to face me."

Marcus said, "He knows you're pissed off?"

"You're not listening," Alan said.

"The fuck if he even had a plan. I have no idea."

"Listen," Alan said, his calm tone slipping away under an edge of frustration. "He isn't here because he was having too much trouble controlling his instincts while I was trying to take care of you, and it wasn't safe. You needed me more than you needed him at the time. Trey ordered him to leave. And when the first alpha gives an order—"

"It's the bond thing. He knows I know how guilty he feels. Well, he ought to feel guilty. That woman turned out to be—"

"Okay, that's enough!" Alan's demand cut through Mason's rant with the sharpness of a blade. "I don't know what bond thing you're talking about but your mate wanted to be here, he tried everything to convince Trey to let him stay, but it was just too risky right now. Too many distractions, too much shit going on with a couple of the other packs, and too many humans here in the den who probably shouldn't be here. He sent him out on a mission and told him to stay the fuck away until he was called back."

Mason was sure he looked as disbelieving as he felt when he said, "The leader of the wolves actually said 'stay the fuck away'?"

"Not exactly like that, no, but—"

"Alright. I get the point." Mason rubbed between his eyebrows. "I'm sorry. I'm just pissed off right now. But I'm sorry. I should've been listening."

"Fucking unbelievable," Marcus said. "You actually know how to apologize. Wait until I tell Momma."

Mason raised his head. Then he raised his middle finger.

Marcus returned the gesture.

"For fuck's sake," Alan said. He dragged his hands through his hair and looked as if he were about to start pulling at it.

Marcus grinned. "Now you know why Momma sent us outside every morning and told us not to come home until supper."

Mason added, "And sometimes even then she sent us back out."

"We're probably the reason she had to take that treatment for thinning hair."

"What the hell, Marcus? You know how sensitive she is about that. You don't bring that shit up in front of strangers."

Marcus waved toward Alan. "He's a doctor!"

Alan looked at that moment like he'd rather be anywhere in the world other than stuck in a small room with Marcus and Mason.

Mason scrubbed his hands over his face and refused to be baited into another argument. "Okay, okay."

"So what did you mean about a bond thing?" Marcus asked.

Mason looked up again. "You know, that bond thing with the pack." He patted his chest. "That stuff you feel."

"Uhm…sure?" Marcus looked furtively toward Alan.

Alan responded with a subtle shake of his head, but Mason picked up on it anyway.

"What?" he asked.

"Nothing," Alan said.

And at the same time, Marcus said, "No idea what you're talking about. I don't know anything about a bond thing." But he looked curious, his eyes bright and his forehead furrowed.

"Never mind," Mason said.

"No, tell me," Marcus said. "I want to know."

Mason thought about how he would explain it and couldn't come up with a good place to start. He glanced at Alan, whose gaze had gone sharp on Mason.

Mason put his hand on his chest. "It's just this tight feeling I get, that's all."

"I should check your heart again," Alan said, "just in case I missed something."

Mason fought back a scowl. "I feel fine. Except for maybe a headache." He hesitated, and noticed that Alan was watching him a little too closely. "And, yeah, my shoulder is a little stiff."

Which wasn't quite true, because what was really happening was that every time he moved his right arm a little too quickly a shock of pain darted all the way from his shoulder to his fingertips. Just because the pain faded almost immediately afterward didn't mean he was eager to feel it in the first place.

"Anything else?"

"Not really."

"Good. We'll do plenty of tests over the next few days. We'll figure out what's going on."

"Could the alien technology be messing with his heart, making him think there's something else going on?"

Mason pinched his lips tight for a solid ten seconds before saying, "There's nothing wrong with my heart. This isn't my heart. It's some kind of pack bond. I can feel some of the emotions coming off those wolves of Five's—they were in my goddamned head. Trust me, I know what I felt. Five didn't act like it was any big deal, definitely not out of the ordinary."

"I'll need to talk to some people about this," Alan said. "No one's told me anything about this kind of feel-ing before."

But Mason was still watching Marcus, because Ma-son had seen that look on Marcus's face plenty of times.

"Goddammit, Marcus, you don't believe me." Mason dropped back against the headboard, covering his eyes with his left arm so he wasn't looking up at either Mar-cus or Alan.

"I believe you," Marcus said. "You say there's a bond, there's a goddamned bond. I told you I believe you."

"You're such a fucking liar."

A hard punch landed right on the bony part of Ma-son's ankle.

"Ow!" He jerked his leg out of Marcus's reach. "You fucking shitbrain."

Alan put his hand up. "Hey! Guys…"

"I'm not a liar, dipshit. It's just I've never felt anything like what you described. It's hard to take in without evidence."

"You've never ignored that feeling you get when you think I'm in trouble. This is the last thing you should need evidence for."

"That's different."

"It's not that different."

"Of course it is. We're brothers. Twins. We share the same goddamned DNA. Those experiments in the twenties—"

Mason scoffed. "They were stupid. You're the one who told me they didn't use a valid control. They didn't prove anything."

"Maybe I was wrong."

"Goddamn," Mason said. He looked over at Alan. "You sure I didn't die? Because I'm feeling a little like I might be dead now."

"You fucking idiot," Marcus said, but without any real heat. "Shut up."

"Not a chance," Mason said. "This might be as close to heaven as I ever get."

Alan wisely kept whatever thoughts were going through his head at that moment to himself.

Marcus smacked at Mason's leg again, and this time Mason was able to catch Marcus by the wrist. The pull in his back made him grunt. Maybe he wasn't ready to start roughhousing with Marcus just yet.

Marcus tried to pull free, but Mason could tell he was

holding back, as if he wasn't sure just how stubborn Mason was going to be about it.

Mason held on. "Just admit it's the same damn thing. If you can believe you get a feeling whenever I'm in trouble and that it's real, you can believe there might be some kind of bond developing between me and Five and his pack."

"I told you I believe you."

"And in the next breath you told me you need evidence!"

"It would help, that's all. But I believe you about the bond, whatever it is. If you say it's real, it's real. But you definitely need to let Alan here check out your heart. Just in case."

"It's not my fucking heart! It's Five, wallowing in a shit load of guilt over something he shouldn't have done, and he fucking knows it. Your problem is you just don't want to admit there could be some kind of psychic thing going on here that you don't understand."

"Guys," Alan tried to interrupt, "I seriously doubt there's anything psychic about—"

Marcus had that stubborn look—the same one he got when he knew he was right and no one else did. "Believing in the thing between us just isn't the same as believing in whatever this bond thing is you're talking about, that's all I'm saying. I'm not calling you a liar."

The pointed look that followed seemed to be meant as a reminder to Mason that Mason had, in fact, called Marcus a liar.

Mason let out an aggravated growl and finally released Marcus's wrist. "Now I'm feeling sorry for Five for having to put up with that shit from me. It's annoying." He eased back on the bed, paying for his sudden movements earlier with a few sharp twinges of pain, most of them in his right shoulder. "Just go back to your wolf and leave me alone."

Marcus grinned, unrepentant, and slapped the side of Mason's foot. "I'll just come back later."

"You do that. Go get some rest. I'm too pissed off right now for company." Then, glaring at his bare toes, Mason muttered, "That goddamned son of a bitch."

He didn't figure he needed to explain to anyone who he was talking about. Five should've been there. He could have explained the whole thing, and instead, Mason had been stuck trying to explain something he didn't even understand himself.

"I can't tell if you hate the guy or if this is what it looks like when you're in love."

Mason directed a flat stare at Marcus.

Marcus laughed, but it was a tired laugh. On closer look, it was easy to see the fatigue around his eyes, and for half a second, Mason was sorry that he'd spent the last ten minutes arguing with his brother, especially after everything they'd been through.

Mason waved Marcus away. "Go on. Get out of here. The doctor has those tests to run."

Marcus started for the door. When he reached it, he looked back to Mason. "So it's the second one, huh?"

"Fuck you," Mason said just as Marcus stepped through the door.

"That would be illegal," Marcus called out from the hallway just before the door closed with a solid thud.

"Goddammit." Mason looked over at a patiently waiting Alan. "He gets on my last nerve sometimes."

Chapter 36

LESS THAN AN HOUR later, Mason was side-eyeing the syringe Alan was preparing. His stomach did a little flip every time his gaze caught on the needle. It wasn't that he didn't like needles, but…this one looked long enough to go clean through his shoulder.

Mason pulled his leg in until his foot was flat on the bed so he could rest his arm across his knee. "You sure this is really necessary?"

Alan stepped up to the bed.

Mason gestured. "You just told me not ten minutes ago how my shoulder is healing remarkably well. Your exact words."

"The wolves' healing technology can work miracles, but sometimes even a miracle isn't enough to do the job right. This particular mix'll give the biotech inside you a little something extra to work with so the healing doesn't stall out. Your body only has so many resources available. With as much accelerated healing as you've had to do over the last week, you need this. Sit up."

Mason pushed himself away from the headboard.

"It won't hurt much. Just take a deep breath."

"What good will—" He cut off abruptly, hissing through his teeth.

"Just another second."

The needle slid out as easily as it had gone in.

Mason glowered at Alan and rubbed at the spot where the needle had gone into his shoulder. Alan stepped back to the small table beside the bed where the metal tray of medical tools and supplies were and started tidying up.

Despite the hour they'd spent together, Mason had learned almost nothing about Alan that he hadn't already known—that was to say, nothing.

After a moment of silence, Mason fluffed a pillow into the space behind him and leaned back again and asked, "Are you mated to one of the wolves here? You didn't say."

Alan's hand stilled over the collection of tools. "I just take care of the medical needs of the humans here. No one's tried to claim me yet, and probably won't from what I hear. Order comes straight from the first alpha."

"You lucky bastard."

Alan raised his head. "You have a mate. You're not happy with that?"

Mason suddenly wished he'd kept his mouth shut. "Forget it. It was just something to say."

Alan was watching him too closely. "If you have a problem with your mate—"

"I'm not gay."

Alan fumbled the device he was repositioning. It was square, white, and small enough to fit in his palm, and the faint clack it made against the metal tray echoed in the silent room. He picked up the device again, then looked over at Mason with an expression too neutral to be trusted.

Just to be sure Alan had heard, Mason said again, "I'm not gay."

"You're...sure?"

Mason stared hard at Alan.

"Ah, okay." Alan cleared his throat. "I've never had this situation come up before, actually."

"Never?"

Alan didn't seem to notice he'd taken to flipping the piece of tech he held end over end. "I know all the wolves here who've taken human mates but there are definite gaps in my knowledge. I've only been working with the wolves for a few years. But I know they try not to claim humans as mates. It's not as common as you might've been led to think."

"That's hard to believe, considering what happened to me—and Brendan, and Brendan's pain in the ass friends—"

"Okay, okay, I get it."

"And Marcus—"

Alan shook his head.

"And that nurse of yours—"

"Okay," Alan said, "you can stop being a smartass and listen."

"He left me out there in the woods with that woman. Do you think he was trying to tell me something, like the fact that he's changed his mind?"

Alan rested his hip against the table his tools were on and crossed his arms. The move emphasized the surprising bulk of his biceps. "He had to leave you behind. It was the only safe choice."

"Really?" Mason waited but Alan didn't explain further. "Come on."

Alan shook his head. "Not my place to decide what you're allowed to know and I don't have time to start asking around. So that's all you're getting out of me. I just wouldn't count on him leaving you in peace for long if that's what you're hoping for. You're his mate."

"What I'm hoping for? You think I want him to just walk away after what he started?" Mason threaded his fingers together over his stomach—gently so as not to jostle his shoulder. "Letting him walk away is the furthest thing from my mind right now. He doesn't get to do that. He started this shit and he's going to finish it."

"Why?"

Mason frowned at Alan.

"You're not gay," Alan said. "If you're never going to be able to love him—"

"Whoa the fuck down," Mason interrupted. "It's been three—what—four?—days. Okay, a week and a half if you count my—" He waved his hand in a vague way to encompass everything. "—whatever you'd call it."

"Recovery?"

"Sure. Recovery. I've never had a serious gay thought in my life. But that fucker did something to me that's really messed with my head."

"I see. You're talking about sex."

"I'm not talking about—well, I am, but—ah fuck." He hadn't meant to allow himself to get flustered but his face was hot and his tongue tied. He leaned his head back to rest comfortably on the headboard so he didn't have to meet Alan's gaze.

"So you two had sex and now you're confused."

"It's not—" Mason forced his voice lower. "I want

things from him I don't want from anybody else. And I don't know why the fuck that is. It doesn't make any sense. The first time I saw him—" He lifted his head and met Alan's gaze head on. "Do you believe in destiny?"

Alan straightened away from the table, clearing his throat. "Not in so many words."

"Yes or no?"

Alan shook his head.

"I don't either," Mason said. "But there's something about Five that's been different from the beginning." He let out a hard little laugh. "I have a lot to be ashamed of. I've been a coward more than once in my life and it hasn't done me any favors. I'm not leaving this place with one more regret tucked under my belt. I've got enough of those to last me a lifetime. I want to know what he started. I want to know where it's going. I feel like I'm on the verge of something I'll never get another chance at if I start running scared now."

Alan's mouth quirked up at the corner as he uncrossed his arms. "I'm not sure when you had the time, but it sounds like you've been doing a lot of thinking."

"I don't want to look back in ten, maybe twenty, years and be the same goddamned coward I was three years ago." Mason lowered his head, staring at his toes again. "He makes me think I don't have to be."

"So you are attracted to him on some level, I assume, even if not physically. How was the sex?"

Just the thought of answering that question made Mason's heart thud against his rib cage.

"You don't have to answer." Alan rubbed his hands together. "Not today anyway."

Mason gave Alan a side-eye, then just gave up and met that knowing gaze.

Alan smiled. "It's my job. Sorry. There will be an exam." His accompanying laugh was gentle but it was clear he wasn't joking.

"Goddammit."

"You don't get mated without sex. At least not as far as I know. So it's not like this is news to me or anyone else."

"That doesn't mean I'm willing to talk about it."

Alan folded his hand together and tapped his chin thoughtfully. "I'm not sure how I can help you, but... Have you ever gotten aroused thinking about a man in a sexual way?"

"I didn't tell you any of this so you could help me." Mason's voice came out uncomfortably high. He cleared his throat.

"I like helping people," Alan said. "So have you?"

"I do my best not to think about men in a sexual way," Mason said. "It hasn't been that hard."

He didn't realize how that was going to sound until after he said it, and he felt a slow flush crawl into his face.

But Alan didn't give him shit over it, not like Marcus would have. "So what do you think of Five? Most people can appreciate how attractive the wolves are as a species."

"They're alright," Mason said as he adjusted his position to something more comfortable for his back.

Funny how easy that made it to avoid meeting Alan's gaze.

Alan didn't say anything, so Mason looked up. Alan had a piercing gaze leveled right at Mason.

"Alright, goddammit. I can see the appeal, but I've never thought 'Hey, he sure looks good. Wish I could fuck him.'"

He *hadn't*. Only now, with that thought at the forefront of his mind, he knew it could happen.

Alan tutted. "They really don't like it when you call mating fucking."

"They call mating fucking all the time."

Alan's eyebrows rose.

"They do," Mason said.

Alan didn't argue, just moved to pull a chair up to the bed. He sat, leaned forward, and clasped his hands in front of him. "So tell me about your first gay experience."

"We're not having this conversation."

Alan leaned in, the lines in his face firming up. "In a lot of ways the wolves think they understand us—but they don't. I think it's worse than we realize. The same can be said about us, I don't doubt that one bit. But they think these mating rituals and instincts they have are perfectly natural—and they might be, for them. But there are things they do and think that we just don't and it makes for some complicated consent issues that, frankly, are over my head. I'm not a psychologist—I just treat injuries the best way I know how. I wasn't even finished with my education when—well, you can guess that."

"Can't say I'm surprised. The only real doctors I know of are a lot older than you."

Alan smiled, deepening the creases around his eyes. "I'm probably older than you think I am, but yeah, I was in my last year when the first heat came."

Mason nodded, but didn't prod.

Alan's smile dropped away again. "Are you okay with what happened?"

"And if I'm not, what? What are you going to do about it, really?"

The calm concern in Alan's eyes was enough to twist Mason's stomach.

Mason made a sound of disgust and lowered his gaze. He started picking at the fabric over his knee. "I don't want to talk about this."

"I don't want to let you out of here if you're going to have to go back into a situation where you feel like you're being—"

"Don't say it!" Mason dragged his hands down his face, the words he hadn't been able to stop Alan from saying ringing in his ears.

"Look—" He lowered his hands. "At first I wasn't comfortable. I'm not going to pretend I was. It's a fucking mess, what this heat has done to us—and what it's done to them—"

It felt significant that he had to say that, but he couldn't ignore the truth the way he had in the past, couldn't keep blaming Five and the rest of them for something that had always been out of everyone's control.

Everyone.

He sighed, hard. "It was a fucking joke. On me. I thought I would hate it. I didn't. He was…different. It was different." He gave Alan a hard look meant to fend off any sudden questions. "I'm still not gay. But if there's anybody in this world that has a chance of making me want to be, it's probably Five."

"So you're okay?"

"I'm okay."

"If things were rough, I'm going to need to check you out. Anal sex is—"

"Whoa!" Mason couldn't keep the outrage out of his voice. "I'm not talking about anal sex with you. Forget it. Besides, I've got that healing shit inside me."

Alan didn't say a word. Marcus would have. Mason was just glad he'd wasn't there.

"That wasn't supposed to be funny," Mason said, his face hot with embarrassment.

"It was pretty damn funny." But Alan's expression hadn't changed at all.

"Is patient confidentiality still a thing?"

"Of course. It was what I was taught and I mean to do things the way they're supposed to be done."

"Good. Marcus can't ever find out I said that."

Alan smiled. Then he sat back, clapping his hands against his thighs. "I just need to know you're okay. I'm your doctor."

"I'm fine."

"If you're sure…" Alan gave him an inquiring look.

"I said I'm fine."

Alan looked over at a screen on the wall just to the left of Mason's bed. "You don't sound fine. And your blood pressure's a little high. Your heart rate's up. Nothing big, but it could mean something. Maybe I should run a few more tests…"

"Alright, fine. You want the truth? I'm not okay. That goddamned shitbrain ran off just when I was about to tell him—" Memories surged to the fore. Mason tried to shut them down, but it wasn't easy.

He clenched his hand into a fist over his knee and just sat there for a moment, feeling again that emptiness he'd first experienced when he'd come back from his trip into the woods to find Five and the others gone.

Alan eyed him with concern, his gaze flickering between Mason and that screen that was obviously telling him things about Mason's physical state. "Go on."

"These are things I need to talk to him about, not you. Sorry. This just isn't any of your business." Mason pushed his hands down into the mattress and moved to the side of the bed, swinging his legs over. "How do I get in touch with him?"

Alan started to answer, only to make an odd face and reach into his front pocket. "I'm sorry. I need to check this. It's set to emergency contact only."

He pulled out a phone and took a look at the screen. A fiercely satisfied expression came over his face. He looked up. "Can you give me a second?"

"Sure."

Alan got up from the chair and moved to the other side of the room, pulling up what looked like a holographic display from the small phone.

Mason quirked one eyebrow, a little surprised to see that kind of tech on what had looked like one of the standard cheap phones that still worked with the sats. Then he heard Alan say "Devon won't" and suddenly he knew why.

Devon Fletcher was an old friend of Brendan's and he was one of the men who'd had a wolf take him for a mate three years ago in the midst of the shitstorm Brendan had created. Fletcher knew tech, and with access to the wolves' technologies, there was no doubt he could probably do some amazing things given half the chance.

From Mason's position, he couldn't see whatever it was Alan was watching, but he heard Alan say, "Excellent…that's what I thought was going on…yeah, it's a good sign…don't let him push too hard…okay, I'll be over soon, but I have some work to finish up first…"

The next pause lasted long enough to feel out of place.

Then Alan said, "Just send Ethan. He'll know what to do. He's a smart kid."

Another pause, this one even longer.

"Listen, I know. Don't—" He glanced over his shoulder at Mason. "I'm not in a position to go into this right now, okay? We'll talk about it later."

The call ended and Alan pocketed his phone and turned to Mason.

Mason pushed off the side of the bed and stood.

Alan's gaze lingered on the tray of medical supplies, his brow furrowing.

"Problem?" Mason asked, squeezing his toes against the cool oak boards of the floor.

"You could say that. I forgot to make you aware of one of the potential side-effects of the drug I put in your shoulder. I should've told you. I'm sorry."

"Yeah?"

"If you'd known, you might have tried harder not to talk." Alan grimaced. "It's one of the drugs the wolves created for us. Some of them make it more difficult for humans to control impulsive behaviors."

No wonder Alan had been so easy to talk to.

"Forget it," Mason said. "I feel fine. You were going to tell me how to get in touch with Five."

"The effect of the drug'll last for several hours. Now might not be the best time to—"

"There's something I need to get off my chest with that bastard and I might as well do it while I've got a little chemical help. Tell me how to contact him."

"It's a potential side-effect. It's not a given—Ah. Okay."

Mason had thought that glare might do the trick.

Chapter 37

THREE HOURS LATER, and Mason was sitting at the dining table in a small house, drumming his thumbs against the dark wood top. He'd been moved, without a clue where he was going, into what he assumed was somebody's home.

The dining table was in a central location in the house and pillows were piled high in the rooms flanking it, and no matter which direction he looked, there were either large windows or wide open doorways that made him feel as if the whole world could look inside and watch him doing whatever it was he was supposed to be doing.

The wolves appeared to like their open spaces, but Mason had a feeling Five might not be so comfortable here. This little house, cozy as it was, had no reminders of the lives the wolves must have lived on their ships.

He'd been sitting there for nearly an hour, waiting. The sound of his thumbs against the table's top was a dull thud in the silent space. His heart was pounding louder than that in his ears, and his right knee hadn't stopped jittering for more than a few minutes.

His attempt to contact Five hadn't gone as he'd hoped and he couldn't stop thinking about what he'd seen during the attempt and speculating over what it might mean.

Six had answered the communication, and the image quality had been so crisp and clear that Mason had felt like he could reach through the screen and touch him. But that was after Alan had brought in Ian and a wolf, who'd led Mason to a building where he'd been allowed to use a communication station of obvious alien design.

Ian had placed the call, and there Six had appeared, right in front of Mason, in a nearly three-dimensional image that jumped right out from the screen. The weirdest part had been the fact that he was almost certain the smell in the room had changed. Just a subtle difference, but noticeable, because the musky scent had made him think of sex.

The smell had distracted him for several seconds as his brain made the connection with the view.

A wall and a door showed behind Six, and Mason recognized the doorframe as a match for the one in Five's bedroom in the house Mason had left just over a week ago to set off on a mission with Five and the others.

Seeing that door had tightened Mason's stomach and then chest.

"I want to talk to Five."

Six had said, "I'll let Alpha know you're well. He'll want to see you."

The communication had ended before Mason could actually ask any questions.

He really regretted his tone with Six, but it was far too late for that now.

Immediately after the call, Ian and the wolf had accompanied Mason to where he was now. The wolf had stayed outside, but Ian had come in to wait for a message.

Mason had taken a seat. Ian hadn't.

"I need to stretch my legs," Ian had said after Mason gave him a look. "It's heat season."

As if that explained everything.

Mason thought it might.

The silence stretched too long, and Mason finally broke it by asking, "Did you smell that—in that room?"

"It's the technology."

"So it was real? I wasn't imagining it?"

Ian shrugged. "Probably not. Smell is like body language to them. They build it into their communications wherever they can. It's pretty fascinating, to be honest. You have to be within the zone to pick it up and it can be really subtle, sometimes we can't smell it even knowing it's there."

Ian went into more detail, but Mason hadn't cared. He'd stared at his hands clenched on the table in front of him and listened with only half an ear, his thoughts tied up by other things.

Then the message Ian had been waiting on came, and Mason forced himself to pay closer attention.

"Five's on his way," Ian said, already tucking his phone away. "Make yourself at home. It'll be another hour, but Matthew's planning to come by, as long as he can get permission and an escort."

"Permission?" Mason asked.

"Rules," Ian said, managing to look like he was smiling with his eyes. "There are lots of rules right now that we follow, so no one gets hurt. Just stay inside and you shouldn't get into trouble."

Mason nodded, and Ian left after that, neither one of them having said a word about the past.

Matthew showed up not more than fifteen minutes later.

Mason got up and hugged his cousin, slapping him hard on the back, before letting out a grunt and wince when Matthew did the same to Mason and clipped his shoulder.

"Sorry!" Matthew said, pulling away and giving Mason a wide-eyed look. But Mason waved his apology off and sat, and Matthew sat too. They talked for a while, Mason telling Matthew how Gillie and Brecken and his mom had been doing lately, Matthew asking lots of questions about a few of the stories Marcus had been filling his head with for the last week while Mason was sleeping off his injuries.

"He's been lying his head off," Mason said. "His hands were shaking like a leaf when he tried to get that bullet out. I'd have been better off doing it myself."

Matthew laughed, then rubbed his hand down his mouth. "He said you were the only reason he got out alive."

"That's bullshit. He didn't need me for anything back there. Moral support maybe. He's a goddamned miracle worker."

"You're not moral support, asshole. You two—"

"Are better than one. I know." Mason rubbed his finger against the smooth wood of the table. "He doesn't need me. He probably never did. And now…"

"He's got Hawk."

Mason wasn't able to hold back a hard laugh. "Hawk?"

The corner of Matthew's mouth quirked up. "Ash says it's a strong name. More than one wolf tried to lay claim to it."

"Hawk. I'm going to rub that in Marcus's face every time I see him. What a name."

Matthew laughed again. "I wouldn't be an asshole about it. You're mated to a wolf who calls himself Five and has a pack full of wolves who decided to follow the leader."

Mason was quiet for a second. "Fuck."

It was nice to sit with family and not have anything to argue about. And Five had been right. Matthew was alive and he was safe. He was, in fact, in great health and he smiled and laughed more than Mason had seen him do in years.

Of course, Matthew wasn't the only one who hadn't been happy for a long time. None of them had been. Matthew had lost his mother to the first heat season, the same as Mason and Marcus had lost their father in the year after. Joining the renegades had seemed like the only way to honor their deaths—and stop the aliens responsible from doing it again. And he'd let Brendan drag Matthew into it, at nineteen years old.

He'd been such a goddamned fool.

But Matthew was doing okay. He was happy. And somehow, between the last time Mason had seen him and that moment, Matthew had found himself a mate—a wolf named Ash.

Mason hadn't fucked up Matthew's life, despite everything, and at that realization, something inside him loosened just a little.

But none of that had stopped Mason's thoughts from wandering back to that door. He'd been almost grateful when Matthew had told him it was time for him to go. He'd left, and Mason had gone back to staring at his hands against the dark wood of the table and thinking about that fucking door.

What did it mean? Why was Six answering communications in Five's bedroom? Why had his forehead and cheeks looked flushed and his hair damp at the temples? Why had his teeth flashed in just that way when Mason had stared too long, suspicion probably written in every line of his face?

Why had Six answered Mason's gruff request to speak to Five so abruptly and then shut off communications?

Mason realized he was digging his thumbnails into the table and stopped. Unfortunately not before he'd left two ugly little marks behind. He stared at those marks. They were the only things that marred the dark wood.

"Goddammit," he muttered.

He'd just put his hand over the marks in an effort to hide from his own guilt when the door behind him opened, making him jump.

He turned, then rose, his movement pushing the chair across the hardwood with a loud screak.

Five stood in front of the door he'd already closed, watching Mason. He took in a deep, slow breath. He exhaled just as slowly, while his eyes burned with an incandescent heat. "I've missed your scent."

"Why did you leave me there alone?"

As soon as the words left his mouth, Mason regretted them. Of all the questions he could have asked—of all the answers he damn well deserved—that one was the one that gave the most away.

He could have asked about Five's pack. There was still so much he didn't know about the final confrontation with Cecily and her people. He still didn't know if he'd been hearing things when he heard that Gray and Francis had been locked up. He didn't know if Lake and Rain and Cord were okay.

He thought they were—he felt something shimmer inside every time he thought of them, even though he couldn't understand the feeling.

He could have demanded to know if Five had been fucking Six—or anyone else—while he waited for Mason to recover. Even thinking about it made him feel a little spark of jealousy he had no right to feel.

Five's eyes flickered. He pushed away from the door and walked toward Mason, his every step a reminder of the alpha predator he was.

"My former alpha needed my assistance. I couldn't resist his call. But the situation was unknown and dangerous and I could not take you with me."

"So you just left me there—thinking—" Mason exhaled roughly, dragging his hand through his hair. He'd done it enough times already to know his hair was probably sticking up in all the wrong ways, but he couldn't stop the need to be doing something—anything—to dispel the frustration that wanted to eat its way out of him.

Five said, "I tried to communicate my intention to come back to you."

Mason didn't mean to laugh but the strangled sound came out before he could stop it. "Communication not one of your strengths, is it?"

Five's hot gaze continued to bore into him. "Apparently not."

Guilt pulsed in the air between them. It was the

weirdest sensation Mason had ever felt. He shuffled one foot and let his gaze drop to the floor.

Five wasn't wearing shoes. Mason hadn't even noticed it earlier, but he couldn't take his eyes off the dark material of Five's alien toenails and the long toes curled against the hardwood. Strange how similar to human toes they were in some respects. A light dusting of hair, sharply defined bones at the joints. Mason wanted to touch them, and he didn't understand why. He wanted to trace the bones and feel the smooth skin and fine hair under his palm.

He cleared his throat and made himself look up—to meet Five's fierce gaze.

"That was the worst possible moment for you to do something that goddamned—" *Stupid*, he wanted to say, but that wasn't the right word. He couldn't find the right one.

He rubbed his mouth and looked through his lashes at Five. "You still don't trust me. I get it. You shouldn't, I told you that myself, but—"

Mason stopped speaking as Five grasped the back of Mason's neck, his hold firm but gentle.

"I would have never mated you if I hadn't realized already I could trust you, Mason Waters."

Mated. That strange inflection was back. He knew Five wasn't talking about fucking or mates in the way of something casual and impermanent.

"You mated me," he said. "In the woods—that's what was different."

Five's gaze burned even hotter than before. "Yes."

"You made me your mate for life without me having a clue that that's what was going on."

"You chose the time and place of our mating. You knew the moment had come."

"I did what?"

"You expressed your regret for your past actions and sought forgiveness through submission. You were ready to mate."

"That's—" *Pretty damn close to the truth.* Mason felt his shoulders slump as he thought back to those moments and couldn't come up with anything to negate Five's claim.

"Hell," he muttered.

He stared at Five's lips and then couldn't seem to tear his gaze away. Had Six been kissing them? Had the others done the same? How many of his wolves had Five fucked? Did Mason care?

He thought he did. That was the scariest thing he'd learned since his call with Six.

He cared too goddamned much what Five might have been doing.

Chapter 38

FIVE LEANED IN, dragging his nose up the side of Mason's neck. "Your scent sets fire to my senses even now. I've spent too much time imagining you beneath me again to have the control I need around you."

The prick of claws tickled Mason's skin and made him shiver; the drawl of Five's voice tightened his groin.

"You're my mate, and I've missed you and worried for you. I've also longed for you and needed you, and now we're together again. It's hard to think of anything other than you and your intoxicating scent."

Mason found it difficult to take his next breath. He wasn't sure exactly what the emotion was that made his stomach flip or his body suddenly come alive, but it felt a whole hell of a lot like sexual interest.

But no, there was no point denying it. It was sexual interest. His body remembered how Five could make it feel. He remembered.

He wanted to feel that way again. And again.

And again.

No end in sight.

If it wasn't about sex before, it sure the hell is now.

That goddamned voice in his head was back, and more smug than ever.

You're so fucking gone for this wolf you'd lick his ass if he wanted you too, wouldn't you?

There was no point fighting the truth. Whatever had happened to him, whether it was all in his head or if some physical change had come over him to go along with the bond he'd felt forming between him and Five and Five's pack, Mason knew only one thing: it wasn't something he would undo.

Move forward, his father had always told him and Marcus. *You can't undo the past and you can't hold back the future. So you just keep moving forward, because the only thing you have any control over is the present. Make the most of it, boys.*

Destiny, fate, whatever anyone called it, those weren't things Mason believed in. He believed in coincidence and the random nature of the universe. And yet...he could remember the row of fives on the side of his dad's last drone. His own goddamned private number for his phone contained five fives. He'd picked the number himself at thirteen and somehow managed to hang on to it in all the turbulent years since. He'd been born at five fifty-five a.m. and he knew that because he'd wanted to know who came first, him or Marcus? Turned out he'd come into the world four minutes too damn late to be firstborn.

It was coincidence, and Mason knew it, but he couldn't escape how it made him feel.

Like he was looking at the future and his next thought could determine the fate of his world.

It seemed fitting that the only thing he could think about was how Five's mouth would feel against his.

"I want to kiss you," Mason said. He wanted to wipe away the memories Five might have made with someone else.

Five raised his head, his hands clamped hard around Mason's upper arms. Mason felt the faintest twinge of pain in his shoulder but it wasn't even enough to pull a wince out of him.

Five noticed. He released Mason and stepped back.

Mason watched him, then rubbed his hand over his face, trying to bring sense back into his brain. "So that's not happening, then."

"You don't have to shield me from your true feelings. I deserve your anger and your disappointment."

"Shield you from my—what the hell are you talking about?"

The guilt was back, a wash of it so strong goose bumps rose on Mason's arms.

"I've made choices that put you in danger. I'm your alpha and your mate and I'm responsible for the injuries that almost killed you. You're human, and fragile, and you needed my protection, and I have a deep regret for assuming you would be safer without me than with me. I was wrong. I can't accept your submission as your alpha and mate until I ask for and earn your forgiveness for my lack of care. You deserve no less."

"All I wanted was a kiss."

"You deserve to know why I made the choice I made."

"Yeah, I do, but—"

"If I had told you we needed to leave, you might have argued with me. You might have wanted to come with us. With our mating so fresh in my mind, I knew my own weakness. I would not have been able to leave you behind. If I had told you to stay behind and wait for me, would you have trusted me to return—or would you have tried to follow me?"

Mason breathed softly through his nose. He didn't have to answer; Five knew.

The reflections in Five's eyes seemed to darken. "My assumption was that I would return quickly. But my mission was complicated by the discovery of a human trying to leave the area. His scent was unusually strong. Gray and Francis fought. Rain gave chase. I had to intervene. Jordan became lost in his heat cycle and was drawn away by a scent I realized too late belonged to the humans with the rogue wolves. By the time we were able to transmit my former alpha's communications and return for you and the female…"

Five sighed, a quiet, gentle sound of resignation. "I had faith that you were strong and resilient and could hold your own with your own people if the female was more than she appeared—I did not account for the rogues returning to the area. It's a mistake I've spent every moment since regretting."

At some point, Mason had started rubbing his left thumb and fingers together, over and over. He stopped the motion. His face was warm, mostly because he'd always found it hard to accept compliments, and those words Five had said—they had sounded a hell of a lot like compliments to him.

He cleared the tightness from his throat. "Sounds like all hell broke loose."

"It was a difficult journey, made more so by several unexpected complications."

"Can't say I wouldn't have done the same in your situation. I don't know. But…I'm not a fucking kid. I know shit happens. We make choices we shouldn't sometimes. I thought that was pretty clear after everything that's happened to put us here. You should have told me you were leaving and risked a goddamned argument. But you did what you did—and it's done. There's nothing to forgive. I wanted to understand. Now I do."

He tried a smile. His face felt stiff and uncomfortable but he wanted Five to know he wasn't holding a grudge.

Five's expression didn't soften at all. "I submit to your judgment, Mason Waters. Allow me to earn forgiveness."

Mason dropped the smile. "I told you there's nothing to forgive. You did what you thought you had to do."

"I hurt you. I almost killed you. If your kin hadn't saved your life, your death would have been my burden to carry for the rest of my—"

"Alright," Mason interrupted in as hard a tone as he'd ever used with Five. "Listen here, you arrogant bastard, I'm responsible for my own actions. You weren't there and you don't get to take credit for any of that shit. Alan made it clear my head injury was caused by multiple hits to the back of the head, not one, and you didn't slam me into that goddamn railing on the stairs, that fucker that wanted to rape and kill me did. As for the second hit, all I remember is you throwing yourself in front of me. You stopped him from getting hold of me and tearing me open with his claws."

Five's lips pressed together in an obstinate look.

Mason plowed on. "Here's a lesson for you. Consider it an opportunity to earn some extra credit. If somebody tries to tell me what to do, and I do it, that's my own damn problem. There is no alpha who gets the blame—

or the goddamn credit. Not in the world I grew up in. I get the reward—or the goddamn punishment. That's the way it's supposed to be. When it isn't like that, that's when you know something's wrong and it's time to get out, however the hell you can. The fact that you don't see things that way—that you blame yourself for me getting hurt—because I chose to stick my nose into the middle of your goddamn fight—that's one place we'll probably never see eye-to-eye. I don't need to forgive you. My injuries weren't your goddamn fault."

A heavy silence followed.

Then—

"Irrelevant. I am your alpha and your mate. I was responsible for your care and I failed you. This weakness you have for claiming responsibility for the actions of others is something I'll have to help you learn to overcome."

"You goddamned—" Words failed him. "—*ugghhh*!"

Blue eyes stared back at him, unreadable. "Your kin told me you have a guilt complex. I didn't understand his meaning then, but I understand now. Unlike him, I won't allow you to wallow in guilt and regret that does not belong to you."

"You're still the same goddamned arrogant bastard you were a week ago!"

Five flashed a smile at Mason, showing enough of those sharp eyeteeth to make Mason's heart lurch heavily inside his chest. "You will adapt. You enjoy submission, and I enjoy giving you pleasure. We're already starting to see eye-to-eye on a great many things, and you will eventually see eye-to-eye with me on this. Now that we're mated, our lives will continue to intertwine, and our fates to converge, and we will receive our reward for accepting the universe's great gift. We are *mated*."

The words—spoken in the wolves' language—set off a deep sense of satisfaction inside Mason, one that rolled over him like a wave. Warmth spread through him with a tingling pleasure. His eyes fixed on Five's fiercely satisfied expression and breathing became a chore as the pressure inside his chest increased. He knew on some level the feeling came from Five and that the pressure wasn't *real*. But it didn't matter in that moment. The feeling consumed him—and it was truth.

They were mated and they were mates and they would be mates.

The fact that the only experience Mason had loving another man was as a brother or a friend was irrelevant.

He could love Five. He knew it in that moment. Someday, he *would* love Five. Only time stood between where he was and where he would end up.

Five ran his hand over Mason's shoulder and down his arm.

A shiver built under Mason's skin.

"I don't know what you expect from me," Mason said, then added, "as a mate."

"Companionship. Affection. Loyalty. Truth."

"And submission?"

"Only after I have redeemed myself to you and shown you I can be the kind of mate you deserve. Only then do I deserve your submission."

"I forgive you."

Five's eyes narrowed and his hand stilled at Mason's elbow. "You forgive too easily."

Mason gave Five a sharp smile, this one feeling entirely at home on his face. It had been a long shot that

Five would accept so easy an out, but it had been worth a try. He had another idea, one that might satisfy Five's requirement for forgiveness and give Mason a small taste of revenge for a wrong Five probably didn't even remember.

Because whatever Five thought, Mason might forgive easily, but he didn't forget nearly so fast.

"I don't want you to protect me if it means leaving me in the dark like that again," Mason said. "Can we at least agree on that?"

Five's mouth pulled back at one corner, showing a flash of pointed eyetooth. He sounded almost pained as he said, "I can agree to consider every other option first, should the need arise."

"Is that the best you can do?"

A short, soft growl came out of Five's throat, only to end as abruptly as it had started. His eyes glittered more fiercely than ever. "It's my responsibility to offer protection to my betas—and to my mate. I won't ignore that instinct. Although I will try to be more aware of your strengths and act accordingly."

"My strengths."

"You're an intelligent human. You're loyal—to your kin and to your pack. You have an ability to communicate with us on a deeper level than most of your kind because of the gift, but the gift alone isn't enough to account for that. You seek to help others, even when offering that help isn't in your own best interests. You are capable of change—and that is a strength more important than any other."

Warmth flooded Mason's face but he bit back the urge to brush off Five's praise.

He glanced around. "Ian told me to make myself at home. This place looks fully furnished." He turned his gaze toward the stairs. "I bet there's a bed up there somewhere."

He heard Five's indrawn breath and looked over to him just in time to see a spark of heat darken his blue eyes.

Mason jerked his chin in the direction of the door Five had entered earlier. "How about you go find some rope? I bet I can get this urge you have to earn forgiveness out of your system before the goddamn sun sets."

This time Five's soft growl raised every hair on Mason's body.

Mason smiled. "Don't like that idea much, do you?"

"Your brash challenge does intrigue me. But I do not think you would enjoy the things I particularly want to do to you at this moment."

"I've said it before and I guess I'll have to say it again, you really don't know me at all."

Mason's grin was just as sharp as Five's sudden flash of teeth.

Chapter 39

THERE WERE NO ropes. Mason found himself uncere-
moniously upended and carried over Five's shoulder up
the stairs.

Five carried him into a sunlit room with too many
windows fast enough to make Mason's head spin. But
once inside, he set Mason on his feet much more gently
than Mason expected.

Almost as if he knew what Mason was thinking, he
straightened and said, "You've been healing well. I
wouldn't want to hurt you by being careless with you."

Mason glanced over his shoulder to see a square bed
large enough for several people resting in the center of
the room. Afternoon sun streaked across a quilt made of
shimmering fabrics and a pile of fluffy pillows in colors
as vibrant as the wolves' alien eyes.

"Whoa. That's an interesting bed."

"Your beds are too small. We adapted a design of our
own."

"A prince could sleep on that bed and not feel out of
place."

"Prince? Yes, this house is meant for an alpha."

"Right," Mason drawled out, then, "Wait. So alpha means prince?"

"It can. It doesn't always."

An awkward silence followed.

Mason glanced toward the door, rubbing his palms against his thighs. "Are we waiting on something?"

"I'm waiting on you, Mason Waters."

Mason caught Five's gaze. "I talk big. I don't do so well when I have to follow through."

Five stepped closer. He reached out and touched Mason's cheek with one hand and took Mason's hand in his other and raised it to his chest. "You don't have any reason to be afraid. I came prepared to submit. My heat cycle will not come."

Mason's fingers curled against Five's warmth as something ugly and painful twisted inside him. He'd always been so goddamned replaceable; he didn't want to be replaceable any more. "Are the drugs really that good now, or…are you trying to tell me you fucked it out with your pack?"

Mason had tried not to sound hurt and jealous, but he was so fucking sure he hadn't succeeded that he couldn't even swallow.

Five's gaze flickered.

The air hung heavy in Mason's lungs, the world full of confusion and uncertainty as Five studied him.

Finally, Five asked, "Why do you doubt me?"

Mason had to clear his throat to answer. "I don't doubt you. I just don't understand your ways. There's a difference. Maybe fucking other people when you can't have the one you want is the way you guys do things. How am I supposed to know if I don't ask?"

Five's implacable stare wavered. He stepped back. Then, in one abrupt movement, he shucked his shirt.

Mason watched warily.

Five flicked the small button holding his trousers closed and the fly fell open. He pushed the trousers down his legs and stepped out of them, then tossed them aside.

He was wearing undershorts, but nothing like the boxers Mason wore. The fabric covered the lower part of Five's abdomen, cradled his cock and balls, and continued to mid-thigh.

Five removed the undershorts.

His cock and balls were bound tightly to his body with a few strips of some flexible material that slipped between his thighs and around his hips.

"What the fuck is that?"

"It is a——" Five said something in the wolves' language that Mason didn't recognize. "There is no translation."

Five touched the material looped snugly around his soft cock. "It's a medical device."

Mason couldn't stop staring at the way the strips of material seemed to be cutting off Five's circulation. He could see the pinch of skin that made it clear something under the material below Five's cock was piercing his body. "What's it for?"

"It's the only way to keep my body from healing."

"Healing from what?"

"It's our way of dealing with the heat when we have a mate who can't mate but no wish to claim another."

"What did you do?"

"My reproductive organs have been—how would a human say it?—neutered."

"Goddammit, Five! Why would you—why in the fucking hell would you do something like that?"

"I can still give you pleasure—"

"Please, God above, tell me this is temporary."

Five's mouth tightened and Mason felt a twinge of shame for interrupting like a total asshole.

"It is temporary," Five said. "I won't be able to fuck you unless I remove the device, but if I remove the device—"

"Remove it."

"If I remove the device, I'll go into my next heat cycle almost immediately. I won't have any control over my instincts. You already tempt me as I am. Every faint trace of your scent calls to me, reminding me that you are mine and we are mated. Without this device, I will not submit." His look became pointed. "You will."

"I don't care. Take it out. I never would have asked you to do something like this. It's fucking barbaric."

A sudden rumbling came from deep in Five's chest, and Mason snapped his mouth closed before he could say more.

"And yet you would have been disappointed if I had, in fact, 'fucked it out' with my pack."

Defiantly, Mason said, "You're the one who thought I'd make a good mate."

"I accept your apology."

"I didn't apologize, goddammit."

"You were going to before your emotions distracted you."

"Fuck you."

"And that's why I didn't remove the device before I came to you. I'm prepared to submit. Let me prove to you how strong I am."

"Get that fucking thing off, now."

"Submission takes strength. You'll see how—"

"Goddammit." Mason reached for the strip in the crease of Five's left thigh.

Five caught Mason by the wrist. "Do not."

"I swear to God, Five, I'm going to kick your ass if you don't get this thing off."

"This is that big talk you mentioned earlier, correct?"

"Goddamn you."

"Goddamn you," Five said.

Mason stopped trying to get at the device and just stared at Five.

Five flashed his teeth in a predatory smile. "If I'm to be damned for a lack of submission to your wishes, it's only fair you be damned with me since you refuse to submit to the wishes of your alpha and mate."

It shouldn't have been funny. Mason let out a choked laugh, then covered the bottom half of his face and laughed until his ribs ached.

Five watched him curiously but didn't move.

Mason plopped down on the edge of the bed, and when he could breathe without gasping, he put his hands on his knees, elbows out. He looked up at Five, wonder in his voice. "I swear to God, Five, I can't decide if I'm doomed or if you're the best thing that ever happened to me."

"I can't promise it will always be easy for you to reconcile our ways to yours, but I can promise to do my best to make it worth the effort."

Maybe honesty would work where nothing else had.

"Come here."

Five stepped forward and Mason spread his legs, letting Five step between them. He put his hands on Five's hips, feeling the masculine grace there and the hard lines that made Five different from anyone else Mason had ever held in that way. He let his hands linger, then drew his palms down until his fingers were so, so close to the crease of Five's ass.

His mouth was only inches away from the taut muscle of Five's abdomen. He leaned in and kissed the smooth skin there. He could feel the brush of dark hair against his lips, fine and soft, and the smell of sweat and warm skin filled his lungs.

Five's body vibrated under Mason's hands but Five somehow managed to stand as still as a statue.

"Five…" Mason drew the name out, let it hang in the air for a long moment. "I don't know what to do with you. You have a hell of a body. You're attractive. But I'm just…I'm learning. I need more time before I'm put in charge of making you feel good—and sex isn't any good when you're not trying to make somebody feel good."

"Your touch makes me feel good. I need nothing more."

"Yeah, you do. But I don't know anything about gay sex except what you've taught me so far." Mason moistened his lips and leaned in for another low kiss, this one closer to the top of Five's pubic hair. He heard Five suck in his breath at the same time that he felt the clenching of muscle under his lips.

"You—are accomplished. You do not need to be taught."

The catch in Five's voice was gratifying, to say the least, but Mason wasn't sure what he should do next.

"Do you—can I—" Mason moved toward Five's cock, then stopped, looking up through his lashes.

"I won't harden. But I would enjoy the feeling of your mouth on my cock."

"What about the thing?"

"Kiss me. Do not worry about the device."

Maybe it was all Mason was ready for anyway, so he just leaned in and let his lips trace across the exposed flesh of Five's dick.

It was weird.

Really weird.

But Five's skin was clean and tasted of warmth and musk and after about three seconds of weirdness, Mason had no doubt that he could have fun playing with Five's cock in the future.

He would taste it first, then draw it deep into his mouth the way he liked it, and then he would—

Five's hand landed in his hair, tugging a little sharply.

Mason pulled back, a line of spit drawing out between them before breaking and dripping down his chin. He swiped it away.

Five spoke breathlessly, "I hadn't realized I would become so sensitive with the device inserted."

"I'm sorry."

"You were correct. I should remove the device."

Mason eyed Five's bright eyes and flushed cheeks suspiciously. "I don't think so. I've changed my mind. Lay down on the bed."

Five's hands were already moving toward the strips of material. "After I—"

Mason grabbed both Five's wrists.

The soft growl he got in response was more exciting than he expected. His dick started getting hard.

"You wanted to submit," Mason said. "This was your idea. Now submit."

When Mason started pulling Five toward the bed with his wrists, Five resisted only momentarily. Mason had to release Five so he could climb onto the bed, and he watched Five's back and ass as he crawled his way to the center before letting out a growl and raking his hand through the pile of pillows.

Pillows went flying off the side of the bed.

Five turned and flopped onto the mattress.

Mason didn't even try to hold back his grin. "Got a weakness there I see needs worked on."

Five's eyes narrowed on Mason and the sharp points of his eyeteeth appeared. "When the device is removed, we will see who is alpha here."

Mason scoffed, but wasted no time yanking off his shirt and unfastening his jeans before he climbed onto the bed with Five. "I have no idea if the shit I like is universal for all men or if it's just me, so you're going to have to tell me if I fuck this up."

Five spread his arms on the bed. Heavy veins cut across his biceps and down his forearms. Dark hair grew at his underarms and across his muscled chest and tapered down to a thin line before reaching his groin.

Five's belly trembled when Mason flattened his hand there, and a deep rumble started in Five's chest.

Mason felt his way across the peaks of Five's dark nipples and fluffed the hair under his palm.

"You sure as hell have plenty of muscle," Mason said. He leaned down on his arm and dropped a kiss on Five's collar.

Five sucked in his breath.

"For somebody who can't get it up, you sure do act like you're getting wound up."

"My body would discover…a way around the damage to my…ahhhh…"

Five breathed out in a rush as Mason kissed his way down toward Five's cock.

"Go on," Mason said against Five's belly. He could taste more sweat now and feel the heat flushing Five's skin.

"I would heal quickly if the...device...wasn't continually severing the..."

Mason raised his head, a sudden flicker of concern unsettling him. "What do you mean, severing?"

Five let out a shaky breath and curled his hands into fists. "The device has to allow me to partially heal each time so that it can perform the dissection needed to—"

Mason sat back on his heels. "Goddammit."

"Don't stop what you were doing."

"I can't do that knowing you're being tortured." Mason raked his hair back from his forehead with his hands and stared down at Five. "This is fucked up."

"I'm not being tortured. I barely feel it when the dissection occurs. It's a twinge of pain so minor—"

But at just that moment, Five took in a halting breath and tensed, and Mason knew—knew in the way he'd known Five was lying to him seconds before—that the pain of dissection might be fleeting, but it was a goddamned fiery stab of pain the moment it occurred.

The tension pulling Five's muscles taut eased.

"We'll spend the rest of our days together," Five said, "and you'll have plenty of time to learn these things. The den we'll share will have access to many of the medical texts related to devices such as this."

"Let's not get carried away here. I'm just getting used to the idea of being mated. Now you want to move in together."

Five gave Mason a steady look. "You will stay."

"I damn well might, you arrogant bastard, but right now, let's not talk about that. Just get that thing out of you."

"If you insist."

Mason gritted his teeth and glared at Five.

Five reached down and released two strips of material in a deft move, pulled one leg up, and then yanked. His back bowed as he sucked in a harsh gasp.

He flung the device across the room. The device banged hard against the window, startling a jump out of Mason.

Mason watched it fall to the floor, eyes wide. The needle-like projections sticking out of the base of the thing were as long as his fingers.

His gaze stuttered its way back to Five.

Five was breathing heavily, staring up at the ceiling.

"Prepare yourself with the lubricant. Hurry. I'll heal quickly without the repression drugs to interfere. I should have waited." Five's back bowed again and a low whine came out of his chest.

Mason scrambled off the bed, already looking around. The only table in the room was clear and the low dresser near the door was an empty surface. "I don't see any god-damn lube. Where is it?"

Five raised his head. His eyes had gone dark and shiny and he was breathing fast and shallow. "Under the bed. There are drawers."

Mason bent and felt around on the smooth wood. A drawer slid out. He found several jars of lube.

"Got—"

Two hundred pounds of roaring wolf knocked him on his ass.

Chapter 40

MASON HAD NEVER unscrewed a jar so fast in his life as he did that jar of lube. And then he almost let it fall right out of his hand as Five picked him up bodily and spread him out on the bed on his stomach. He clutched at the jar, but he was too busy trying to move into the motion of the bed as Five hauled him onto his knees and dragged Mason's jeans right off his ass.

Five's hard cock slid along the crease of Mason's ass and he was just about to panic when Five stilled behind him.

The bed jostled and Mason hurried to get as big a glob of lube onto his fingers as he could.

Then smeared it all over the quilt as a hot mouth closed over his asshole.

"Oh fuck," he said.

He spent the next several minutes gasping, trying the entire time to stay focused enough to get another glob of lube onto his fingers so he would be ready when Five—

He barely made it. He felt the glide of hot skin and thick cock against the backside of his fingers as he smeared lube all over his hole and then the hard push of thick cock stretching out his asshole well before he was ready.

"Uunnhhh…" he said, breathing hard through his teeth.

His forehead and knees dug into the bed and his thighs trembled as Five slid deep.

The hot pleasure of the stretch and the fullness of having that cock inside him reminded him of just how much he'd liked this the last time. Everything felt at least as good as he remembered, if not better.

Five thrust forward.

Mason groaned.

Better. It was so goddamn much better. Maybe in part because he could have sworn he felt a little spark of something coming from Five every time he buried himself in Mason's ass.

Mason's cock hardened a little more with every thrust and soon he was gasping almost as fast as Five. He dug his toes into the bed and tried to gain some leverage so he could stop sliding up the bed. He grabbed for one of the few remaining pillows on the bed, wrapped his arm around it, and wedged it under him, then grabbed a handful of quilt in the other.

If he didn't, he was going to take his dick in hand and jerk off way too early.

He held out for a while. He wasn't sure how long.

Long enough for Five to come in his ass and then on his ass and then in his ass again. He had alien semen dripping down the backs of his thighs and drying behind his knees, and Five didn't seem to be anywhere near finishing.

Mason had just started sliding his lubed hand along his dick when Five roared.

"Mine," Five said, then pulled out of Mason's ass and flipped Mason onto his back.

Mason didn't even have time to catch his breath. Five jostled his way between Mason's thighs, pushing them toward Mason's chest, and thrust his cock right back inside Mason's ass.

The air jolted out of Mason's lungs. Five curled over Mason, dragging his nose up under Mason's arm, and with back curled and arms straining, he started fucking Mason again.

Mason smoothed Five's hair off his forehead, breath hitching every time Five fucked into him.

"You're beautiful like this," Mason said, not sure Five would even understand him. Five was consumed by his heat, and his rutting had a frantic quality to it that touched at Mason's soul.

He didn't know how he knew what Five wanted—maybe it was the bond, maybe intuition—but instead of reaching for his own dick again, he put his arm around Five and held on to the nape of Five's neck, letting his fingers dig in against Five's skull.

Five made a soft sound and after a few moments passed, his thrusts lost that frantic quality, and he started to calm down.

Before Mason could decide if he was going to reach for his dick again, Five pushed up on one arm and reached for Mason.

Mason's eyes fell closed as Five's warm hand pulled at his dick. He came within moments, the shivery rush of release dragging a long, low groan out of him.

Later, he was staring across the room and trying to decide if taking a piss was worth the effort of climbing off the warm bed—and out of Five's warm embrace—when Five stirred from the heavy sleep he'd fallen into long after Mason came.

"I'm going to stay," Mason said, before Five could say anything. "But if you say I told you so, swear to God, I'm never letting you fuck me again."

Five just sniffed along Mason's back and said, "I've never doubted you would come to realize the benefits of being my mate."

"Goddamn you."

Chapter 41

MASON STIFFENED his back as Five looked down at the table's top. He tilted his head, studying the small marks Mason's thumbnails had left behind the day before.

"I didn't mean to do it," Mason said. "You think it'll matter? Or should I—"

Five clawed five long scratches into the wood.

Mason was so shocked he couldn't move for a good three seconds. "I—that's just—goddammit, Five."

"You were upset. Now there's no reason for you to feel responsible for scarring the table."

"So this was you trying to make me feel better."

Mason felt a slight increase in pressure in his chest, lasting only a fraction of a second.

Five's expression turned wary. "You don't feel better."

"No, I fucking do not."

Five sighed and glanced down at his claws. "Impulsive behavior is one of my weaknesses. I'll work harder to correct it."

Mason eyed him for a moment, then finished pulling out the chair he'd started to pull out earlier before giving in to the almost compulsive desire to make his guilty confession about the marks on the table. He sat and pointed at the chair sitting closest to his. "Sit. I haven't eaten in I don't know how long and I want food."

The table was piled high with fresh rolls and hot stew, and even though it was early morning, Mason's stomach was already grumbling.

Five fed him while Mason asked questions. He learned that Gray and Francis had, in fact, been locked up, but it had been temporary because Gray had developed a resistance to the repression drugs and needed to mate to calm his heat and Francis had been set on returning to the last known location of the human they'd come across during their side mission and had to be held back.

He also learned that some humans might have escaped the area of the laboratory, but the wolves were making every effort to track down anyone who could have had contact with the people responsible for the deadly virus.

However, the rogue wolves and their humans were gone. The wolf who'd attacked Mason had already been dead when help arrived. But two had escaped the ambush by Cecily's people and left the area. Only one wolf had remained behind, and he would have to face the First Alpha.

"He'll die then," Mason said. "All those wolves were part of the group trying to overthrow the First Alpha—those that Brendan tried to make that deal with three years ago, right?"

"They are rogues, yes. But he will choose to submit and swear fealty to *Traesikeille*."

"Why are you so sure?"

"He is the third from *Traesikeille*'s third, if I'm not mistaken. Without his alpha to interfere, he will submit."

"I have no idea what that means."

"They are kin."

"Related?"

"He is one of Trey's many children."

"Oh."

After that, the conversation changed direction for a little while, and Mason learned everything he'd wanted to know about what had happened after he'd been knocked out on the stairs.

But he still had one question related to the rogues and it came back to him as he was watching Five tear small pieces off the last half of one of the last rolls.

"Those rogue wolves mentioned a prophecy. Do you know anything about that?"

Five stopped what he was doing and watched Mason with curiously bright eyes. "The prophecy saved us from extinction and gave us purpose."

"Ah. A religion then. I've always wondered."

Five laid the roll aside. "It is not a religion. I don't expect you to understand, but we found Earth because of the prophecy. Without it, we would never have asked you to share your world with us. The Diviners try to interpret and explain the prophecy, but it is complicated. We all have our part to play. You brought us your former alpha —"

"The hell I did. And I don't have a former alpha. We talked about that."

"Then your former friend."

"Wasn't really my friend, either," Mason grumbled.

Five picked up one of the pieces of roll and dipped it into the remaining stew, then offered the bite to Mason.

"Irrelevant. The point is that the prophecy predicted you would bring him to us, and it predicts he will bring peace. His son—"

"Whoa the fuck down. First, if I know anything about Brendan Greer, it's that he isn't the kind of guy who has kids. Second, how am I responsible for bringing him to you?"

"Alpha *Craeigoer* said you and your brother were questioned after you were brought into the den. The information you gave his pack helped them find his mate and Brendan Greer more quickly after they were lost."

"I don't remember anything like that."

Five's pause seemed overly long. "Interesting."

Suspicious now, Mason sat back and crossed his arms. "Why is that interesting?"

"You would have been drugged. There's no reason for you not to remember. But I'm certain it happened, unless…"

"Marcus told them he was me when he went off with that wolf. He let them question him twice, trying to protect me. Goddammit." But then Mason frowned. "The timing on that wouldn't have been right, would it? When did they bring in Brendan?"

"Irrelevant."

"It's not irrelevant."

"It is irrelevant, because it's unlikely he could impersonate you while being questioned under the influence of the drugs."

"So why don't I remember this then?"

"There are drugs that erase memories."

Mason's breath stuttered in his chest. "Why would someone use those drugs on me?"

"I don't know. It's unlikely." Five scooped another

piece of bread through the hearty stew and offered it to Mason. "Eat."

Mason lowered his arms but didn't take the bite. "I'm pretty damn uncomfortable with the idea that something happened to me that I can't remember."

"Eat," Five said again.

"Would you not want to know? How would you feel if you couldn't remember something that might be important to you?"

"I don't remember much of what happened to me after the death of my heat mate during the last heat season. I've accepted that I will not remember. Whatever happened is in the past. Do you believe it's really necessary to know this now?"

"I don't know. How can I know if I don't know what happened?"

"How can you assume it's something you should know if you don't know what it was?"

"Now you're just being a difficult asshole." Mason stared stubbornly at Five, who stared right back.

Five pressed the stew-soaked bread to Mason's lips. Mason finally gave in and took the bite.

"You suggested Brendan Greer isn't the type of man to have children. But you are wrong. He will have a child. The prophecy isn't clear how that will happen. We have many people who would be willing to act as a surrogate for him and *Traesikeille*. No one can overlook the fact that the universe sent a human doctor to us even before First Alpha had claimed his mate."

"Alan?" Mason said around his mouthful. "He's just a guy who was in the wrong place at the wrong time. Coincidence. He's not even a real doctor—I mean, he is, but he didn't finish, so he's really not. In case that matters."

"The prophecy doesn't care about technicalities." Said as if Mason were really trying his patience.

Mason swallowed his food, then grinned. "Hey, you're the one who thought I'd make a good mate."

"You keep saying that as if you're hoping I'll change my mind. I will not."

Mason laughed.

After another few bites, he said, "So about this kid…"

"We've discussed the prophecy enough for now. We have a mission to discuss."

A spark of interest shot through Mason. "Another mission?"

"We'll search for any indication that people might have returned to the lab since we collected the dead and cleared it of the virus. Nothing more."

"It's still a mission."

The corner of Five's mouth turned up. "It is."

Meaning clearly that it was probably just something Five had come up with to distract Mason, but Mason let that pass. "Do I get a weapon this time?"

"I will be your weapon."

Mason snorted. Then—

"You're not kidding. Goddammit, Five!"

"The heat season hasn't ended."

"How much you want to bet we spend as much time fighting as we spend fucking?"

Five leaned forward and touched Mason's cheek with the tip of his finger, so gentle. "I am your life, and you are mine. The anger I felt when I first realized who you were, what you were…it is gone. The scars of your past, like the scars on this table, make you what you are today, just as they've made me what I am. We'll find joy in this mating. I do not doubt that at all. Do you?"

Mason swallowed, feeling caught in a storm by Five's ocean-deep gaze. "We'll probably do okay."

A predatory smile exposed a flash of sharp eyeteeth. "If that's the way you express all your great affections, it's little wonder you've had so few mates."

"Great affections? You're such a goddamned arrogant bastard."

"Yet you do not see it as a weakness."

"There's this old saying about fast cars and faster women. Swap out difficult for fast and you pretty much know everything about me you'll ever need to know."

Five studied him with narrowed eyes. "I cannot decide if I've been insulted or complimented."

"A little bit of both, but only in the best way possible."

About Odessa Lynne

Odessa Lynne writes male/male romance. After years of reading romance, fantasy, and science fiction novels, she discovered she liked romance in her fantasy, sex in her science fiction, and love between her heroes best of all, and that's exactly what she puts in all her own stories now, for readers who enjoy the same. Odessa lives in the southeastern United States.

Visit odessalynne.com for information about current or upcoming releases or to sign up to Odessa Lynne's new releases email list.

Made in the USA
Middletown, DE
04 May 2022